"What's that?" asked M_____, _____ Lych strained his ears. It sounded like rustling. Occasionally there was a low moan. He opened the driver's door and switched on the headlights. Suddenly illuminated, several hunched figures turned their faces away.

Lych let out an involuntary gasp of horror. Marian stuffed her hand in her mouth to stifle a scream.

There, all across the road, a strange procession had appeared.

Some walked almost like men, others shuffled with difficulty while still more crawled across the ground like snakes. What Lych and Marian could see of their faces filled them with terror.

So far, the creatures had ignored them. Something inside Lych told him they should seize the opportunity to flee.

"Quick!" whispered Lych, climbing into the car. Marian followed suit, closing the door quickly. Taking advantage of their good fortune, Lych started the engine, put the car in reverse and began crawling backwards an inch at a time. He dared go no faster for fear of tipping them over the edge of the narrow track.

Ahead, in the receding light of the headlamps, they could see more of the foul creatures climb over the lip of the road and cross over towards the hill.

"The Children of Yig?" Marian whispered the question.

Lych looked pale in the faint light from the dashboard. He merely nodded, slowly.

The Book of Yig: Revelations of the Serpent

A CTHULHU MYTHOS ANTHOLOGY

EDITED BY

DAVID HAMBLING & PETER RAWLIK

DEDICATION

This book is respectfully dedicated to Brian Stableford

CONTENTS

THE SNAKE IN THE GARDEN

A HARRY STUBBS ADVENTURE

"I hate and fear snakes, because if you look into the eyes of any snake you will see that it knows all and more of the mystery of man's fall, and that it feels all the contempt that the Devil felt when Adam was evicted from Eden."
Rudyard Kipling

"He's shapen like a man, except ye look at him clost."
Zealia Bishop, "The Curse of Yig"

South London, 1927

The events of a case rarely present themselves in neat chronological sequence. It is not the habit of the world to deliver the pieces of a puzzle all the right way up and in the right order like a jigsaw; rather we get a jumble of odd incidents, most of them part of some other puzzle altogether. The investigator must pick out the correct pieces and assemble these as best he can.

If I were to narrate matters as they occurred in real life, then the reader might be as baffled as the investigator, and moreover the stream of irrelevancy would make for tiresome reading. Therefore, it is up to the writer to fillet the facts and prepare them for easy consumption, as a good butcher prepares meat, removing the bone and gristle and leaving just enough fat for good cooking. While this preparation makes for an easier read, it also makes the thing look far more straightforward than it actually was. The reader should bear in mind then, that the case presented to them on a platter, as it were, bears the same resemblance as a roast fowl does to a bird in the bush.

Though I did not know it at the time, my involvement in the matter started then when I was proceeding down Westow Street towards my office one morning. I was accosted from a doorway.

"Hist! Mr Stubbs—hist!"

I could not determine the source of this utterance, until an unprepossessing figure emerged from the shadows. Daylight revealed a patched and filthy army greatcoat, secured at the waist with twine. He shuffled forward on boots stuffed with newspaper, waving a hand at me.

"Good morning, Slingsby," I said, pausing in my step.

"Mr Stubbs," he said, with a black-toothed grin. "So glad I caught you, sir. I've something for you."

I was expecting to be solicited for a copper or two. Slingsby, propertyless as any homeless individual was not the sort to have anything for anybody. Not in the usual run of things.

"And what might that be?" I asked.

Slingsby waved a packet wrapped in brown paper, then held it possessively to his bosom.

"I can't show you here," he confided. "This wants somewhere private."

I folded my arms.

"Maybe you had better tell me what this is all about, Slingsby."

"It's a long story," he said. "But I wouldn't go wasting your time, Mr Stubbs. You know that. This is a business matter."

We were only two minutes from my office. While Slingsby might be no more than a tramp with a tramp's taste for drink, I doubted he would importune me without good reason. I was far from sure that his notion of good reason would coincide with mine, but in my game it pays to listen to everyone.

"You'd better come with me," I said. "But I will hold you to account."

I would never physically abuse someone in his position, but I dare say my appearance—'brutish' being among the mildest epithet that have been applied—belies my essentially reasonable nature.

"Surely," he agreed.

We approached my place of business. The downstairs, entered through the main road, is a shop. The upper floor of the building, accessed by a rear staircase on the mews, is given over to a concern selling pottery and ceramic items by post. Except, that is, for the one room with a hand-lettered sign, Lantern Insurance.

"Morning, Mr Stubbs," said Kitty, the first to see me, and was echoed by the other women from their places by sawdust-filled packing crates. But they fell silent when they saw Slingsby's figure trailing after.

"Corporal Slingsby is assisting me with a case," I explained. Generally speaking, Kitty would have obliged with two cups of tea when she saw me with a visitor, but I did not feel that courtesy could be extended this morning without a special request. "If you could bring us both a cuppa, it'd be much appreciated, Miss Albright."

My office is nothing much to look at. It would not disgrace a plumber or any other honest tradesman though, and Slingsby was hardly the fussy sort. Decent if worn secondhand furniture, a few rugs, the walls livened with sporting prints.

"You want me to sit down?" he asked.

"Make yourself at home," I said, hanging up my bowler and moving to my accustomed seat by the solid table that served as my desk. He put the brown paper packet in the middle of the table between us. Almost as though he wanted to be rid of it. A suspicion grew in my breast.

"Would this be human remains, body parts, or any article of that description?" I asked.

"Well, it is, and it isn't," he said.

Slingsby's face was mainly obscured by an untidy beard, his cheeks smudged and dirty, the nose covered with broken veins, eyes bloodshot. I may not be a picture, but I wondered what Slingsby thought when he saw himself in a mirror. Or maybe he preferred to avoid his reflection.

"You've a lot of books here, Mr Stubbs," said Slingsby. He had made no move to remove his coat, or even his hat. They were not so much clothes to him as skin.

"You can drop the 'mister' in here," I said. "We know each other of old."

I'd been acquainted with Slingsby since the end of the war, when there had been a great deal of camaraderie and fellow-feeling between all us ex-servicemen. We had a few years of drinking to catch up on, and we made up for lost time in the pubs and bars. Slingsby had been one of the regulars down in the Conquering Hero, The Horns and some of the other watering holes. He had been in Army from '14 and invalided out some time before the end. As the victim of a gas attack, he drew the heartfelt sympathy of all of us who had made it through with wind and limb intact.

"This little library here is just a few odd reference works," I said. "Mainly timetables and business directories and suchlike. Surprising how quickly they mount up."

Indeed, I had recently acquired a bookcase to house them all. A closer look would have shown that not all the books were equally reputable; on the lower shelves were a number of volumes of folklore, ghost stories and similarly lurid material, hidden behind plain dustjackets. Questionable perhaps. But in my experience, not without their value as reference material.

Close up, you could smell Slingsby. The same smell all tramps acquire, an unwholesome brew of animal odours, one that made me want to open the window at once. It is not just the smell of unwashed skin, of sweat and mould, though that's a great part of it. I knew that smell from the war, when you get two pints a day for washing and shaving until you finally get rotated out and you can sluice it away in a good bath. It was a vile smell and it momentarily robbed me of the power of speech.

"I'm not holding out," he said, mistaking my silence for hostility. "But it requires some explanation. I'll tell you the story and you can decide for yourself."

"Just tell me about it in your own words," I said.

Kitty came in just then with two cups, which she put down on the table without a word, not looking at Slingsby or me. Her expression was eloquent, and I was grateful she refrained from sniffing or wrinkling her nose.

Slingsby held his teacup with grimy fingers, dirt encrusted under every nail, and blew on it.

"You ain't got a gasper?" he asked.

I have never smoked myself, but kept a case of cigarettes for those who do, as the friendly gesture is often appreciated. I offered Slingsby one, and provided a light.

"I shouldn't," he said, and burst into a fit of coughing at the first lungful. "But I do."

It was painful to watch. I had heard all the stories of gas attacks, men swimming through the green fog of chlorine gas, of masks dropped or broken, men drowning in the green froth that filled their lungs, of burned eyes and nasal passages stripped out by acid. Slingsby had a milder dose than many, but it had left him without strength.

"Steady on," I said when he was about to take a second puff. "I want to hear this story of yours before you kill yourself."

"You will—you will," he said, between coughs, then settled down, contemplating the white tube and its glowing red tip. "This was two nights ago—Tuesday that would be."

"Tuesday the twelfth," I said, writing in my notebook.

"Here," said Slingsby. "You don't need anything in writing. I don't want this getting out."

"Your confidentiality assured," I said. "My method of working requires written records, but the identity of my informants is known only to myself, and I will use a cipher for your name. In my notes you will merely be referred to as Mr S."

"If that's how it's done," said Slingsby. He did not look a happy man. Anything about him in writing, anything that smacked of official records, set him on edge.

"Or we can terminate this interview here and now and you can go on your way, " I said.

"No, no, I want to tell you."

"Tuesday night then," I prompted.

"Dry evening with no wind, or maybe just a little breeze, and mild as you like. Moon just past full. I was making the most of it, taking a stroll down Church Street."

"Are you in the habit of nocturnal perambulations?" I asked.

"There's nobody about at night. I can pick fag ends and anything else I can find out of the gutter without being bothered," said Slingsby. "You, you don't know what it's like. A man in my position is fair game for anyone. Officious shopkeepers threatening me with the law. Schoolboys throwing stones. Biting dogs, and their owners 'you get away from my dog!'. Women with disapproving looks, shepherding children away like I was a leper—that's hurtful. Nobody ever does anything, except the sanctimonious buggers who want to give me a ha'penny so I can listen to a lecture about the evils of drink. They know where they can stick their ha'penny."

"You find it more congenial when the streets are less inhabited?"

"Just me and the cats. Lovely creatures, cats. They don't bark. Cats'll keep you company...anyway, I was prospecting for trifles when I heard someone coming, so I just stepped back out of sight."

Not much need to ask why he might do that. Anybody he met, whether it was drunken revellers or the law itself, would be unwelcome company.

"It was just this one bloke, and he was furtive," said Slingsby. "No doubt about it, he was furtive. Not walking along boldly like an honest citizen. And he had this bundle under one arm." Slingsby leaned forward and tapped the brown paper packet with a dirty finger.

"What did he look like now, this individual?" I asked, pencil poised.

"Hard to say. It was dark, of course, and he was wearing a coat and a cap. I never got a look at his face. But he did have a very furtive walk, I'll say that."

"Was he big, small, tall, fat...?"

"He was a small fellow," said Slingsby. "Shorter than me. And the way he moved; he didn't have much flesh on him."

Slingsby, whose wrists showed more bones than they should have, and legs like broomsticks under his trousers, did not see himself in the category of skinny men.

"So, a short, slightly-built man. Or perhaps it could have been a woman?"

"Dressed like a man," said Slingsby. "A man, definitely, or maybe a youth. His coat was in good nick. Shoes, too. A man, from how he was dressed."

"But no stick or cane?"

"I'd have noticed that."

"Gloves?"

"No gloves. I could see his hands distinctly."

"What was he doing with his hands?"

"I was just getting to that, if you don't keep interrupting with all these questions. He stops, just outside the grocers. They've got their bins outside on Tuesday night, see, because Wednesday is the collection day for the dustcart. This man, he takes a look around—and he doesn't see me—and he takes the lid off a bin, and puts this parcel in. And then, and this is the suspicious thing, if you ask me, he goes back. Right back in the direction he just come in, instead of continuing on."

"That is rather suggestive," I said, and took a sip of tea,

"I wait until he's out of sight," said Slingsby, "and then I go and have a look for myself. And lo and behold, there's this package he left there. And what do you think is in it?"

"I haven't the foggiest idea," I said. "Perhaps you'd better tell me before my patience wears any thinner."

He slurped his tea, prolonging the delay before resuming.

"I open it up and I see, in the moonlight, clear as anything—a face!"

"A what?"

Slingsby nodded gravely. "A face looking back at me with empty eyes. I said you'd be interested! I took the whole thing out, and well, you can see for yourself. In the light of day it ain't so shocking, but it gave me a turn."

From the paper parcel he took something that looked at first like a thin sheet or a shroud, or a filmy ladies' nightdress, but as he unwrapped it the shape of the thing became apparent. It has arms and legs, a body and a head—and the face of a death mask, with holes for the mouth and the nostrils.

"It's a flayed human skin," said Slingsby.

"I can see that," I said.

"A whole body, peeled like an orange all in one piece." He

drew my attention to one limb. "Look, you can see five fingers and a thumb, like it was a glove."

"I have never seen an anatomic specimen like it," I said.

Slingsby supped tea, satisfied that he had surprised and baffled me with his find.

From my butchering days I was familiar enough with the process of removing the hide from a carcase, but this skin did not seem to have been flayed by any normal instrument. It was much too fine for that, just the very outer layer of the dermis. Shed like a snakeskin.

"Assuming," I said, "That it is in fact skin and not some facsimile." I ran the material through my fingers. It was somewhat like skin, and could not have been even the finest fabric. It might, though, have been some sort of rubberised substance made into the likeness of a human skin. Certainly, there was not the slightest sign of hair anywhere on it, not on the scalp or anywhere else. Either it had been treated for the removal of hair, or the thing was a manufactured product.

"It's a human skin," said Slingsby.

"And why didn't you go to the police with it?"

"Police! Why don't I paint my face green and sing Old MacDonald, why don't you ask me that?" said Slingsby, with the addition of some uncouth language.

"Failing that, you might have let Mr Renville know. He likes to be informed of everything that occurs in this parish."

Arthur Renville, my patron, was a key figure in what might be termed the informal economy of Norwood. He regulated those activities which are not regulated by the normal legal mechanisms. If anything happened that he was not informed of, so much the worse for those doing it.

"That's what I'm doing, isn't it?" protested Slingsby. "I don't have to make an application to him in person, do I? You'll pass it on up the chain."

I was a little taken aback by this. I have no formal business relationship with Arthur Renville, and while he has employed me directly on a few occasions, I am very much a free agent. I did not expect that long-established members of the local community such as Slingsby would see me as his henchman.

"I suppose so," I said.

"Because this is in your line, Stubbs, ain't it? You're the one as deals with all the funny business for Mr Renville. Anything that ain't normal, you're his first port of call. Like that funny business with the Chinese bloke and those Irishman and—my coat getting stolen, and that."

"I was going to ask you about that," I said.

The patches were clearly visible over the bullet-holes that had perforated Slingsby's greatcoat. He claimed to have been asleep when the coat was taken from him. Taken by something which was not exactly a human being. Maybe he had been in a drunken stupor, but I had always suspected Slingsby had seen a deal more than he let on, and had lain doggo while his coat was stolen.

"I've got nothing to say," he said. "I don't want anything to do with that business."

"But what about this?" I asked, poking the laid-out skin with a forefinger. "You seem to be keen enough to get yourself involved."

"For a small consideration," said Slingsby hesitantly. "You'll reimburse me for my trouble, won't you? You don't get something like this brought in every day."

"I see, now we're getting to it, Slingsby. You're after money. Shouldn't have expected it wasn't because you were suddenly feeling public-spirited."

"Five shillings isn't too much to ask," he wheedled.

"Two bob, and I'll keep your name out of it," I said.

"That'd be very good of you, Stubbs," he said, flashing his ugly, blackened smile again.

"Here you go," I said, holding out the coins. "I needn't ask where you're going to spend it."

"Give over, Stubbs," he said, weighing them in his hand. "I don't need no morality from you. Just you leave me in peace and I'll leave you in peace."

"Fair enough. No offence, Slingsby."

"None taken. Couldn't spare another smoke, could you?"

I duly handed over a cigarette, which Slingsby tucked behind his ear as he rose to his feet. He needed one arm on the chair to help him up. Although no older than me, Slingsby had the body of a frail old man.

"Good luck with this little mystery," he said. "And I'll keep an eye out for anything else for you."

"I'd be much obliged if you did," I said.

Slingsby shuffled out. After one more look, I carefully rolled up the human skin and replaced it in the package. Then I opened the windows. Miss Kitty came in; she said nothing but rather pointedly wiped the chair and the table where Slingsby had been sitting with a damp cloth. There were no actual marks on them, but she obviously felt it was called-for.

"Sorry about that," I said. "I won't be inviting him in again— it's just there wasn't any alternative locale."

"Who you invite in is your business, Mr Stubbs," she said primly, picking up Slingsby's mug using the cloth so she did not have to touch it. "But we had thought better of you."

I felt bad for not speaking up for Slingsby. Perhaps he had not chosen to be what he was today, but there was nothing that would convince people like Kitty that he was anything more than a tramp and a drunkard.

That skin bothered me though. Perhaps it was nothing, but my instincts suggested otherwise. I drafted a brief telegram to Miss de Vere advising her of the find and requesting instructions. If it was something serious she might be able to provide guidance.

A piano warehouse is an eerie place to be at midnight. The high doors make you feel tiny, and the vast, shrouded shapes through the barred windows are uncomfortably reminiscent of giant, sleeping animals. A single electric light burned feebly overhead. The acoustics were peculiar for some reason; perhaps it's all those wires capturing and echoing sounds. Whatever the underlying cause, it gives a distinct impression that one noise would wake the whole lot up.

Things were not quiet for long though, as two vans drew up smartly and men piled out and set to opening the doors.

"Evening, Stubbsy," said Arthur Renville, clapping me on the shoulder. "Thanks for attending."

The men were moving fast, as men will when overseen

directly by a man like Arthur. They started shifting boxes from the vans into an empty corner of the warehouse.

"Teddy, when you're stacking those boxes, remember the pile has to be the size and shape of a piano. Don't do it any old how. There're dustsheets over there by the door to drape 'em with. Piano-shape."

"I didn't know you used this place," I said.

"Normally I wouldn't," he said. "It's a question of needs must when the devil drives, necessity being the mother of invention, et cetera. My preference would be somewhere less public, but I've got two vanloads of goods needing a home until Wednesday. They can stay here incognito as pianos until then. But that's not why I asked you here."

"Isn't it?" I had been all ready to roll up my sleeves and do some heavy lifting. I had made a few bob now and then helping move consignments for Arthur, and if it was a little bit below my current station I knew Arthur would not have asked me without good reason.

"Oh, Lord no," he said. "You've left all that behind you, stepped up a rung or two. Respectable businessman— respectable *married* businessman in a month or two. You're not a youngster to be engaged in clandestine activities."

Arthur's tongue was firmly in his cheek. Clandestine activities were his meat and drink, and he did not have so much respect for the respectable men who profited from the trade.

"Something else then?"

"I'm afraid so. I'm here, there and everywhere at the moment, so it's catch as catch can and this was the nearest thing to a convenient rendezvous I could find to see you." Arthur's face was suddenly serious. "It's something bad, I'm afraid. Murder most foul, as the bard has it. You hear about the fellow stabbed to death in the Dog and Duck the other day?"

"Only the essentials," I said. The story had been splashed all over the newspapers, but the coverage was thin when you sifted through it. One unidentified man killing another seemed to be the gist of it.

"It's a messy one," he said. "This bloke reserves a private room with the landlord the day before for a little business

David Hambling

meeting, giving the name 'Smith,' if you can credit that. He goes in, and another man turns up a bit later. Twenty minutes later, the second man walks out, without anyone noticing anything particular. Except that he left, it later transpires, our 'Smith' dead with ten knife wounds in his neck and chest, and enough blood to redecorate half the room."

The men from the van were hurrying to and fro. This was a situation where the removal work needed to be done as swiftly and cleanly as possible, else Arthur would not have felt a need to be there.

"That is bad," I said. "A murder like that would bring half Scotland Yard."

"Too ruddy right, Stubbsy. Not a little domestic killing, or even one of your gang-against-gang murders where everyone knows who's behind it. This one is mystery end-to-end, so of course the coppers are swarming over it, poking in everywhere. Asking questions."

This was Arthur's nightmare. What he wanted was a quiet neighbourhood with nothing to attract official attention, and no reason for the police to be knocking on doors or looking inside locked garages. With both the victim and the suspect unknown, there could be any amount of prodding and prying.

"I've called Blaine in to look into it," he said. "I don't like him any more than anyone else does, but he gets results. He'll be able to turn up things the boys in blue will miss."

I said nothing. Blaine was an unsavoury individual. I did not like to see Arthur relying on him, however well-qualified he was.

"I'm sure we'll put a proper name to Mr Smith," he went on. "His wallet was gone but he had a cigarette case from a particular regiment. There were initials on his handkerchief. And a wedding ring. He was the sort of man who will be missed pretty quickly, mark my words. As to the other—by all accounts the barman is the only one who got a good look at the man, and he did a bunk. As soon as the bluebottles came buzzing round, he made himself scarce and hasn't been seen since."

"Somewhat suspicious behaviour," I observed. "Or was there another reason for his unscheduled departure?"

"You've hit the nail on the head there. This particular drawer of pints has a record as long as your arm, being a thief of the common-or-garden unskilled variety." Arthur shook his head at the senseless villainy of it. Few things riled him so much as petty pilferage. "So they won't be getting anything from him."

"The police won't. But he might talk to Blaine, I suppose."

"He's gone. When a man like that pulls a disappearing act, he drops out of circulation," said Arthur. "Blaine's made enquiries. Not a sniff."

Now the word was out, if the missing barman were anywhere in Norwood, his appearance would have been seen, marked, noted, and reported back to Arthur within the hour.

"If you can find him, you'll win a prize," he went on. "But that wasn't what I wanted you for. Normally I wouldn't trouble you. But I just thought I'd drop a word to the wise, as this might just be in your bailiwick. This is a copy of a note found in the back pocket of the deceased."

He produced a folded slip of paper and passed it over.

"The light isn't very good here," I said, trying to make it out.

"Doesn't make much difference," he said. "If it looks like squiggles, it's because it is squiggles, however much you look at it."

After a few seconds squinting, I understood his meaning. A row of blocky shapes marched across the page, not like any alphabet I recognised.

"What sort of writing is that?"

"That is the question which has them all scratching their heads," said Arthur sagely. "The consensus of opinion among those who know about these things is that it is a cipher code of some sort. But nobody has seen anything like it, and that includes some gentlemen formerly of the Intelligence Corps."

Clearly Arthur had been pulling strings and calling in favours to get expert opinions on the matter.

"And you think this note might be germane?"

"Blaine doesn't think much of it. He likes things more straightforward. But there is another small mystery, inasmuch as Mr Smith seems to have been expecting trouble."

"How do you know that?"

"He had armed himself with a second-hand automatic. He had it in his hand, under the table, when he was stabbed. Loaded and cocked with the safety off. Never fired a shot while he got stabbed in the face and neck with a cheap clasp-knife from Woolworths."

I tried to visualise how quickly a man could draw a knife and stab you across a table. No more than the blink of an eye if he did not fumble it. Long enough to react though, if not by ducking out of the way then by squeezing a trigger.

"How could that happen?"

"Unfortunately, the late Mr Smith is not able to furnish that information," said Arthur drily. "All we can say for sure is that he failed to do the one thing that would have saved his life, despite having planned to do it."

"There's many a slip 'twixt the cup and the lip," I observed.

"Maybe his attention was distracted, or he hesitated for whatever reason."

"What I don't quite understand yet is—how can I be of help in the matter?"

"I don't know that you can be," he admitted. "I'm clutching at straws. I have precious little faith in His Majesty's Constabulary, and Blaine won't change the odds much. The one concrete suggestion that came back from our little gathering of code experts was that it resembled secret writing used by alchemists five hundred years ago."

"I see," I said, and I did. Arthur had me pigeonholed as the man who deals with the occult and out-of the-ordinary. In fact, it was his insistence on this point that had resulted in my gaining some expertise in that exact field, and not without some difficulty and personal danger on my part.

"So I'm wondering whether this is less a simple criminal matter that Blaine can help with, or more—" he shrugged and smiled wanly up at me. "More esoteric. Something more in Harry Stubbs' line."

The question of why Smith had not shot his assailant may also have hinted that something unusual was afoot. I had personal experience with what they call the Evil Eye, which can root you helpless to the spot, but of course there were much simpler explanations.

"I wouldn't know where to begin," I said.

"I like that about you, Stubbsy—not overconfident. You start slow and cautious but you finish strong." He patted me on the arm again. "You put on your thinking cap. If you can come up with anything, you will be amply rewarded. Amply."

"No need for that," I said. "I'm always happy to help."

"Good man! Blaine will be in touch to see what you find. Mind how you go, Stubbsy."

With that Arthur was off, stepping in to supervise the last few boxes being put in place to form the outline of a pretend grand piano.

I tucked the slip of paper between the pages of my notebook and walked to my lodgings. I had not gone twenty paces before I was arrested in my progress by a voice from nowhere.

"Evening, Mr Stubbs. You well?"

Slingsby slunk out of an alley mouth, greatcoat swishing. I had not seen him, but then I never seemed to see him until he wanted to be seen. He was used to avoiding the public gaze.

"Evening Slingsby. Well enough—and you?"

He spat on the ground in answer. "Wouldn't happen to have any fags on you?"

"Here, " I said, reaching for my Woodbines. "Did you hear about the knifing in the Dog and Duck the other night?"

"Gentleman got his throat cut for his wallet, even though he had a shooter in his hand. Proper vicious killing by the sound of it—and bold as brass." Slingsby held the cigarette, waiting for a light. "Things like that didn't happen before the war."

"Not much they didn't," I said. I did not hold with this rosy view that London was an Elysium where nothing bad happened before 1914. I came up with a match and lit the cigarette. His hand trembled violently, making the job somewhat difficult.

"Bloody shakes," he said. "Thank you, Mr Stubbs, you're a gentleman."

"If you see anything…"

He took an experimental puff, and coughed lightly a few times.

"Yes, yes, I'll let it be known. But unless he's got the mark of Cain on him and wanders about at night I'm going to have my work cut out spotting him."

It was, I had to admit, a fair comment.

"Keep an eye out anyway. Good evening to you," I said, and left before he could start himself coughing and choking again.

My mind went back to the Roslyn D'Onston affair. There had been letters intercepted then between an ancient brotherhood of black magicians, trading the secrets of their dark arts. I had stumbled across other secret groups too, not least the people who called themselves TDS and who were, in a sense, my employers.

A motor-cycle passed, sweeping the road ahead with a brilliant cone of light, and was gone again. An idea had come to me and gone.

The next morning found me down West Norwood Public Library as soon as it opened. A request from Arthur demanded attention immediately if not sooner, and I immersed myself in the world of alchemical mysteries.

Alchemists were always great ones for secrets, understandable enough when they believed they had the formula for making gold from lead or achieving eternal youth. Mostly this took the form of using code words for certain vital ingredients of their work. For example, a recipe may call for starting with Prima Materia, or First Material, except that nobody now knows that the substance is. Some say that prima materia is dew, others that it means vinegar, others still that it is caustic lye, while another group contends that it is nothing but urine. Without knowing what the First material, the White Stone, the Green Dragon or other ingredients are, the complex alchemical recipes are completely useless. The alchemists' secret code remains unbroken to this day.

Other alchemists were more subtle. Some left recipes which were entirely fake, like Paracelsus claiming that laudanum was made of crushed pearls when the important ingredient was opium.

A rare few, such as the German Martin Roesel, wrote in actual cipher. Hence there are only a handful of books on the esoteric topic of alchemists' ciphers. A few years back I would have had to go to the British Library or somewhere, not that they would open their doors to someone without a string of letters after his name and a bona fide academic reason to be there. However, thanks to the wonders of modern communication, now all I had to do was fill in a form and Mr Hoade, the assistant chief librarian, and a personal friend, would take care of the rest.

"It's nine-thirty now," he said. "And this volume is held in West Dulwich. If I mark the request as urgent I should be able to place Schoenwetter in your hands by four o'clock."

"I would be extremely grateful if you could, Mr Hoade."

"No trouble at all. Another one of your 'interesting' cases, I assume?" A faint smile played around his lips. "But of course, your interests are your own affair, and I don't make a habit of prying."

Hoade suspected something of my involvement with matters out of the ordinary. He was well-informed of local news and could correlate my reading with certain subsequent events. I had always endeavoured to keep him safely away from my operations, but I may have kindled in him a dangerous interest in the esoteric. I had seen too many scholarly gentlemen lured into dangerous literary waters and destroyed by the things that lurked in the depths of old books to feel entirely comfortable about involving even a man as level-headed as Mr Hoade any more than necessary.

Hoade might have been less co-operative if he knew that in this instance I was investigating a brutal killing—and doing so without the cognisance of the proper authorities. Even if there was nothing illegal about what I was doing.

Hoade was as good as his word and later that day I was able to sit down in my office with Schoenwetter's *The Devils Doctors— Secrets of the Great Alchemists*. It is not an easy book to find, but for some reason West Dulwich Public Library has quite a trove of books of this type. Schoenwetter is well-illustrated with many of the various ciphers used by alchemical practitioners, mostly traditional symbols of the zodiac and established occult signs and sigils. I leafed through it like a bloodhound searching for a scent trail, and three-quarters of the way through I was rewarded with a row of characters looking decidedly familiar.

I compared the book side by side with the slip of paper Arthur had given me. The resemblance was not complete, in the same way that a child's copybook does not quite match the teacher's exact original, but they were near enough for my money.

"*Used in an invocation attributed to Albertus Magnus c. 1275. Believed to have been copied from an original supposedly from Arabia. Highly doubtful. Possible decorative surround copied and recopied in error. No known correlates.*"

The text went on to give three supposed translations of the coded text, one which was chemical in nature, one more of a spiritual-religious bent, and the third frankly sexual. The author suggested that these translations told us more about the lenses of personal obsession through which the cipher was being read than the contents of the cipher itself. I was prone to believe him.

I would at least have to take my hat off to Arthur's friend from military intelligence. He must have had a great acquaintance with codes to remember that this particular script was associated with alchemists. No doubt they tried to solve it for an exercise, but there was no sign that this alphabet had been used for centuries.

I was not looking forward to conveying this information to Blaine. Like a shark attracted by the smell of blood, my apprehension seemed to draw him. Voices were raised in the next room and the door opened without the preface of a knock. Blaine stepped through, closing the door on Kitty who was trailing behind.

"Inspector," I said, according him his former title and rising to my feet.

"Stubbs," he said, affording me the briefest look before glancing about the room. "Very fancy office you have."

He laughed at his own joke, more of a bark than a laugh.

"It is modest, but sufficient for my needs," I said.

Blaine circled the room, making a show of looking at the items on the shelves and the walls. He held his hat in both hands; he was a bull-necked, bald-headed character, powerful but running to fat. His raincoat was of good quality, as were the new leather shoes. Better than a serving police inspector could afford.

In the ring I would have made short work of Blaine, but he preferred to hit people who could not hit back. He might not have the power of arrest anymore, but the ex-policeman had a wealth of contacts inside the force. He was an authority on unofficial ways of supplementing income, and rumour had it that even the higher-ups were wary of him.

"You can't catch many fish with this set-up," he said. "I've heard about your racket, chasing away ghosts for old ladies. You didn't think that up on your own, did you? It was that rat Skinner. Where is he these days, gone back to the sewers?"

I was not about to give Blaine any information about my former partner. Blaine continued circling.

"I believe you're helping Mr Renville with certain enquiries," I said.

"You don't look like a confidence trickster," he said. "That must be a help. But still, is this all you can do?" He stopped and held his hands up with a pitying smile. He was one of those men for whom success is not enough: it was important to him that others should fail.

"Mr Renville asked me about this cipher," I said, pulling out the slip of paper.

"Oh yes, the secret cipher," he said. "And tell me, are the Tibetan masters planning to overthrow the government with psychic emanations?"

"It is a genuine cipher, dating back to the thirteenth century."

"How fascinating." He turned to me suddenly, raising his eyebrows. "And what does it say, Stubbs?"

"I can't tell you that. Not yet, anyway."

Blaine laughed properly this time, a real guffaw that shook his shoulders.

"I'm too early, aren't I? Should have given you a couple more days to come up with something." His mirth was cruel but genuine. "Dear oh dear...Renville must have made a lot of money on you in the boxing ring, because I can't see what use you are out of it."

"My investigation is continuing," I said.

I was still standing, and had not offered Blaine a seat. He seemed to prefer prowling around in any case. I felt better being able to look down on him.

"Look here, Stubbs," he said. "There's a lot of talk about this killing, about how Atkinson was mesmerised—"

"Atkinson?"

"The dead man. Thomas Atkinson. Kept a hat shop on Church Street. You obviously hadn't heard. Wife, two kids, no known criminal associates—unusual for this neighbourhood." Blaine clearly felt that any information needed to be accompanied by a dig. "There's talk he was in a trance when he was stabbed, so it must have been done by a magician. Stupid talk by stupid people."

"Do you have a theory of how it was done?"

"'Theory?' All you need to know is not to fan any wild ideas with talk about alchemists and wizards," he said. "I'm pursuing leads, and I don't want you muddying the waters and throwing obscurities into a simple murder case."

"If I can be of any help," I offered.

"Help by not interfering. Keep your hocus pocus for the nervous ladies who want you to exorcise their pantries of servants helping themselves to the cheese in the small hours."

"I understand, Inspector," I said.

"Atkinson may not have had a record, but that doesn't mean he was on the level," said Blaine. "I reckon I know what he was up to and how it got him killed. People are not very original in their crimes, and it won't take but a few days to get to the bottom of it."

"You have a suspect?"

"Near enough. And when I nab him, I'm not going to have you sounding off to Renville with stupid ideas of your own." He was facing me directly now, and at closer range than I found comfortable. "This is cold-blooded murder, not goblins in the cellar. I deal in facts, however unpalatable they may be."

"You have quite a reputation as a private investigator," I said. Blaine was, in a way, the man I wished to be. He was an independent agent, investigating crimes in his own way, with no fear of the authorities. On the other hand, he was universally hated.

"Yes I do," he said, not without satisfaction. "They know me in Scotland Yard, they know me in the courts. They know I get results. Whereas your reputation...is as a failed boxer and associate of criminals."

"I'm aware of our relative standings."

"Good," he said, and took a final look about and moved towards the door, pausing on the threshold to deliver a final shot. "I hear you're going to marry that tart." A short laugh again. "Each to his own, I suppose."

I could have crossed the space in a heartbeat and broken his nose before he was out the door. Blaine knew well enough I would not do such a thing, even with such a great provocation. I did not catch what he said to the packing girls on the way out, but the tone was dismissive. None of them answered back as they would have done to another visitor; he was that sort of man.

A quiet knock and Kitty opened the door a crack.

"Do you want a cup of tea after that, Harry?" she asked. "So rude!"

"That would be very kind of you," I said, as calmly as I could.

My blood was boiling and I would not calm down until I had worked out some of my anger in a good long session down at the gym that evening, battering the heavy bag until my arms were on fire.

Of course I poured out my feelings to Sally, even reluctantly recounting his parting words. Sally is rather persistent at times. She knew Blaine from the old days when she was forced to work on the streets. Her eyes narrowed when I repeated his words.

"That man is rotten through and through," she said after a count of three. "Do you think he'll catch the murderer?"

"By reputation he's none too gentle," I said. "He has none of the constraints applied to serving police officers, and he never picks on anyone who is going to complain to the law—not that it would do them any good. That gives him something of an edge."

"I'm sure he'll get someone, but who's to say it's the right man?"

"I doubt whether even Blaine is unscrupulous enough to point the finger at an innocent man."

She gave me a look indicating that she had no such faith, and that I was a fool for thinking otherwise.

"If he's Inspector Lestrade," she said. "You can be Sherlock Holmes. That would be the best revenge. You're an investigator after all—that's why he's so upset, because he knows there's a rival on the case."

"I'm hardly a rival to Blaine," I said.

"He hasn't solved the cases you have," she said. "Mr Renville has faith in you—and so do I. This Blaine is all hot air. He wants to ignore the important evidence for a start."

"I've never investigated a crime," I said. "Not as such. Doing it without Blaine noticing is hardly feasible. And the cipher isn't going to give up its secrets. There's nothing we can do."

"Fiddlesticks," said Sally, ideas already crystallising into plans behind her eyes. "We'll start with that pub."

"I'm not sure—"

"I'll do it myself then," she said.

And she did.

LANTERN INSURANCE CO Ltd:
Norwood London SE Branch
OFFICIAL USE ONLY—FIELD INVESTIGATION REPORT
To be completed as soon as possible following investigation. Contemporaneous notes to be attached.
NAME OF OPERATIVE: *The soon-to-be Mrs Sally Stubbs*
DATE AND TIME OF INVESTIGATION: *Yesterday evening*
ADDRESS OF INVESTIGATION: *The Dog & Duck Pub*
SUBJECT OF INVESTIGATION: *MURDER!*
OBSERVATIONS:

After a brief introduction to my place of work and being tested by pulling a few pints—a test which I passed with flying colours—I settled down to tending the bar and getting to know the regulars. I have never worked as a barmaid before, but I've spent enough time with Elsie to know the ins and outs, and she gave me a few tips before I went.

There was no chance of staying 'undercover', as you say, for long. I had not been there ten minutes before somebody calls to his mate "Mind you don't get saucy now Bernie—that's Harry Stubbs' lady friend. He'll knock your block off if you try anything on with her!"

The disclosure of my identify was quite an icebreaker, as there was quite some interest about your activities in the area, and they all got to telling stories. The funny thing is that after the topic was introduced nobody asked me anything, although I knew more than any of them, they all preferred to tell stories of their own. Anyway things took one turn and another and soon we were talking about the Murder. And of course just like before everyone knew more about it than everyone else and they were all vying for who got the closest look at The Murderer.

"As soon as he came in I knew he was up to no good," said Bernie, who had a red nose and not much hair to speak of. "He sneaked in. And he had his cap pulled down like that."

"All you saw was the back of his head, and you can do a character reading," said his friend Wally, whose whole face was red, and who had a paunch like a pillow on his lap to boot. "You didn't even see his hand."

"I saw his hand," said Bernie.

"You never, you just heard about it from Robbie," said another who was leaning over from the other end of the bar. He was an older gent, rather upright, and clearly thought himself a cut above Wally and Bernie. He had been sipping at a whisky at a slow but steady pace, and smoking a big smelly pipe. For your future reference, I do not care for the smell of pipe tobacco. He added for my benefit, "Robbie's the usual barman."

"Decided to take himself off on holiday," said Bernie, with a wink. "Before the police could ask him about his hobbies."

"Or something else," said Wally.

"You don't really think that," said Bernie.

"All I'm saying," said Wally, appealing to me, "is that you don't stab someone across a table like that. Not if he's awake. A few knock-out drops in his beer though...that'd do the job."

"That's slander," said the man with the pipe. "You've got it in for

Robbie. Just because he stops serving you when you've had too many." *He turned to me. "When Bernie starts slurring, he's had enough. Don't give him any after that."*

"That Robbie is a tinpot tyrant. I wouldn't put anything past him."

"You think he keeps a Mickey Finn behind the bar?" The older gent sneered with the authority of one who knew. "I've been coming here twenty years, and there's never been anything like that in here. D'you see any bottles with a skull and crossbones there under the bar, my dear?"

"Nothing like that," I said. There was a big, battered truncheon hanging there for when things got rough, but that was all.

"If his drink wasn't doctored, how the other cove stab him so easy?" asked Wally.

"He didn't," said Bernie. "There must have been a third man hiding in the room."

"What a load of rubbish you talk," scoffed the pipe-smoker. "Nobody could have got in and out."

"You don't know anything about it."

"Excuse me! Wasn't I sitting right here on this very stool? I was close enough to see his hand."

"What about his hand?" I asked.

"He was missing two fingers," said Bernie, holding up his hand with the ring and little fingers curled in so it looked like he only had three fingers.

"He was missing part of two fingers," corrected the man with the pipe. "Just the top joint, on his left hand. Robbie remarked on it when he'd gone, and I said that I'd noticed it myself. Picked up his drink with his three-fingered hand instead of the good one. If Robbie knew the man, he wouldn't have been surprised at that, would he?"

"The Case of the Three-Fingered Assassin," said Bernie. "That's what they ought to have called it."

"So many people in here and nobody even saw the killer's face," I commented.

"I didn't notice his face," admitted the pipe-smoker. "But I heard him. The voice, not the words. He was very quiet-spoken—took him

two goes to tell Robbie he was looking for Mr Smith. He didn't sound like a foreigner—just ordinary. And that's what makes him so hard to find."

"Not many men missing two fingers," said Bernie.

"There's thousands," objected Wally. "Half the men in the war lost a finger or two to shrapnel or gangrene. Or accidents. Frostbite, even."

"Not half of them," said Bernie. "Only a few."

"Thousands," repeated Wally. "Even if the police knew, it wouldn't help them."

"They probably do know," said the man with the pipe.

"I haven't told them," said Bernie. "Are you implying I'm a squealer?"

"Haven't you heard of forensic science?" jeered the older man. "There was three plain-clothes men with black bags and fingerprint powder and cameras and everything the next morning. They went over every square inch of that room."

"That's modern policing methods for you," said Wally.

"See, they don't have to beat a confession out of somebody these days," the man with the pipe went on, talking to me. "All they need is a single hair from the crime scene and they can prove you did it. Just a speck of dirt the size of grain of salt and they can tell it was you."

"That won't help them find him," said Bernie. "He'll have made himself scarce. Could be in the colonies by now. Anywhere."

"Doesn't need to go that far," said the pipe-smoker. "Just get himself out of London."

The others nodded their heads wisely.

"But won't the police be looking for a suspicious man with three fingers coming from London?" I asked.

"He could wear gloves to hide them," said the pipe smoker. "That's the beauty of it. We both noticed the fingers and we forgot to look at the face."

"Or even a wax fingertip," said Bernie. "Some war veterans have them made."

"There's a bloke with an ivory hand walks in the park," said Wally. "Unless you look closely you'd never know."

"You don't think they'll catch him then?" I asked.

"Better if they don't," said the man with the pipe, with heavy emphasis. "With a man like that."

An uncomfortable silence followed until Bernie spoke up.

"That's all rot," he said. "There's got to be a simple explanation."

"We're better off not knowing," said the man with the pipe. "He came, and he did his business and he's gone. As far as I'm concerned we can leave it at that and it can be another one of those unsolved murders."

He spoke with some conviction. He would not elaborate on whether he thought the murderer was an agent of the devil or just what he was. The brutality, the sudden and inexplicable nature of the killing, had made an impression on him. The killer was something not quite normal and best left alone.

Seeing that nobody was going to contradict him again, he sighed, drained his glass and pushed it in my direction for a refill. By common consent the subject was closed, and the company moved on to talking about the football at great length.

REMARKS AND CONCLUSIONS

The Dog & Duck is a friendly sort of place, and it would not take much tidying and redecorating to make it altogether quite pleasant, for a pub. The clientele is by and large polite and well-mannered, without much use of coarse language.

As regards the Murderer, nobody seems to have noticed him very much except for his three fingers. He was what you would call a nondescript, without any distinguishing features. He ordered a half of bitter, which Robbie drew for him, and then went into the room at the back as directed.

There were mixed opinions on the matter of Robbie the barman, with a sizeable minority willing to suspect that he was in some way involved or colluding with the Murderer, though he was not universally popular. Also there are some people that will say anything once a body's back is turned, and some people who just like telling stories, and some people who do not have any sense to start with. So I don't set much store by what any of them say.

Robbie must have had a better look at the Murderer than anyone else, but I honestly don't think that anybody there knows anything more than they're saying. And if you asked them more, even if you paid them, they'd just start making things up so it's not worth it.

All in all, it was not a difficult evening's work, and the extra money will go towards my wedding trousseau. Not nearly as pleasant as factory work though, and men's conversations do not half get boring after a while—I'd rather watch paint dry than listen to them! With all the smoke and the lack of home comforts I'm sure I don't know what the attraction of a pub is.

Arthur had said that if I could locate the fugitive barman I would win a prize. Sally suggested I check the obvious place, which she was sure Blaine would have overlooked.

In Mr Edgar Allan Poe's classic story, "The Purloined Letter," the police fail to find a missing letter because it is in a letter rack, not stashed in a hiding place as they expected. The barman, the one witness who had seen the murderer, had apparently fled the area. Everyone accepted this as obvious. But perhaps, like Mr Poe, the subject of the search had simply decided to hide in the most obvious place of all. In which case I might be able to have a quiet word with him.

Norwood, it has been remarked, had its heyday in the last century, when it was a desirable address and many grand mansions were erected. Since then, most of them have been put to institutional use, becoming schools, orphanages, offices, hospitals or even asylums. Most, though, have been divided up into flats, such as the building I now approached.

The police had not been here before me; how could they have been? The pub landlord, Mr Robert Cahill's employer, had told them he had no idea where his employee lived. A wave of amnesia rolled in when official enquiries were made. Unofficial channels were far more satisfactory, and Arthur Renville's name worked like a charm when I asked.

I gave the bell-pull a hearty tug, and heard it jangle in the upstairs flat. After the fourth pull, I heard a door on the ground floor open, and a minute later the front door opened to reveal a stooped old fellow in a dirty undershirt. Judging from the name under the bell, this would be Mr Eaton.

"He's gone," said the putative Eaton, holding on to the door with one hand. "Slung his hook. No use your wearing out the bell."

"Good afternoon," I said, tipping my hat. "I'm looking for Mr Cahill, who I believe occupies flat Number D, on the upper floor. He is the barman at the Dog and Duck public house."

"Who d'you think I'm talking about?" he demanded. "And who are you anyway—a debt collector?"

"As a matter of fact I am," I said. "But in this instance I just wished to have a private word with Mr Cahill."

"That bird has flown," said Eaton. "What did you want to talk to him about anyway?"

"He is a material witness in a rather unpleasant murder," I said.

"That again." He stroked his cheek. "All I know is this. He came back all of a hurry, told me to look after the aspidistras, and he was going and he couldn't say how long it would be."

"Aspidistras?"

"Very valuable plants, and they take a bit of looking after." He said this with a perfectly straight face. "I've done it before, when he had to go 'abroad,' like. He told me he was going and said I might need to look after them for some considerable time."

As an explanation it was far too convenient. It was also ridiculous. I put my hand on the door in what might at the least be seen as an assertive gesture. Plenty of people make fun of me, but this seemed unwarranted.

"I've been perfectly reasonable with you, Mr Eaton," I said, balancing politeness with assertiveness. "There's no call for you to go wasting my time. You may think I look like a fool, but I assure you I am not going to be taken in by stories about 'aspidistras.' Tell me the truth now, did Cahill ask you to put off anyone who came after him?"

"It's God's own truth," he protested. "Really and truly, he left me to look after his aspidistras. He has quite a collection."

"Codswallop," I said firmly. "My view is that Mr Cahill has not gone anywhere, he's lying low in his own flat. And you're covering for him, giving me a cock and bull story—now, looking after a dog, I could believe, or even a parrot. But Mr Eaton—this tale of vegetation-minding carries no credibility."

I could have gone on to say how well-known it was, even to the likes of me, that the aspidistra is a tough customer that can withstand any amount of bad treatment, but I did not want to stoop that far.

"Very well, I'll show you," he said, opening the door.

He admitted me into a narrow hallway.

"Meredith, we're in," I whispered to myself.

"I'm just showing a gentleman into the flat upstairs!" he shouted through an open door. "My wife—bedridden."

"I'm sorry to hear that," I said.

"Don't be long," croaked a female voice behind us.

Eaton led me up three flights of stairs. As we went up he trudged slower and slower and the carpeting grew thinner with each floor until we arrived at the entrance to the top-floor apartment. Eaton paused, breathing heavily and jangling keys about until he found the right one.

"See, I have the keys," he said. "How d'you explain that if I'm not watering his plants?"

I had expected gaining access to be more difficult than this. At the same time I realised that because it was easy, it was most likely futile. Eaton would not have been half so eager to let me in if Cahill really was hiding up there.

"Everyone thinks you can neglect an aspidistra all you like," he said. "But that's not so. Not when they're young."

A cramped entrance hall opened into a larger space with a sharply angled ceiling, punctuated with three dormer windows, two of which were open. It was living room, bedroom, dining room and kitchen all rolled into one, though it was as much conservatory as anything, with a veritable forest of potted plants sprouting from every available surface.

"See?" said Eaton. "Best collection of aspidistras in Norwood, bar none."

The enormous plants with their leathery green leaves gave the apartment the feeling of a jungle clearing. They have always been a popular centrepiece in middle-class drawing rooms, but you only see them singly. You seldom see several of them in one place. This gathering felt strange, like the members of a secret cult meeting for some clandestine communion.

"Plant-lover, is he?"

"Money-lover, more like," said Eaton. "These specimens will be worth a pretty penny, once they get to a certain size. Cahill reckons next year he'll cash 'em all in."

"There's not much light for them."

"Aspidistras are shade plants."

"Well, now I've seen everything," I said. "It really is an aspidistra farm."

Eaton picked up a feather duster, obviously kept on hand for the purpose, and whisked the nearest plant with a proprietary air.

"The adult plant is a robust sort," he said, with the confidence of a man repeating something he has only just learned. "That's what makes them so popular. But in their early days they are tender creatures that need nurturing. Once they reach a certain stage they're tough as old boots, you just have to get 'em past that and you're quids in."

He indicated a side table crowded with bottles of assorted shapes and sizes, sprays large and small loaded with formulations to stave off insects, fungus and blight. An entire chemist's shop for the care and cultivation of aspidistras. Below them were two tin watering cans, and a kind of umbrella-stand with trowels and forks. But my attention was had been caught by something else.

"What's that smell?" I asked. Beneath the earthy odours of damp potting compost and the sharpness of plant-feeding formula was something harsher and more metallic, something I knew well from my days in the butcher's shop.

I pushed past Eaton and opened the bathroom door. The smell was stronger in here, and overlaid with top notes of meat going off. Towels obscured the contents of the bathtub. I tossed them aside; the towelling was covered in dark, wet stains. A body lay face-down in the empty tub.

"Look here," I said. "Would this be Mr Cahill?"

Eaton was speechless for a moment, just gulping.

"Is it him?"

The old man nodded, still tongue-tied.

I rolled the body over, and the cause of death was readily apparent. Cahill's throat had been slashed, not ear-to-ear but a deep gouge that had efficiently severed some vital artery—the jugular, I suppose. The vast majority of Cahill's blood had run down the plug hole. Something tinkled against the bath: a bloodied open razor. What they aptly call a cut-throat razor.

I surveyed the bathroom, the white plaster walls and the tiling around the wash basin, the mirror above it. Not a drop of blood anywhere, but there was a mark just about five feet above the ground next to the mirror. Cahill had been placed, or forced, face-down in the bath and his throat had been cut in situ like a slaughtered pig.

There was a discoloured patch on Cahill's forehead. It would take a coroner to say for sure whether that had been there before he was killed. My guess, though, was that Cahill had been standing in the bathroom when he had been assaulted. Either he had been hit with a blunt instrument, or else his head bashed against the wall leaving that smudge. While stunned, he had been thrown or toppled into the bath where he suffered the fatal injury.

It reminded me of the way we stun animals before slaughter.

"Oh my Lord," said Eaton, supporting himself as though he was the one struck on the head. "He was here all the time."

"Just you calm down now." I guided him to an armchair, and went to fetch a glass of water. The last thing I needed was my only witness having a funny turn. Or a heart attack.

As the last one to have seen his neighbour alive, Eaton was the obvious suspect. He was not a powerful man, but even seemingly-weak individuals can have a burst of strength when driven by passion or desperation.

He gulped the water gratefully while I tried to formulate my line of questioning.

"Mr Cahill told you he was going away, and then he gave you his keys," I said.

"No, I've always had a spare set."

"He told you he was going away, and consequently you've been coming up here to look after the plants for the last four days. And in all that time you never noticed there was a corpse in the bathtub."

"The kitchen tap is closer for filling the watering cans," he said. "I never had any call to go in the bathroom."

"So when would have been the last time you spoke to him?"

"That very night, like I said. He came back, late as usual, and told me there had been some trouble at the pub, somebody stabbed. And he was going away because he didn't want no trouble."

"What time was this? Did he wake you?"

Eaton opened and closed his hands as though trying to clutch a fragment of historical time to better examine it.

"About ten o'clock. I was awake anyway, I'm always awake. Because of my wife, you know. I looked out to see who it was, and I saw him on the stairs, and we chatted for a bit, and he reminded me about the care routine for the plants. And he went up, and that was the last I saw of him."

I made a circuit of the room, avoiding the potted plants as a racing-driver avoids obstacles, and noted an open valise on the bed, stuffed with shirts and underwear. Mr Cahill had been partway through packing when he had been interrupted. Perhaps he had gone to get his things from the bathroom.

"Did you hear somebody go up after him?"

"No, nobody."

"And you didn't think it strange you never heard him come down?"

"I didn't think about it," said Eaton, wringing his hands. "I just thought he must have gone out quietly."

I stuck my head out the dormer window. The roof sloped down steeply to the guttering. I made a note of the exact layout so I would be able to identify it when I surveyed the building from below. Then I made another circuit of the apartment, paying particular attention to the floor, which was scattered with crumbs of black compost.

Eaton looked up beseechingly. As though I had the answer.

"Well now, Mr Eaton," I said. "This is the manner in which we will proceed. Once you've calmed down a little, I'll go and talk to a friend of mine and he'll arrange things. Maybe we will have to involve the police, but we may not."

"But I have the only key!" he said, his hands chasing each other over his lap. "They'll think I did it for the aspidistras. These plants are worth money. He always said so."

"Don't worry, Mr Eaton. Just tell Mr Renville what you know and you've nothing to fear."

I escorted Eaton back downstairs, and even exchanged a couple of words with his bedridden wife to assure her that all was well and her husband would calm down soon. Getting the two of them back together did seem to soothe him and he fell into his natural role of carer. I declined the offer of a cup of tea and bade them farewell.

Eaton did not have much to worry about. I guessed that Arthur would keep the police out of it. They were kicking up enough fuss over the one murder; having a double murder would inflame things even more, and probably get the newspaper reporters out in force out to boot.

I was not looking forward to the interview. I had been hoping to impress Arthur with a discovery, perhaps even a lead pointing directly to the killer before Blaine found him. Instead of new information all I had uncovered was a new corpse for him to worry about. It was better for him to have the news rather than the authorities, but I could not expect very much thanks.

Sally and I walked arm-in-arm through the Crystal Palace Park, past the boating lake and the dinosaurs. Seeing the lifelike recreations of those long-dead monsters, things that no human has ever seen, gives me a certain satisfaction. For centuries men thought there were no such things as dragons, until science proved that there were. Similarly, the things that I had seen, things that nobody else would ever believe—one day they too would be proved by science, and people would walk round them in parks.

"It's like the 'Murders in the Rue Morgue'," said Sally. "That had an open window and a cut-throat razor as the murder weapon. It was a gorilla that did it."

"The murderer must have been as agile as a monkey," I said. "My reasoning is that he followed Cahill to the building and went up the outside, and in through the window which had been left open to give the plants sufficient ventilation. Then he waited in the bathroom, and ambushed Cahill with his own razor when he came in."

"You don't think it was Eaton then?"

I shook my head. There was no logical reason why the old man could not have been the culprit. Except that it would be odd behaviour for the murderer to invite someone in to discover their crime. Some criminals do delight in taunting the authorities and flaunting their crimes, but he did not seem the sort.

"I think it was whoever committed the previous murder. My reason for wanting to talk to Cahill was that he was the one person who might be able to identify the man. And it seems I was not alone in my reasoning. Furthermore, from the circular impressions left on the rug, I noted that some of the plant pots had been moved. Moved in exactly a way so as to provide convenient access to one of the windows."

"If he's not a monkey, he's one of those cat-burglars," said Sally. "There can't be many of those around. Or a circus acrobat. Or a steeplejack."

"I hope it helps Blaine in his investigation," I said.

Sally drew in her breath over her teeth with a hiss at the mention of his name, and I elected to change the subject.

I stopped by the Ichthyosaurus, an enormous, fish-like creature with a long snout, a row of pointed teeth and huge saucer eyes, basking in the shallow water among the lily pads.

"Have you ever heard of the theory of parallel evolution?" I asked.

"Course not," she said. "And I'll bet you hadn't either until you went to the library this afternoon."

Sally's knack for seeing through me was disconcerting. I supposed that this was a foretaste of married life.

"Be that as it may," I said, "the theory is that evolution shapes things according to their particular niche, whatever they originally looked like. So this ichthyosaur, which was originally descended from land-dwelling quadruped reptiles, ends up looking almost the same as a dolphin, which similarly evolved from four-footed terrestrial creatures."

"That's a lot of long words in one sentence, Harry," she said, "But I think I see what you mean. They all look like fish when they've been living in the water a while."

"Not just fish, but practically identical to each other."

She tilted her head on one side. "If you say so, *Professore*, but you'd have more luck passing off a mastiff as a greyhound than selling that one as a dolphin."

"More striking examples exist," I said. "This is just what we have to hand here for purposes of illustration. The wombat of the Antipodes is remarkably similar to the groundhog of North America, though they are completely unrelated. Environmental factors moulded them both to the same shape."

"Don't know what either of them looks like," she said. "Do you?"

I rose above her rather pointed observation.

"The Malagassy Fossa looks exactly like a domestic cat, although it is in fact a species of mongoose. Because there are no cats native to Madagascar, it has evolved to occupy the same niche as the cat does in Europe."

"Oh well, that proves it then," she said.

A couple passed by pushing a perambulator, and Sally bestowed a fond look on the baby waving its little fists in the air. He could not see the towering monsters on the island just a few yards away. How traumatic might it be for him to get a glimpse of them at such a tender age? Probably not at all; he was too young to see them as anything but strange-shaped blocks of stone.

"They're still arguing about whether evolution exists in America. Trying to get the schools to stop teaching it. It's well-established as a scientific fact though. Mr Charles Darwin proved it."

"So I've heard."

"It is a lovely evening" I said, patting her arm. "And I shouldn't be wasting it boring on about matters I don't even understand myself."

"You've evolving into a detective," she said, with a certain pride. "That's what this is about, isn't it? That murder case."

"I shouldn't bring work home with me."

"I wouldn't be here if you hadn't," she said, with a light laugh. "But I know what you mean about evolution. We get the same thing happening all the time with the girls at the pickle factory."

"How's that?"

"We get new girls coming all the time. They start out looking different, with dowdy clothes, long hair all over the place and that. Some of them have odd accents, you know, girls from the country—" she put on an exaggerated Kentish burr, "I ha'ant a-seen her since Chewsday last." Adopting her usual voice, "And you know, within three months they're just like everyone else. Artificial silk stockings, shingled hair, and talking like they was born Londoners."

"That's just imitation, though."

"Not the way I look at it," she said, shaking her head emphatically. "It's what you call the niche, the environmental pressures shaping them. When they've got the same money as everyone else, they can afford the same things, like nice clothes. And if they want to attract a mate, they've got to have the right hair and make-up. And you've got to talk London or nobody can understand you. It's what you'd call the evolutionary niche of the pickle factory girl."

"You make it all a lot easier than those books," I said. "You should be a teacher, Sally, not working a machine putting tops on jars."

"I'm a senior now," she reminded me. "I've moved up the ladder. Don't know if I like the sound of teaching."

"You're very good with children."

"Your brother's little ones are lovely," she said fondly. "The little devils you get in schools though—pickle factory's much more fun."

We chatted on about her job prospects and what she would do after we were married. Ideas about dinosaurs and convergent evolution sunk into the deeper recesses of my brain, there to marinate for a while until I was ready to inspect them again.

Now, the celebrated Occam's Razor might argue against such a wild flight of fancy as I had in mind. There is no need to go inventing new things when all can be explained well enough without resorting to outrageous novelties unknown to science. But my visit to the library, and my conversation with Sally, had set me to wondering something I had not previously considered: could there be a being which walked like a man, and talked like a man, but which was not in fact anything like human?

I was deep in thought on this matter when Sally returned to the previous topic.

"I almost forgot," she said. "I was asking around if anyone knew anyone who was good with codes. And there's maybe someone who lives next door to one of the girls in the factory who can help."

I could hardly turn down an offer of help, though when she explained it sounded like a rather unlikely source of assistance.

I never know what to say to children. And I am not at my best when interviewing women. You might imagine, perhaps, my discomfort at the prospect of interviewing a fourteen-year-old girl, especially when her own aunt refused to be present.

The front room was average enough, a fine carriage clock ticking away on the mantelpiece, flanked by three Dresden shepherdesses on either side. A coal fire glowed in the grate, two views of Paris and His Majesty's visage looking down from the walls. The headrests of the chairs were protected by antimacassars with a lot of fussy lace; I did not dare lean back on mine.

The temperature might have been pleasant, but the atmosphere was frigid.

Miss Frey sat stiffly in her chair, looking ahead with iron-blue eyes. I was not sure if she was staring at the clock, willing the minutes to pass, or glowering at the china shepherdesses. They were pretty and graceful and feminine; she was not.

Miss Frey did not look like a polite young lady. Her hair had been chopped short, and not by a hairdresser. I am no expert on ladies' fashion, but the brown dress which enveloped her looked like a cast-off which had been in the back of a wardrobe for a generation.

I had been ushered in here with a cup of weak tea. I could barely taste it, so strong was the smell of furniture polish. My attempts to start a conversation had elicited monosyllables and Miss Frey had yet to meet my eye.

The ticking of the clock became louder as the silence between us grew.

Miss Frey was by all accounts a prodigy, but she was also more troubled than I had been given to understand. I gathered from her aunt that the niece had flashes of brilliance at school, especially in mathematics and language, but also that she repeatedly got into trouble by trying to correct her teachers. And that she preferred the company of books to that of her peers. She was clearly not the social type, and everything about her manner suggested that this meeting was not her choice. She positively radiated hostility, so I was not entirely caught unprepared for what happened next.

She turned suddenly, steel glinting in her hand, and thrust at my face.

I ducked my head to one side, caught her wrist in one hand, and with the other plucked the scissors from her grip. She let out a small cry of surprise, and I pushed her, not too hard, back into her armchair.

My inclination was to end the interview at that. Actions speak louder than words, and if she could not express herself any other way, she had made her feelings known. I was not willing to give up so easily, though. It was not simply perversity on my part, but a sense that she was motivated more by unhappiness than actual anger.

"That's really not necessary, Miss Frey," I said, placing the scissors beside my tea. They were small but sharp, stolen no doubt from the sewing-box.

She rubbed the red imprint of my grip around her wrist, looking daggers at me, daring me to slap her. I had no intention of doing any such thing. Violence was uncalled-for.

"Your auntie was telling me," I started. "That you won a newspaper competition."

"So?"

She packed a deal of hostility into that one syllable. I hesitated to go on.

"I'm a freak," she added. "What did you expect?"

That rather brought the conversation to a standstill again. Miss Frey fixed her gaze on the far wall once more.

"You've seen me now," she said. "You can go any time you want."

"As a matter of fact, I wanted to ask you something."

"What? You want help with a crossword?"

Her words rattled like granite chips down a metal chute.

"I'm not really a crossword-puzzle enthusiast," I said. "I do have a puzzle though, one which is somewhat more complex."

She gave no sign of interest. But she did not say anything discouraging either.

"You won a newspaper competition—"

"I wish I'd never done it!"

She sounded entirely sincere. I slipped the piece of paper from my pocket, unfolded it.

"Nevertheless, you show a remarkable natural talent for breaking codes. I was wondering if you—"

"Why should I?" she shot back.

"That's a reasonable question, Miss Frey," I admitted. "I haven't really thought about it."

"Well?"

She was quick, and she was sharp. And not overly polite. A difficult customer for someone like her aunt, who was more the slow, conventional sort who would not take to be answered back to.

"Well, in the milieu in which I operate, there's always an understanding of what they call quid pro quo—something for something else. You do me a favour, and I owe you a favour in return. Favours are the common currency."

"Huh. I thought you were going to offer me a bonnet or a handbag, or something stupid like that," she said. For the first time her tone was almost conversational.

Perhaps I would have offered her some item of female attire, if I had been thinking about it. But somehow I had not been considering her as a girl at all.

"You don't want a hat," I said.

"What sort of favour would you do—do you beat people up?"

"What has you aunt told you?" I said.

"*She* didn't say anything. I just thought. You know."

"To the uninitiated I may look like the sort of person who 'beats people up'," I said. "But looks can be highly misleading. I dare say there's more than meets the eye to all of us."

"Pity," she said. "There's people I'd like to see beaten up."

"I don't do beatings. But I can menace," I said. "Like this."

I straightened my back and put on an absurd gargoyle face. In spite of herself Miss Frey giggled.

"Or this." I made an even more grotesque expression, one that always got a laugh from my little nephew, but there was no laugh this time.

"I've got a better idea." She nodded to the mantelpiece. "Would you break those? They're too perfect. I hate them."

The shepherdesses posed elegantly mid-twirl, indifferent to Miss Frey's feelings and their danger. Miss Frey had been willing enough to attack me, but had not smashed the china figures when she had a chance. Either she feared the consequences from her aunt of breaking one, or she wanted to test me.

"You help me, and I'll help you," I said.

She took the sheet of paper and stared at it intently. She went to a shelf to retrieve a school exercise book and a pencil. She folded the book open on itself and, resting it on the arm of her chair, started copying out symbols.

I watched the clock and allowed her to work undisturbed.

"It's too short for a cipher," she said. "It's a code."

"What does that mean?"

She did not reply for a minute but continued copying out characters. A tiny vertical line had appeared between her eyebrows.

"A cipher is where each character stands in for a letter," she said. "Like a substitute alphabet. There are seventy-three characters here, so that would only be about fifteen words. And there are too many of them and not enough repetitions."

"Repetitions of what?"

"English writing is one-fifth e's and a's," she said. "So you look for those first. But there's no more than two of anything.

And most of them are unique. That's impossible for English. Was this copied properly?"

"As far as I know."

"Even if it's copied wrong…that could be a tail, that one and that one might be the same…it doesn't make it any better." She looked up. "It's definitely a code rather than a cipher."

"Which means what?"

"Each character stands for a word, or a phrase," she said.

"I noticed how some of the characters are similar but different, like Christmas trees with different number of branches," I said.

Miss Frey turned the page and started sketching.

"There are these six basic roots or bodies," she said. "And then they each get extra lines and squiggles and dots added. Lots of different ones. Vertical, horizontal. And this one has little v's added."

She carried on sketching and I let her work for a few minutes more.

"It's strange," she said. "I don't understand how this works."

"I suppose that's how codes are supposed to work."

"No! I mean, it's really strange." She shook her head as though trying to shake something off. "It's not a code, is it? It's in some foreign language."

"I don't honestly know," I said.

"You can tell. Or I can. With codes it always keeps the same shape as English, even if it's completely different. Even backwards. This isn't like that."

"So it's maybe another language, like German, and then turned into code." My heart sank. It was sounding increasingly unlike that the enigma would be unravelled.

"No, no, not like German." Another vigorous shake of the head. "German's just like English, really."

"If you say so. But if it isn't German, what sort of language is it? Chinese?"

She shook her head again, more slowly.

"You'll have to give me some sort of clue," I said. "Because I don't know what you're talking about."

"Look at it," she said, as though I hadn't already stared long enough to give me a headache.

She scribbled more, then stopped abruptly.

"I can't do this," she said. "It's not fair!"

"I'm afraid—"

"It's not fair!" she said, even louder, lunging for the scissors. Instead of attacking me again she snipped at the offending scrap of paper with a series of violent movements, not efficiently but expressively. "It's not fair!"

After a minute of furious activity she had cut the paper to shreds, during which times tears started to run down her cheeks. Confetti littered the floor around her feet; Miss Frey's aunt would not be pleased.

"I see," I said, in a calming tone. "Your considered conclusion, then, Miss Frey is that the message represents an unknown language, rather than being a simple cipher or coded communication."

She sniffed and swallowed. She looked a little embarrassed.

"I suppose so. Yes."

I took a china figure from the mantelpiece, weighed it in my hand, tossed up in the air a couple of times. Once I was sure I had her attention, I tossed it up again and let it fall. It shattered on the tiled fireplace surround, sending bits of china shooting in all directions.

Miss Frey's mouth gaped, then she grinned delightedly.

"Quid pro quo. I do know what you mean about those statuettes," I said. "They can be a bit...smug, I suppose you'd say. Not my choice of decoration."

"But I couldn't help," she said, her smile vanishing.

"I wouldn't say that exactly. In fact, I'd say you've saved me a great deal of time in going down blind alleys. And indicated that I am very much on the right path. Your suggestion that the writing does not resemble any human language makes perfect sense."

The line appeared between her eyebrows again.

"So what is it?"

"Inhuman language, Miss Frey," I said. "I'm so sorry it caused you so much distress."

"No, no," she said, and I was not quite sure what she meant. She was looking at her notes again. "Inhuman language?"

"Something from brains quite unlike our own. No wonder your finely-tuned intellect had trouble digesting something so alien. Had I known, I wouldn't have sprung it on you without any preamble."

She laughed at that, which I took as a good sign.

"I didn't give you much chance!" She put her notes down. "I'm sorry. If you can get any more writing like this I might be able to start getting a sense for it. If you've got any clue what it's about..."

"I'm sorry, Miss Frey, I'm very much in the dark. But it's good to have some confirmation of my theory."

"My pleasure," she said, shrugging, confused, half-sarcastic. Almost like any other fourteen-year-old.

I took a step towards the door, groping for a suitable exit line.

"Do be careful with scissors now, don't go hurting someone." I paused, wanting to say more, filling the gap by unwrapping a toffee for myself. "If people call you a freak—and that's not an unfamiliar experience to me—that's simply their very impolite way of expressing that you have qualities they lack."

I gave her what I hoped was a cheery wink, and went to confront Miss Frey's aunt.

"Of course," I told Sally later, "I had to apologise several times to the aunt for breaking the china piece, and I paid suitable recompense."

"That poor girl," said Sally.

We were walking to the pictures for our evening's entertainment. Well-earned entertainment, in my case, not that the day had been exactly a productive one.

"I'll remind you that she did attack me with a pair of scissors," I said. I had expected a bit more sympathy.

"Oh, you poor man," said Sally in mock pity. "You don't fool me Harry Stubbs. Remember how that bloke came at you with an axe once? You weren't bothered by that. Pulled it right out of his hands. A little girl with a tiny pair of scissors wouldn't bother you."

"A small, quick assailant can be very dangerous, especially one armed with a sharp implement," I said. "She could have had my eye out."

"Oh very likely," Sally scoffed. "But you did the right thing." She patted my arm. "Nine men out of ten would have slapped her and left then and there. But you saw all she wanted was a little kindness."

"I believe that girl has a special talent," I said. "I would have preferred it if she had been able to crack the code and tell us what it said. But if she couldn't do it, well I don't believe anyone could. Which is an interesting fact in its own right."

"They even broke that German code in the war," said Sally. "The telegram about the Americans."

"I believe this one may be uncrackable. It's a genuine unknown language. Not much use to Arthur, maybe, but it might be an indication that this really is an unusual sort of a case."

In the library, I was alerted to a presence at my shoulder by the rank smell.

"Afternoon, Mr Stubbs," said Slingsby, nodding at the volumes piled up around me. "You're set yourself a lot of reading with all those books."

"Slingsby—I didn't know you came in here," I said.

"I like reading," he said defensively. "Especially about sailing ships, and the great age of discovery and that." He held up a book with his grubby fingers—*Samuel Pepys and the making of the Royal Navy.* "So long as I don't bother anyone, they leave me be. I just tuck myself in a corner and nobody notices."

I found that hard to believe. The smell alone must have cleared out a good radius around him. More likely the librarians did not want to get their hands dirty and make a scene throwing him out. I let it pass.

"Sailing ships, eh? Each to his own."

"You look like you were looking for something," he said. "I kept hearing you riffling through those pages and thumping books down. I thought I might offer my services, like, give you another pair of eyes."

Certainly, I could have used some help, but I needed someone sober, studious and reliable. I did not make an immediate answer, and he seized on my hesitation.

"I know what you're thinking," he said. "But all I'm asking

for is payment on results. If I'm no use, you don't give me anything. If I am—well, you've got a half-pack of cigs, and you don't even smoke."

Paying Slingsby off with tobacco would stop him from bothering me further, but I was reluctant to get him involved.

"I'm afraid this a case for a confidential client," I said. "I can't—"

"Mr Stubbs," he said, and waved a forefinger from himself to me and back. "You and me, we have an understanding. We already share secrets—you can trust me." He indicated the patched gunshot holes in his greatcoat. "Come on, Mr Stubbs, give a man a chance to do an honest job for once."

I leaned back and pulled a chair over. Lord knew what sort of trouble I would get into for consorting with Slingsby, but I was not going to sit here and argue with him. I shoved the nearest pile of books in front of him, volumes I had already scoured without turning up a single grain of gold. He sat down, placing his own book to one side.

"What you need to do is look through these for references to—to lizard men."

"Oho," he said, showing his blackened teeth in a quick smile. "Lizard men. The sort as might shed their skins, you mean."

"Lizard men, humanoid reptiles, snake people, anything else of that ilk. Anything you find, you mark the place with a slip of paper for me to read. No folding of pages or defacing of the volumes, you understand."

"I know the library rules, Mr Stubbs," he said. "I'll see what I can find for you."

Slingsby was not a quiet library companion. He wheezed, and he mumbled to himself sometimes when reading. He was restless and kept changing position in his seat. And I could not help noticing the smell. But his presence was enough to make me redouble my own effort. Knowing that you are under scrutiny is a good way of preventing daydreaming, especially where poring through a deal of tedious written material.

When I was finished with a book I added it to his pile.

"I prefer the pictures," he remarked, thumbing through

some plates in a book about explorers in the Middle East. "I like pictures of old ships best."

I did not comment, but continued diligently reading through a summary of Mesoamerican mythology, made almost unreadable with tongue-twinging polysyllabic names. The ancient Aztecs—or Mayans or someone in that part of the globe— venerated snakes, and had a snake-god who was considered to be their ancestor of their people. He was not what you would call a snake-man though, and he was invariably described as feathered which was unhelpful.

I paused at an illustration of a peculiar idol: the figure of a man composed of many snakes. Or perhaps it represented a priest covered in sacred snakes; the scholars were unclear.

"There's one," said Slingsby. "Have a look at this, Mr Stubbs."

"Put a placemark in it," I said.

"Come on, have a look now."

I marked my own place and he turned his book around. I checked the cover—it was Col. F.W. Phelan's *The Lone and Level Sands: An Expedition to the Heart of Arabia*.

Strokes had singled out one of the photographic plates.

XII—"Three clay tablets recovered from the excavations at Al-Manzafar. See pp115-118"

Two of the tablets in the picture were unadorned oblongs covered with cuneiform, but the third was quite different. In the four corners of the tablet were grotesque figures. They walked on two legs, but they had long tails and grotesque heads somewhere between a crocodile and a seal.

"What do you call that," said Slingsby, "if not a lizard man?"

"You've got a keen eye," I admitted. Sharpened, no doubt, by all those days of searching for fag-ends in the gutter. I took a magnifying glass from my pocket to inspect the photograph more closely.

"Four lizard men, in fact," he said. He stretched and rose to his feet. "Four successes. Enough book-work for the day, eh? I'll take my pay now if you don't mind."

Slingsby was not one for sustained effort, and I was more than glad to see him go, shuffling out with the prized pack of cigarettes clamped in his dirty hand.

The figures adorning the corners of the tablet were undoubtedly meant to depict lizard men of some sort.

I turned to the relevant passage in the book. The tablet was considered to be unique, its place of origin unknown, but likely Mesopotamian. It had been found in the tomb of a scholar-king of the first century, part of his most treasured collection, but was probably much older. Its meaning and significance, and even the pictographic alphabet it was written in, were all unknown. It was said to have come from a nameless city somewhere towards the interior of Arabia, but this had never been identified.

I turned back to the photograph to inspect the text on the tablet. It was difficult to tell, but under the magnifying glass peculiar writing resolved itself into a series of more distinct shapes.

My jaw dropped open.

I fumbled the scrap of paper which Arthur had given me, with the copied symbols, and looked from one to the other. At first I was not sure; the overall pattern was similar, but none of the actual pictograms seemed to match. Then I turned the paper upside-down, and the resemblance jumped out at me.

The letter was written in an alphabet which had been unknown for eighteen hundred years. An alphabet associated with lizard men. A secret writing which had remained impenetrable for millennia—and which was still in use.

"They arrested him then," said Sally. "Your murderer."

"I hadn't heard. How did you know?"

"It'll be in the evening papers, I expect. I got it from Joan in the factory. Her neighbour's sister is married to a policeman who heard it at the station."

"How did they catch him?"

"It was a post-office box number." She leaned forward confidentially. "You see, the man who was stabbed, he was using his shop as a postal address for a bit of extra income. Only he didn't leave it at that. He reckoned that anyone who wanted a PO box had something to hide, so he steamed open all their letters, and he was blackmailing them."

"That's pretty low," I said. "Clever, though."

"Now the police had traced all the PO box holders save one, this man called Jigson. They found forwarding addresses for them in his notebook, but some of them came in and picked up their post personally. None of them fits the description until this last man Jigson comes in—"

"Jigson? What sort of name is that?"

"—and the police were waiting for him. Six of them, ready with revolvers in their hands. He didn't have any chance. They had him in handcuffs and into the van before he knew what hit him, she said."

"Why would a murderer give himself away like that?" It did not ring true to me at all. "In fiction, they always return to the scene of the crime, but…"

"Maybe he thought it would look more suspicious if he didn't come," she said after a moment's thought.

"But the police wouldn't have been able to trace him if he'd stayed away. Not just from a name, which is surely an alias anyway."

"Or he was expecting an important communication."

I thought of the pictograph-letters, their uncrackable code.

"Then he could have sent a boy to get it," I said. "And checked the boy wasn't followed when he came back."

"All I can say is that he was the last one, and he matched the description exactly—not that they had much of a description."

Something was very wrong here. A man who was prepared to cover his tracks by murdering a second time, one who communicated in unbreakable code via a post office box…a man like that would not make the elementary mistake of walking into such an obvious police trap.

"I do hope they've got the right man," I said.

"Who else could it be?" she asked. "They've eliminated everyone else. Maybe Jigson just got over-confident, thought he'd got away with it. It happens, you know. Criminals are not all masterminds."

"They'll have to get a confession. There're no good witnesses, not from what you said. The only two men who got a good look at him are both dead. If he keeps his mouth shut they won't be able to pin anything on him."

"He could be a professional killer with a previous history. They'll be matching his fingerprints with every other unsolved murder. Checking his alibi. Interviewing his associates and seeing if any of them squeal."

I never went much beyond Holmes, but Sally was an avid reader of modern crime fiction, among other things. I have never been a fan of Agatha Christie, but Sally was well-informed on current methods.

"I suppose the police know what they're doing," I said. "Presumably, he did at the least have parts of two of his fingers missing? Not that such a thing would on its own be enough to convict him."

"It depends on the jury," she said pensively.

Even in police custody, the murderer would be safe so long as he kept a cool head and told them nothing. They rely on breaking a man down by constant pressure, browbeating and a little rough treatment—enough for him to know what's in store if he doesn't co-operate. Or maybe they'd put him in with a cellmate who would pump him for information in exchange for his own charges being dropped. A man who was resolute and determined, one who could resist the psychological pressure, would survive unscathed.

"Fingerprints again, though," she said. "He should have worn gloves. He left his fingerprints on the knife."

"And he was just a normal person?" I asked.

"Not a lizard man. Not as far as anyone can tell," she said. "We don't know how good his disguise is."

I could not tell if Sally was joking with me, but she saw the look on my face and patted my hand.

"I do believe in them," she said, adding unexpectedly, "it's in the Bible."

"Is it?"

"In the Garden of Eden, the serpent talks to Eve. And later on God cursed it so it couldn't walk upright but had to slither on its belly. So before it must have been a walking, talking serpent. A very cunning one. Maybe one that can hypnotise people like a snake hypnotises rabbits. That fits the bill, doesn't it?"

"I suppose so," I said.

I was pleased that Sally was taking my side, though as far as the case went it seemed less relevant than ever.

Some friends were meeting at The Horns, a local public house, to watch a darts match. Otherwise I should never have been there. The contest was just getting interesting when I felt an insistent tap on my shoulder.

"Put your drink down, Stubbs, I want a word with you outside."

I turned to see Blaine's ruddy and none-too-handsome visage.

Grudgingly, because the match was so gripping, I passed my pint to a friend and followed the former police inspector through the door. Outside it was cool and clear and quiet.

"I'm not having you upstaging me," he said. "I've heard about what you've been up to. Very clever."

"I'm not upstaging you," I said. "I've followed a few lines but—the case is over, isn't it? I haven't had anything to do with it."

He held my gaze for a long second. Blaine was breathing heavily; he looked like he wanted to hit me. I found myself bending my knees and raising my arms a little, ready to dodge or block.

"It's over, is it?" he asked.

"That was very much my understanding. Unless…"

He allowed me to trail off, and make the connection.

"The suspect will be released tomorrow, due to lack of supporting evidence," said Blaine. "As your all-seeing intelligence sources have not informed you of the fact."

"I didn't know that."

"Now you do know it, you'll know to stay well away," he said. "My colleagues on the force have failed signally to get any purchase on the suspect. So as soon as he's freed I'm going to tackle him myself with my own personal approach. And you're not going to be involved."

"Of course not," I said.

"Of course not," he mimicked.

"Have you got some evidence that the police missed?" I asked, unable to resist.

He looked at me pityingly.

"How this works is, I'm going to have a little chat with him, and he's going to give me all the evidence I want," Blaine said. "In fact he's going to be begging to tell me all about it."

I was not so sure. Clearly Jigson was a tough customer, and if the police had a scrap of good evidence they would have held on to him.

"I should let you come along to see how it's done," said Blaine, seeing my doubt. "It'd be an education for you. You think it's all about physical pain, like in the ring. It isn't. Breaking a man is all about what's inside here." He tapped his head. "But maybe you're a bit too soft-hearted to witness something like that."

"He is a dangerous man," I said.

I did not like to say that Jigson might not be a man at all, might be something other than human.

"So am I," Blaine said.

Whatever Blaine had in mind for Jigson, I did not wish to be part of it. Even if the man on the receiving end was a double murderer.

"I'll keep out of your way."

"'I'll keep out of your way, *Mr Blaine*,' you mean," he said.

This was too much for me. I had imbibed a couple of drinks, and my evening's entertainment had been interrupted just so Blaine could throw his weight around. I leaned back and looked down on him.

"I know what I mean," I said.

Instead of getting angry, Blaine barked his laugh. My show of defiance was merely amusing.

"I expect you do," he said. He went on in a less friendly tone. "And afterwards, I'll be letting Renville know just exactly how useless you've been to me this whole case. Just in case he still has any illusions. So long, Stubbs."

With that, Blaine turned on his heel and strode off. I watched him go. I did not have any rejoinder ready even if he had stayed, so I went back to the darts match, feeling that on the whole, the encounter could have ended very much worse.

I was sufficiently worried that later on that evening I had sought out Arthur, hoping to inoculate him against any lies that Blaine might be planning to tell about me. I found him supervising affairs in the dairy yard, where an assorted bunch of labourers and drivers were loitering after being paid off. I waited my turn to speak to Arthur, who listened attentively.

"Don't worry about Blaine," Arthur said reassuringly. "He's like a stick, one I pick up when I need to give something a prod. It's a useful implement, but I know it's covered in muck and I act accordingly when I handle it."

"I do appreciate your understanding, Arthur," I said.

"The thing about Blaine, Stubbsy—he's not one of us," said Arthur. "He might want to work with us, but he'll always be an outsider here."

That put the seal on it. Arthur did not need to explain a word more.

I heard nothing from or about Blaine the next day, when I expected he would be making his move. When I did eventually get word it was from an unexpected quarter.

"I told you that Blaine isn't as clever as he thinks he is," Sally said the next evening, as we were taking our evening stroll in Crystal Palace Park. "Oh, hadn't you heard? That Jigson gave him the slip."

Her smile was a little smug, but still not unattractive. I was prepared to let her be one up on me if she was providing information.

"No I hadn't heard," I said. "This is from your friend-of-a-friend in the force, is it?"

"That's right."

We stopped to admire the boating pond, now occupied only by numbers of ducks and a couple of swans, drifting ghosts in the twilight.

"It seems," Sally went on, "that Blaine had a couple of off-duty coppers with him when he went to apprehend Jigson. They took him to an old railway shed."

At least Blaine had accepted that Jigson really was dangerous, and not somebody that should be tackled without assistance.

How he had persuaded the police officers, with threats or bribery, I could not begin to guess. But it was dirty business; the law should not be involved in such matters.

"The blue shed down by Norwood Junction," I said. The place was known to be unoccupied, and had been used for a variety of more of less nefarious purposes, the most innocuous of which was the storage of boxes of coconuts awaiting transhipment by Arthur's concern.

"I suppose so. Jigson went along like a lamb—same way he did when he was arrested. Blaine probably showed him a badge and pretended it was another arrest. But Jigson won't tell them anything, and Blaine gets rough with him, as you can imagine, and what do you think happens next?"

"I wouldn't mind hearing he picked up a chair and knocked seven bells out of all three of them," I said.

"He dived out the window," she said. "Blaine turned his back for a moment, and the others weren't paying attention, and Jigson just literally leaped out the window. He went from sitting in a chair to a flying jump like he was spring-loaded."

"And they couldn't catch him," I said.

"They got out the shed just in time to see him going around the corner," she said, nodding. "It's a blind alley and they thought they had him, but when they got there—not a sign."

"They should have looked up. I told Blaine that Jigson was a climber. A fast climber by the sound of it."

"Like a monkey," she said. "Or a gorilla."

"Or a lizard. That's the last we'll see of him then," I concluded. "I suppose that makes it a draw; I didn't get him, but Blaine didn't get him either. And if we've seen the back of Jigson for good and all, I suppose Arthur will settle for that."

It appeared to put a cap on the whole thing. I was quite looking forward to seeing Blaine though, and asking him innocently how he had got on with his plan, but that pleasant encounter never happened. Arthur heard nothing from Blaine, and for the next few days the common assumption was that Blaine was out somewhere tracking Jigson down. The longer things went on, though, the less likely this seemed.

I sought out Arthur the next morning in the Electric Café,

where he was addressing a soft-boiled egg with his usual concentration.

"Blaine may not want to come back and tell me he's failed," Arthur told me. "But I'm paying him and I expect some ruddy service for my money."

"There's something else," I said. "I got the address of Jigson's lodgings. If Blaine's busy in hot pursuit, I thought I'd go around there and see if Jigson had left anything that might give a clue, especially as he must've left in a hurry."

"Good thinking Stubbsy," said Arthur, dipping a toast soldier and coating it on both sides before looking up in anticipation.

"Except—Arthur, he didn't leave in a hurry. He didn't leave at all. The landlady told me Jigson is still living there. She expects him back this evening."

"Does she now?" said Arthur, crunching his toast.

"So we have a situation where Jigson is apparently still with us, and Blaine as, as far as anyone knows, mysteriously disappeared. He was seen in a post-office shortly after the incident when Jigson escaped, but nothing since then."

"You think something may have befallen our Mr Blaine? Something like what befell what's-his-name the barman."

"Robert Cahill," I supplied. "Murdered in his own home."

"Couldn't happen to a nicer bloke than Blaine." Arthur dipped another piece of toast meditatively. "I hope Jigson hid the body a bit better this time so we don't have to clear up."

"If you have a home address for Blaine—"

Arthur cut me off with a shake of his head.

"Blaine's not your problem," he said. "What you need to deal with—what we need to deal with—is Jigson."

"Yes."

Arthur sat back and looked at me expectantly.

"So, tell me Stubbsy, what course of action would you recommend at this juncture?"

The question surprised me. Arthur was usually so decisive, like a general commanding his army. I expected him to tell me what to do, but was in what he deemed to be my area of expertise: dealing with the out-of-the-ordinary, the truly uncanny which did not conform to normal laws.

"I would approach him in a public place," I said, after a judicious pause. "Let him know the game is up. No confrontation. No threats. Just a quiet word."

"I could get a few of the boys—but you don't need any assistance then?—No? I'll leave that to you. Just you watch yourself with this one, Stubbsy."

Arranging an encounter with Jigson was simple enough. His landlady said he usually ate at the dining rooms on Westow Street in the evening. I watched from a discreet distance as he took a table and was served.

To be correct, I would describe Jigson as a man of roughly twenty-five years of age and of medium build, with brown hair. He was not in any way unusual. There was no scaly skin, flicking tongue or lizard blinking of translucent eyelids. He would have passed anywhere without comment, and indeed had done so. There were several more remarkable-looking individuals in the room, including, I suppose, myself.

To all externals Jigson seemed perfectly normal. But if you were to look beneath the surface, it would be like whipping the dustcover off a grand piano and discovering a piano-shaped arrangement of boxes of pilchards.

He was eating a bowl of oxtail soup, accompanied by a crusty bread roll split open and thickly smeared with butter. His manner of eating was not bestial, but, as with everything else, quite ordinary. He did not have any freckles, moles or scars that I could see, being as unmarked as a tailor's mannequin, which is perhaps unusual but difficult to make into a point of singularity.

"Excuse me," I said. "May I take this seat?"

"Suit yourself, friend," said he, busy at his soup.

I pulled the chair back, scraping the legs on the uncarpeted floor, and sat down facing him. He did not trouble to look up at me.

"There is something to which I would wish to draw to your attention."

He looked up now.

"You're one of Renville's vigilantes," he said. His voice was quiet and even, educated but not affected. "Another one."

"My name is Stubbs, Mr Jigson," I said, not offering my hand. I placed the folded skin carefully on the table in front of me.

I was expecting surprise, suspicion and anger, or maybe even fear. I was ready for puzzled curiosity, either real or feigned, at the sight of the peculiar object. I was not prepared for a total absence of reaction, not so much as a blink or a moment's pause in the spoon going to his mouth. He just looked at me, his face devoid of expression, having barely glanced at the skin.

"I know just what you are," I said in a low voice.

He laughed pleasantly, as though I was a friend and had just said something absurd to amuse him. It was a jolly laugh, and just as I thought he was carrying it on longer than necessary, the mirth cut off completely, like a light being switched off. The effect was disconcerting.

"No," he said, without a trace of humour. "You don't. You never will, my friend."

"This—skin—tells me something," I said.

"That tells you nothing," he said with quiet authority. "Listen, Stubbs. I could take you to a city—a city which your kind have never visited—with a library with more books by our kind than you could imagine—in a language which none of your kind can even read. If you lived long enough to read every one of those books, you would know nothing about me and my kind."

"Is that so?"

I never worked out afterwards why Jigson decided to engage me in conversation, rather than ignoring me or simply walking out. Was he sounding me out to see how much I knew, or attempting to assess me in some other way? Or did he think he could put me off the trail?

"Let me ask you something," Jigson said, leaning forward again. "What kind of tile can't you stick to the wall?"

"I don't know," I said, nonplussed at this sudden change in direction.

"A rep-tile," he said, with a laugh, so cheery and so unexpected I could not help but laugh too. "How do you tell how much a lizard weighs?"

"I don't know."

"By the scales," he said, and we both chuckled. "I could tell jokes all day and laugh along with you. But I will never know why you laugh, or what laughing means."

"Nobody knows that," I said.

"But I can make you laugh. Not because I am a natural comedian, but because I am a natural chameleon." he said. "We have no humour. Nor any parental love, nor romantic attachment, nor patriotism, the things that drive you to love and hate. We are built differently. But we do have emotions, equally deep emotions, ones that you have no concepts of or words to express. Ones you could never understand."

"The basics though are the same for any race," I said.

He shook his head.

"You have an affinity for dogs; we love snakes, which you loathe. And the relations between you—you would kill any man, if he was wearing the wrong uniform," he said. "You all would." I could hardly deny this, given the scale and scope of the late war, and I nodded reluctantly.

"Of course."

"'Of course', to you, my friend," he said. "We are different. We have our loyalties, our politics, our religions even, but they are beyond your understanding. Your kind—to us, you are a pack of noisy, over-excitable children let loose on a beach, thinking they own it, oblivious to their elders quietly enjoying it. And the next day the children are gone and the tide has swept away all trace they were ever there, and the elders abide."

"We may be children, but killing a child is odious to anyone," I said.

"Others view things differently," he said. "A child is an unformed thing, only half there. And, while you strain to produce children one at a time, if you hatched vast broods of them you would not value them so much. And children with a fatal illness so they never grow up—" he looked at me meaningfully "—some say it's a mercy to kill them."

His tone was casual, but the words themselves, especially now I see them in black and white, were a stark warning.

"You are getting rather philosophical now," I said, not wanting to get side-tracked. I indicated to the skin on the table.

"Will you accept for starters that you are not, shall we say, as other men?"

"Certainly, my friend. But the difference is that you are all amateurs, whereas I am a professional. Nobody ever taught you how to be a human being. I have had a thorough course of instruction—a longer one than you might imagine—and I have learned all there is to know. I can read the subtleties of expressions, pick out nuance. I may never truly know what goes on behind them, but I know how A leads to B. Fully half of you are clueless social outcasts, shunned by the others, unable to make their way in the world. Wherever I go I can make friends, seduce women, get on in society."

He might have been boasting, or mocking me, though his tone was neutral enough. He may simply have been making his case that any attempt to catch him would be futile. Or, in the light of subsequent events, he may have been trying to distract my attention by giving me more things to think about.

"But you're not…medically speaking…"

He raised one eyebrow. Of course I could not say exactly now he might differ from anyone else. Possibly his people had mastered a deeper art than my limited knowledge could conceive, and no medical test would reveal his true origin.

"Ordinary humans do not shed their skins," I said, trying another tack. "If you were to have to do so on a regular basis it would be somewhat of an inconvenience—and rather likely to give you away, sooner or later. So perhaps skin-shedding is something you save for a special occasion."

He supped again, with no sign of interest in what I was saying.

"It might for example, be a way of shedding your fingerprints for a new set," I said. "I believe you may have other unusual talents. Humans are not in the habit of regrowing missing fingers, which again might give you away as not being of our stock. But lizards do, perhaps you can do it to, if and when you wish."

"You have an inkling," he said. "The faintest glimpse of vistas opening up above and beyond this little world of yours. Just an inkling. Best to stop there, my friend. If you discovered the truth about this world and your place in it, you'd be driven to howling madness." He took another spoonful of soup.

"I have seen things not of this world," I said. "Beings outside the ordinary run. Had to fight some of them, in my time. You don't hear me howling about it."

He bit a piece from his bread roll, chewed unhurriedly and swallowed.

"And what was it you wanted from me?"

"If I had a free choice I'd enlarge that 'inkling,' as you call it," I said. "Peer a little further into those vistas, risk a step towards that howling madness. Ask you a few questions."

He laughed again, exactly the same laugh, as though it was being played on a gramophone player, again cut off short.

"You wouldn't understand the answers," he said. "If I tried to tell you what I was about—it would be like trying to explain the theft of the Koh-i-Noor to a mongoose."

The Koh-i-Noor is of course a famous diamond from India, the largest in the world and part of the Crown Jewels. It has incalculable value, not just as a gemstone but as a cultural relic and a symbol of British rule over India. There is also some superstition attached to it, as the stone is supposedly unlucky for any male ruler. I supposed he was referring to some equivalently prized object among his people, but he was not about to enlighten me.

"In any case it's not your concern," he said, apparently forgetting that we take the murder of other humans as a serious matter. "There's no malice towards your kind. In fact, we raised you to the civilised state—your ancestors were barely sentient before we intervened. Not that you ever forgave us for sharing the fruit of the tree of wisdom...my point is that I'm not going to share my business with you, which you could not understand anyway."

"In that case," I said, "my only task is to let you know that we know." I put one hand over the skin. "Then you can depart quietly and I'll dispose of this little curiosity with no fuss."

He supped, shaking his head as though it was nothing to do with him.

"We also happen to have a rather unique letter," I said. "One written in an unusual and suggestive script."

"The police showed me one like it. They didn't have any idea what it said. Nor do you."

"Experts are examining it now," I said, which was not exactly true, but I wanted him to think that there was something at stake. "Talented people with broader minds and more esoteric knowledge than Scotland Yard."

"You know the police can't touch me," he said. "What are you threatening—murder? What you might call cold-blooded murder?"

He did not seem alarmed by the prospect.

I leaned forward across the table.

"Something worse for you and your kind—exposure," I said. "Your covert scheme cannot remain covert, not here. Too many people are wise to it and are watching for you. Time to call it a day and leave the good people of Norwood alone. I don't care about your business, but I will not tolerate murder."

Jigson might not care about his own life; I had the impression that life and death, his own or others, meant nothing to him. But secrecy was something that mattered to them. They had remained hidden for centuries, and now I was threatening, not necessarily plausibly, to dent that secrecy.

Instead of responding Jigson took another spoonful of soup, looking straight through me. Human beings cannot simply ignore one another's presence, however much they try, but he had the gift of making a person disappear. It was eerily like being a ghost with no bodily form.

"I think..." I said, but the words died on my lips. It was not just the absence of eye contact; there was no contact on any level. He could interact with humans like a human when he chose to, but when he chose not to he was beyond reach.

"Good evening then, Mr Jigson," I said quietly, replacing my bowler and stuffing the skin into an outer coat pocket. I wrapped a thick scarf around my neck on the way out to the chilly night.

I believe I had conveyed to Jigson that I was just one of many, and that silencing me would achieve nothing. I was aware though, that as with Cahill, he might decide to deal with me in his own swift and lethal fashion.

Pausing at the first corner, I looked back to see if he was following me. I turned off the main road down Carberry Road, a residential street. Halfway down the road, something made me look back over my shoulder.

A small figure was twenty steps behind me. He must have dropped the soup spoon and grabbed his coat before I was even out of the door, and ducked away when I looked back the first time.

Another man might have smiled, or given some sort of acknowledgement of the situation, but Jigson's face was blank as he came towards me. He flipped his hand, and the knife he must have concealed in the sleeve jumped into it. Not a clasp-knife or an assassin's stiletto, but a dinner knife picked up from the dining rooms. Hardly a dagger, but sharp enough to deal with the dining room's tough braising steaks. Dangerous in the right hands.

I did not know, and do not know yet, why Jigson attacked me. His logic and his motivations are unguessable. It may be that it was a matter of honour, that I had insulted him in some mortal fashion that demanded revenge. It might have been a matter of simple hygiene and the desire to cut off a loose end that had been left dangling, one which might cause complications if left unattended. My hunch though, was that it was neither of those. That it was more a question of humour, that my murder was in the nature of a practical joke or prank for his own self-satisfaction.

I turned, knees bending, my fists raising themselves automatically into a boxing stance. My body was anticipating what would happen next, even if my conscious brain was not quite ready to accept it. There are norms in human behaviour, and while attacks do sometimes come out of the blue, even if there is none of the usual shouting and gesturing, you can tell if someone is heading for you or just hurrying to get past. This man just walked rapidly as though he was going to go through me.

My reach far exceeded his, and keeping him at a distance should not have been difficult. That's the way you deal with boxers who are faster than you, especially if they are smaller. Distance gives you the time to see their attacks coming.

I timed my punch to hit Jigson as soon as he was within my reach, and well before he would have a chance to strike at me. But it did not happen like that.

Before my arm even started moving, I was struck twice in the neck, not powerful blows but quick ones that I did not even see. A striking snake is one of the fastest things in nature. They say a mamba can strike three times in the time it takes you to blink, and this man was as fast as that.

Now I knew how Jigson had killed Atkinson in the pub, even though the other man had him covered with a gun. He had no need for hypnosis with such superhuman speed.

My reflexes saved me—those and the leather collar Sally had stitched inside my scarf. I pushed Jigson away rather than hitting him, recoiling three steps as I did so, my hat flying off.

The shove practically launched him into the air, but rather than falling Jigson spun and regained balance faster than I did. He stood, frozen in place, watching. He was still wearing his cap.

I could not quite believe what had just happened. Three empty milk bottles stood on the stairs beside me in front of someone's front door. I grabbed them and pitched them one after the other at Jigson as he came forward.

They slowed him hardly at all; he ducked and dodged out of the way so they shattered behind him. That noise at least ought to get someone.

I should have shouted for help, that would have been the sensible thing to do, but somehow it never even occurred to me.

As he closed I decided I was not going to make myself a sitting duck this time. I retreated, dodging left and right, throwing out a couple of feints just on the chance he would run into one. He was too canny for that—or else my movements were too obvious for his accelerated senses.

Still backing away I pulled off a dustbin lid and held it up for a shield.

It seemed ridiculous. I towered over Jigson, like a gladiator facing a pygmy.

Jigson moved a little to the left, and then a little to the right, the knife held low, gauging my responses. I held my shield well away from me and kept it at waist height, covering as much of my body as possible.

"There's no need for this," I said.

He moved, and I instinctively leaped back, fearing he was going to come in close and get around my shield. I was not fast enough; I felt the dustbin lid plucked out of my hand. It flew away and rolled down the street with a metallic grinding before coming noisily to a halt against the kerb. Again his movement had been too quick to follow.

We faced each other again.

Jigson always went for the neck. That was his modus operandi, and a practical one too. Our combat instructors always told us it was the quickest and most reliable way to kill a sentry. You can stab him in the heart, but there is a lot of ribcage to get through and if you strike bone the blade may be turned away. Was he going to have another stab at my neck, or would he try some other body part next time? My life might well depend on guessing the answer.

"Killing me won't help you," I said.

Jigson said nothing, but circled around to the left to prevent me from edging back towards the main road. Perhaps running might be my best chance of survival, even if I risked a stab in the back. Jigson was waiting for me to make a move that would leave me open, knowing that I could not just stand there.

"Lots of others know about you as well," I said.

Jigson moved forward, seeming almost to glide, knife lowered. Getting close enough for me to step in for a long right at his chin.

Instead I backed away, past a shadowed doorway. If I could back off another thirty yards I might be able to make a run for it. But Jigson was pressing me close.

Jigson was quick, but he was not all-seeing, and his attention was fixed on me. He was still pretty acute though. I saw something burst out of the shadows behind Jigson; no man would have had a chance to react, but Jigson whipped around just as the other man hit him, and a shout rent the air.

"Gah!"

I could not see what happened in the shadows, but the next thing I knew I was facing the tramp Slingsby, swearing and holding a hand to his face.

At our feet was my assailant, stretched full-length on the pavement, twitching and jerking in a most disturbing fashion. A dull cylinder of grey metal lay next to him. It took me a moment to recognise a length of lead pipe.

I tried to find Jigson's hand with the knife in to kick it away, but then I saw the whole side of Jigson's head had caved in, with an impression deep enough to put your fist into. Slingsby had obviously struck him a tremendous blow. Maybe Jigson's skull was thinner than that of normal men.

Almost as soon as I saw the injury, the horrible twitching ceased forever.

Slingsby looked stunned.

"Move your hand," I told him. He was cut across the lower part of his jaw, and the slash was down to the bone. Blood was welling up all over.

"It's a messy one," he said. "But I couldn't just let him kill you, could I?"

"Put pressure on that," I said, wadding up my scarf to staunch the wound.

"I saw you following him, and I thought—" he paused to cough slightly, "I thought, that Stubbs is going to have his hands full if he's doing what I think he's doing."

"We'll get you to a doctor."

"No doctors," croaked Slingsby. "Just leave me."

Blood was already leaking out around his fingers.

"You'll do what you're told, Slingsby." I said. "Press that down tighter. Now, just you sit down on these steps a minute. Nobody is leaving anybody."

Slingsby was swaying where he sat. A window opened across the street, and I saw a figure silhouetted with a light behind him.

"What's all this racket?" he bellowed.

"Call an ambulance!" I roared back. "There's a man been stabbed!"

The next evening I was waiting outside the pickle factory, dressed up and ready to escort Sally to the pictures. I was spruced up, a box of chocolates under my arm and a fresh flower in my buttonhole.

All the other factory girls were coming out at the end of the shift. I attracted many curious looks, and I did not kiss Sally in front of all those eyes, but she took my arm and we strolled on like any other couple.

Sally immediately started quizzing me on what had transpired since the previous night. I had sent a note round to her lodgings in the early hours to let her know that all was well, and the bush telegraph of friends-of-friends, and the afternoon newspaper editions, had supplied her with some of the details.

"Once more I'm indebted to Arthur," I said.

"He's indebted to you, more like," she said. "He asked you to catch a murderer and you did. One who slipped through everyone else's fingers. Including the police and that Blaine. Has he showed up yet?"

"Not yet," I said.

Or at least, not that I knew about. Arthur might well have information, may have sent someone around to Blaine's known addresses, and may have made a grisly discovery. But he had not shared any information with me, for which I was grateful. The less you know, the less you can let slip. I doubted I would be seeing Blaine again.

I had slung Jigson's body out of sight behind a garden hedge before the ambulance arrived; he was surprisingly light, like a bag of feathers. Arthur had been in two minds about whether to sink Jigson's corpse in the Thames in a weighted sack and call it quits, or whether to allow it to be discovered. But Arthur is a fine exponent of the principle of least effort, and as soon as I explained things to him he saw a tidier solution. He did not laugh at my revelations about lizard men.

"So your idea," he said, "is that Jigson shed his fingerprints, so the ones he left in the pub don't correspond with what he has now?"

Arthur fumbled around with the skin for some time. I could

not tell what he was doing until he wormed his hand around in the thin material, and held it up, wearing the right hand like a glove and inspecting his fingertips.

"It's worth a try," he concluded.

"What is?"

"Seeing if we can get these to leave prints." Calculation whirred by behind his eyes as he fitted all the pieces into place. Arthur was less interested in the real story than the story that would work best for him. "It'll be a bit of bother for you I'm afraid Stubbsy, but I know a friendly policeman who'll give us a hearing. Tell him all you want, just leave out the hocus pocus and it'll all come right."

Arthur's friendly policeman was an inspector, one who, unlike Blaine was still on the force. He did however have an eye to the main chance rather than the letter of the law. He arrived swiftly in response to Arthur's summons, and showed a keen interest when Arthur raised the topic of solving an unsolved murder and showing up some of his colleagues as being less than astute.

"The long and the short of it," I told Sally, "Is that in the official version, our murderer used special gloves to disguise his fingerprints, gloves which were discovered on his body post-mortem. And tomorrow morning a parcel of illicit cocaine will arrive at Jigson's PO Box, the one Atkinson rented him, showing conclusively that Jigson was involved in the drugs trade, thus explaining his motive for the murders and the secret letters."

Having Atkinson's murder assigned to a dead man who tried to blackmail him tidied things up neatly, and left nobody to be questioned about anything.

"But what about the barman, Cahill? Why did Jigson kill him?"

I spread my hands.

"That, we will never know. Surely nothing to do with aspidistras! I still don't know what Jigson thought he could gain by killing me. All I can think is—humans don't need much of an excuse to kill snakes, and maybe they feel the same about us."

"And what was Jigson doing here in the first place?"

"Equally mysterious. They found copies of more coded

letters in Atkinson's effects, which I have passed on to Miss Frey for her entertainment. I told her if she can make any sense of them, I'll make a clean sweep of the mantelpiece and her aunt will have to collect china dogs instead. One other clue, if it be such, was a program for a talk at Spurgeon's College which he evidently attended."

Spurgeon's College is a local establishment of some renown where they train missionaries. Many of these go try their hand at converting the heathen in India, which put me in mind of the Koh-i-Noor again. But without any further clues, I could not begin to guess what Jigson's interest would have been there or who he had seen.

"So we don't have any answers," Sally concluded. "I told you it was like the 'Murders in the Rue Morgue'. The inspector in that one went with the convenient explanation instead of the true one. Only this time it's your lizard-man in the morgue."

"And Slingsby in the hospital."

"That poor, brave man," said Sally. "How is he?"

"He lost a lot of blood, and he was in a poor way to start with. They say there's a risk of infection, but Slingsby is a tough old soldier. And Arthur will see him right."

Arthur never forgot a favour or a debt, and saving me—or killing Jigson—was no small matter. While Slingsby might complain about being in hospital, the treatment that Arthur was paying for had doubtless saved his life. They were feeding him up now, and he'd probably leave the place healthier than he had been in years. That wouldn't stop him ruining it all by smoking every cigarette he could cadge. Slingsby was not destined for old age. In fact, he might well have preferred to go out in a blaze of glory.

"I suppose he'll get a reward from the police for bravery," said Sally.

"Slingsby doesn't want anything to do with the police, and Arthur thought it was tidier if he wasn't involved. In the official version, you see, Jigson attacked me, and I hit him back, and his head hit the kerb, resulting in fatal injury et cetera."

"They're making you into a killer," she said, clutching my arm tighter.

"It's being treated as self-defence," I said. "Any court proceedings will be a formality,"

Certainly, nobody was stepping up to make Jigson's case, and the law had already decided he was a murderer.

"And you, Harry Stubbs," Sally said, turning on me. "I hope you've learned your lesson after nearly getting yourself killed by tangling with the wrong man. Lucky I made you wear that scarf!"

"I don't know what lesson I've learned," I said. "But we won."

In truth I had been considering the matter. One thing that bothered me especially was that they might be a genuinely superior race, one which was right to look down on us. They were undoubtedly older than mankind, with who-knows-what science and art behind them, and were not far wrong in viewing us as destructive, upstart savages. Not that this would justify their killing us—but then we kill lesser animals without any compunction, so the example has been set.

And I had seen one of these beings dispatched by a tramp administering a blow to the head with a blunt instrument.

I do not like to think that the human race triumphs only because of our capacity for brute violence. Rather, I take solace in the fact that even Slingsby, a social leper whose personal hygiene rendered him literally untouchable as far as most people were concerned, even in him there beat so a true heart that he would risk his own life for the sake of a slight acquaintance.

I hardly knew Slingsby. All he owed me were a few cigarettes, but if I had been his blood brother I could not have asked for a swifter or braver response. All of which is a roundabout way of saying that perhaps humanity does have some qualities that make us equal to the lizard-people.

I do not doubt that they abide. Whatever plot or scheme Jigson was part of must surely continue somewhere. At best we may have thrown the schedule off by a few years. All I can say is that I do not hope to see any murderous human reptiles around these parts ever again.

ANDREW DORAN
AND THE JOURNEY TO THE SERPENT TEMPLE

BY MATTHEW DAVENPORT

Anchorage 1938

The Idol of Tsathoggua was in the hands of the Germans and I could feel the occult war between the nations slipping out of America's hands.

I was sitting in a bar in Anchorage and sipping a strong whiskey. An hour previously, I had lost a race to a plane carrying the ugly statue. The plane was, inevitably, headed to Berlin to deliver the idol to the Führer. It was only one more occult piece out in the wild that would be used to convert human soldiers into frog-like monstrosities with an insatiable appetite and the strength of ten men.

My dismay made me sound like a member of the American military, but I wasn't anything of the sort. Instead, I was a man fighting a never-ending war to keep the aliens and ghosts from beyond the veil out of our world. The more monsters that our world had, the easier it would be for them to consume us all. Today I lamented a lost battle. Tomorrow the battle would continue.

"Dr. Andrew Doran?" a voice asked from behind me.

I turned away from my drink and took in the couple that obviously didn't belong in this place.

The gentleman on the left wore a long grey coat covering a matching grey suit. In his hands he held a fedora that would normally cover his receding hairline.

On the right was a woman. She wore an equally grey dress with a gold necklace that hung low. Her hair was pulled back into a ponytail. She was the one who had asked for me.

"Maybe not so much today," I answered, "but he might show up tomorrow." I took another sip of my drink and asked, "Who's asking?"

"My name is Elena Cantor. My colleague is Nathan Rusch," she answered. "We represent a group with a specific lineage that has bequeathed us with responsibilities too big for us to handle on our own."

I laughed and turned back to the bar. "That sounds really important. I don't know that Doctor Doran can help you out."

"Don't you turn your back on us." Rage filled Nathan's voice. I slid from the stool as his hands passed through where I had been. It looked like he had been trying to grab me, but I hadn't drank enough to slow me down, yet.

My movement continued and I punched him across the jaw.

Or at least, I would have, except Elena's hand caught mine with surprising speed and strength, halting my attack before it could land.

"Alright," my eyes never left Nathan, but I spoke to Elena, "you have my attention, but keep your dog on his leash."

We took a table at the corner of the bar. They sat across from me, Nathan sitting closest to the wall.

"Your story was missing some key details," I waited until after the waitress had departed before speaking. "You're from a long line of what? And what are these responsibilities that are too big for your tiny shoes?"

Elena smiled, but I could see her struggling to read me. She was earnest in wanting help and she didn't know if my reputation was myth or not. "We're-"

She was interrupted by her companion grabbing her wrist and barking, "He is not to know that."

Elena yanked her wrist from Nathan's hand and shot him a glare. "If he is to help us, we will need him to trust us." She returned her attention to me. "We are from a long line of ancient wizards and we are being hunted because of it."

"Wizards?" In the past, I had been called a wizard, among other things. I don't know that it was wrong or right, but every other wizard I had ever met was a greedy monster hellbent on trading deals with demons for more power in our world. My right hand found the pistol hidden in my jacket while my left raised my glass closer to my mouth. "I've never known a wizard who didn't earn the trouble that found them."

Elena must have sensed the tensions rise and held up her hands in a slow gesture. "We, and the people we represent are untrained and mostly powerless. None of us want our ancestry, but we are stuck with the results of it."

"And those are?" I released the grip of my pistol but my hand didn't drift far.

"Do you know about those that worship the serpent god, Yig?"

The question hit me like a ton of bricks. I was more than aware of the serpent god. Yig was similar to Dagon, in that he chose to mate with his followers and their offspring were numerous across the Earth. Yig was a selfish creature that was only into converting the human race. His hybrid children rarely found themselves accepted by humanity and their way of life was forced upon them. It was an indoctrination from birth and few of his children left the pit.

Of the ones that did, their status of being from both worlds made them valuable allies and I had made friends with several of Yig's hybrid children. Of the ones that I had failed to ally myself with, they tended to find themselves in the employ of those same militaries currently fighting for occult sides of the current global conflict.

Elena and her friend were both new to me, and they didn't need to know everything that I did.

"I have heard of them," I put a puzzled look on my face. "What do they have to do with this?"

"Our common ancestor broke a deal with their god and he managed to avoid his punishment by dying and hiding his heirs," Elena explained. "We have since been discovered and they are aiming to end us all."

"Where do I come in?"

Nathan glared at Elena and then myself. "I have been asking that same question since your name was first brought up."

Elena didn't even bother to shoot a glare at Nathan that time. "There's a stone central to Yig culture that would protect us from them. Our people can't get anywhere near it without Yig and his followers becoming aware." She leaned back and waved her hand in my direction. "Whereas you are Andrew Doran, and finding difficult occult artifacts is your entire reputation."

"Not my entire reputation," I shook my head. "I have friends that are related to Yig. I won't help you procure a weapon to use against them." I made to leave the table, but Elena grabbed my wrist. This time her grip was gentle.

"No harm will come to any of the Yig followers. The artifact will only keep them from finding us." She released my wrist. "If you don't help us, we and our people will die."

She said 'our people' as if they were a unified family or tribe and it seemed less formal than her claim that they only shared one ancestor from hundreds of years ago. I doubted that it was important, but I filed it in the back of my mind for later. There was at least more to her familiarity with her distant cousins than Elena was letting on.

"I'm going to need more than a plea for help. Do you have any idea where this stone is?" I sat back down and held my empty glass up in the bartender's direction.

"You will help us, then?" Elena's face lit up with surprise. Whatever she knew of my reputation, it must have implied that I would be a harder person to sell.

"As long as you're being honest about this stone," I answered. "I can't stand by and watch people get murdered for the sins of their great-great-grandfather."

"Wonderful," Elena clasped her hands together. "And you're absolutely right. You will need to know more if you are to get the artifact, and that is why I brought Nathan."

"Oh," I grinned, "I thought it was for his award-winning personality."

Nathan smirked at that, proving to me that he wasn't entirely humorless.

"The stone is being held in the Temple of the Serpent in a

remote jungle location in Northern India." He unfolded a piece of paper that I hadn't seen him retrieve. It was a map of India that seemed older than everyone at the table, combined. I was only mildly familiar with the location that Nathan indicated. There was a Yig cult in that area, but that was the extent of my knowledge without any additional research.

"Can we put this against a modern map?" I asked. "It's going to be difficult enough to find on my own."

Nathan shook his head. "Elena and I will be going with you. As will some of our … cousins."

"You just told me that you can't get anywhere near this artifact," I countered, only growing more confused by the minute. "How are you going to take me someplace that you can't actually go?"

Elena shook her head. "We can't get within the Temple of the Snake without the Yig priests and attendants becoming aware of our presence. We are not fighters and they will kill us if we try. We can get you close, though."

That made more sense to me than them not being able to pick up the stone. Magic was useful and could restrain, harm, or curse someone because of their lineage, but it took a lot of power to make something like that happen. Even for a god, they would rather not have to waste a ton of power over one mortal family if they didn't need to. It was simpler just to make your worshipers protect your powerful relics than it was to pour that magic away on them.

Besides, it gave the worshipers something to do in the hundreds of years between when Yig would show up to woo their maidens.

"Alright, then we're going together," I said. "When do we leave?"

Nathan glanced at my glass and then back to me. "We would like to leave in the morning."

I downed the whiskey and put the glass on the edge of the table. "No problem, but these drinks aren't free. Were you thinking of paying me for this trip?"

Elena gave me a tight-lipped smile and waved at the bartender who grabbed a large bag and brought it to her.

"We believe you lost something of great importance, recently. Perhaps this will pay the balance in full?"

She slid the bag to me and I opened it, letting it slide down to reveal the heavy object inside.

I was looking at the frog-shaped body of a hairy beast. It had short arms, many eyes, and a tongue carved to look as though it was sliding out from between its many teeth.

"The Idol of Tsathoggua," I gasped. Nodding, I indicated that we were square. While I was relieved that the idol wasn't in the hands of the Germans, I was suddenly filled with questions.

When did the bartender get the bag with the idol?

When did Elena and her angry companion get it?

Why wasn't the bar being stormed by German soldiers?

I was beginning to think there was a lot more to this situation than I fully understood.

I wasn't prepared to head directly to India in search of Elena's snake stone and she understood that. On the other hand, Nathan was anything but pleased. I explained that I would need research materials and the means to secure our safe passage once we arrived there. The British Empire still had a strong influence in that region and any travel into Delhi would involve me and my new compatriots being given special passage. I couldn't secure that without talking to allies in Arkham.

Nathan was quick to explain that he and Elena didn't need any special certificates. Elena jumped to my defense by explaining that I was obviously not either of them. With my doctorate in archaeology, all I needed was to call a friend of mine in London to secure me a research pass, but I also wanted to use the time to research my new friends.

For reasons that neither of them wanted to explain to me, I was to travel alone and they would meet me in Arkham in two weeks to begin the journey to Delhi. I couldn't imagine there were many vessels moving between Anchorage and the continental United States, but they insisted that they would find another means of travel.

Archaeology isn't the profession of the rich, so I wasn't boarding any passenger ships to get home. Instead, I managed to trade labor for passage on a fishing boat that was going along the coast. The journey took six days when I had been promised it would take only five, but I wasn't upset. The hard work and times I had with the crew of the *Carpie* were some of the best of my life.

The *Carpie* dropped me off in Bellingham, Washington where I had to hire a car to take me to the station in Seattle. The train ride from Seattle to Chicago was pleasant. I read my well-worn copy of Edgar Rice Burrough's *A Princess of Mars* and achieved some much-needed rest after the adventure in Alaska and my five days as a fisherman. By contrast, the two days on the train to Chicago was a small slice of Heaven compared to the Hell that was the day and a half ride from Chicago to Arkham.

The Chicago train was more crowded than any vehicle I had ever ridden before. The man next to me should have been classified as an Eldritch abomination by how loud he snored and the odd hours he kept when he migrated between the drink car and his seat. Reading was just as impossible as sleeping and I spent the majority of my time with my attention aimed out the window.

Having lived among suicidal cultists and murderous wizards, I can honestly say that I never felt my soul so incredibly depleted as I did when I finally arrived in Arkham, Massachusetts. The relief that flooded me as I stepped off the train and onto the grimy platform was euphoric.

I was home.

Ten days had passed since I had left Anchorage and only four remained for me to conduct my research, call my friend in London, and meet up with my new associates. It sounded like a lot of time, but I had no idea how or if any of my contacts or research would have enough time to locate information on Nathan or Elena with how little I had to go on.

My home was more accurately described as a small storage room with a window and a cot. While Arkham had become my home during my school days, it was clear that the local academics weren't fond of me. Between their animosity and my desire to learn everything that they never taught me, I barely used the apartment.

I wasted no time unpacking my gear and instead picked up the phone and requested a transatlantic connection.

It wasn't too long before the operator connected me with my friend. Captain Cross was an ex-soldier who acquired and sold rare and forbidden books, as well as being a sometime operative of Britain's military intelligence. It made him valuable as an ally and unpleasant as an adversary.

Many of his acquisitions tended to have more of an occult history than not and we had run into each other on multiple occasions. His connections ran deeper than mine and he could be incredibly useful in both of my needs.

"Dr. Doran," his voice crackled over the long-distance phone call. "Always a pleasant surprise."

I smiled despite myself. He was already using what I considered his "salesman voice," knowing that for me to call was a rare thing indeed.

"How have you been, Cross?" I asked.

"Well enough, considering."

There was a momentary delay as he responded. The distance between us being echoed over the call. He let out a short sigh.

"I hurt my foot this morning." The captain had lost one leg from the knee down in 1917. As always with the captain, there was more to the story. "I was looking at a sixteenth century volume of alchemy, supposedly cursed. Would you believe it, a translucent, luminous spider dropped out. Nasty little thing! Kept coming after me -- bullets wouldn't stop it. I reasoned that the best way to stop a ghost spider was a ghost foot. Stamped on it with my foot that isn't there. Squashed it flat but hurt my heel in the process. Turns out whisky is just the thing for phantom pain, but the thing is --"

"I could use your help," I said, jumping right in. The captain's stories could go on forever, and transatlantic calls are not cheap.

"My services are at your disposal, Doctor."

"First," I explained, "I'm traveling to India to do some research and I'll be using the Imperial Airways to get there." The Imperial Airways were the British commercial flights.

Getting to India wasn't as much of a hassle as it had been even a decade ago thanks to the Airways having come into being but going as myself was the biggest hassle.

"Some people I recently ran into like to keep an eye on the flights for my name, and I was hoping to get there unnoticed."

"Ah, you need papers," Cross hesitated. "As a matter of fact, I know a chap who used to travel there regularly and has all the passes and permits you'll need. He doesn't need them anymore, he swears he's never going to leave his village in Sussex again. You see, the last time he was in India he had a run-in with this rakshasa—"

"And I need information on two people: Elena Cantor and Nathan Rusch," I cut in, and spelled the names out for him so as to not be lost over the distant connection. "I need as much information as you can get. Especially anything to do with their families."

"Are they Americans?"

I could tell he was taking notes. "I think so," I thought back to their accents, "but I'm willing to bet one of your government contacts has heard of them."

"Anything else?" He pressed.

"No, that's all I have." I quickly told Cross about their unexplained retrieval of the Idol of Tsathoggua and how they found me. Cross's smile could be heard in his voice.

"They are well connected to move so quickly. Considering the nature of the idol, perhaps I'd better make enquiries in the esoteric antiquities field as well, see if the names set any bells ringing. Do you think the Germans hunting the Idol worked for them?"

"Again, I don't know," I answered, "but I'm open to theories."

"I'll see what I can do for you."

I gave him directions to send any responses via post or telegram to the Delhi office.

"Certainly. Oh, and I'll drop in a list of some books the War Office have been showing an interest in. They're not in the published Miskatonic library catalog, but I've a feeling some of them might be lurking on a forgotten shelf somewhere. I can get you some good prices—or swaps, if you're looking for anything."

Cross knew as well as I did that Miskatonic University held

a number of books they did not want the world to know about. But cooperation is a two-way street. That being said, he knew that my relationship with my alma mater was strained at best.

"I'll see what I can do for you too," I said.

His parting words were always the same, but they seemed more grave when he said them this time. "Watch your back, Doctor."

I took only one day to rest and recuperate before I packed up a new bag with fresh supplies and took a bus to New York City. The New York Harbor was the best option for getting a ship to London and it would be where my new associates were planning to meet me.

If I had owned a car the trip would have taken around four hours. Since I didn't, I was forced to survive six hours by bus to the city.

I've never been a fan of New York, mostly because I knew what was hiding within it. I loved the people and the architecture and the city that everyone thought they knew, but that was only a fantasy that I wasn't permitted to share. Large cities like New York attracted horrors of the occult that knew how easy a person could vanish in a crowd. They became feeding grounds for creatures who fed for pleasure, used entrails for spells, and believed that it was their city first.

On the one hand, it made it a great city for collecting information. On the other, nothing you ever got in the Big Apple was worth the price that the monsters would demand.

How can you ever feel safe when every large building is channeling the esoteric energies of the veil and any apartment building could be the focal point for a rift between dimensions?

The answer was simple: just ignore it, and New York had enough glitz and glamor to make ignoring it easy enough.

Unfortunately, I've never been one for glitz and glamor, either. As I waited on the docks for my new companions, I found myself cataloging all of the unfortunate things hiding at the edges of everyone's perceptions.

Two women had the energies of Dagon's lineage exuding from them as well as the jewelry they tried to sell people passing by.

Several of the rats scurrying by were just a little too big and had faces that looked more human than anything.

A man selling squid paid no attention as a tentacle regularly shot out from his cart and pickpocketed anyone who got too close.

Then there was the music like nothing I had ever heard before. It seemed to be drilling past my brain and deep into my soul...

"Pleased you could make it, Dr. Doran." The voice startled me out of the trance I seemed to be falling into. It was odd in that while I was aware I shouldn't be listening to the music, I was still angry at the interruption.

Elena stood before me with a carpet bag and nothing else. Behind her was Nathan, wearing as pained a face as the last time I had seen him. Behind him were five other men and one more woman, each carrying their own luggage.

"You too," I waved at the people behind Nathan. "Who are your friends?"

"Family," Nathan sneered at me. "You will do well to remember that."

I held up my hands in surrender. "I meant no offense. You hadn't mentioned them before, and I was caught by surprise." I shot Elena a look. "I don't like to be caught by surprise."

Elena nodded, "There should be no more surprises from us. We assumed you understood that we were not the only members of the wizard's family who wanted your assistance. They are coming with us as support as well as for protection." Her voice grew quieter. "None of us are safe until we have the artifact."

Elena went ahead and introduced them to me, but I didn't hear their names. They all had an odd look about them. They shifted and scratched while trying to remain still, as if they didn't want anyone to notice. It looked like they were uncomfortable in their own skins.

I wasn't ready to dismiss the odd reaction yet and chose to instead file it away with the other things I planned to corner Elena and ask her about. Hopefully without Nathan around.

"Shall we board the boat?" Nathan encouraged us.

Agreeing, I followed my companions to the ramp and waited through the lengthy line with them. I spent that time trying to find more oddities, not only among the new arrivals, but also among Elena and Nathan as well. While I had my doubts about the six newcomers, there was nothing about Elena and Nathan that led me to believe they were anything but human.

That didn't mean that they were, though. I wasn't about to discount whatever setup had occurred with the Idol of Tsathoggua or the quirky weirdness of their friends. Those facts alone were enough to make them suspect, but nothing about them as individuals was adding to that collected information.

My cabin was small, but larger than what I had shared on the Carpie. The tickets that Elena and her companion had acquired for me spared every expense and I had to bend my knees to fit on the bunk. I wasn't complaining, though, as I had stayed in places much more uncomfortable than this one. I was fortunate enough to be a creature of adaptability and could fall asleep just about anywhere when the need hit me.

Sleep wasn't on my mind as I set forth from my room at the first sign of sunset. Our destination was London, where we would find our way to India by means of the Imperial Airways. Until then I planned on using our several days of sea travel to learn more about my newest companions.

The ship was large enough to make a blind search impossible, but I wasn't looking for only one person and I had a general idea where their cabins were. I made my way in that direction, on the same level, but practically on the other side of the boat. The halls were cramped, and I had to turn to the side to make my way past the crowds of people trying to get to either their cabins, the dining hall, or the deck.

When I reached what I thought to be Elena's room, I stopped before knocking. Inside, there seemed to be intense whispering. Loud enough that I could hear it through the door, but with enough air that I couldn't make out the words. Briefly, I caught a syllable or two that sounded familiar but still unintelligible. I finally decided that I wasn't gaining anything by listening in and knocked.

I was shocked to see that it was not Elena's room at all. The door opened and I was greeted by one of their newer associates, a tall man with bald hair. He wasn't wearing a shirt and his face was devoid of emotion. Behind him was another of their friends with dark and thick hair. While smaller, he also wasn't showing any emotion on his face. He was wearing a dark jacket and thick leather gloves. I couldn't remember if he had been wearing them earlier or if it even mattered.

"Can we help you?" the bald one who had greeted me asked.

"Uh," I was still trying to take in the full scene and was caught off guard by the question. Every bit of information that I could collect from them would help me to figure out why I was having such a difficult time trusting Elena and Nathan. "Yes, I was looking for Elena."

He nodded in the direction I had originally been walking. "She is in suite 114, in that direction."

I gave my thanks and tried to ignore him as he watched me turn and walk away. I could feel his eyes on me for several seconds before I heard the door shut. This was the first time I had to wonder if these wizard descendants were finding it as hard to trust me as I was to trust them.

Elena's room was further from mine than I had previously assumed. When I finally reached it, I noticed the door was ajar. With her entire cadre of cousins floating around the ship, I didn't see this as amiss. I knocked and waited for a response.

When nothing came, I reached for the door to push it open. Before I could, I heard a choking sound on the other side.

I threw open the door and saw Elena on the bed with a short, thin man standing over her. His hands were around her neck. He was only half of my size and wore unkempt blonde hair. His clothes fit him poorly and hung loose on his frame. My eyes only briefly registered the length of wire on the floor, presumably a garrote.

I reached for his shoulders to pull him off, but he met me in the middle of the attempt. His speed was incredible. Leaving one hand to pin Elena by the throat, the other shot out and grabbed me by the wrist. He twisted as he did and the combination of my shock at the speed of his counterattack and his incredible strength spun me off my feet and into the opposite wall of her cabin.

Whoever this was, he was stronger and faster than me and if I didn't act soon, my benefactor would be dead. If I couldn't match his strength and speed, I was going to have to match his wit.

The immediate problem was that he was choking Elena. If I could free her, she could potentially help me in the attack. To that effort the small cabin was a great benefit. I charged from my prone position and slammed the entirety of my body into the lanky man.

Before I had even hit him, his fists and fingers jabbed at me at least three times in my neck and side. All of his hits happened while his one arm continued to choke the life from Elena. I had expected that, with his speed, he would be able to hit me and possibly even incapacitate me in my assault. That's why I had put all of my attack behind my momentum.

I wasn't a large man but I was at least twice this man's size and my mass combined with my momentum was enough to crash him into the wall that the bunk rested against. I heard Elena let out a coughing gasp for air but I couldn't revel in my small amount of success. Her attacker never stopped moving when I hit him and with both hands free he was pummeling my head, chest, and abdomen with increased ferocity. He wasn't choking me, but I was unable to catch my breath just the same.

Grasping at the first thing I could, I yanked up the blanket from the bed and blindly attempted to twist it around his head or his hands or anything I could grab. He didn't make it easy, but as he fought to keep from letting me grab him my feet found purchase and I slammed my shoulder into him again.

This time I was rewarded with a gasp. I couldn't afford to stop moving, no matter how badly my body was aching, and twisted the blanket up and around his head. I twisted the blanket over my shoulder and put the attacker between my back and the wall. Pulling on the blanket with all of my strength, I attempted to pin him against me as I knocked him back against the wall over and over again.

I thought that I was getting the upper hand on him until he

launched me off him with a hard shove, reminding me of how much stronger his small frame was than mine.

I fell into Elena who was starting to get up. She groaned but was on her feet before I was. Her attacker had already removed the blanket from his head and was stepping over me to grab her again. I didn't hesitate and punched him as hard as I could in the knee.

I was finally rewarded with a howl of pain that ended with him falling on top of me. Elena pulled a suitcase from a pile near the door and started bashing him on the head repeatedly as I continued to punch him in the chest.

After what seemed like forever, he stopped moving and we began to relax our attacks. Elena and I took a moment to catch our breaths and I put my hand to his chest to check for breath. Our attacker was dead.

"Thank you," Elena said through deep breaths and rubbed her throat which, thankfully, wasn't showing any signs of the struggle.

Nathan came crashing in before I could offer her my returned thanks over clubbing the man to death.

He glared at me and demanded, "What did you do?"

My blood was still churning from the fight and I wasn't about to let anyone take their shots at me.

"I was doing your job," I stood up and got in his face. "Aren't you supposed to keep her safe?"

Elena was also still feeling the after-effects of the fight and came to her own rescue.

"No one is supposed to be protecting me," she exclaimed. "I am fully capable of taking care of myself."

I didn't tear my glare from Nathan until he looked away. I pointed at the body. "Do you know who he is?"

Elena shook her head. "I have no idea, but I would place a large wager on him being an acolyte of Yig."

"An acolyte?" I asked. "Or a Child of Yig?" I pointed to his eye, where I could see a scaly patch underneath peeking out. Reaching down, I tugged at the flesh near the scales and was rewarded by the face pulling away. A quick tug tore the flesh-like mask from his face.

What I was looking down at was a fully-grown Child of Yig. He had already gone through the full transformation known to happen to their kind when they reached adulthood. His general shape was like our own, but instead of smooth skin, he had scales in beautiful shades of black and red. His eyes were entirely human-looking, but the followers of Yig had ways of hiding their normally snake-like eyes.

Elena and Nathan both stared at the corpse with discomfort on their faces. While I had expected shock, it was entirely possible that being hunted had put the Children of Yig into their visibility before. On the other hand, it takes more than a small amount of knowledge to safely handle the Idol of Tsathoggua. Elena and Nathan both seemed to carry more of their ancestor's skills than I had assumed. Judging by the assumed level of knowledge into the esoteric reality of our world, I wouldn't be surprised if they were powerful wizards in their own right.

Then why did they need me?

"Who is he?" I demanded of Elena. My words broke the silent tension filling the room.

Elena glared at me. "I told you that I don't know."

"And I'm telling you," I said with all of the annoyance of a person who had only barely won a dangerous fight, "that I don't believe you."

"How dare you question me," Elena was suddenly in my face with her adrenaline-fueled rage. To both of our surprise, Nathan's hand grabbed Elena's arm and pulled her back.

"I know him," he said it so quietly that we could only barely hear what he was saying.

"And?" I demanded.

Nathan addressed his explanation to Elena. "The night that I came to you and I told you that we were being hunted, he was there. He revealed himself to me and asked if I knew what he was." He shrugged. "I told him that I did and he warned me from the course that we are on. He said that Yig demanded he warn us that the road ahead would not be easy." Nathan turned his attention to me. "He suggested we let them kill us in our homes instead of so far from them."

I don't know if it was Nathan or the way he said it, but I

didn't believe a single syllable of that story.

"Alright, I believe you," I lied. "He won't be the only one on this ship."

Elena seemed to buy everything Nathan was selling. "Why didn't you tell me about this before?"

"It is why we hired this one," Nathan waved at me. "Isn't it? His knowledge in these matters are to protect us and his skills are to take the artifact. I thought Yig would be blind to us, but it would seem that his is not."

"No," Elena said, addressing my statement. "He won't be the only one, but I don't know what we can do about the rest of them until we know who they are."

"That is a problem for later." I waved at the body. "We need to get him somewhere that he won't be found."

Nathan nodded. "We will put his mask back on and our cousins can help us sneak him to the deck. If we move quickly, the few people we pass will assume he is drunk. Once on deck, we can throw him overboard."

I patted Nathan on the shoulder and put my elbow out for Elena to, reluctantly, take.

"I'm glad you have that handled," I ushered my benefactor from the room. "We will be taking on the scenery and building an alibi far from here." I winked at Nathan, "Just in case."

Dining was slightly less extravagant than I had expected from the ship's size. There was a large room that looked as if it could be made a little dressier if the occasion permitted, but now it was just the essentials. Not nearly enough wait staff were running around and taking orders while we took our seats.

"I don't like my honesty to be challenged, Dr. Doran." Elena didn't afford me any pleasantries, choosing instead to get directly to what bothered her.

"I wasn't questioning your honesty," I explained. "I was questioning your lies." Before she could counter with whatever rage-filled remark she had intended, I cut her off. "You have been lying to me from the moment you found me and I don't enjoy risking my life for people who only wish to use me and discard me."

Elena took a deep breath, "You aren't wrong."

"The truth, then?" I demanded.

She opened her mouth to answer, but I stopped her.

"Lie. Try again."

Again, she moved to speak and again, I interrupted.

"Also a lie. You have a tell that I don't think you're entirely aware of."

"What is that?" her frustration filled her voice.

"Your face doesn't move when you're unsure of what to say. You put in more effort for the truth, as if you're trying to convince me of something I should already know," I explained. "Your lies, on the other hand, register almost no emotion."

She smiled, "Perhaps I simply find it too difficult to lie to such a handsome man."

I returned her smile, but even I could tell I wasn't feeling it. "Lady, I've been flirted with by the best, and that was the biggest lie you've told me tonight."

For the first time since we had met, Elena gave a genuine laugh. "Very well," she said. "You have caught the liar. What would you like to know?"

"Everything."

"Too bad," Elena surprised me with her answer. "I paid you to do a job and the information hasn't changed. I need your help to save me and my companions from the followers of Yig. The stone will help us do that. No Yig are going to die, at least not intentionally, through our actions. So, unless you're operating on some sort of truth-detector, I would assume that our contract is still valid."

I mulled over her words for a moment and swigged the glass of water that had been placed in front of me. It would be easy to say no and walk away from the entire job. I could enjoy the boat ride, get off in London, and maybe let Cross tell me more about that phantom spider over a pint.

That would be the safest route, but I couldn't convince myself to do it. I was far enough along in this snake heist to realize that if Elena and her friends weren't on the side of right, then they were likely to be a force to be reckoned with. I would rather see this through to the end and be there to spoil whatever plan might be working in the background than to let them find another way to reach their goal and turn out to be entirely on the side of darkness.

"I am still here and prepared to get you your stone," I answered. "I can't do my job if lies are going to lead to you getting killed. There are things you will have to tell me, and I would prefer it be sooner rather than later."

Elena picked up her menu. "It will most likely be much later, if at all, so I suggest you order something."

"Let's hope that 'later' comes much sooner than the next assassination attempt." I didn't even look at my menu.

Elena slammed hers down. "Don't threaten me, Dr. Doran. While one snake man was able to catch me by surprise, I promise that you will not." She jabbed a finger into the menu. "Now we can sit and have dinner like polite adults, or you can continue to pout like a child. Either way, I am going to eat."

My goal had been to push Elena and see what she was capable of, but I could see that this conversation had run its course. I didn't want to lose my chance to claim the artifact before we were halfway through our journey. I would have to be content with Elena knowing that I was on to her.

Without my knowledge of when or how, the mood around us shifted and Elena was talking as though we hadn't just had an argument on morality and verbal agreements.

"A temple with a magical stone that carries the power of Yig sounds ominously familiar to me," I said, changing the subject from the décor of the room where we had just killed a snake-man. "Would I be right in assuming that you have discovered the location of the lost Temple of Mu?"

The Yig Temple of Mu was an ancient city said to be the actual home of Yig on our plane of existence. Lost to the jungles of wherever years ago, it was assumed that Mu had either been destroyed by colonial Europeans or had suffered a cataclysmic shift into a different reality. If it still existed and housed artifacts of the serpent beast, then it was likely to be a bastion of Yig worshippers and their weapons. It could be home to a culture older than humanity itself and twice as deadly.

Elena smirked. "Mu is a myth, passed down by a thousand generations of Yig acolytes to keep the great snake god mysterious." She leaned back as her food was delivered. After nodding her thanks to the waiter and waiting for me to do the same, she continued. "Everything from the wizard's notes lead us to believe that this is the Temple of Rthan."

"I'm unfamiliar with Rthan," I said.

"Rthan is where the factions of Yig would congregate every few years to discuss their relationship with man," Elena explained. "While Yig has been considered a benefactor of humanity, Yig's Children have been broken into various groups based on how deserving of his gift they all believe us normal people to be."

"How bad could it be?" I pressed, knowing that people that wanted to fight often found a way to justify it.

"Humanity has walked over this planet and laid claim, whether it had it or not, on most of it." She began cutting into her food while she explained. "Even the acolytes who believe humanity deserves Yig's grace consider themselves to be the chosen race. Many have found humanity to be undeserving and disagree. They regularly commune in Rthan in hopes of receiving a new mandate from their god."

"To go to war?" I asked.

Elena smirked, "Something like that." She let out a small giggle. "I'm sorry. I only laugh because the term 'war' implies a battle of somewhat equal measures with uncertainty over who the winner of such a conflict would be. It's a hardly fitting description in this case, but perhaps the best one available." She took a sip of her wine and stared into the glass as she said, "The Yig Children outnumber us two to one, have the powers of a deity at their disposal, and are all at least as strong and fast as the one we just dealt with. Not to mention that they have thousands of years of technological advancement over us. They may seem like country folk with funny skin, but don't be fooled. They are an advanced culture that tolerates our presence."

She set the glass on the table. "If humanity ever loses Yig's favor, every trace of us will be wiped from existence before we could figure out what was happening."

Returning to my room that evening was an exercise in Holmesian deduction. I couldn't look at anyone without wondering if they were a cleverly disguised snake-person or just the average traveler. I had already been suspicious of my travel companions, now I was suspicious of everyone.

That suspicion only grew when I found Nathan sitting on the top bunk in my cabin. Originally, I had been bunked with a young man in his later teenage years. He had seemed pleasant enough but, more importantly, he kept to himself and ignored me.

"It would seem that you were in need of my assistance earlier and I was too far away to provide it," he said as I entered the room. "I traded rooms with the boy so that I could be readily available if the need arrives again."

"Is this your idea or Elena's?" I demanded.

"I don't know what you're talking about," he smirked at me.

Through gritted teeth I asked, "Why do I feel more like your prisoner than your contracted guide?"

Nathan's smirk disappeared. "You are not our prisoner," his voice filled with the weight of stress and exhaustion. "We need your help and we have secrets. You don't need to know our secrets and we don't need to know yours. That does not change our need of your aid."

This new Nathan was lacking all of the aggression and combativeness of the one I had known for such a short time. He looked like he was getting tired of whatever road we were actually traveling down.

"We are looking to intrude on the territory of an ancient god whose followers are undecided on whether or not humanity deserves to continue on this planet." I removed the annoyed tone from my voice. "That's the reason that I'm concerned about your secrets. I don't want them getting me killed."

"We cannot get the stone without you," Nathan laid down on his bunk. "Therefore, it does not matter what our secrets are. We can't let you die."

My new roommate let his tone complete his last sentence for me.

We can't let you die until we have that for which you were hired.

The rest of the journey to London wasn't nearly as complicated.

I had to learn to get comfortable with Nathan or whoever else they had decided to pair me with. They continued to insist that it was for my protection and companionship on this long voyage. It was clearly a lie, but I had nothing to hide. It was in my best interest to let them stay near me.

While they were watching me, I was watching them.

We arrived in London by way of rails on a rainy day after the ship delivered us to Southampton. We made our way to Croydon by way of two taxicabs. From there it was only a short trip to the airfield for our flight on the Imperial Airways. I was beginning to get nervous that Captain Cross's man was going to miss me when a young Chinese girl in a flatcap came riding up to me on a bicycle.

"Dr. Doran?" she asked. "Are you really him?"

I answered in the affirmative and realized that she was clutching a yellow envelope. "My name is Lily. The captain likes to tell me stories." She shrugged. "He tells everyone stories. Your stories are always my favorite." She suddenly remembered that she had the envelope and held it out to me. "From the captain. He said you owe him and that you knew what that meant."

I smirked. "It means I'll have to give him something that I don't actually have."

The young woman returned my smile. "Ah, so you do know the captain."

With that, she rode back the way she had come.

Elena and Nathan had watched the entire exchange while their friends, whose names I had still not wasted my time on learning, continued working on getting the luggage aboard the plane.

I was worried that they might figure out that I had asked Cross to look into them, but as I opened the package to inspect my papers, I saw that my concerns were wasted.

On top of my documents claiming me to be a researcher dispatched by the British Museum was a small slip of paper with a number and a note.

Call me when you get to Delhi. — *Cross*

"Is everything in order?" Elena asked a little louder since I had chosen not to acknowledge her previous question.

I nodded and held up the packet. "I'm cleared to arrive in India." I glanced at the name on the paper. "My name is Dr. Walton Ford, of the British Museum."

Elena smiled and Nathan rolled his eyes.

"Can we get moving then, please?" He asked before turning toward the plane and joining the rest of our group in boarding.

I couldn't help but feel anxious about the Captain's note. He wanted me to call him, which meant that it wasn't something he could have passed to me in the open with the courier. Instead, he needed to tell me directly.

He knew who they were and they were potentially as dangerous as I thought they were.

Unlike the transatlantic trip, there was nothing notable that happened on the flight. The entire trip took us about two and a half days with several stops in which we switched to a different plane. I could see how this could have been a bother to some, but I enjoyed the adventure that was traveling by plane. I wished that we could have stayed longer in Cairo. That city of ancient cultures and delights held the fancy of my most archaeological fantasies. I managed to see a cat as I waited for our next flight to fuel and couldn't help but be entertained by the question of whether it was just another cat, perhaps a long dead pharaoh, or maybe a ferryman to the long-missing city of Ulthar.

The flight offered a pleasant chance to relax and I slept for most of it. I had no idea how much my services were about to be put to the test, and saw no reason not to rest. At the very least, I was certain at this point that while my life was expendable after the fact, Elena still needed me for now.

We were greeted as we got off the plane by a Deputy Commissioner Jackson. He was there long enough to welcome us to India and inspect our papers. With how quickly he glanced at mine I had to doubt if he even read them. Our presence was mostly ignored by everyone around us and I had a hard time believing that the Germans had anyone watching arrivals. It seemed as if I hadn't needed Captain Cross's help.

That wasn't exactly the case, though, as I still needed to find a telephone.

The Deputy Commissioner had begun to walk away when I

went after him to ask for the nearest phone. He directed me to a small post office and told me to ask for Mr. Patel.

"Phone?" Nathan asked. "Does the great Dr. Doran have friends, or is he calling his mother to let her know he landed safely?"

I knew that my call to Cross wouldn't go unnoticed, but I still hadn't thought of what I was going to say. At the last second, I decided on a half-truth. "I'm calling a researcher of mine. He was hunting for a ghoul nest in Norwood." I pieced together some esoterica from the back of my head and hoped that it would float. I let out an exaggerated sigh, "You're not the only people I'm working for."

"I'll go with you," Elena said. "I have a call to make as well."

I knew I wasn't going to make my call alone, but I had still held out hope.

After we found the phone, I began dialing while Elena leaned against the desk it rested on. This entire distrust thing was getting annoying. I wished that she could at least pretend she wasn't listening in.

I dialed the number that was on the paper Cross had sent me and waited for the operator to ask me who I was reaching. Instead of the captain's name, I gave his address and waited for it to connect.

"Doran, is that you?" Cross's voice cut through a bit of static coming across the line.

"Yes, Mr. Hoade," I answered the name of a librarian we were both familiar with. I doubted that Elena was aware of who Captain Cross was, but I didn't want to put him on her radar. "What have you found for me?"

After the delay, I could hear the smile in Cross's voice. "They are right next to you, are they? I do enjoy a good secret conversation. It reminds me of this time that I was traveling across Spain and-"

"Hoade," I hissed into the phone. "Could you please tell me what you found?"

"Nothing," Cross answered. "They didn't exist before two months ago."

That told me nothing at all. "What does that mean?"

"It means they aren't just lying to you; they *are* the lies."

I smiled at Elena and said into the phone, "Is that all you found?"

The static-filled delay was just long enough that I began to worry that we had been disconnected.

Finally, Cross answered. "That's all of it, but I can keep looking. I just came across a large leather-bound French copy of Geoffery's *The People of the Monolith*. The man who owns it is a recluse who only recently came out of a coma. It's possible that he—"

"Keep looking," I cut him off, but the delay meant that he continued his story for a moment longer. "I've got to go. Thanks for all of your help."

I hung up the phone and stepped back, waving my hand to indicate that Elena could use it.

"Did your friend find what you were looking for?" She made no move for the phone.

I shook my head. "I'm worried that it slipped through his grasp. I don't know what it will mean if he can't find it."

Elena stood and went to the door of the shop. I pointed at the phone again, "What about your call?"

She smiled back at me as she opened the door. "For the life of me, I can't remember who I was going to call."

I rolled my eyes as I followed her out and back to the rest of our cadre.

Aside from the high temperature, the streets were crowded with merchants, rickshaws, and varying animals from cattle to baskets filled with chickens. Every corner of the street served as both a means of travel as well as a marketplace. The noise seemed both incredibly human in that it was a conglomeration of life, yet entirely indefinable in regards to individual words, vehicles, or tones.

Through the crowd, I could make out two cars being loaded with the meager luggage Elena's friends had and everyone was loading into them. I had only brought with me my own small bag that I wasn't letting out of my sight if at all possible, and therefore I left them to their work.

The cars, much like the tickets and most of the cost behind

this venture, were supplied by Elena. According to Cross, she didn't exist, so I wasn't sure how she was affording any of this.

I didn't wait for seats to be called out like we were going on some trip to Grandma's house. Instead, I climbed into the driver's seat of the first car and waited for everyone to finish loading their things. While it might have seemed petulant, I was using the time to examine the bustling crowd as they swarmed around us. This close to our destination I was expecting increased resistance.

It was because of this observation that I saw the three men step out of the crowd with machine guns.

"Everybody down!" I shouted and was rewarded by Nathan, Elena, and the two of their companions who I initially met on the Gemini, diving into my car. I gunned the engine and hoped not to hit anyone as I glanced over my shoulder. Behind us, I watched as the three gunmen opened fire on the remaining four of Elena's cousins before commandeering their car.

The roads were anything but clear, even after we left the market area. It took all my concentration to drive through the city at such a speed while avoiding the pedestrians and the rest of the bustling city.

"How did they find us?" Elena demanded from the back seat.

"They know where you're going," I shouted. "They were waiting for us."

Bullets slammed into the back of the car and I grew a new concern for the pedestrians I was trying desperately not to hit. Between people in the streets, their animals, and all of the trucks loading and unloading their wares, Delhi was not the ideal place for a car chase. People were going to get shot. I had to get this away from the city.

There was an easy way to keep the people of Delhi safe, but they weren't going to like me for it.

Behind the buildings on our left was a large farm, fenced off to keep the animals inside. Past that, I could only barely make out the edges of the tropical dry forest that surrounded the city.

Another hail of gunfire almost distracted me from making my next turn. Instead of turning right and deeper into the city,

I yanked the wheel to the left. The sides of the car screeched as we barely fit between the two buildings. Plaster and stone rained down on the car as I gunned the engine and crashed out of the alleyway and through the fence of the farm I had just been observing.

We were given a short respite from our attackers' gunfire as they had to readjust and work their own path out of Delhi and into the farm.

"Why aren't we shooting back?" I demanded in the sudden rush of silence.

"Shock," Elena answered, "I would presume."

Nathan waved behind us to indicate the car chasing us. "Most of our weapons are in that car."

"That's just wonderful," I shouted as a hail of bullets alerted us to the other car's closing proximity to us. I looked at Nathan and then over my shoulder into the back seat. Returning my look to Nathan and partially to the lack of road before us, I said, "Take the wheel."

"What?" was all he had to say as he stared at me with an expression of complete confusion.

I grabbed him by the wrist and slapped his hand onto the steering wheel. "The wheel. Take it," I explained. "We're going to bust through that fence and if there isn't any road you're going to need to watch for trees. Keep us moving and try to keep it straight."

"Where are you going?" Elena demanded as Nathan finally gripped the steering wheel of his own accord.

Turning around, I dug around on the floor for my own bag and pulled into my lap. I smirked at Elena as I found what I knew had been in the bag this entire trip.

Holding up my revolver, I answered, "I'm just stepping out for a bit."

The other car had already caught up to us, as I knew it would. When I first told Nathan to take control of the vehicle, I had lifted my foot from the accelerator. I needed them to catch up to us. It wasn't a safe gamble, but we were going to die if we didn't stop them.

I slid out of my window and shimmied onto the roof. I

dropped flat as they saw me and began shooting. I remained there until I felt, and heard, Nathan crash our car through the fencing.

My plan was simple enough, if I could pull it off. I waited until the driver was already in a maneuver to hit our car, either with the hopes of knocking me off or to crash us. Having started the maneuver, it was going to be difficult, even with his inhuman reflexes, to adjust as I leapt from one vehicle to the other.

I almost slid off the back of the car but managed to get a grip before I did. There wouldn't be room for me to fight any of the three snake men from the front seats. I fired four rounds from my revolver into the passenger seat and then rolled toward the right side of the vehicle. Bullets pierced the roof as I only barely got out of the way in time.

Using my momentum, I clumsily climbed in through the back passenger-side window. I fired my last two shots as I did to prevent the snake man in the back seat from killing me before I was in the car.

It worked, but he recovered more quickly than I could. Before I was able to do anything, he was bringing his machine gun down, aiming it at me.

I kicked it up as he fired. Holes riddled the roof of the car and he lunged at me. I used my now-empty pistol as a set of knuckle-dusters and punched the snake man in the face. His own body twisted within the confines of the car in a way that gave him a huge advantage. Unfortunately for him, all the twisting in the world couldn't help you see through blood pouring over your eyes. His flesh mask was trapping his injuries inside but, instead of acting like a bandage, it funneled the blood directly into his vision.

He was still a wild snake, biting and grabbing at me with incredible speed. I tried to ignore his titan strikes to my abdomen and took advantage of his blindness by hitting him again with the pistol. By the fourth hit to the side of his head he had slowed down to where I could get my arm wrapped around his throat. Once I had, it was only a short time before he blacked out.

His machine gun had fallen to the floor of the car during

our struggle. I grabbed it and aimed it at the driver. "I'm sorry about your friend," I nodded to the passenger whose bloodied head was resting against the console. "Keep driving and no one else has to die." I reached over the unconscious snake man and opened the door next. Then I pushed him out. Before the driver could react, I said, "He's more durable than a human and we both know that fall won't kill him. You can go back and pick him up soon."

My companions were still to the left of the snake man's vehicle and only a few yards ahead. We had already reached the forest and were mostly sliding between trees and shrubs to stay on some semblance of a path.

"Listen," I explained. "I don't think you're the bad guys here, but I also don't know that you're the good guys. I think people have been lying to me and I think that you can help me set the record straight." I directed him toward a set of trees to the right. "I'm going to shoot this gun into the roof. When I do, scrape the car against some of those trees and take us out of their line of sight."

I waited for him to nod his understanding and then fired three shots into the roof.

The snake man driver sold his part very well. As soon as the gun went off, he swerved the car to the right and dragged us along a line of trees. Once we were out of sight from my companions, he slowed the car until the hood rested against a tree.

As we touched the tree, he said to me, "For realism, when they come to find you." He took the blood of his compatriot and smeared it all over his flesh mask.

"Good idea," I said. "Now, tell me everything you know."

The snake man's hearing was better than mine, and he ended our conversation and rested his bloodied head against the steering wheel.

"Thank you," I whispered as Elena, Nathan, and their cousin pulled up next to us. "Praise be to Yig."

I unlatched the door and kicked it open as they approached, indicating that it must have been stuck. When I got out of the car, I fell to one knee and hoped that they thought I was injured. It wasn't a huge leap from the truth. Leaping between cars and fighting snake men wasn't easy and my body was bruised and exhausted.

Nathan came to my side and helped me to my feet while Elena looked me over for injury.

"How did you fight and survive three of them?" Elena's voice was filled with shock.

I shrugged. "It was really only the one. The driver was occupied, and I shot the passenger."

I didn't want them lingering around the 'corpse' in the 'crashed' car, so I walked past her and slid into the driver's seat of our vehicle.

Nathan and the nondescript, and now I knew why, cousin followed me as Elena waved at the crashed car. "What about the map?"

"I already looked, and it isn't in there, but we don't need it anyway," I answered.

She put her hands on her hips, "And why is that?"

"Don't take me for a fool, Elena," annoyance filled my voice. "You've gone through my bag three times since we first left America and you're well aware that I have researched and know the location of the Temple of Rthan."

"Very good, Dr. Doran." She walked back to the car and got in. "I guess you have now become our guide in a more traditional sense."

I grabbed my notebook and map from my own bag and began working out where we were in relation to the Temple of Rthan while trying to still act like everything was normal. It wasn't time for them to know what I knew.

From all my notes and research, from the few texts I had kept on me when I traveled, I was able to piece together a general idea of where the Temple of Rthan was in relation to our arrival. Generally speaking, Rthan wasn't far from the city but had remained hidden by a combination of thousands of years of foliage, local superstition, and small acts of specific violence to keep the local populace in enough of a state of fear to not look for it.

Unlike the locals, we were actively trying to find it and it would therefore take more than a small and precise attack to warn us away.

We drove through the forest for about a mile before we came across a road traveling Northwest to Southeast. A quick glance at my notes was all I needed to confirm my direction. We turned Southeast and enjoyed the relatively less jarring ride that a road gave us over the forest floor.

We drove for about an hour in complete silence. This trip had seen at least a marginal amount of casual conversation between the 'cousins' during times like these, but nothing of the sort was happening. It was this complete silence that made me wonder how much Elena suspected that I knew. Either that, or I was being paranoid. It was also likely that everyone was nervous about visiting the temple.

A quick kick to my bag, followed by the soft jingle of bullets, helped to ease my tensions. Everyone else would need to find their own ways to cope.

Checking my notes while keeping my eyes on the road was simpler than I had expected it to be in the heart of India. It was how I knew we were getting close to the Temple of Rthan.

According to my notes, as well as information that I had gleaned from my new snake man friend, I decided that we had come as close to the Temple of Rthan as the road would allow us. Pulling the car over, I helped Elena, Nathan, and their "cousin" to grab their bags. We weren't going to need much besides a few canteens and our wits.

The forest before us was dry, but dense. Pushing through it was a task and I caught more than a few doubtful glances from my travel companions. As we worked through the woods, we managed to discover a small path, either made from an animal or the locals, and we began traveling down that. I wondered if my companions could feel the eyes that watched us.

When we had traveled about a mile or so from where we had parked the car, I dug around in my bag and pulled out my compass and notebook.

"Are we lost, Dr. Doran?" Nathan demanded.

"Nathan," I lowered my tools and looked him directly in

the eyes, "Your tone and complete lack of respect for the only person with any idea of which direction to go isn't going to work in your favor. I suggest you try talking to me with a modicum of appreciation." I dropped my notebook on the ground. "Otherwise, you can find the damned temple on your own."

He stepped toward me with his arms raised. Before he could close the distance between us, I had a small knife out. I twisted and slashed, taking a step back as I did.

"Now's as good a time as any, I suppose," I said to no one specifically. "Did I cut you, Nathan? Why don't you show me what I already know?"

As he straightened, I could see that my blow had struck home. His cheek was hanging off of his face by the line of his jaw. There was no blood and underneath was an entirely different surprise.

Scales that were black and red.

Elena gasped in shock. "What is the meaning of this? Nathan," she slowed her speech to indicate her own understanding of the situation, "are you … one of them?"

She had stepped up next to me and was looking at him closely. As quickly as I could move, I snapped my wrist out to cut her as well.

Elena's grip wrapped around my wrist faster than a human that wasn't looking at me should have been able to move.

"Got you," I grunted as she squeezed my wrist with inhuman strength.

"All you got," she smiled and showed no exertion on her fake face, "is indentured servitude. We still need your assistance."

"What is the deal with this stone?" I demanded.

"The Stone of Rthan, to use one of its less-exciting names, will allow us the opportunity to commune with our god and implore his favor," Elena explained.

My wrist bones were popping as her grip only tightened. "To what end? Yig can hear your prayers without the stone."

Nathan tore off the loose piece of flesh and laughed. "We don't want to pray to Yig. We want him as an ally in our holy war to end humanity."

Hask, the driver who faked his death, had called Elena and

her friends the "unruly American cousins." He had told me
that they wanted the powers of Yig to replace humanity as the
benefactors of Yig's gifts. Why should Yig be as pleased with
humanity as he was with his own children.

"Shouldn't the children be favored?" I asked, repeating
what Hask had told me.

"Oh," Elena smiled and finally released my aching wrist.
"That's how you knew. You spoke to our local cousin."

"And the wizard story was entirely fake?" I already knew
the answer.

Elena shrugged. "While you claim to be a friend to the
Children of Yig, there was no doubt whose side you would take
if you knew that a holy fire was about to wash over humanity.
That same friendship will allow you passage into Rthan and
the blessing of Yig, allowing you to touch his stone and bring
it to us."

I sheathed my knife and rubbed at my wrist. "And you think
your god will help you wipe out humanity if you ask nicely?
He's a god that's older than most of the gods on this planet. He
doesn't just do what he's told."

"We are a species that ages much slower than yours," Elena
said. "First we will discover the means to communicate with
him, and we will worry about the rest at a later time."

It was a half-baked plan but you didn't eat an elephant, or
coerce a god, in one big bite. Small bites over time was the smart
play, but trying to get a god to back your own motivations was
a dangerous game anyway. They were gambling a lot for a slim
chance at success.

"And your local cousins are against the idea?"

"We originally tried to convince them to help us," Nathan
said. "That was a mistake."

I smirked. "Yig deemed humanity as beneficial children, as
long as we do less harm than good he won't ever side against
us."

"Then it will be our job to convince him, and our cousins,
of the blight on this world that you and your species are. Now
take us to Rthan." Elena stooped to pick up my notebook and
compass.

I swung my fist down and dropped the full amount of my weight behind the punch. I was surprised when it connected with the back of Elena's skull. Part of me had expected her to expect the attack.

At the same time, a gunshot rang out from out of sight and Elena's remaining American cousin, whose name I was never going to remember, jerked and fell to the ground in a spray of blood.

Nathan dove behind a tree while I made no move.

The gunman was Husk. The snake man from the car had agreed to follow me at a distance and to assist however he could. Obviously, his idea of assistance was to eliminate his distant family at the earliest convenience.

I wasn't about to argue. I had been lucky in my fights with Children of Yig up to this point. Being clever only got you so far when you were physically outmatched in both strength and speed.

To that point, my biggest mistake was thinking that a snake person wasn't able to attack me just because they were on the ground at my feet.

Where snakes were most at home.

Elena wrapped her arms around my legs and twisted with the kind of strength only a hybrid snake person could possess. I was on the ground and wrestling with her as I heard Husk's step cutting through the forest toward us.

She wasn't punching or biting at me and I couldn't figure out her end goal until it was too late.

At my belt, she yanked the knife from my sheath and twisted, throwing it into Husk's throat. He fell to the ground with a bloody gurgle before he died.

Nathan ran over and pressed his hand to his fallen companion's chest. I didn't see heartbreak the way I would have in a human face. Instead, what I saw was a deep familial bond being shattered. He was moved and upset at the passing, but he also saw no point in mourning him. When his moment had passed, Nathan shifted his attention to Husk's corpse. For a moment, I expected a repeat of the same behavior but Nathan ignored Husk's corpse and picked up the machine gun he had been carrying.

Aside from their speed, strength, and numbers, I was now outgunned.

In another hasty movement that my eyes didn't catch, Elena was on her feet and had brought me to a standing position as well. Eyeing me, she picked up my compass and notebook and slammed them into my chest.

"Take us to Rthan or I will kill you where you stand."

I opened the notebook and said, "You're such a charmer." She didn't respond as I looked at the compass and tried to ignore our proximity to Husk's body. Another poor soul who had died trying to help me.

After about five minutes of letting my heartbeat calm down while I pretended to look at the notes, I waved in the direction that we had already been traveling.

Nathan, now with his false face entirely removed, jabbed me with Husk's machine gun.

I walked about 300 meters before it became apparent that we were standing in the courtyard of the Temple of Rthan.

Unlike humanity, whose natural tendencies had been beaten out of us with evolution and civilization, the Children of Yig had no reason to shed their roots. To me, the courtyard looked overgrown with vines, trees, and plant life to the point that would give your average gardener a heart attack. To the Children of Yig, who saw overgrowth and plant life as necessary, this looked like home.

Behind the trees and foliage was the temple. It was built lower than most human temples were, with height being of less importance as cool air. Without exploring, I knew that the temple went deeper into the ground, allowing for the place to remain cool so that the inhabitants could sleep.

Of the inhabitants, a few could readily be seen. They each carried two small spears, about the same length as their forearms. With their speed and lithe physicality, they could be dangerous melee weapons, or lethal ranged weapons.

"Welcome to the Temple of Rthan," I said. "Now how do you plan to get past the guards?"

As if my words had called them to our attention, more of the snake people arrived. They lined the walls of the temple each with a different type of weapon. The weapons were a mix of clubs, knives, and spears and the blades and blunt implements were all made from a metal that I couldn't recognize.

Until this journey, I had yet to fully examine the Children of Yig. The friends that I had were either products of a hybrid relationship and retained mostly human features, or were entirely human by visual standards, having not yet gone through the metamorphosis.

"I believe that you forget, Dr. Doran," Elena's voice went up in pitch as she took on the superior tone of someone who knows more than everyone else in the room. "We hired you to go in and get the stone. We don't have to get past the guards; you do."

I let out a long and slow gust of air. "Fine." I started walking forward and toward what I assumed to be the main entrance to the temple. It was a large set of double doors covered with serpent imagery. The same silver-yet-not metal that made up the dangerous ends of their weapons seemed to also be the medium for their door. It gave the illusion that the images of snakes covering the door were writhing and crawling across it.

Nathan grabbed my arm. "What are you doing? They will kill you."

"No they won't," I said. "The same reason you hate them is the same reason that I won't be attacked."

"The Serpent God gives safe passage to the humans who offer him a boon," Elena's smile had a pained edge to it and didn't reach her eyes. "The good doctor thinks that he's in Yig's favor."

"You had better hope that I am," I said. "Otherwise you've wasted an entire trip here."

I was more in Yig's favor than my patrons knew. I had spent the evening beforehand saying the rites to Yig and his pantheon. It was a simple incantation during which I invoked his name and made a promise to deliver to him more than I would receive if only he could provide me safe passage into his temple. He knew my intentions and he knew that I had no intentions of handing over some powerful artifact to the bastards who had dragged me out here.

Nathan let go of me and I continued forward. When I got to

the double doors I whispered my promise to Yig.

"I will bring you what was promised." My voice was so quiet, I doubted anyone could hear what I said.

The doors swung toward me and I had to step back to avoid getting hit by them. Without knowing what material they were made of, I had no idea how heavy the doors were. From their size, I had to assume they would have crushed me if I was hit.

Glancing over my shoulder showed me that Elena was excited that everything was going to plan while Nathan was keeping his eyes on the locals. They hadn't stepped on the temple grounds yet and were therefore not offending anyone. In addition, I wouldn't be surprised to find out that they were protected by having me in their employ. Attacking us on the road was one thing, but if everything Elena and my research had shown was correct, the Temple of Rthan was intended to be a peaceful meeting place for the Children of Yig. They wouldn't attack unless provoked.

The temple was surprisingly well-lit. Every 10 feet there were panes of what looked like glass, but contours in it led me to believe it was an organic substance. Behind them were fires, providing ambient heat and light to the entire place. This made the temple warmer than I was comfortable with, but was perfect for people who were cold-blooded.

I reached into my pocket and pulled out a folded sheet of paper from my notes. The Children of Yig were not going to take me to their prized stone. The paper had crude instructions on how to find it within the temple and any sort of traps that awaited me.

There was a slant to the floor that was only barely perceptible and as I followed my notes I could sense the halls getting mildly cooler. I was traveling deeper into the ground. It was difficult to tell how deep I had gone but after about twenty minutes of switching directions, comparing my notes to the engravings on the walls, and beginning to doubt my directions, I stepped into a mile-wide chamber.

The vast cavern was filled with serpent people, dwellings carved out of the stone, and a much larger temple in its center.

This was the true Temple of Rthan.

I stepped forward and into the chamber and was greeted by a fast-moving guard. Before I knew what was happening he had slashed my palm with a blade and grabbed me by the wrist.

He never took his eyes off of me as he stretched my hand toward his face against my will. I didn't want to lose my favor with Yig and the attacking this guard would likely do that. Instead, I stood there and waited for him to take whatever action he wished.

A darting of his forked tongue lapped blood from my hand. As he released me he spoke in a quiet whisper.

"I know your scent. Visit us in peace. Leave us in peace." He leaned in for the last part. "Otherwise, I shall hunt you and know your scent again."

It did not sound like a threat so much as a curse. His people would hunt me for the rest of my life if I broke my pact with Yig.

Even without my notes, it was obvious that I needed to head to the center temple. While their snake-like species didn't need the same kind of paths as we did, they still had them. This was most likely to facilitate their pre-metamorphosis family. I feared breaking some unspoken rule about running in proximity to the temple and therefore I walked with a brisk pace. It was a childish fear, but there was nothing wrong with being overly cautious.

As I made my way through the village, because no other name would suffice, I did my best to ignore the stares and looks of disgust. While Yig had welcomed me, that didn't mean his family had to like it. This was their home and sacred place of gathering and I was the equivalent of the neighbor's dirty pet shaking his mud-soaked fur in the living room. That being said, they left me entirely alone.

I stood at the foot of the actual Temple of Rthan and tried to look at where it joined the ceiling. Even though I wasn't anywhere near deep enough, I couldn't see the top. Whatever this place was, it broke the laws of physics and was trying to take my mind with it.

The doors to the temple were the first test that I was going to have to pass. There was a riddle written in Indian.

Translated, it read: How can you tell if a snake is poisonous or not?

Not only was it a generally simple riddle because of its being the first, but it set a precedent. To answer this riddle you needed to think less like a man and more like a serpent.

Clearly, yet quietly, I answered. "You let it bite you."

The doors shifted slightly and I took that to mean that they had unlocked, but not that they would be opening of their own accord. Any time you watched a snake move through an opening, the animal would press its way through it and take only the amount of space that it needed.

I pressed my hand into the small gap created by the door unlocking. Wiggling my fingers, the gap stretched to permit my hand, and then my arm, and soon my entire body was through without opening the door as wide as would be the norm in the human world.

The room behind the door was completely dark, with no light except the small amount from the barely-open door. In that dim shaft of luminescence, I could see a rope and anchor system that touched the door. If I had opened it much further it would have triggered some sort of trap that I most likely wouldn't have survived.

There's something inherently terrifying about the dark. Children have a fear of it for a reason. You can't see what it holds, but also there's something primal. In my travels, I had become aware of foreign monstrosities and alien demons that used the dark for either camouflage or things more sinister. These things could use it as a portal between their world and ours or as a weapon into our realm of existence. The stories that accompanied these creatures traveled back thousands of years.

So, it was entirely the work of thousands of years of human ancestry being hunted by inconceivable horrors and not a generic fear of dark spaces that made me hesitant to move forward within the chamber.

The silence was permeated by a low hiss that sounded as though it was coming from all around me. As I forced my feet forward, a feeling of something pushing past my leg made me freeze in place. Waiting where I stood, I let three more instances of something slide by my foot before my rational brain reminded me that we were in the Temple of Rthan and these were very likely to be snakes.

"Tell me, Dr. Doran," a thousand snakes spoke with one voice, "what will you do with Yig's stone?"

It didn't take a genius to know that the thing that spoke to me through a room full of snakes was likely the serpent god himself.

"I plan to betray my captors. I will use the stone for leverage before returning it to the temple and its people."

"If the stone is how the children speak to their god, then who am I?" The voices were almost too loud and I cringed as they spoke.

"That's what Elena said it was," I answered honestly. "I believe it to be more of a conduit to Yig's power." I shrugged, hoping the thing could see the movement. "Either way, the children being limited to speaking to Yig through the stone doesn't demand that Yig is equally limited. I believe you are Yig, or possibly as close as I will get to talking to him today."

There was a pronounced hiss that almost drove me to my knees with its volume before turning to a soft hum.

Finally, the voice said, "That is possibly as close to correct as you will get today, as well." The voice rolled into a snickering sound.

In the darkness, I hadn't been aware of what the size of the room was that we were in or how it was decorated. The snickering turned into a rolling laughter as the room was bathed in fiery lighting.

The room itself was made of the same rough stone as the rest of the temple. The more surprising thing was that the room itself was huge. It had to take up the entire base of the temple with barely any room for the walls.

In the center of the chamber was a small box. Obviously, with nowhere else to hide, the stone had to be inside it.

That wasn't what had caught my full attention, though. Every snake that had slithered by my leg in the dark, and a great many more that I hadn't known were in the room, had formed into a large pile that was taking on a shape. This snake conglomeration was forming into the rough outline of an oversized man. It wasn't enough that it was a man the size of at least two of me but did it have to be made entirely out of snakes?

Again, I wasn't a person who had an overly strong fear of snakes so much as I preferred to be a realist. Fighting a handful of snakes wasn't so bad and could get done simply enough if you knew what to do and how to do it. The part that stirred my more primitive senses was the coordination of such a large number of the creatures.

To my benefit, I had been in so many situations that were in many ways very similar to this that I wasn't frozen in my sudden fear. Instead, I was galvanized into action.

While this was obviously another of Yig's tests, I wasn't certain exactly how I was expected to pass it. My tenuous truce with the serpent god meant that I was to leave all snakes unharmed, yet here was a beast made entirely out of them.

It was in my best interest to not fight this amalgamation, but to retrieve the box.

I ran directly at the lumbering pile of creatures and dropped my knee in what I hoped would be my most successfully copied baseball move to date. I went into a slide that was aimed directly between the thing's "legs."

Snakes shot out of those same legs and grabbed me in a mix of teeth and wrapping my limbs. My momentum halted before reversing with added velocity. I slammed into the ground about forty yards from my target.

I groaned less from the impact with the temple floor and more from the small amounts of venom that were now coursing through my veins. My faith in my truce with Yig gave me hope that these poisons wouldn't be my end, but I couldn't help but wonder if I had made an error in trusting in the snake god.

The edges of my vision began to blur but I felt no slower than before I had been bitten. I leapt to my feet and tried again, this time feinting to the left before rolling to the right.

Instead of snakes reaching out to bite or grab me, the beast raised one of its writhing arms and extended it in my direction. A tentacle made entirely of snakes stretched from the arm and defied gravity by slamming into my chest and sending me sailing through the air.

This time, I hit the wall near one of the sconces. The wall knocked the wind from my chest, or perhaps the venom was making it more difficult to breathe. Either way, I was gasping for air as I landed on the ground.

I used the wall to climb to my feet and my eyes caught sight again of the sconce. It had been knocked askew by my impact. In the haze of my venom addled mind, an idea surfaced.

While I couldn't hurt the snakes, there was nothing in my deal about scaring them.

I took off my shirt as quickly as I could and used it to grab the large saucer of burning material that had rested within the wall. Carrying it awkwardly, I slowly advanced on the monster.

With each step I could feel my body going numb and slowing down. I was going to need to be fast to do this right and the longer I took, the slower I'd become.

The snake thing stepped to the side, providing an open path to my target that was also an obvious trap. We were at a stalemate, but only if the thing would react the way I was hoping it would. If I had miscalculated my quarry's mettle, then I was doomed.

I took the bait and ran directly at the box. All of my muscles either screamed as I pushed them to their limits or were entirely numb as the poisons in my blood took effect.

The beast's lightning reflexes came at me as it tried to smother me in gnashing serpents. I turned up the sconce and threw the lit material in an arc that I hoped would block the creature's path of attack. Fortune smiled on me as the snakes, remembering their basic instincts, recoiled and fell from the creature in an attempt to avoid the fire.

I released both the sconce and my shirt and dove on the box, coming up in a roll that showed the beast that it was in my hand.

It was at that moment that I realized this might not have been a contest that ended when I retrieved my prize.

As I stared at Yig's chosen form on this plane of existence, time seemed to stop entirely.

Finally, the thing fell to the temple floor and the individual snakes dispersed. I clutched the box to my bare chest as I watched the snakes slither into the cracks and seams before disappearing from my sight.

My gasps for air turned into gulps as the venom receded from my system along with Yig's family.

When I was able to stand, I put my shirt back on and looked inside the box. What I saw there made me smile the first genuine smile I had found appropriate this entire trip. I left the temple and began my march back to the surface.

The daylight blinded me for only a moment as I came out of the faux temple's doors. I held up the box and I could tell that Elena only had eyes for the prize while Nathan, who's reptilian face was difficult to read, showed clear signs of surprise at the amount of blood on me. Judging by his subtle look, I figured that I must have looked much worse than I thought I had.

"Give me the stone," Elena pointed at the box. It was obvious that she wanted to step closer, but Yig's boon was only given to me. She could start an all-out war with her own species if she stepped any closer without permission.

"That's not going to happen." I took a seat on a fallen tree right near where I imagined Yig's line was. It was only a few feet past where the closest of his children were standing, poised and ready for a fight.

"Excuse me?" Elena and Nathan raised their guns at me.

The Children of Yig all tensed.

I raised a hand as I clutched the small wooden box under my other arm.

"Hold on, just a minute," I said. "There're a couple of things we need to discuss before you start war with your cousins or I decide to hand this over."

"Such as what?" Nathan demanded.

"My freedom, for starters," I answered. "I'm not dumb enough to think I'll make it back to Delhi in one piece once I give you the box." I shook the box to indicate the prize.

"Very well," Elena said. "You stay with your new friends until we take off. After that all bets are off. What else are you demanding?"

"Well, that's the problem," I said. "I kind of like Earth without it being run by snake men, so I am not entirely sure that the bets would necessarily be off. Even if I never saw you again and you were able to use the stone to convince Yig to provide you with his boon over humanity," I gestured to the snake men behind me, "or his other children who obviously want no piece of what you're offering, there will be war. A whole lot of war. War with humanity and war with your cousins. Millions, if not billions, will be killed as you try to exert your control over the world's lands. Giving you this stone," I held up the box again, "isn't worth any one life, including mine."

"If you won't give us the stone," Elena's voice was filled with rage, "then why did you go in there to get it?"

"I didn't go in there to get the stone," I answered. "I went in there to give you a chance to see what it was like to live with Yig," I waved, again indicating Elena and Nathan's Indian cousins, "instead of using him as a tool. They have everything they could want. Community, family, and power. Or haven't you noticed that they are working with the local governments to run the cities?"

"We don't want to run cities," Nathan shouted, "we want to replace humanity as the ruling species on every continent."

"They won't allow that," I said.

"They won't have a choice," Elena pointed at the box. "With that, Yig will demand that his people all move as one. There won't be a war so much as a quick and bloody replacement."

"Well," I smirked, "when you put it that way…" I patted the box. "You're not giving me much incentive to give this thing to you."

"What is it you want?" She tried to dial back some of her anger. "We are so close to our goal," she held up a machine gun. "We won't let spears stop us from getting our prize."

"No," I agreed. "I didn't think that you would, and the last thing I want, here or anywhere, is bloodshed. So, here's what I'm thinking." I stood up from the log and walked forward. "I will give this box to you, and you will stay here for one month. Learn from your family. Learn the rites of the Children of Yig and earn the right to use the stone of Rthan. I will give you this box right now if you can promise me that you will try."

I turned to the nearest Child of Yig. She clutched her spear in hands that were green and orange in scales. Her beautiful pattern stretched over her entire body and made me wonder if she had changed while still among people. If so, that had to have been an incredibly difficult life.

"Is that a deal that your people will honor?"

The orange and green warrior looked down at the box and then back at me. Then she shot a glance toward a large collection of her people near the fake Temple of Rthan. There were silent communications between them before she returned her attention to me and gave me a nod of approval.

"There you have it," I said to Elena and Nathan. "Is that an agreement that you can honor?"

She hesitated, casting looks at Nathan as their own nonverbal communication transpired.

After a moment that seemed to last forever, she nodded.

"We agree. Give us the box and we will do as you say."

I set the box down on the ground and sprinted past them and into the woods. As I did, Nathan spun toward me, exactly as I knew he would, and opened fire with his gun. I dove behind the first tree that I came across and only peeked out when the shooting stopped.

The locals were brandishing their spears and prepared to fight but hadn't made a move yet. Elena had scooped up the box and was just opening it as I watched.

The look on her face was priceless.

She was just discovering what I had after my battle inside the Temple of Rthan.

Someone else had stolen the stone before we got here.

She let out a scream of anger that I thought would tear down the forest. As she did she clawed at the flesh mask on her face and revealed turquoise scales beneath. She then did the next thing I had been predicting she would do.

Elena grabbed the gun from Nathan and shot one of the local Children of Yig.

Even if she hadn't shot them, our deal had been binding. She had promised to stay in peace for a month with her more devout cousins in exchange for the box, not the stone, of which I had made perfectly clear. Even if she had intended to keep that promise, which I wouldn't have bet on, she would never have stayed the course once she saw that the box was empty.

Breaking an oath made on temple land beneath the watch of Yig and then killing one of his children on that same land made her and Nathan blasphemers against their own people. Before the spears pierced her chest, I knew she would never lay eyes on the real stone of Rthan.

What seemed like hundreds of spears impaled both Nathan and Elena. As if that wasn't enough, Yig sent his emissaries. Thousands of snakes came from the trees and every direction to swarm over and devour the two betrayers.

When I was certain that Yig wouldn't see me as one of the betrayers as well, I made my slow trek back toward the car and Delhi.

I planned on stopping in London on the way home, and this time I would be the one telling the captain the story.

STILL LIFE WITH DEATH

BY MARK HOWARD JONES

The Northeastern United States—1955

Light filled the generous space as the two men stood before a pair of small display easels. One wore a thoroughly perplexed expression while the other stood to one side, listening glumly.

"None of the proportions are right, man. Nobody looks like that. Your portraits have always been beautiful, even exquisite, but these are just... well, shoddy, Lyall."

"If you're going to use words like 'shoddy' then I'll thank you to call me *Mister Lych*." He didn't know if his attempt to mask his genuine irritation with a mildly jocular attitude was working or not.

The well-dressed man took a cigarette out of his gold, initialed case. "But seriously, Lyall, what were you thinking? Have you suddenly been infected by the Avant Garde?" He extended the engraved gold case towards the other man.

Lych shook his head, then sat on the canvas chair that waited in front of the two paintings. "I wanted to try something... new!"

The visitor issued a chuckle which turned into a sigh. "Well, alright... but *this*?!" He toyed with the handkerchief sticking out of his breast pocket, tugging at it as if impatiently straightening the clothes of an untidy child.

Lych stood up again, restlessly. He ran his hand through his dark hair. "Yes! That!" He pointed to the canvases while arching an eyebrow at the critic. "I just wanted to give you a sneak preview of what to expect at the private view next week. Thought you might like an 'exclusive'. I wish I hadn't bothered now."

The other man's expression softened. "Well, don't get me wrong. I do appreciate that, believe me. I just don't know what to make of it, Lyall." He walked over to a large armoire, picked up his hat and flourished it in a foppish manner before putting it on his head. "I'm sure I'll think of something to write!"

Lych led him to the door. "Be kind, Adam, please. My bank account would never survive your harsh words."

The man chuckled. "Well, okaaay. I'll go with you on this one. See you at the gallery next week then."

Lych nodded and smiled before clicking the door firmly shut. He sighed heavily.

Another man emerged from a half-closed door at the end of the room. He looked ill and disheveled, haunted by an air of exhaustion. "Who was that?"

"Adam Rodenghast. He's a critic," said Lych. Fiddling with some brushes, he selected, then rejected them each in turn.

"Well, I don't like him."

"Oh, they're all like that from time to time." Lych reached out and rubbed the sleeve of the other man in reassurance. "Don't let him bother you. Nothing's going to change. No serious artist ever listens to a critic. Certainly not me. OK, he's a snake... but he's an influential one, and I can't afford to ignore him."

He indicated the straight-backed chair that faced the huge window. "Shall we continue?"

The ill-looking man poured himself onto the chair and did his best to sit still. Lych removed the cover from the canvas he was working on and selected a brush.

Later that day, he answered the bell to see a small, dark-haired woman in an elegant light green jacket and knee-length skirt standing there. She feigned distraction for a moment before suddenly pretending to notice him and craning her neck up to kiss him.

"Hi!" she said, smiling. Lych returned the greeting and

stepped back to allow her in. An expensive-looking handbag was tucked under her arm.

His on-off relationship with Marian Elder was back on at the moment, which meant that his mood was good but his pockets were a lot lighter that he'd have liked.

"Did I ever tell you how much I hate your carpet, darling?" Marian lifted one foot off the floor, as if it caused her pain to walk on the gaudily-patterned floor covering.

"Only every time you see it," said Lych wearily.

"Well, it always clashes with my outfit," she replied, in mock outrage.

Lych bowed low in front of her. "I'll have it ripped up at once, Your Majesty."

Marian giggled and settled herself into a comfortable chair, depositing her bag on the offending carpet at her feet.

Lych objected at once. "Hey, don't sit down. I want to show you my latest big project. I'm hoping to finish it in time for next week's show. I've already warned Alex at the gallery to leave space for it. Just hope I can finish it in time—a blank wall doesn't look so good at a private view."

Marian followed dutifully. She'd been allowed into Lych's holy of holies just twice before. It was where he kept what he considered to be his most important work.

He unlocked the door. Then he seemed hesitant, opening it just an inch at a time as if unsure he wanted to show her what lay on the other side of it.

"This painting is too big to ever be confined in a glass cage." He led her into the room and they stood before the huge canvas. It reached nearly to the ceiling and was at least 15 feet wide. It was illuminated by a large skylight and a step ladder stood abandoned to one side.

The canvas was covered with bright patches of pigment that looped and curved around each other. In the center were two more carefully delineated figures, seemingly engaged in either a wrestling match or a bout of love-making.

"My God," she muttered. "What is it?'

"It's called 'Eve and The Serpent'! Not even Rodenghast's seen this. He'd hate it, I'm sure."

"She looks uncomfortable," was all Marian had to say.

"But wouldn't you say it was beautiful?" he prodded.

"Only if I was using the word 'beautiful' in a new and interesting way," replied Marian. Thinking better of her jibe, she smiled at him. "It's wonderful, Lyall. Really. You're like Van Gogh... but with two ears."

He stared at her in hot contempt for a moment before turning away and snatching up a paintbrush. He toyed with it a moment before replacing it.

Conscious that she'd upset him, Marian wandered back into the other room.

"What are these?" she asked, standing before the two small easels. She'd tugged the dust covers off and was examining them closely. "Oh God... how horrible!"

"Careful! They're still wet." Lych steered her away from the paintings. "Those aren't finished yet. Not ready to be seen."

"But, Lyall—they're grotesque. Not like your usual work at all!" She seemed genuinely unsettled by them.

He appeared to be suddenly upset by her words. "Perhaps I can't paint anymore, eh? Maybe this act is over. Maybe I should turn my back on the audience, bring down the curtain, burn the theatre to the ground?"

"That'd be a bit... dramatic, darling!" She smirked, pleased with her pun. "I'm sorry, darling. I didn't mean to upset you. I'll wait until they're both finished and you're ready to show them to me."

Sensing how upset he was, Marian went over and took his hands in hers. "Listen, I'm meeting Janice for lunch at the Shalimar. Why don't you join us? I'm sure she'd love to see you." She gazed up into his frowning face.

"I'd love to, but I've got a guest staying. And he's in pretty bad shape. I don't want to leave him alone right now," said Lych.

"Not another of your old army buddies who's fallen off the wagon, is it?"

Lych shook his head. "No, he's an engineer. He's done some work for the army, though. His problem is a little more serious than drink, Marian."

Hearing that, she knew it must be serious. He never called her by her first name.

She nodded. "Oh, right. Well, shouldn't he be in hospital if he's that bad?"

Again Lych shook his head. "I don't think any hospital could help him, somehow. I've been doing some portraits of him, at his request. It does seem to help calm him down, somehow."

"Sounds like you're both benefitting, one way or another."

The frown didn't leave Lych's brow, so Marian decided it was time for a tactical withdrawal. "Well, I'll leave you to it. I'll see you tomorrow."

After seeing her out, Lych stood watching the door behind which Fant was supposedly sleeping.

Mid-morning came and went before Lych decided it was definitely time for work. He'd made a few phone calls and wasted as much time as he could. Now he'd run out of convincing excuses.

He left the living room and went into the small studio.

Fant was already there, standing by the window. He looked even more dishevelled and withered than usual. "We had visitors!" he croaked.

The latch closure on the frame had obviously been broken.

"Damn! Have you noticed if anything is missing? We're two floors up, for God's sake. What did they want?" Lych examined the damaged window.

"Me, probably," said Fant.

Lych opened the window fully and looked down into the alley that ran between his building and the next. It was empty, as he'd expected.

There were no tell-tale boot marks on the window ledge but there was something else. He reached out and picked it off the grimy surface. Holding it up, he turned it in his fingers. It was a few inches across and roughly triangular in shape, with rounded edges. It felt slightly rough between his fingers.

Fant hadn't noticed that he'd found something, so Lych quickly wrapped it in his handkerchief and secreted it in his pocket.

It was time to play down his suspicions for Fant's benefit, he decided. The man was in a distraught enough state as it was, without adding a fresh mystery to his problems.

"Probably just opportunist burglars," said Lych. "Well, if they were looking for money or valuables, they came to the wrong place. I'll get a guy in to fix this window tomorrow."

"I shouldn't stay here, Lyall. It's causing trouble for you. Maybe even putting you in danger."

Lych tried to get the window to stay closed in a bid to keep out the chill night air. "Don't be absurd, Franklin. It's probably just a common-or-garden burglar who picked the wrong place," he lied.

"No. I think they knew I was here. I think they're coming for me." He paced in agitation.

"Calm down. We'll work everything out, OK?" Lych left his task and crossed to his friend.

"My life is a ruin cobbled together from bits of failure—it's a filthy remnant of what it should be. I can tell you this because I trust you… and I think you trust me." Fant looked into his eyes, almost begging for confirmation.

"Yes. Yes, sure." Lych nodded, unsure if he was telling the truth or not. But it was what Fant needed to hear.

Fant ran his hands along the windowsill, agitated. "I've never told you the full story of why the things that are happening to me began in the first place."

Lych shook his head. "No. But I didn't want to pry. You asked me to paint you and that's my profession, so… I doubt I'll ever get a chance like this again."

Fant laughed sourly. "Yes. Enlightened self-interest, I suppose you'd call that."

He went over to a leather carry-all and came back with a book bound in well-worn black leather. There was no writing on either the front cover or the spine. He held it in his hands as if it was the heaviest thing in the world. A few beads of sweat showed on his upper lip.

"This book is one of several left by my father. It contains… certain ancient and obscure writings. They have been used for centuries by scholars and occultists to effect results that…" He trailed off, seemingly lost for words, then gazed at the floor.

"Are you OK? Do you want to sit down?" Lych grabbed the only chair in the room and swung it round towards Fant.

Fant looked up, as if from some spell. "No. No, I'm alright." His fingers ran along the page edges of the book. Suddenly, he opened it, selected a particular page and held it out to Lych. "Perhaps you'd better read this—it partly explains things." Lych took the book and sat on the chair himself. The page was covered in fading print with some odd illustrations dotted throughout the text. The worn leather felt slightly gritty in his fingers as he began to read.

Marian had 'just popped in' on her way to her dressmaker. Of course, Lych had been expected to drop whatever he was doing—in this case, he'd been working on the large painting for his impending show.

He forced himself to hide his impatience as he made coffee for the two of them. Fant was asleep in the spare bedroom and he needed that more than he needed coffee, thought Lych.

He placed Marian's coffee down in front of her and proceeded to pace around the living room.

"Please sit down, Lyall, you're making me dizzy. How is your friend now, by the way?"

"He's a victim of his own success, if you will." Lych flopped down into a chair, which complained under his bulk. "He claims to have succeeded in loosening the bonds that bind everything together, partially eroding the walls between realities. The laws that keep things as they are no longer seem to apply to him. That's why he changes appearance so often, I'm convinced of it. He talked about 'tiny pockets of everything surrounded by a vast sea of nothing'. I'm trying to help him."

Marian stared at him. "But how are you helping him? You're not—you're just exploiting him. He's a helpless victim, if what you say is true."

"I'm trying to fix an image of him. He seems to think that if enough of these images are captured, he may be able to use them to somehow undo what he's done to himself."

"No, no. I don't believe any of this. How on earth did he

unlock this secret? And how is it we've never heard anything about scientists doing anything similar in the past?"

Lych leaned forward, tangling his fingers together as he talked. "Well, what he did wasn't exactly scientific. You've heard about his father."

Marian let out an exclamation of disgust. "That old letch! My mother and aunt told me all about him, thank you very much. And he had the nerve to call himself a man of God—a missionary, no less!"

Lych nodded in sympathy. "As far as I can make out, he left a lot of old volumes and notebooks behind that Fant used... unwisely. I don't think he fully grasped what he was doing but somehow... somehow... obviously by accident, he succeeded where the old man failed."

"But what was he trying to do?"

Lych sighed heavily. "God alone knows. But now he's asked me to paint these 'images of power' so he can return to normal."

Marian sat down in the chair next to Lych. "Do you think it will work, Lyall?"

"At first I thought it might," said Lych, placing his hand over hers. "But it's been over two months now, and the transformations keep happening. On Monday he changed into something foul—serpentine, worm-eaten, barely alive. Fortunately it lasted only for a few hours. I couldn't paint that. I just couldn't."

"How often does he change?"

"It depends. Some evenings I've been working in the studio and Fant's been in the room next door. He hasn't been in my line of sight, he's been hidden by the wall, so the only way I know he's undergone any change is when the light casts a shadow on the far wall. Once the shadow cast was so cruel, positively malign, that I slammed the door and locked it until the next morning.

"I barely slept that night, and once... I thought I heard something enormous scraping against the door."

Lych leapt to his feet and with two steps was at a pile of canvases leaning against the wall. "Yet other times, he looks normal. Almost handsome." He held up a small oil sketch for Marian to see. It showed a man of Fant's rough appearance but with fine, attractive features.

She nodded. "So the different men I've caught glimpses of you with over the last six months... they've all been Franklin?"

"That's right."

Marian put her hand to her throat. "My God! That's awful. No wonder he looks half dead all the time."

Lych remained silent, mulling over how best to help Fant. Then he remembered the object he'd found on the window ledge.

All desire to paint now gone, he decided to find out what he could about the mysterious object.

"Listen, Marian. I have to go and see a friend at the university. Do you want to come along for the ride?"

"But I was just on my way for a fitting. Can I ring my dressmaker and re-arrange?"

Lych lifted the telephone and held it out to her.

They reached the bottom of the steps at the parking garage near Lych's apartment. Marian knew he'd bought a new car recently but she hadn't seen it yet. Her anticipation had grown on the short walk over.

When Lych stopped at a big, ugly black car, her heart sank at the same time as her face dropped. "What's this heap of junk?"

Lych looked at her through narrowed eyes. "This is a Packard 120 Touring Sedan. What's wrong with you, don't you recognise an American classic when you see it?"

"Classic, huh? I guess that's another way of saying museum piece."

Lych climbed inside and unlocked the passenger door. "Are you getting in?"

Marian pulled a face. "Hmmm. I suppose I'll have to, unless I want to walk. And I *don't* want to walk." Settling herself into the seat, she smirked slightly at her companion.

"You can carry a lot in the back," he commented, jerking his thumb in the direction of the spacious back seat.

Marian raised an eyebrow at him.

"I got a good deal on it," he said, defensively.

"Oh yes, I'm sure you did, my boy. You'd have had to!" she said, then giggled.

Lych started the engine and gunned it loudly. The roar echoed off the concrete walls of the garage, drowning out any further sarcasm.

Lych and Marian had to wait outside Dr. Chin's laboratory when they arrived. He was deep in conversation with two important-looking people in suits.

Eventually, the men left, shooting mildly suspicious glances at the pair of lurkers in the corridor. Lych smiled, hoping it would allay their suspicions. Judging from the men's unchanging expressions, it didn't seem to work.

Lych knocked gently and opened the door when given the OK.

"So what were the police doing here?" he asked the dark-haired Chinese man sat at the lab bench.

The man rose and walked across to shake Lych's hand. "Lyall! Hey, haven't seen you for a dog's age—how are you?"

"So what did the police want, Gary? Have they caught up with you at long last?"

The man chuckled. "Oh, that—my head of department and the Vice-Chancellor. They think I've been a naughty boy. I was getting a telling off. Not for the first time, mind you. Damned bureaucracy!"

Marian, who had been standing behind Lych, coughed softly. "Oh, I'd like you to meet Miss Marian Elder—a very good friend of mine. Marian, this is Dr Garrett Chin."

"Pleased to meet you, Dr. Chin." She extended her hand, which he shook eagerly.

"Please, call me Gary." He beamed broadly at her, holding on to her hand for a little too long. The scientist was clearly dazzled by Marian's charms.

She perched on a lab stool while Lych fished the minor treasure from his pocket. "I've got a little something here for you, Gary. I was hoping you might be able to tell us something about it." He carefully unfolded it from his handkerchief and placed it on the wooden surface at the scientist's elbow.

"Hmmmm. Typical. I only ever see you when you want to pick my brains." Lych made an apologetic face as Dr. Chin prepared a microscope slide.

Marian had seen the mystery object on the ride over and was equally eager to solve the enigma.

"It would be great if you could help us, Gary," she offered, hoping some extra encouragement might ease things along.

Gary smiled at her. "I'll see what I can do, shall I?" His eyes lingered on Marian's smile.

"Hey Doc, eyes on the microscope, if you please," chided Lych.

Dr. Chin seemed slightly dazed. "Oh, yes... right." He peered down the microscope at the specimen they'd brought him, occasionally adjusting the focus and moving the slide. He muttered inaudibly to himself.

After several minutes had passed, Lych coughed softly but pointedly. "Any news, Gary?"

Dr. Chin looked up from his task, a slight frown crinkling his forehead. "Well... it's not quite right but it looks very like an oversized scale of an Ophiophagus hannah."

"Hannah who?" inquired Lych. "What's that in plain English?"

"It's the Hamadryad, more commonly referred to as the King Cobra. Where on earth did you find it? It's magnificent... could be an entirely new variation of the species."

Lych frowned. "It could well be, I suppose. I can't tell you right now where I found it, but I promise I'll reveal all as soon as I can." He felt he had to offer his friend something.

"What neighbourhood does it come from?" asked Marian.

Garrett smiled at her again. "Oh well, all over South East Asia really."

"India, maybe?"

"Yes, certainly India. I believe they figure quite prominently in mythology and folk traditions in India—though that's not my specialist area, obviously."

Marian looked at Lych. "Franklin's father!" she said, jumping down from the stool.

"What... Franklin? Do you mean Franklin Fant? What...?" Gary looked from one to the other, desperate to be let in on their dark secret. As a scientist, unsolved puzzles, hidden secrets and mysteries in general drove him mad—and Lych knew it.

"Thanks, Gary! We've got to dash but I'll ring you later, I promise," said Lych as he and Marian headed out the door. "Wait! Come back!" Gary shouted after them, equally frustrated at being kept in the dark and at having Marian snatched away so quickly.

Lych sat across from his guest. The early afternoon light gave the latter a strange halo but Lych wasn't prepared to attribute any holy status to him, despite his saintly suffering.

"Tell me, do you think there's *any* way to reverse what's happening to you?" Lych put on a cold, detached air.

"You read the book. You know what's happening! I've read it and read it—as well as other papers my father left—and I can't find a single thing that will help."

"Well, that load of old mumbo-jumbo didn't mean a lot to me, I'm afraid. All I really know is what you've told me." He was deliberately trying to provoke Fant into revealing what he knew.

"It's not exactly as if I can look up anyone in the phone book to help. Where the hell would I start?"

Lych nodded slowly. "Are you sure there's nothing that your father left that might be of help? He seemed to have a lot of knowledge of the occult. I mean, are you sure you've explored everything he left you?"

Fant shifted uneasily in his seat. "Come with me to my apartment, Lyall. There's something I need to show you."

"What... now?" Lych was surprised by the sudden invitation. Maybe he was going to get a little closer to the truth after all.

"Yes. I want to know what you think. Please."

Heading across town, Lych felt as if he was carrying a volatile cargo that might go off at any moment. If Fant began one of his transformations he'd have to find a quiet side street or back alley and sit tight until the whole thing was over.

Fant's apartment was in a much more select part of town. On the way over Lych noticed that there were far fewer people in the street, but far more expensive-looking cars parked at the side of the road.

Lych's older car looked like a poor country cousin next to the sleek new autos. He parked it neatly outside Fant's apartment building and tried to pretend he was delivering it to a classic car collector who lived nearby.

The elevator delivered them to the tastefully-decorated second floor. As they walked down the corridor, they heard a commotion coming from the other side of the wall. "Is that coming from your place?" asked Lych.

"I think so. We'd better watch our step here."

Fant slipped the key in the lock quietly and walked in. Lych stood at his elbow. The room was in disarray. Pieces of furniture had been upended and there were books and clothes strewn everywhere. There were sounds coming from the bedroom.

Lych went over to the window and stood in the mild breeze blowing in from outside. The clasp was broken, along with one pane of glass. He began to close it when he heard Fant gasp.

Turning, he saw a large man heading towards Fant. He was over six feet tall and seemed almost as wide. "You! Where is it?!" he demanded.

He dug his fists into Fant's clothing and began to shake him around. "Where!?" he bellowed.

Lych realised the man hadn't seen him. Two large steps and he was by the man's side. His fist connected with the side of the man's head and he went down. Lych nursed his knuckles—he'd forgotten how much hitting a man hurt.

The man was on his feet again almost at once and Lych realised he had a real fight on his hands. Fant was in no fit state to help him, either.

Throwing his bulk forward, the man passed right by as Lych sidestepped quickly. The man sprang back up and headed towards Lych once more. His fists were huge. If one of them connected with him, Lych knew he'd be out of the contest. He had to try and protect Fant.

Grabbing a straight-backed wooden chair, Lych used it like a lion tamer to keep the man at bay. To his astonishment, Lych saw Fant grab the twin to the chair he was using and raise it above his head. It came down on the man's head with a sickening thud. The big man fell forward like a sack of potatoes, clearly unconscious as he hit the floor.

Lych leant over the man and began to search his pockets in the hope of finding out who he was. He'd searched his outside pockets and was about to look for his wallet when the man opened his eyes. He must have a skull like rock, thought Lych, moving back cautiously and reaching for the chair again.

The man saw the chair in Lych's hands and half ran, half fell out of the door, bouncing off the far wall and disappearing around the corner. Fant began to follow him.

"Leave him," said Lych. Fant turned and saw what Lych had already witnessed. He made a weak noise in the back of his throat.

The thing that stood in the doorway before them was huge. It looked like a man dressed in a grey robe, except its head wasn't properly human at all.

Lych couldn't make out what he was looking at for a second. The head was flatter and wider than it should have been with barely any nose and a broad slit for a mouth.

His mind raced—at first thinking the figure that stood before them must have some sort of inherited deformity. But it seemed too extreme for that. Maybe…

Lych had no time for further speculation as the figure lunged towards him at unbelievable speed. He managed to swing a punch as he pivoted sideways on one foot. It caught the thing on the side of the head as it passed. A sound of sibilant irritation reached Lych's ear.

He made to follow the figure, intending to spin it round and land a proper blow. Maybe that would persuade it to be more reasonable, he thought.

Then he lurched backwards in shock as the figure leaped at the wall and stayed there, clinging three feet off the ground. He'd been expecting it to rebound at him and had tensed his muscles to expect the attack. Now he didn't know what to expect.

The figure began to ascend the wall. When it reached the tall ceiling it reached out, clinging to it, then scuttled towards the window. Behind him, Lych heard Fant gibbering. "No! No!… Not here!"

Before it reached the open window, the figure turned its

head to look directly at Lych. He couldn't tell if the glint in its half-human eyes was hatred or not, but he was appalled to see the creature's mouth open wider than should have been possible. Two thin jets of liquid shot forth, Lych twisted to one side to try and avoid them.

The creature then turned its head, pivoted its body downwards and disappeared through the window.

Lych was too stunned to move for a second or two. Then he hurried across to the window and looked out. At first he saw nothing, but then he caught a swift movement in the corner of his eye. Turning his head, he was astonished to see the creature walking on all fours diagonally down the wall, avoiding two windows before disappearing around the corner.

He pulled his head back inside and stood dumbfounded. Fant stared at him as if recovering from an electric shock.

Lych looked around at the debris in the room. Whoever they were, they had clearly been looking for something. Hopefully, they'd been disturbed before they found it.

One arm of his jacket was almost entirely covered in the sticky substance. He raised his arm to try and wipe it off.

"Don't touch it!" yelled Fant.

Lych turned to face him. "Why not?"

Fant was leaning against the wall, clearly shaken by the whole incident. "I've seen that before. In India. One of my father's colleagues got some of it on him and accidentally touched it."

"And?" Lych shrugged his shoulders in challenge.

"He died gasping for breath within 15 minutes. The doctor said he had a huge amount of snake venom in his body."

Lych looked down at his jacket, self-consciously holding his arm stiffly by his side. "Snake venom? But... this amount? There's just too much of it. It can't be possible."

"You saw that thing!" said Fant. "It was the size of a man! Bigger!"

"Now hold on, I don't know exactly what I saw. As far as I'm concerned, it *was* a man—in some fancy costume." Fant looked at him with a degree of despair. Lych decided it was best not to take any chances where possible asphyxiation was concerned.

"Then how do you explain it walking across the ceiling?"

challenged Fant. Lych didn't let on that he'd also seen the creature walking down the wall outside.

"Look, just help me get this off. Carefully." Lych held his arm out straight and undid the jacket's buttons, then lowered his arm and slid the one sleeve off while Fant prevented it from falling to the floor. They bundled the jacket into a large paper bag and left it in the corner of the room.

"I don't suppose I can get THAT dry cleaned," mused Lych. "I can't afford to go wasting jackets like that. Next time I'll come in a suit of armour."

Fant sighed heavily. "I doubt that would help." He sounded exhausted, physically and mentally.

Lych found a bottle of half-decent whiskey in the kitchen and poured them both a glass. Fant knocked it back and coughed in distress. Lych slapped him on the back.

"Now, what was it you wanted me to see, Franklin?"

"No, never mind now. Can't we just get out of this place? I'm beginning to hate the sight of it."

Two broken windows in two days, thought Lych, closing the door behind him. He was going to be very popular with the local glaziers.

The rest of the day was spent in a state of unspoken tension. Fant was afraid for his own safety, of course, thought Lych, but felt sure he was keeping something to himself.

Lych stuck his head around the kitchen door. "I'm going to the grocery store. Is there anything you want?"

Fant had a tin of beans in his hand, glaring at it. In the other hand was a can opener. He held it like it was a lethal weapon. "This isn't a can opener, it's a can't opener!" he spat, throwing it across the room. "Lend me your knife."

Lyall stopped and looked at him. Fant saw the expression on his face and grew suddenly angry. "What?! Don't you trust me with it?"

Shamefacedly, Lyall dug in his pocket and took out his folding knife. "Here."

Fant massacred the tin with the knife, spilling as many beans over the countertop as he managed to get into the saucepan. He threw the pan onto the gas and lit it.

"You want some, too?" he asked. Lyall politely declined.

There was a knock at the door just then. When Lych opened it, two large men in overalls were standing there. One consulted a piece of paper. "Uuuhh... Mr Luke. We've come to fix your window."

"The name is Lych and the window is this way." He turned to show the pair where they'd be working when he felt a sudden pain at the back of his head. He lay down very suddenly and everything went black.

"The door was open, and I found you just lying here." Marian's face came into focus. It was crumpled by a deep frown.

He touched his head and winced. Then a terrible thought surfaced from under the pain. "Where's Fant?!"

"I—I don't know. I just got here this second," she replied.

"Help me up, will you?" Marian grabbed his arm and after a few seconds of hilarious pantomime in which Lych and gravity had a serious disagreement, he managed to stand up.

They searched the apartment and the studio but there was no sign of him. "They've taken him. Damn! I promised him he'd be safe here."

"Lyall, sit down. There's blood running down the back of your neck. I'll take a look at it."

She went into the bathroom and returned with some cotton wadding and a bottle of iodine. "What happened to you?"

"I had visitors. They tried the direct approach—last time they came in through the window, this time they tried coming in through my head." He flinched as she dabbed at the wound.

"Try to stay still. I know it hurts, but I've got to clean it." Marian swabbed the cut as gently as she could with the wad of cotton wool.

"I know he's your friend, sweetheart, but you can't take all the responsibility. You should get the police involved now. Kidnap is a serious matter—and you've already done a lot for Franklin. Is he really worth getting your brains bashed out for?"

Lyall almost exploded with impatience. "Oh Marian, stop this melodramatic dimwittery. Surely you know he's my half-brother?"

"Whaaat?! No, I didn't… but, you don't look anything alike. How was I supposed to know?"

"I thought it was common knowledge. My mother re-married after dad died. Her second husband was Reverend Fant," he explained.

Marian nodded. "I see. I'm sorry. I just didn't know. Now I understand why you're so keen to help him."

"Sorry to snap at you. I'm just angry at myself for being caught off guard. I promised he'd be safe, damn it!"

Marian finished cleaning his wound and dressed it with a small piece of gauze. "The bleeding's stopped, at least."

"Thanks. I'm sorry you've been dragged into this, Marian. Maybe you should stay away for a while until this business is over—I don't want you to be in danger."

Marian smiled. "That's sweet of you. Really. But I never leave a candle burning in a paper house, Lyall. I know what I'm doing." She leaned over and kissed him on the head, making sure not to graze any sore spots.

He smiled up at her. "I know, I know… you're a big girl now. But seriously, I just don't know what these people will do!"

"I'm my father's daughter. You should know that by now." Marian knew that he'd find that some comfort.

"Oh, speaking of which, I'm supposed to be meeting him for lunch—I just popped in quickly after my Italian class. If I dash, will you be OK?"

"Sure. I doubt they'll come back for me. I'm no use to them." They kissed and promised to speak later.

She left him wondering how on earth he was going to find his half-brother, and praying to God that he'd be safe until then.

Marian was back, again. Lych's work was on hold, again.

"I didn't expect to see you until tonight," he said, trying to hide his mild annoyance.

"Well, I've been doing some detective work while you've been busy daubing away," she said.

Lych gave her a weary look. "I've had precious little time for daubing, as you put it. I've been too worried about Fant. That wall is going to be bare at next week's opening, I know it."

Marian moaned softly in pretended assent or sympathy. "Anyway, I've found out who we need to speak to if we want to find out more about your lizard cult, or whatever it is. I borrowed this from the library for you." She placed a heavy hardback book down in front of him.

Lych picked it up and read the spine. "Let's see. 'Myth and Folklore in the Early Americas'... does that mean before breakfast?"

"Ha ha. According to an article in last month's 'Art and Archaeology', Professor Marius Lingard is one of the world's foremost experts on religious cults, and he doesn't live far away. In fact, he teaches at the university here."

Lych continued staring at the book jacket.

"And check out the publisher," prodded Marian.

His eyes flicked to the bottom of the spine. He silently mouthed the words 'Elder and Keyes', then chuckled to himself. "How remarkably convenient."

Her father's company printed mainly academic books and school textbooks, both of which helped to pay for Marian's expensive education and keep her in the style she felt most comfortable with.

"OK. Let's track down this Professor Lingard. He's bound to know more about man-sized lizards that walk upright than we do." Lych sighed heavily.

"Let me do it. I can use my charm," said Marian, putting on a forced smile that was more of a snarl.

A few hours spent on the phone got Marian nowhere. The University department had been easy enough to contact but the professor's secretary seemed to be on a permanent coffee break. When she finally spoke to the woman, things didn't go well.

Marian threw her notebook onto the sofa, where it bounced for a moment like an excited dog. "His secretary says he's on sabbatical—working on a new book. Snooty so-and-so wouldn't even give me his phone number."

"Okay. Well, maybe we should deploy our secret weapon in that case."

Marian put on her puzzled expression, hoping Lych wasn't thinking of doing something stupid.

He waited several seconds for the penny to drop. When it didn't, he leaned forward and grimaced at her. "Your father." Marian snapped her fingers. "Of course. Let's go."

Her father's formidable secretary, Greta, was no match for Marian and she and Lyall were standing in his office within the hour.

There was lots of wood and a very deep-pile carpet. Lyall thought it not very advisable for an office, but appreciated how comfortable it felt beneath his feet. He felt like he'd done a lot of walking in the past few days.

A stylish aluminium cigar holder caught his attention on the wide desk. The elder Elder certainly knows how to make an impression, he thought.

Behind his desk hung the portrait Lych had painted of him three years ago. It made him smile with satisfaction. The somewhat protracted portrait sittings at Elder's large house outside town was where he'd first met Marian.

After several minutes the door opened and a shortish man with iron grey hair entered the room. He was smartly dressed with a rather bright tie around his neck. "We-eell, this is a surprise...," he began, going over to his daughter and kissing her on the cheek.

"Hello, Daddy," purred Marian.

"Hello, Lyall. Good to see you again," said the man, extending his hand. "What can I do for you young gadabouts?"

"Mr Elder, I ha -," began Lych.

"It's Norman!" corrected the older man, poking Lych gently in the chest.

"Lych nodded. "OK... Norman, I have a favour to ask of you."

"You can have anything you want as long as it's not my daughter," he chuckled.

Marian nudged her father in irritation. "Oh, Daddy."

"Anyway, sit down, both of you." Norman slumped in the large leather armchair behind his desk. "Cigar?" The aluminium object was pushed in Lych's direction. He declined politely.

"You know what your doctor said about those things, don't you? If Mother was still alive, she'd chew your ear off," chided Marian.

Her father puffed to get the thing lit. "Yes, well," he said, through clouds of smoke. "You make a very good stand-in, my dear. Now what is it I can do for you, Lyall?"

"This may sound a bit odd, but we'd like to speak to one of your authors. The trouble is he's not too keen to speak to us and we really need his help. It's a professor called Marius Lingard."

Norman's eyebrows danced on his brow for a second. "Oh, him. Right, well. Is this research for a painting then, Lyall?"

Lych felt a lie was in order. "Yes, that's it. I need some information about him so I can get some of the details right... I've decided to try a mythological subject for a change, and I believe he's an expert in the particular subject I've chosen."

The older man nodded. "OK. Well, if you think that's what you need. I should warn you; his ideas are a little *speculative*, let's say. Still, it gets column inches in the papers. All helps to sell books."

"Do you think you'll be able to persuade him to see us, Norman?"

The older man nodded. "Oh, yes. I'll have someone give him a ring. I'm sure he'll co-operate."

Just then there was a buzz and Greta's fussy voice came over the intercom. "Your son is here to see you, Mr Elder. Shall I show him in?"

Norman moved the toggle. "Yes, please do, Greta. Thank you." He looked up at Marian, eyebrows raised. "Well, two surprises from my beloved children in one day. You'd better get my heart medicine ready."

Greta's plump form pushed open the double doors and led the way into her boss's office in a very formal manner. Behind her, walking slowly, came a thin young man with sandy hair and a peculiar glint in his eyes.

His father nodded to the secretary. "Thank you, Greta." Like all secretaries, Greta had to be thanked at every possible opportunity.

The older man got up from his plush leather chair and came around to the front of the desk. "Robert, my boy. How are you? What a nice surprise." He shook his son's hand before Marian got in on the act.

"Hi, Robbie. You having fun?" she asked, kissing him on the cheek. Lych had only met the boy once before but his first impression still held—that he must follow his mother, as he looked to be cut from entirely different cloth than either his father or his sister.

Once the introductions were over, Robert stood with his back to the window, leaning on the sill. Lych had the unaccountable feeling that the boy meant to leave by that route.

Two flies were using the window to court each other. Lych watched them fuss and buzz up and down the glass for a second or two. Robert had noticed them, too.

As Lych looked away he was sure he caught the boy's head move out of the corner of his eye. The movement was astonishingly quick. Puzzled, Lych looked back at Robert, who stared back at him with a distinct lack of politeness. The flies were nowhere to be seen.

Marian and her father had been indulging in some verbal jousting over a minor family matter. They obviously hadn't noticed anything strange.

Norman turned to Lych. "Well, this is an occasion, I must say. Both my children in my office at the same time. Perhaps you'd better paint a portrait of the three of us together, Lyall."

Lych already knew which side of the family Marian got her sarcastic streak from. It's certainly on display today, he thought.

Changing his tone of voice entirely, Norman suddenly made an announcement. "Robert is going into politics," he looked directly at the boy. "Aren't you, son?"

The boy nodded slowly, never taking his eyes off Lych.

"Well, good luck in that snake pit," quipped Lych. Norman chuckled in agreement.

The boy's presence unsettled Lych, but he couldn't put his finger on exactly why. He wasn't even sure what he'd seen a moment or two ago, but he knew he didn't like it much.

"Well, we'll let you two get on and talk about changing

the world between you. Just make sure it's for the better, OK?" Marian turned her toes towards the door. Lych followed suit.

Goodbyes were said and the pair managed to pass by the fearsome Greta without getting singed.

As they were walking to the elevator, Lych couldn't get Marian's brother out of his mind. Unsure whether it was a wise idea, he decided to start prying.

"Does your brother ever seem... slow, to you?"

"Slow? Are you trying to imply that Robert is retarded in some way?" snapped Marian, outraged.

"No, I mean his movements. Just his movements. He never seems to hurry himself."

Marian shook her head vigorously. "No. But he could certainly move quick enough when Daddy tried to swat him during 'tag' when we were kids. He was as quick as a whippet."

Lych chuckled. "He didn't ever climb the walls?"

Marian laughed. "No, that was Daddy's trick. But what an extraordinary question. What's wrong with you today, Lyall?"

Her comment about her father hadn't steadied his nerves. "Sorry. Sometimes I speak without thinking."

"Maybe you should try thinking without speaking from time to time," she said.

Just then, the elevator door clunked open, allowing Lych an easy escape from the conversation.

As Lych and Marian stepped into the dusty lobby of his building an hour-and-a-half later, they were met by the caretaker, George.

"Ah, Mr Lych. Your phone rang as I was passing earlier, so I let myself in and took a message for you. Hope you don't mind." The slightly stooped figure rummaged in his pockets, before handing over the crumpled paper.

Lych took the paper with a smile. "Thanks, George. That was good of you. I'll see you right at the end of the month."

"Just pay your rent on time and that'll be fine. Then I won't get complaints from the landlord again," said George, nodding for emphasis.

"Yeah. That too, George. Thanks again." Lych let them into his studio before uncrumpling the paper. He turned it round in his hands before handing it to Marian. "Here—you can read his writing. What does it say?"

Marian scanned it for a few seconds before announcing "Professor Lingard can see us tomorrow at 11 at his cottage. That's great, isn't it?"

Lych nodded. "Sure. We might get some answers then."

"Hurray! Daddy came through for us!"

"One of Daddy's minions came through for us, more like. What's the address?"

After Marian read it out to him, Lych dug out a battered copy of the 1953 city directory.

"Hey, that thing's nearly two years old," protested Marian.

Lych raised his eyebrows in her direction. "And you think they've changed all the streets in that time, do you?"

Marian wrinkled her nose and pursed her lips at him, silently acknowledging that he had a point.

"Hmmm. It's fairly remote. We'd best make an early start. Off you go, head home and get your beauty sleep, you."

"But Lyall, you said you'd take me to dinner!"

"I will. Just not today." He smirked at her and she pouted back unhappily.

He grinned back triumphantly. "I'll call you a cab."

Although it had been described as a cottage, the professor's retreat was actually a large, spacious bungalow. It had a garage to one side and a decorative bird bath at the front, which visitors were no doubt expected not to hit with their cars as they parked. Lyall did his best to comply with the unspoken request.

A middle-aged woman in a smart maid's overall answered the door to them. Once inside, Marian enquired after the professor.

"Oh, no, Professor Lingard isn't here," said the maid politely.

"But we were told he'd be expecting us," said Lych. The frown in his voice was quite audible.

The maid smiled. "I simply meant that he's at the cottage, sir."

"This isn't the cottage, then?" asked Marian.

"No miss." The maid walked over to the window and

beckoned them over. She pointed to a small single-storey wood and brick house just visible through the trees. "If you just follow the path around the side of the house, it'll take you there. I'll ring the professor to let him know you're coming."

After thanks and smiles, the pair left on their journey. "It looks like something from a fairy tale," said Marian, peering through the trees.

The path took them around the side of the house and in a direction away from the cottage. Then, it wound back towards it and ran parallel with it for a while before the building was once again hidden by some trees. "I think we're being led up the garden path here. My feet hurt," complained Marian.

"Poor princess. Shall I pick you up and carry you?" Lych chuckled at her.

"Don't you dare," she said, her hackles rising at the suggestion.

Eventually they saw the cottage straight ahead. A sense of slight relief filled them when they actually reached the professor's door.

Marian knocked. When the professor opened the door, he didn't look at all pleased. "Professor Lingard? I'm Marian Elder. This is my friend, Lyall Lych… the painter."

The professor shook her hand out of politeness and ushered them inside. It was clear that he wasn't used to visitors of any sort, let alone those that had been imposed on him.

At first, he didn't seem too comfortable. Courtesy demanded that he ask if they wanted coffee and then ring through to ask the maid to bring it.

But he sat on the edge of his seat, as if expecting their stay to be a short one. He ran his hand through his greying hair several times, as if unsure how to treat the daughter of his publisher. And her friend… the painter.

He sat smiling rather idiotically until the maid brought the coffee through. Marian didn't envy the poor woman having to carry the tray all the way along that winding path.

After the formalities, Marian felt she'd best get things started. She turned on her smile. "Professor Lingard, we can't thank you enough for agreeing to see us at such short notice," she beamed.

The professor seemed at least partly charmed. "Oh, well, umm... that's alright, Miss Elder. Though I don't have a great deal of time to spare, I'm afraid."

Marian nodded, understandingly. "Of course. We'll try to be brief."

"In fact, we have some information that might be of interest to you, professor," said Lyall. "Something that you might never have come across before."

It was the first time Lych had spoken since they met, and the professor seemed quite surprised that he could speak. He also appeared slightly annoyed that a layman should presume to tell him what he should or should not be interested in.

"Oh, really? And what might that be?" The professor's forced politeness was almost visible in the air between them.

"It's evidence of a sort," began Lych. "An eye-witness account of a strange encounter with a supposedly impossible creature."

This obviously piqued the old man's attention as the temperature of his hospitality seemed to rise a degree or two. "A sighting of a cryptozoological specimen, you say. That's very rare. But can this witness be relied upon? I mean neither alcohol or drugs were involved, were they? Because that's definitely not my field."

"I can assure you that wasn't the case, professor. And the witness is highly reliable, as far as I'm concerned—it's me. But, to assure me that I'm not going crazy, please will you tell me what you know about serpents?"

"Serpents. You mean mythologically speaking, I presume?"

Lych nodded. He and Marian both hoped they could draw him out enough to discover the solution to the mystery facing them.

"You know the Biblical story, of course. Mankind's fall from grace has been attributed—in large part, at least—to a serpent." As the professor spoke he seemed to relax in their company, obviously feeling on safe ground as the keeper of arcane knowledge.

In a bid to steer the professor onto less well-trodden ground, Lych shot him a question. "What about non-Christian myths— say snake gods?"

"Snake gods. Yes, there are many, many of them. The Ancient Egyptians for instance—Wadjet was the cobra goddess of Lower Egypt. And the upright cobra seen on their funerary ware was known as the Iaret. It was a symbol of royalty and divine authority," said the professor.

"And the Celts dedicated a special day of divination called Imbolc each February to serpents, among other beasts. Their goddess Brigid was thought to have some special connection with snakes, you see."

Marian leaned forward and tried to meet the professor's eyes. "What about India?"

The man nodded. "Yes, India is rife with snake gods and cults devoted to them. There are a lot of snakes in India, of course."

Lych sat forward, too. Now they seemed to be getting somewhere. "And snake men?"

"Snake men?!" The professor half stood before sitting down again very suddenly. "I assume you mean a hybrid being—part-man, part-snake?"

Lych nodded. "You're going to think I'm crazy, professor, but I think I've seen something that stood upright like man … that had arms and hands and legs and … well, this thing had what looked like a snake's head!"

The professor coughed softly. "No, not crazy, Mr Lych. Some people might send you away to speak to a psychiatrist. But not me. And India… yes.

"Snake symbols form an important part of the Hindu religion. But several Indian intellectuals I'm in contact with are convinced there is another branch of snake worship that adheres to a much more obscure, a much *older* religion, you understand."

The professor stopped speaking. Lych and Marian leaned forward so much they almost lost their balance. "Go on, please," said Marian, hoarsely.

"Well, there are a few hints in ancient texts, most notably The Book Of Eibon. It's said to date back to pre-history, though some *experts* claim it to be a hoax entirely." The word 'experts' was pronounced with more than a note of irony.

Lych and Marian glanced at each other. "But surely, Professor, you are an expert. That's why we've come to you."

"Yes, well… not *expert* enough for some, it seems." He seemed to reflect for a moment before moving on.

"Yes, serpents appear in human mythology and art far more than any other creature, it seems. I firmly believe that this is all down to some ancient race memory, embedded deeply in our minds.

"It can't be any memory of our meeting with dinosaurs, of course, but maybe our pre-human ancestors…" There he trailed off, becoming lost in himself once more.

Suddenly, he sat up straight and looked directly at them. "But that is all speculation. And I'm afraid that's the problem, most of this is mere speculation. Facts are very hard to come by. And maybe that's been planned deliberately, eh?

"You see, references—enticing references, in my opinion—to a race of half-lizard men crop up again and again in human culture. Too often, I believe, for it to be a coincidence."

He pulled open a drawer and rummaged around inside for several moments before pulling out a light brown folder. "I have a letter here from a certain well-known Indian scholar—I shan't name him, I'm sure you understand—but he claims to have found evidence of recent abductions in a northern Indian province that is linked to a continuing snake cult.

"He says in one passage 'The parents of one girl claim to have woken in the night to hear their daughter's screams as she was taken away by this certain cult' and then later, 'The father told the local police commissioner that he tried to pursue, but his way was blocked by several enormous snake-men'. There!"

"When was this supposed to have happened?" asked Lych.

The professor scanned the paper. "This letter is dated last summer and… ah, here it is… he claims one of his researchers came across the story in official police records just two years prior to that."

"Oooh. That's too close for comfort. When you said recent, I was hoping you were talking about the last decade or so," said Marian.

"Yes, yes. It is a trifle worrying, I agree. These cults are often very unpleasant, some would say evil. Of course, there have been no recent reports similar to that in America for quite some time.

"Some would attribute that to the light of reason driving out the darkness of superstition, or some such nonsense. But personally I think it's just down to them being careful."

Marian looked uncomfortable. "I hope you're wrong, professor. But…"

"Oooh!" Professor Lingard leaped up from his chair suddenly, as if someone had stuck a huge pin in him. Marian, startled, nearly lost her perch on the arm of the large lounger.

The professor shot past her to a set of deep shelves. Rummaging for a moment or two, he came back with a grin on his face. "And here, we even have an example of the influence of the snake cult in popular culture."

He held up a magazine so Lych and Marian could see. It looked old and the cover was chipped and folded, but the cover painting was clearly visible and quite lurid.

The magazine was called 'Startling Snake-Head Stories' and it showed a crudely-done painting of a cowboy, both guns drawn, blasting away at something lunging from between two large bushes.

Lych took it from the professor and laid it on the edge of a small table between him and Marian. They both leaned over, peering down at the sickly-coloured image of a man-sized figure in tattered clothing and an enormous snake's head, flinging itself at the figure of the cowboy. Scaly skin covered the arms of the creature as it reached out with claw-like hands.

"Extraordinary, isn't it? It's almost exactly an illustration of what you've been talking about," said the professor.

"It's extraordinarily badly-painted," said Lyall. "But, yes, it is very like the creature I saw." He noticed that the pulp magazine was dated March 1942.

"May I?" asked Marian, reaching out to open the magazine. She presumed that the illustration was relevant to a particular story inside, and there, halfway down the contents page, it read 'Snake Man of The Lost Canyon' by R. M. Simpson. The other stories all had more mundane titles to do with confronting rattlesnakes and cottonmouths. An ophidiophobe's nightmare, she thought.

"I've read the story, of course," said the professor. "I even mention it in one of my books. There is nothing remarkable about it, unfortunately. Certainly, the author seemed to have no special knowledge of any manifestation of any of the snake cults—it's all pure invention.

"It turns out that R. M. Simpson is a pseudonym for a much better-known author who, presumably, wrote the story for a quick profit."

The professor retrieved the magazine, carefully returning it to his collection. "But the cover is... amusing."

Lych nodded. "Certainly. If you've got the right sense of humour."

"Now if you please, Mr Lych. Tell me about your own encounter with this snake-man you say you encountered. In some detail, if you please."

It was another hour before Marian and Lych left the professor's cottage. He seemed very interested in the encounter with the creature in Fant's apartment, asking detailed questions that Lych was often unable to answer.

Disappointingly, the professor seemed to know very little of the activities of Yig and his followers. But at least Lych now knew he wasn't just seeing things.

Rather than wander along the winding path again, the pair decided to cut through the trees. Although the woods were too small to get lost in, they soon became confused as to which direction they were headed in.

Marian began to notice movement on the ground all around them. "Lyall!" she gasped, gripping his arm too hard. "What's that?"

From all around them, long shapes began to emerge from behind trees and under dark bushes. Slowly, sinuously, the shapes slithered along the ground towards the small clearing. Eventually they all met and began writhing around and over each other in a large ball.

"Lyall, what's going on?" Marian dug her fingers into her

companion's arm, her dislike of snakes beginning to get the better of her.

"I don't know,'" said Lych in a distracted voice. He couldn't tear his eyes away from the wriggling mass. There must have been almost two dozen snakes of various sizes and colours gathered together.

"Watch them, Mr Lych," said an unseen voice, ignoring Marian's presence. "Watch what they are capable of."

The serpents began to writhe even faster, moving under and around each other's bodies, in a never-ending dance. It was hypnotic and unsettling as the normally slow-moving beasts began to further increase the speed of their bizarre dance.

A column of snakes began to form as they drew together ever closer, climbing and squirming over each other to gain height. Gradually each snake came to a halt, staying stock still as its companions continued to twist and climb.

When the last snake had taken its place atop the others, they froze into one solid-looking pillar of serpentine flesh. Their varicolored scales shone slightly in the mild gloom.

The unnatural pillar stood about four feet in height and about eight inches across. At times it looked like a carved piece of art. Then one of the snakes would flick its tongue out to taste the air and the illusion was ruined.

Several of the snakes were pointed towards Lych and Marian and their glinting, dark eyes held their gaze in a hypnotic trap.

After a second or two, Lych regained his senses. "A nice trick, whoever you are. Did it take long to train them, huh?" There was no reply to his taunt.

He looked around him quickly, careful not to drop his guard. Some of the snakes might be venomous and could attack at any second.

"Why don't you come out and talk, eh? Why all the mystery and the sideshow tricks?"

Lych's comments were ignored for several seconds before the voice started speaking again. "Impressive, aren't they? Just imagine what they could achieve if they were directed against you and your companion in anger, Mr Lych. Once their work was done, you'd be unrecognisable."

Lych didn't know how much of it was a bluff, or even how many of the snakes were actually dangerous, but he thought it best to play along. "All right, I'm imagining. What do you want from us?"

"Give us the stone, Mr Lych. Destroy your paintings—Yig does not permit icons to be made of such desecrators."

Lyall was taken aback. "What do you know of my paintings?!"

"I... we know all we need to know. They are abominable things and must cease to exist!"

"Where's Franklin Fant?" demanded Lych, raising his voice to a shout. He continued to peer between the trees, convinced their tormentor must be nearby. Marian continued to stare in horrified fascination at the living serpentine column.

"We have him. The stone and the paintings, Mr Lych. If you comply with our demands, he will be returned to you."

At those words, the snakes making up the bizarre pillar began to crawl over each other, gradually descending to the ground before disappearing into the undergrowth.

Marian shuddered. "My God, I hate snakes!"

Lych put his arm around her shoulders. "Well, I think you might have come to the wrong party, in that case. Come on, let's get back to the car."

They began threading their way back to where they'd left the car, scanning the ground all the while for signs of any snakes. In the future, always stick to the path, he told himself.

Marian picked her way carefully, with exaggeratedly high footsteps, almost as if she was loathe to touch the ground at all. "What painting was he talking about, Lyall?"

"Those small portraits that you saw."

"Those things in your studio?!" She grimaced up at him.

He sighed. "You're not being paid by Rodenghast, by any chance, are you?"

After several long minutes, they saw the dark bulk of the car appear through the trees. "I've never been so glad to see this wreck," said Marian, climbing into the passenger seat.

Lyall climbed in and sat staring silently out of the side window for a moment. He played with his lower lip, deep in thought. Then he started the car up, listening to the reassuring growl of its big Detroit engine for a second or two before driving off.

Back at Lych's apartment they both had a stiff drink, followed by another.

Lych took Marian's glass off her as she was reaching for the bottle a third time. "I think we need to keep a clear head right now, don't you?"

She pouted at him before handing him the bottle, too.

Lych sat down heavily in his battered armchair. Marian leaned over the back of it. "Boy, that scared me half to death," she said. "How on earth can anyone make snakes do that?"

"Some form of hypnotism, maybe," muttered Lych.

"Us, or the snakes?" She laughed, mirthlessly.

"I don't know. Both, perhaps? What I want to know is how he knew about my paintings? Unless he—or some of his friends—broke in here the other night for a little light art appreciation.

"We need to get over to Fant's place. Find out if there's anything hidden there."

"What you need is rest, Lyall. You've got dark bags under your eyes," she said.

"Yes, well... They're where I keep all my sleepless nights." He stood up, stretched and reached for his coat.

"OK. But I'm driving," insisted Marian, taking the car keys out of his hand.

The pair let themselves into Fant's apartment, courtesy of a stiff piece of celluloid that Lych always carried with him.

"Another trick you picked up in the army?" asked Marian in a low voice. Lych grinned and nodded.

"So what kind of stone are we looking for?" She lifted the cushions out of the way and felt down the back of the sofa.

"I don't know. You heard exactly what I did. The voice just said, 'the stone'." He opened a few drawers and hunted around inside boxes.

"Well, diamonds are sometimes called stones. Like the ones you put on your finger!" There was nothing hidden under any of the chairs.

"Trust you to think of that." He upended a small table to

check there was nothing taped to the bottom.

"Yes, trust me…" There was nothing hidden in the messy kitchen's food cupboards. Or the half-empty refrigerator.

Marian stood in the middle of the freshly dishevelled room. "Well, I can't find anything even slightly stoney."

A series of loud noises issued from the bedroom. "What are you up to in there?"

Lych came out of the bedroom carrying a box that was evidently heavy. "This was hidden behind a false panel at the back of the clothes closet."

The box clunked down on the flat wooden surface of the table. Lych removed a black velvet cloth to reveal an ancient looking object. "The aforementioned stone, I presume."

It sat on the table between them. "That's *it*? That's what all this trouble is about?" asked Marian, clearly unimpressed.

Lych nodded. "Mmmm-hmm. Doesn't look like much, does it? Certainly not worth making death threats or kidnapping people over."

The stone was roughly seven inches across and light brown in colour. It was squared off with the edges chipped irregularly in several places. Here and there were marks where some form of vegetation had once clung to it.

Leaning forward, Lych tipped it up so that the light fell on the front of the stone. Although it was badly worn, some markings could still be made out. He tilted it at various angles as they tried to make out what the markings might be. The details had obviously been finely carved at one time, but the centuries had eroded them badly.

"I can't really make anything out," said Marian.

"Hang on," said Lych, and disappeared into the other room. When he returned he was carrying a small pocket torch. He flicked it on and held it at right angles to the front surface of the stone. Shadows appeared in the dips and hollows, making the images more distinct.

"Hey look, that could be a man with a crocodile's head. And that there… that curved part might be a big snake," said Marian.

"Yeah, they could be. But the rest is too badly eroded to make anything else out."

Marian rummaged around in her handbag. "I know a trick. Got any baking paper?"

After several minutes of searching in the ramshackle kitchen, Lych found what she had asked for. She laid the paper over the surface of the stone and pulled it tight. Then she took a small notebook and pencil set from her handbag. She ran the pencil lightly across the paper.

Images began to appear as if by a primitive form of magic. When she had finished, she carefully lifted it free. "Not quite a brass rubbing but it's the same idea. Careful not to smudge it!"

"Excellent work, Miss Holmes! I should have thought of that myself." Lych grinned at her.

"But you didn't!" She was very pleased to point it out.

They both examined the paper at length. "That part at the top looks like a group of stars, doesn't it? And those dots might represent a number... a date perhaps?" mused Marian.

After several more minutes they gave up straining their eyes. "It's no good. This is like playing chess in boxing gloves. Without knowing what we're looking at—or looking for— anything on this stone could be... *anything* on this stone!" Lych lifted it up, ready to return it to the safety of its box.

"Hey, that's odd. It feels warm," he said. "But it hasn't been near anything hot."

Marian put her hand on it, partly to check that Lych wasn't trying to spook her. "God! It almost feels alive. Quick—put the creepy old thing away!"

Lych lowered it into the sturdy box and covered the top with the black cloth. "I think we'd best take this back to my place. For safe keeping."

It was Saturday morning. Normally Lych rose late and had a leisurely breakfast before getting down to the serious business of doing nothing all day. But sleep was a stranger right now, so he got up quietly. He made sure not to disturb Marian, who had thought it a 'good idea' to stay over.

He sat in the living room in the semi-gloom, waiting for the sun to come up properly, wishing he knew where his half-brother was. The phone, sitting on the table next to his chair, only had the chance to ring once before he snatched up the receiver. It was almost as if he had been expecting it to ring.

He said nothing, waiting for the caller to speak first. When it came, the voice was deliberate and cultured. "Is Mr Lyall Lych there?"

"Speaking. Who's this?" There was an expectant crackle on the line.

"We know you have the artefact, Mr Lych. There's no point denying it. It doesn't belong to you any more than it belongs to Mr Fant... or his father."

Lych stared down at his shoes. "I can't deny that you're right."

"Then you are agreeable. You will meet our... request?" asked the voice.

"Hold on there. I said it didn't belong to Fant or his father, or to me. But how do I know it belongs to you? I mean, who the hell are you people, anyway?"

There was a cold silence at the other end of the line. "Do you honestly think you're the first race to rule this world, Mr Lych? Or the best? No, far from it. There are things beneath your very feet that would astonish and horrify you, believe me.

"The stone was created by us. Therefore, it belongs to us. Surely you must agree with that proposition? You are a reasonable man..."

He wasn't sure whether the words were a statement or a question, but for a second Lych interrogated himself—*was* he a reasonable man?

He scratched his head, sleepily. "I may be reasonable, but you can't say the same—reasonable people aren't kidnappers or blackmailers! But I'll play your game... you let Fant go—unharmed—and I'll let you have the damned thing. I mean, why the hell would I want it, anyway?"

Again, there was coldness seeping down the wires. "No, no—I did not say he would be spared. We will return him to you, but he will die within the month. And first we will make him wear the faces of all those who have stood in our way—those before him who have betrayed us or worked against us.

"In fact, it has already begun, as you have noticed. Destroy your paintings or you will never be safe. Take this warning very seriously. For your own sake and that of Miss Elder."

Lych couldn't speak. He had been wrong about Fant. The changes he was undergoing weren't down to his success in decoding his father's occult texts at all—he was a victim of the old man's failure, rather than his own success. *They* were doing it to him!

Anger welled up from his gut. Who the hell did these people think they were? "Hey, if this damned thing is so important to you, why has it taken you so long to track it down?"

Lych could almost feel the contempt oozing down the phone line towards him. "We do not move to your pace, you fool. We do things in our own time. We do not live lives that are short and chaotic, as you do.

"We are star-marked, blessed. Whereas, you..." The crackling on the line underlined the dead air, left deliberately.

"When Mr Fant began trying to access the power of the stone, we became aware of its whereabouts. We had thought that perhaps he might destroy himself but, as time passed, it became obvious that we had to step in. To help him along, so to speak."

Lych forced himself to remember that Fant's life was the most important thing here. "I don't know why you want this piece of stone so badly, but I've already said that you can have the cursed thing, as far as I'm concerned. When and where do you want it delivered?"

"That is very wise, Mr Lych." The voice now had an unpleasant note of smugness to it. "The east entrance of the Museum of Natural History. Tomorrow night at nine." Suddenly there was a click, and the line went dead.

Lych settled the phone back in its cradle. He didn't know if he was doing the right thing. But if he wasn't, then he didn't know what the right thing was.

And once they had Fant back, maybe they could help him. Maybe the threats the voice had made were empty.

Marian had woken and came into the room, wearing Lych's pyjama top. She looked around the room, as if expecting to see a visitor. "Who were you just talking to?"

"I was on the phone. Our mysterious voice again."
Marian looked puzzled. "That's odd. I didn't hear the phone ring."

The next day passed slowly. Anxiety gnawed at Lych's insides. Marian went home for a change of clothes but was back by early evening. 'To keep an eye on him', she had said. He knew the real reason was that she smelt adventure and wanted some for herself.

At 7.50 Lych was ready. He pulled on his large, warm overcoat and zipped up the beaten-up canvas bag he'd dug out from the back of his wardrobe.

Marian's curiosity got the better of her at that point. "So, what's in the bag?"

"The stone. They can have this hunk of rock in exchange for Fant," he explained.

"OK. Seems like a fair exchange to me. I'll just get my coat on and we can leave," she said.

"I need you to stay here, Marian. Really." There's that name again, she thought.

She smirked at him as if she thought he was teasing her. It was his set expression that convinced her otherwise.

"It's going to be dangerous. And I don't know what state Fant will be in when they hand him over. I'll bring him straight back here, so can you be ready to help me?"

"But what's in it for me?" she asked, staring glumly at Lych as he grabbed his hat and opened the door.

"You can have my 'I Like Ike' button, OK?" He closed the door firmly behind him. He wasn't sure if the 'Damn you, Lyall!' that he thought he heard as he closed the door was his imagination or not.

He drove to the museum and parked a short distance away. He wanted to creep up on this situation, rather than roar into it at full throttle.

He walked the rest of the way. Once he got there, he stood behind a tree for several minutes, scanning the approach to the museum. It was quiet. There was hardly anyone about.

When he was satisfied no unpleasant surprises were waiting

for him, he walked over to the steps at the museum entrance.

He stood a few steps up, making himself conspicuous, and placed the bag down at his feet. He wanted them to see that, too.

After several minutes, a small grey cat appeared and stared at Lych. He tried to ignore it, but it obviously didn't regard him as a threat. It came up to him and rubbed its head against the bag at his feet before curling itself around his left leg.

"At any other time I'd be happy to make friends, kitty," he muttered, half to himself and half to the cat.

But the cat disappeared like fog when a large, dark blue car pulled up. Lych squinted in the poor light and could see someone sitting behind the steering wheel. Then the back door opened and a large man in a hooded coat or cloak looked out at him.

As he got out of the car and walked towards Lych, the shadows clung to him like molasses, seeming to move with him. They weren't dispelled by the streetlights. It made Lych feel even more uneasy.

Finally the man stood one step down from him. Despite the difference, he still matched Lych in height. An odd, strong odour pervaded the air.

Silence reigned for several seconds before the man spoke. "Do you have the Stone of Power, Mr Lych?"

Lych kicked the bag at his feet. This seemed to agitate the man, who swayed back and forth slightly. "Please be careful. It is very precious. We do not want it damaged."

"I don't know if we're talking about the same thing," said Lych. "This one's been through the wars, by the looks of it. You'd better check it out."

He knelt and unzipped the bag, tugging it open and removing the black cloth.

"Yes, that is it," said the man, unmoving.

"But you haven't looked," protested Lych.

"I can tell. I know it. Please close the bag and give it to me. Too much exposure to it is not healthy."

"You didn't seem too concerned about my health when we met at my friend's apartment." Lych was starting to get angry and tried to dial it down.

"We have never met before. You previously encountered one of my brothers, Mr Lych."

He hadn't heard his 'brother' speak, but every time this one spoke, he managed to make his name sound like a bad word—something your mother told you not to say as a kid.

"OK. Bring Fant out and you can have the stone."

The man swayed slightly again. "We did not bring him with us, but he is somewhere very safe. Very safe."

Lych took a step down. Now he had to look up at the man. Now he could see his eyes and he didn't like it—they were large and cold. "Hey, look here—if I don't get Fant—right now—you can kiss this piece of rocky road goodbye!"

The swaying became more pronounced. "Unlike your kind, if we say we will do something then we WILL do it. Mr Fant will be returned to you very soon. You have my word on that."

Lych wanted to carry on making a fuss, play the hard case, refuse to play along. Maybe even claim the cops were in on it. But something in the man's voice and the gleam of his large, dark eyes seemed to hypnotise him.

"O—OK," was all he could manage to say as he watched the bag being handed over by someone...

but it didn't feel like it was him.

The man took the bag down to the car, got in and was driven away quickly by the chauffeur.

Lyall was left standing on the steps, the world swaying slightly before his eyes. His head began to ache. He sat down suddenly on the cold stone steps. After five minutes he'd persuaded the world to stay still.

His mouth was dry. The inside of his head felt the same way. He didn't know what had happened to him, but he knew he needed to clear his head.

Struggling to his feet, he made his way gingerly to a late-night coffee shop that he'd passed earlier.

Managing to get the door open, he half-lurched towards the counter and propped himself there. One leg felt like it was made of clay, while the other was made of granite.

The waitress finished her conversation with the only other

customer in the place. "What can I get you, mister?" she asked in a voice louder than an air-raid siren.

"Cof—fee," croaked Lych. "Just coffee … thanks."

She pulled herself up to her full height and looked at him oddly. "Sure thing. Comin' right up." She pushed a cup in front of him and filled it up slowly. "There you go."

He gulped the bitter brown liquid down gratefully. "Can I have another please?"

The waitress filled his cup quickly this time. "Glad you like our coffee so much, mister." He nodded and emptied the second cup.

He made sure to leave a generous tip when he finally felt he was able to drive. He hoped this was the last time he'd ever have to deal with these serpent people. Somehow, he knew he was kidding himself.

The night was another sleepless one, spent staring at the ceiling. Lych ran it over and over in his head. Why the hell had he just meekly handed the bag over like that?

Around 6.45 there was a thumping at the door, like someone was trying to batter it in. Lych stumbled out of bed and went to answer it.

There, slumped against the door frame, was Franklin Fant, half conscious and clearly unaware of his surroundings.

"Fant! Fant! Are you all right?" Lych knelt beside him, supporting his shoulders. He tensed his muscles and pulled Fant to his feet, wrangling him gradually through the door.

He laid the exhausted man down on a sofa and dashed into the kitchen. Coffee might be part of the solution, at least, he thought.

Holding Fant's head up, he poured coffee down his throat. Two cups. Three cups. Eventually the grogginess seemed to fade. "Lyall… Lyall…" he gasped and gesticulated for more liquid.

He reached out to grasp the cup himself. "It was awful. Like being in a pit. Right at the bottom of a pit. It was dark all the time. Never any light. It felt like I wasn't alone. Ever."

"Do you know where you were?" asked Lych.

"No. It was always dark. I slept a lot. I think maybe they drugged me."

Or twisted your mind, thought Lych. "Well, you're safe now. I think you're a fair exchange for that old chunk of rock!"

Suddenly, Fant was fully himself again. He shot upright. "What? You gave them the stone?!!"

Lych frowned. "Yes. It was the only way to save you! If I'd gone to the police, then who knows what would have happened. They'd probably have found your body sometime around next Christmas."

Fant became more agitated with every second that passed. "No, No, NO! We've got to get it back from them. We've GOT to. You don't know what they can do!"

"Well, what can they do?" asked Lych, incredulously.

Fant pulled an envelope out of his inside pocket and handed it to him. "Read this."

Lych opened the envelope and slid out a sheaf of sturdy papers. Unfolding them, he saw that they were pages from a journal. The first entry had the date November 15th printed at the top of the page. In fading ink next to it, someone had written in the year—1938.

"What is this?" asked Lych.

"They are from the journal of the Reverend Edgar Fant. It might help you understand the reasons behind my decline."

Lych pressed the pages flat on the table and began to read.

"*November 15th, 1938—My beloved Evelyn is gone. I found her in the garden, and she was already cold. It looked like she had been bitten a dozen times. The doctor said it was snake toxin that had stopped her heart. It was hideous. THEY sent the snakes—I know it! Oh Lord, help me in my time of suffering.*"

Something cold ran through Lych's core when he realised he was reading about the death of his own mother. The Rev. Fant had written to him to tell him that his mother had died in India, and that she had been buried there, but he didn't know any of the details. Until now.

He lowered the paper. "Our mother." His voice was strained, hoarse.

Fant nodded. "I know. My father never told me all the details.

He kept me away from her. I didn't see her body—I was just a
kid. Only when I read that after he'd died…"

"*November 17th, 1938—I sought out their supposedly hidden
temple a little outside the town. I took my revolver with me, but the
place was empty. It looked to be in ruins. God forgive me but I would
have had no qualms about gunning one of them down. They have taken
something precious from me so I, in turn, have taken something from
them. An eye for an eye, as it says in Leviticus. I have carried away
one of their 'sacred' stones from that place. It is hardly equivalent to the
taking of a life, but it will have to suffice.*"

"*November 18th, 1938—I know from my work in the Bureau that
each part of their temple is necessary to their foul work. Why they
should leave the place in ruins is beyond me but then they are filthy,
low animals. The lowest sort! I sit staring at the pile of soiled Bibles
piled on my doorstep—the very same ones I had distributed to the
children only weeks ago—and I want to take a hammer and smash the
accursed stone into rubble. But something prevents me.*"

"*November 19th, 1938—The local trader, Mr Patel, has issued me
with a dire warning about the heathen followers of the snake deity,
which he calls Yig (another name to add to the list of others I have heard
it called). He claims they will seek revenge on me for interfering with
their work. There is no way he can know about what I brought back
from their temple. I think he is speaking about the copies of the Holy
Bible that I distributed to the children and to the Bible classes that I
hold each Thursday and Friday. I have no way of knowing if Patel is
one of the devotees of this abominable cult, but he had a particularly
fervid look in his eye while addressing me.*"

"*November 21st, 1938—This last week has been a living nightmare.
The Deputy Commissioner, Jackson, has been sympathetic but says
that India 'isn't for everyone'. He's a pompous English ass. He refuses
to do anything about the snake worshippers, claiming there is no
evidence on which they can act. What about the death of my beautiful
Evelyn? What more proof does he need of their malign activities? May
the Lord help these people—they deserve better than to be mere victims*

of this evil."

"November 22nd, 1938—My son and I leave today. In five days, we shall be in France and from there we shall take a ship home. It will be so good to see home again. I can't let them do to Franklin what they did to Evelyn. Their sacred object is already stowed in my luggage. With it safely an ocean away from them, they will be unable to finish their vile work. Truly, the serpent has chased us from this Eden."

Lych let his hands drop, the papers dangling from his fingers. "My God!"

"A god, certainly. But not the one you and I would recognise," Fant corrected him.

Lych looked up at his half-brother. "What was this work he was talking about? He called it 'their vile work'—what is that?"

A disconsolate shake of the head told Lych all he had to know.

"So was your father ever in the FBI? He mentions his time in 'the Bureau' in this diary."

"No, it was earlier than that. He was with the Bureau of Investigation. I think they were a forerunner of the Feds. Once, when he was drunk, he mentioned a couple of odd cases out west that they had to investigate. Snake worship was involved. Maybe that's what he meant. What started it all…"

"Did he ever talk to you about what happened in India? It obviously left its mark on him."

"It destroyed him! I remember him drinking. And the women he'd bring back. When my aunt came to visit once, she took me back to live with her in Iowa until I left for college. It was the last time I saw him until he was lying in his coffin.

"Those things destroyed my mother. They killed my father, too, in a way. And now they're coming after me. I wish I'd never heard of India—I dream of burning our old house in Meghalaya to the ground.

"My father loved that country—he loved the people, the places, the food—until he came across the cult that he called the Children of Yig."

That evening Lych, Marian and Fant sat down to what they hoped would be a civilised meal. For once, Lych was happy not to have to pander to Fant's favourite diet of burgers, beans or meatloaf.

Marian had helped him to fix a reasonable-sized steak with green beans, potatoes and corn. She had even brought a bottle of wine. In preference, she said, to Lych's usual gut-rot whiskey.

They had just finished the main course, and Marian had promised a surprise for dessert, when Fant suddenly gripped his stomach and hunched forward.

"Hell, Lyall, your cooking's not that bad! Are you okay, Franklin?"

She and Lych crowded around the hunched, seated figure.

"I—I think he's transforming again," said Lych. "Help me."

They each put an arm around his shoulder, attempting to lift him from the table. Fant groaned and rolled off the chair sideways. He grunted loudly, rolling into the middle of the room.

"Nooooooo!" The yell heralded an appalling change in him.

His face began to melt, seething as if worms were burrowing out from within him. He moaned and clawed at his face with both hands, digging his nails into the softening flesh.

As the repellent transformation continued, Marian screamed and dashed into the corner of the room. Lych took two steps backwards, getting ready to run.

"Lyall! Help me..." begged Fant, before his lips meshed into one, silencing him. He fell to his knees, before rolling onto one side, panting hard through his nostrils. Writhing across the floor, he pushed his head against the wall, seeking some relief from his agony.

Lych stepped forward again, wanting to help him but not knowing how. "What can we do, Lyall? What can we do?" wailed Marian.

Eventually, Fant stopped moving and fell back, unconscious. The agony was over, for now.

Lych knelt by his side, unprepared for what he saw. "My God! Come and look, Marian."

Slowly, she crept forward to see what Lych had already

seen. "Oh no—that's his father's face! How on earth…?"
"Come on, help me get him into the bedroom." Marian was
reluctant to touch him at first, but she finally took his feet.
They slung Fant between them and carried him to his bed.

Shaking her head in disbelief, Marian had trouble digesting
what she'd just seen.

"There's something horrible—sadistic even—about making
him wear his father's face. I mean, what sort of people are
they?"

"I don't think they're people at all," said Lych. "At least, some
of them aren't—the ones in control, I mean. They've terrified or
hypnotised some people into helping them, I'm sure, but I don't
think the ones behind Fant's torture are human. They can't be!"

"B-but what do you mean? Not human?" There was a note
of genuine distress in Marian's voice.

"Just what I say. There have been several species of
mankind that are now extinct. You've heard of Neanderthal
Man. Well, it's not unreasonable to suppose that other men…
or things that looked like men… might also have existed in the
past. Some may even have survived. Like these lizard men, for
instance.

"From everything I've heard, I get the impression they've
always lived alongside us, hidden from sight. Maybe they're
not numerous enough to challenge us openly. Perhaps that's
why they move so slowly and deliberately—we were told in the
army that sudden movement always attracts attention. Slow
and stealthy is best, they always said.

"Until the moment comes to strike, that is. I'm just afraid
that they've decided now is their time to strike." Lych looked
genuinely worried.

"The sharp-minded snakes hiding in the back alleys of our
history, nudging us closer and closer to the edge of the
precipice. And look at us now… ready to blow each other to
kingdom come with the press of a button. Yet even that's not
good enough for them!"

The next morning, Fant's bedroom door was open wide and there was no sign of him. Lych guessed that he'd gone back to his apartment.

Concerned about his state of mind, Lych wanted to catch up with Fant before he did something to put himself in danger.

He rang Marian at once. They arranged to meet at her town house and track down Fant as soon as possible.

When Lych arrived 20 minutes later, the maid informed him that her mistress was still breakfasting and would be down shortly. She showed him into a spacious parlour and left him to his own devices.

Marian could spend half the morning breakfasting. He'd once seen her eat toast, coffee, lamb's kidneys, kedgeree with quail's eggs and white asparagus, followed by more toast, and describe it as a 'light breakfast'; he'd only had appetite enough for two small pieces of toast washed down with coffee. How she managed to keep her wonderful figure was a mystery to Lych.

He let his eye wander along a bookshelf containing nothing very interesting, before spending time perusing the several paintings that hung on the walls. There were none of his works there, he noted sourly.

It was three quarters of an hour before Marian emerged. Even then, she was only half dressed.

She walked across and kissed him. "Come and keep me company while I dress."

"We need to get a move on," he said impatiently as he followed her up the wide stairs.

She nodded. "I know. I'll only be a few minutes, I promise."

Several more than a few minutes later, she emerged dressed in a black blouse and jacket with a dark grey skirt. She wore practical and unattractive black shoes, and clutched a small shoulder bag.

"You look as though you're going to a funeral," said Lych.

"Well, I feel as if I am," Marian replied, then bit her tongue. "Sorry. It just slipped out."

"Hmmm. Maybe *you* should try thinking without speaking from time to time," he said.

By the time they got to Fant's apartment it was almost

mid-morning. He would have had time to re-decorate, let alone pack and leave, thought Lych.

A light blue Lincoln Capri pulled out of the underground garage of Fant's building. "Hey, that's him," said Lych, delighted to have caught up with him. He beeped the horn twice.

A brief flash of Fant's sunlit face could be seen through the side window before he accelerated away. Lych was sure Fant had seen them. He was also sure that Fant's face had changed once again, and was now more or less back to normal.

"Hmmm. Looks like he's playing hard to get. I hope he's OK. We'll follow him and hope he pulls over for gas... or something."

"You'd better put your foot down," said Marian as the light blue car disappeared into traffic.

Lych kept his eyes on Fant's tail lights, almost missing a stop sign once. The sun glinted off the smooth lines of the cars all around them. Knowing the darkness they were heading towards, the sunshine came as a cruel taunt.

Fant had obviously spotted them following him and put his foot down. He narrowly missed a large brown van as he hurled the car round a corner. Lych was forced to stop.

Once around the corner, Lych scanned for the light blue car. A mild sense of panic gripped him when he failed to spot it. "There!" cried Marian. "Just on the other side of the blue delivery truck."

Lych saw the number plate and pulled over behind the car directly to Fant's rear.

When the traffic ahead cleared slightly, Fant's car jerked forward and kept accelerating. Unable to overtake the slower car in front, Lych was forced to hang back. "He's driving like he's got the Devil up his tailpipe," he complained.

The light blue car took another corner sharply, narrowly avoiding a woman and child on the kerbside.

Lych pulled the car around, trying to avoid the pair and scraped the passenger side on a roadside signpost.

"Christ, Lyall! Drive it, don't just aim it!" yelled Marian, clearly shaken.

Sweat beaded Lych's brow as he gripped the wheel tightly.

He spoke through his teeth. "Sorry about that."

Another ten minutes of tense, dangerous driving saw them leaving the city. The traffic thinned as miles fell behind them.

"He's heading for the coast," said Lych.

"So where do you think he's going?" asked Marian.

"I don't know. I'm going to hold back a little, make him think he's lost us."

There were hours of straight coast highway with villages nestled at its side. Lych kept the light blue dot in view but held back as far as he dared.

Marian managed to get the old radio to work. The smooth trumpet tones of King Leopardi flowed out of the dashboard speaker. She listened to the station for an hour or two before she got bored and switched it off.

By now the light was going and Lych found it harder to keep Fant's car in sight.

At one point they stopped at a roadside place called The Little Red Cafe. A quick cup of coffee and a burger hit the spot. As they were leaving the cafe, a light blue car dashed by, clearly visible in the light spilling from the forecourt.

"That's him, Lyall. That's Fant's car," yelled Marian. Lych could see his half-brother's face lit up by the dashboard lights, his expression set and determined. Impossibly, it seemed, they had got ahead of him.

"Come on," yapped Lych, rushing to the car. This time he was determined not to lose the other car. He followed him at far less distance, not caring if Fant saw him or not.

Lych hung on to Fant's tail lights like a bloodhound in the pitch black, not prepared to be shaken off again.

It was mostly dark all around them now. The lights of houses at the roadside, or set farther back from the road, became rarer.

The tail lights of the car in front became Lych's only focus. He began to feel tired, worn down. He had no idea where Fant was getting his energy, given that he'd looked like a walking corpse for weeks.

Eventually, Fant slowed and Lych followed suit. "I think he's looking for a turning," said Lych. Sure enough, the car's lights disappeared for a few seconds as they turned almost 90 degrees.

The headlights of Lych's car revealed a rough-looking road. As soon as he turned onto it, his car's suspension began complaining.

"Where on earth is he going?" asked Marian.

"You keep asking me that, but the answer is still the same—I don't know," Lych replied through gritted teeth, struggling with the steering wheel. The road had narrowed considerably and was now little more than a track. The rutted surface tried to tear the wheel out of Lych's hands every few seconds.

Fant's car had disappeared round a bend. Bushes and small trees appeared in the headlights at one side for a few seconds before snatching at the side windows. Marian felt as if they were grabbing at her face and flinched frequently.

Lych glanced out of his side window. There was a steep drop waiting for them if he lost control of the car.

Suddenly, Fant's car showed up in the headlights. Lych slammed on the brakes, muscles straining to prevent the car from skidding sideways.

The light blue car in front was skewed at an angle, blocking the road. Lych and Marian jumped out of their car and hurried over to Fant's abandoned vehicle.

"Why has he just left the car here?" asked Marian. Lych shook his head as he eased around the side of the vehicle. Then the reason became clear. There was a body trapped under the front wheel.

Lych knelt down. It was too dark to see anything much, so he reached in his pocket for a box of matches. In the light he could see the man was dead. Except he wasn't sure if 'man' was the right word. It was dressed like a man, but its face had a hideously wide mouth and skin that looked like it was changing into something else. There was blood pouring from its ear and there was no movement. It was obviously dead.

"What is it?" asked Marian, trying to ease round to where Lych was. He stood up, partly blocking her view. "Don't look. There's a dead body under the wheels."

Marian flinched. "God!" She quickly reversed course and went back to their own car.

"Fant obviously hit the man and fled in panic," said Lych.

"God knows what the poor wretch was doing in such a remote spot at this time of the night ... umm, I mean morning."

"What's that?" asked Marian, suddenly. "Listen!"

Lych strained his ears. It sounded like rustling. Occasionally there was a low moan. He opened the driver's door and switched on the headlights. Suddenly illuminated, several hunched figures turned their faces away.

Lych let out an involuntary gasp of horror. Marian stuffed her hand in her mouth to stifle a scream.

There, all across the road, a procession had appeared within the last few minutes. They seemed to be heading into the bushes that fringed the road and up the hill beyond.

Some walked almost like men, others shuffled with difficulty while still more crawled across the ground like snakes. What Lych and Marian could see of their faces filled them with terror. So far, the creatures had ignored them. Something inside Lych told them they should seize that opportunity.

"Quick!" whispered Lych, climbing into the car. Marian followed suit, closing the door as quickly as possible. Taking advantage of their good fortune, Lych started the engine, put the car in reverse and began crawling backwards an inch at a time. He dared go no faster for fear of tipping them over the edge of the narrow track.

Ahead, in the receding light of the headlamps, they could see more of the foul creatures climb over the lip of the road and cross over it towards the hill.

"The Children of Yig?" Marian had whispered the question. Lych looked pale in the faint light from the dashboard. He merely nodded, slowly.

After they had gathered their thoughts silently for a while, Marian spoke. "What do you want to do, Lyall? We don't know where he's gone... how can we follow him?"

"I think he'll be going where we saw those others going. Up the hill," said Lych. "I don't know what's up there but it certainly seems to be popular, so let's pretend we've had an invitation, too."

They left the car and started to climb the hill that led up from the road. In the darkness they could just make out several figures in light clothing making their way haltingly up the slope.

Marian pressed something into his hand. "Here. From my bag of tricks," she murmured. Lych looked at the small flashlight and nodded his thanks.

They avoided a growth of bushes and found a rough sort of path, though they seemed to be the only ones using it. Lych dared to switch on the flashlight. From all around them, the night seemed to be calling in odd, strangled voices, just barely audible.

Marian grabbed Lych's arm and pointed ahead. "Look—there's a body lying there."

Lying face down in the darkness just ahead was a man wearing Fant's distinctive green jacket. Marian reached him first and tried to roll him over in the torch light. "Franklin. Franklin! Are you all ri -" She stopped mid-sentence and stumbled back in horror.

Lych finally reached the pair and shone the light on Fant's face. He no longer looked like his own father. Now he wore Lych's face.

"He's changed again. It's all speeding up. And it looks like I made it onto their list of personae non grata." Lych lowered the torch and reached into his hip pocket, pulling out a small flask. He flipped the top off and, cradling Fant's head, brought it up to his half-brother's lips.

Fant swallowed gratefully then coughed. "Lyall. You shouldn't have followed me, you shoul -"

"Easy. Easy. You've been through another change. Just take it easy for a moment."

Fant shook his head. "No. There's no time. No time, now. They failed to gain revenge on the father, so now they've come to claim the son! I've got a surprise for them."

"We saw them just now. You hit one of them with your car. But how did you know to come here?" demanded Lych.

Fant put his hand up to his head. "I can feel it. In here. It told me to come."

"This is crazy. What's supposed to be going on here, anyway? For God's sake come back to the city with us, Franklin."

Fant shook his head vigorously. "No. No! You have your art. Art is a glimpse of the real world. This world is a pile of ashes to me now. Let me go on…"

Lych's head spun. It was as if he was talking to himself in the mirror. As if he was trying to convince *himself* of his own case.

Suddenly Fant was on his feet and Lych reached out to help him. Fant pulled his arm away and ran off up the hill.

"Fant—come back! We can help you. We can…" Fant ignored his plea, running into the darkness. Lych's torch beam was too weak to cut through the gloom and his brother soon disappeared.

Marian stroked Lych's arm. "Lyall, shouldn't we go back? You tried to help him—he obviously doesn't want it."

Lych looked at Marian with surprise. "I can't just leave him! You go back to the car if you want to… I'm going on."

Marian gazed into the darkness that lay back the way they'd just come. "Okay, let's go on then, if you must."

They struggled up the increasingly steep slope, listening with increasing trepidation to the strange sounds coming out of the darkness. Sometimes it sounded like muffled yells. At other times it was more like a kind of tuneless singing.

Suddenly the ground dropped away and there, in a natural hollow, they saw a large gathering of figures.

"Get down," hissed Lych, grabbing Marian and pulling her into the long grass. The first of the figures was standing only 20 yards from where they lay.

The pair could see a semicircle of figures, some in elaborate hooded robes while others were clothed in rags. They were all gazing towards the centre of the hollow where a lone figure stood. An odd murmuring filled the air, as if none of the figures dared speak too loudly. It was the same indistinct set of words, over and over. Like a stuck record, thought Lych.

The figure in the centre raised his arms, revealing indecipherable symbols stitched to the underside of his robe. His head remained lowered. He said nothing but, seemingly from nowhere, a host of writhing creatures began to crawl up his body. Snakes were appearing from the grass at his feet and slithering up his body. Some of the smaller ones had already reached his hands and writhed around his fingers like living jewellery, their night-lit eyes glinting like malevolent gems.

Soon his body was a column of living serpents. Only his robed head was visible. Marian gasped in distaste.

As the robed figure raised his head, the moonlight caught the edges of a golden mask covering the upper part of his face. It had slitted serpentine eyes and was etched with more strange symbols, some embedded with peculiar jewels. The lower part of his face was clearly human.

Fascinated by the spectacle, Lych dared to raise himself up on his elbows. He caught his breath when he saw that the stone lay less than a foot in front of the robed man. It seemed to be reflecting more light than merely the moon's illumination.

The line of figures nearest to him threw themselves on the ground, as if suddenly struck down by lightning. Several of them began to wriggle forward on their bellies, then suddenly stopped as if held by an invisible force, unable to continue.

"I don't like the look of this little lot," whispered Lych. "I wish to God I'd got a gun with me."

From the tiny bag slung over her shoulder, Marian slowly eased a large Luger pistol.

Lych's eyes widened so that, even in the poor light, the whites were visible. "Where the hell did you get that thing?"

"My brother brought it home from the war." She smiled nervously.

"And you just decided to borrow it, right?"

She nodded, putting both her hands on the deadly thing.

"Have you ever fired one before?" He asked.

"Tommy showed me how. I'm an OK shot. I nearly winged Daddy's car once, though," she admitted.

He held out his hand. "Give it to me. I got used to handling one in the army."

She hesitated. "But I thought you were in the camouflage and dirty tricks department? You're no sharp-shooter, surely?"

He bridled at being talked to like a child. "I still had to go through basic training. Every soldier has to learn how to shoot. The army isn't just full of overgrown boy scouts, you know."

Although not entirely familiar with the weapon, he slid the box magazine out and checked it. There were still four bullets inside. He'd have preferred a full magazine, but vowed to himself to make sure these four counted.

He had no intention of killing anyone—but he'd found out the hard way that a little gunfire helped enormously to focus the mind of those being shot at.

He held the weapon against his chest, his finger well away from the trigger, and returned his gaze to the bizarre gathering before them.

The serpent priest uttered some clashing syllables that neither Lych nor Marian could understand. The snakes continued to cover his body. Many of them stayed still, but one or two writhed with renewed vigour at his words. He dropped one of his arms and twisted it in what looked like an unnatural manner.

The air a few yards above him seemed to divide and fold in upon itself as he once more altered the angles that his arms made. He continued to spout gibberish, some loudly and some seemingly intended for those closest to him.

The snakes appeared to coil around him more tightly as the air above the priest now seemed to split in two. Again, the priest held his arms in a peculiar manner as a strange reverberation began to fill the night air.

Suddenly, one of the figures closest to the snake-covered priest threw off its cowl and dashed towards him. Kicking the man backwards, he reached down and heaved the stone up onto one shoulder. Lych caught a glimpse of his own face as Fant dashed into the knot of bodies that now blocked his way.

At least two followers yelled in agony, bitten by snakes angry at being flung through the air when their master was toppled.

Perhaps the stone really did have some sort of hidden power, thought Lych. Fant had obviously found a new store of energy from somewhere as he charged forward, pushing the worshippers aside like a professional footballer.

"Stop him!" yelled the priest, shedding serpents as he struggled to his feet.

Lych didn't know what Fant's plan was—or even if he had

one—but he felt he had to help him get away. He stood up, aimed towards the tall serpent priest and pulled the trigger of the big pistol.

The throng fell back in shock as the crash and flash of the gun tore through the night. Several broke into a run, swallowed instantly by the darkness.

The bullet whizzed past the tall figure, which turned, hissing through its teeth. "Too late, Lych!"

Marian looked at Lych, surprised. "He knows you!"

He shook his head, looking puzzled. "Which 'Lych' is he talking to—me, or Fant?"

The snake priest was stalking angrily in the direction of the gunshot, grasping a large snake in his hands. It writhed around them in flowing coils, its eyes always on Lych. He clearly intended to use the creature as a weapon.

"Get behind me, Marian," gabbled Lych, levelling the pistol and ready to fire again. He didn't know if the snake was venomous or if the priest was merely trying to scare them.

Several steps closer and the priest was nearly on them. Then he halted, as if puzzled by something.

"You! But you…" he began, turning his head to gaze in the direction where Fant had run.

"It seems your little trick… your little *torture*… has misfired, you bastard!" spat Lych. Here was a representative of the forces that had put himself, his half-brother and Marian at risk over the past days. All he felt was anger and hatred.

The robed figure raised the large snake above his head for a moment, then lunged forward. The snake's fangs flashed towards Lych's face. He gritted his teeth and pulled the trigger.

The sound was enormous and filled Lych's head for a second. When it had cleared, the man lay at his feet. A large red stain was spreading across his robes.

The snake, seemingly panicked by the gunshot, slithered away quickly from the dying man.

Lych knelt and lifted the golden mask from the man's face. "You!"

"Damn you, Lych. If only you'd stuck to your paint…" The man's voice choked off as he coughed up a gout of blood. Then he fell silent for good.

"Lyall?" Marian's voice was trembling. "Wh-who was he?"

Lych looked down at the corpse. "Rodenghast. He was an art critic for one of the big papers. At least, I thought he was..."

He had no idea how he was going to explain killing the man to the authorities, when the time came. He didn't know if venomous snakes would be considered a deadly weapon by the police. And, without a weapon, his plea of self-defence would be meaningless.

Lych pushed his concerns to the back of his mind. He was worried that Fant was out there, somewhere in the dark, being pursued by an angry horde of Yig's followers.

He knelt to close Rodenghast's eyes. "Come on. We need to find Fant now."

The strange phenomenon that had appeared in the air above the priest was now nowhere to be seen. Yet the odd reverberation that had issued from it could still be heard quite clearly.

Lych stood still in the darkness. He strained to hear from which direction it was coming. He was sure it was important to know.

"This way," he said, heading into the darkness to meet the unknown.

Marian kept pace with him. "What was that language that Rodenghast was speaking back there?"

"Damned if I know," replied Lych. "You're the one who has a gift for language. I struggle with English."

The sea could now be heard in the distance—one moment it was calling to them, the next warning them to stay away. But he knew that they had to carry on.

A man in a light robe could be seen just ahead, struggling to carry something. "Fant! Fant?" At Lych's shout, the figure turned to face them, lit by the faint glow emanating from the heavy load he carried.

"Go back! Get away!" yelled Fant, then lurched off into the night once more.

They struggled to follow him as the night filled their eyes. The feeble flashlight was little use against it.

They kept on in the direction they thought he was heading.

Lych was surprised that they'd encountered none of Yig's followers so far. Maybe courage wasn't one of their strong points, he mused. Or perhaps without Rodenghast to spur them on, they were simply ineffectual. Either way, he didn't really care.

Marian gasped and stopped in her tracks. She seemed unable to take another step, staring straight ahead of her.

"What's wrong?" The sea added its roaring voice to his query.

She pointed to the old lighthouse; its outline picked out clearly by the light of the half moon. "I-it reminds me of the snakes at the professor's house."

Lych looked up at it. "Yes. Or a cobra rearing up to strike." He reached out and gripped her hand firmly, remembering that he only had two bullets left.

They could just make out Fant's figure staggering towards the abandoned structure. Lych was puzzled yet again by his half-brother's behaviour. Surely he couldn't be hoping to climb it in his condition?

The door was hanging open when Fant reached it and he disappeared inside.

Lych and Marian panted up to the door a few minutes behind Fant. The 'No Entry' sign and heavy boards had been ripped down a long time ago, by the looks of things.

Inside, the space was smaller than they'd thought. It stank strongly of bird droppings. From somewhere above they could hear Fant's clattering ascent of the wooden steps than ran around the inner curve of the wall.

Lych's torch beam struggled to penetrate the thick darkness gathered inside the tower. "Fant! Fant!"

There was no reply, but Fant's footsteps could still be heard. Lych climbed the first two steps. He heard a creaking followed by a loud cracking sound. Then another. "Quick—get out!"

They both lunged headlong out of the door, a cloud of dust and debris following hard on their heels. Marian lay next to him on the grass, coughing and picking bits of debris from her hair and clothes.

Lych allowed a couple of minutes for some of the dust to settle, then looked inside. The wooden steps up to the first landing had collapsed completely. He stepped back out into the night air.

"There's no way up. Or down—Fant is trapped up there."

The sound of the waves crashed up against Lych's thoughts. Why had Fant come here? Surely, he hadn't intended to trap himself? Or maybe he thought he was safe up there.

Lych looked up at the sky above the lighthouse again. There was almost nothing to see and yet...

The strangeness in the air—only half-seen but keenly felt—was now stationary above the wrecked lamp room of the lighthouse. It throbbed and roiled with more energy now.

Fant seemed to be struggling to stand up straight. He hunched over, as if in pain.

Lych and Marian watched as he appeared to muster all his strength and force himself upright.

They saw him desperately raise the stone high above his head and hurl it as far as he could out into the night. It arced away from the lighthouse and plunged into the swallowing darkness beyond the cliff edge. The sea sighed its approval as it accepted the unexpected gift.

The air drummed angrily, summoning an odd illumination that suddenly surrounded Fant. He twisted around, clearly battling to escape it or its effects.

There, up on the heights, they saw his silhouette. Dark, deformed, possibly human but now obviously so much more, he turned about once on a strange pivot, then once again, before vanishing in a twist of air.

A faint sound barely reached their ears. It might have been a plea for help or a cry of ecstasy. Whatever it was, it had come and gone in an instant.

Then the night was still, dark and quiet.

It was a portrait of a man. But not quite a portrait.

Everyone who saw it on display during the Portico Gallery's Private View agreed it was a triumph of both technique and inspiration. Yet, as one young visitor put it, the image "left a bad taste in the mouth".

The critics all agreed that the painting, incongruously

entitled 'Still Life With Death', was one of the artist's finest works, despite the odour of decadence and the unworldly that almost palpably emanated from its surface.

It showed a figure from the chest up holding an apple in its hand, proffered towards the viewer. The apple was a healthy red on one side but very obviously worm-eaten on the other.

Something about the figure's eyes seemed only half-human, most agreed. Those who recognised the subject in person were shocked by his degeneration. But overall, the reviews in the September 2nd editions of the papers were glowing.

Lych never had a chance to read them. Marian Elder found his studio empty on the evening of September 1st, his paintbrushes cast to one side and fresh paint still on his palette. There were no signs of a struggle. He just wasn't there.

He hasn't been seen since.

REVELATIONS

BY PETE RAWLIK

Prologue: The Incident at Witch Hill Hospital, May 1960

The storm clouds rolled in, black against a grey sky, as Dr. Wingate Peaslee and his partner pulled off the road that led from Arkham to the coast and onto the long drive that led up to the military facility known as Witch Hill. The government had ordered the structure built three decades earlier to serve Navy personnel that had been injured while occupying Innsmouth. Later—as the occupation dragged on—the staff of the facility found themselves dealing with the detrimental psychological toll of the prolonged and bloody fighting with the bootleggers of Devil Reef, and so the staff of Witch Hill found themselves offering psychiatric care as well as physiological. Working in Innsmouth had an effect on men; they tended to break under the stress and needed care before they could be cycled back to other assignments or, more likely than not, medically discharged from service. Wingate himself had spent time here—briefly, back in 1936—as a member of the staff after he had returned from Australia. Someone in the Navy had read about his work and since Miskatonic University was only a few miles from the hospital, he could serve as faculty at one and clinician at the other.

At least that had been the plan.

By the late Thirties, he wasn't teaching at Miskatonic or treating patients at Witch Hill. He still had rights at both— when he was in town he liked to take advantage of the Faculty

Club—but most of his time—most of his life—was spent working for JACK, the Joint Advisory Commission, Korea—a covert operation officially tasked to support American operatives in North Korea, and, when necessary, rescue and extract downed pilots. Such operations were just a cover though, what Wingate and all of JACK really did was investigate things that made Innsmouth look like a tea party, with the whole goal of preventing anything like that from ever happening again.

That is where Witch Hill Naval Hospital came in.

The facility discreetly provided treatment to those in service to the State who had encountered things that had left them broken both in body and mind. The lower levels, the general wards, were filled with men suffering from various forms of psychoses, manias, neuroses, and a whole ward of the catatonic, and the staff of doctors, nurses, analysts, and therapists that had been trained to ease their suffering and find some way to make them whole, or at least functional again. The upper levels were home to something else. Here were housed a small army of administrators, analysts and directors that acted as a kind of central point for the collection and dissemination of knowledge that was not fit for public consumption. The wards may have been filled with howling men and those tasked with their care, but here, in the upper halls of Witch Hill no word, no dream, no drawing, no screaming howl went unnoticed, and for each there was a specialist waiting to find some advantage, or draw some interpretation and wring out some meaning from the mad ravings, or at least try. And at the very top, were the seven men who sacrificed nearly all in service to their country, and even now—in the face of personal tragedy—still chose to serve; attempting to understand it all, racing to integrate the ranting and random bits of information, and then telling men like Wingate Peaslee where to go and what to do.

On occasion men like Peaslee came back to relate what they had found, and infinitesimally grow what little knowledge mankind had to defend themselves.

The Lerneaum occupied most of the fifth floor. As Peaslee and his partner came off the elevator, he saw the attending nurse approaching, a pretty little thing that he had once taken on a rather enjoyable picnic. It looked as if they'd arrived just in time and would be seen quickly; she had finished her rounds and was leaving. He caught her eye and gave her a smile, and got the same in return. His focus returned to the Lerneaum and the two chairs set up for their arrival. Peaslee grimaced as he considered them, a glance showed him that his partner's face held a commiserate grimace. The two men were intimately familiar with the stark wooden things, completely lacking in character, design, and comfort. Peaslee and his partner, Bishop, set their briefcases on the floor beside their chairs and waited for their presence to be acknowledged.

The thick, velvet curtain that divided the room hung heavy and still, muffling the murmuring conversation that was occurring on the other side. Also interfering with their ability to hear was a noise, something rhythmic and mechanical that ended with a thick kind of wheezing, as if a titanic lung was inhaling and exhaling. Abruptly, the conversation ceased and the cloth divide jerkily slid back and revealed the seven men known as the Hydra.

Just a few feet back from the curtain was another wall, the style of which was inconsistent with the rest of the room. It was made from sheets of aluminum, in a patchwork of sheet metal riveted and welded together. In this makeshift barrier seven large rubber bellows had been mounted and from these protruded the heads of seven men, resting on pillows, supported by steel brackets, staring up at the ceiling. Mirrors mounted on that ceiling provided each of them a full view of the room.

Peaslee knew they hadn't always been like this, but in the summer of '37 each of these men had been stricken with polio and against all the odds, each had failed to recover. The odds of this happening to seven well-educated agents, of contracting the disease, and of therapies not being effective, and finally of showing no signs of recovery, were astronomical. This did not go unnoticed by the more suspicious of minds in the agency. By its very nature the organization was prone to paranoia, and what had happened to these men only served to make that paranoia worse. The running theory was that an enemy had infected these men in an attempt to eliminate them and weaken

JACK. That had been fifteen years ago, and now these men ran the organization, surrounded by machines meant to keep them alive.

The seven heads continued to speak to one another, but the metallic wall, the droning medical equipment, and their condition made understanding what they were saying extremely difficult. It was like listening to music while swimming; Peaslee knew that words were being said but who was saying them and what they were, he could not always tell. He caught a snippet here and there. The word "Caiman" was used several times, but everything else was just gibberish.

Finally, their attention turned to the two waiting men and they were addressed directly. "Dr. Peaslee, Dr. Bishop, please be seated." The two men didn't know who had spoken but it didn't matter. They did as they were told; the chairs were exactly as awful as the men remembered. There was some more mumbling. "We've read your reports. Peaslee, are you prepared to elaborate on your findings?"

"Yes," Peaslee cleared his throat. "Since the twenties, when J. W. Burns began compiling legends, it has become clear that almost every culture has some version of a mythical wild man. These creatures, which Burns himself refers to as sasquatch, have a variety of names including trows, ogres, kallikantzaros, yeti, and mitche. Sightings of these creatures are generally confined to remote areas, and often go unexplained with little to no data collected, at least until the last few years. Following the Townshend Incident, a concerted effort to document ancillary information was initiated and certain patterns have begun to emerge." Peaslee paused, but not long enough for anybody to ask a question. "The pattern we've been able to discern is relatively predictable. Witnesses, usually in remote places, tend to describe encounters with giant insects, sometimes moths or bats, or even birds. Such encounters are often dismissed at first, but then grow in frequency until the evidence of something weird occurring becomes indisputable. This is followed by a lull in activity for a week or so during which the local populace breathes a sigh of relief. However, the reality is that the occurrences have not ceased, but rather have become hyper-localized, being experienced not by the community, but rather by an isolated individual—a loner—whose demeanor is such that they are unlikely to seek assistance from law enforcement or other authorities. This culminates in the loner vanishing, the implication being that the alien influence has abducted the individual." Peaslee stood and began meandering around the room. "Then several months later, sightings of large hairy hominids—sasquatch—begin. Such sightings will be accompanied by strange lights in the sky and in some cases, a resurgence in sightings of the flying monsters. This will go on for several weeks but after culminating in what can be described as a frenzy of sound and violence, the event is often brought to a close. In some cases the cessation of activity is associated with a spectral light show. There are some variations on this, but this is the general pattern."

A slow and phlegmatic voice rasped from the wall. "We are aware of the pattern, Dr., and its variations."

Peaslee nodded. "It's those variations that led Dr. Bishop and I to formulate a theory. Going back to the Townshend event, and the curious case of Avis Long, we came to suspect that the aforementioned abductions did not necessarily involve the entire corpus. We believed that the primary target was the cerebral cortex, and that the rest of the body was left behind after extraction."

A second watery voice interjected. "Brain extraction has always been suspected, but we've never recovered a body from any particular event, not even from Miss Long."

"Indeed," agreed Peaslee. "Which is why when reports of something bird-like started coming out of Washington, Bishop and I went out there as fast as we could."

"Washington?"

"Yes sir, a small town near the border with Canada. In February, a local couple, the Hornes, reported seeing something large with red eyes and wings in the night sky. It pursued them in their car for several miles before they were stopped for speeding by a local deputy. At the time it was thought that the couple had made the story up to try and get out of the ticket. Days later there were several other reports about a giant, red-eyed owl terrorizing both livestock and residents. Despite the strange nature of the affair, the sheriff organized a task force and began systematically staking out the more remote areas and roads and coordinating patrols of some of the more isolated residents. In early March, deputies visited the cabin of Loren Palmer and found it to be unlocked and unoccupied. There was uneaten food on the table and the wood stove had burnt itself out. There was no sign of a struggle but none of his friends or relatives had heard from him in days. On the 23rd his brother filed an official missing persons report. Sasquatch activity began in early April. Initial reports were of strange noises in the woods and around rural houses. The first tracks were discovered on the 12th. It wasn't much after that when the reports of visual sightings came in, particularly in the area known as Ghost Wood." Peaslee took a pause to refresh his memory. "Sightings continued through April and came to our attention on the first of May. Dr. Bishop and I reached the town on the third. We spent one day gathering background information and interviewing witnesses. On the fifth, we entered the Ghost Wood and spent the next several days tracking the creature in the hope that we could either capture or kill it, thereby validating our operating hypothesis."

There was a hissing sound that resolved into a voice. "What exactly was your operating hypothesis?"

"Others have suggested that the bodies were incinerated, dissolved by acid, or broken down by some similar process, but there was no evidence for any of this. Our theory is that following surgical extraction of the brain, the body undergoes a kind of metamorphosis. The entities that we think are responsible for all of this, those from Yuggoth, which are also referred to as the Mi-Go, another traditional name for a mythical hominid, are sometimes referred to as the Fungi from Yuggoth. Dr. Bishop and I think that close contact with the creatures, such as surgical extraction of the brain, might contaminate the human body, causing it to sprout the extraterrestrial equivalent of hypha, fungal hairs. I suspected that the fur of a Sasquatch isn't fur at all, but rather alien fungus growing on a human body."

"And your theory has been validated?"

Peaslee closed his eyes and took a breath. "To my satisfaction, yes. During our time in the Ghost Wood I came into contact with one of the creatures, and was able to place several rounds into its head. This apparently was enough to kill the thing. Upon examination of the body I found that the hair was indeed more similar to fungal strands. Examining the body I found an area of bare skin that contained a disfigured—or more precisely stretched—tattoo of an anchor. Palmer had been in the navy and had such a tattoo."

"And where is this body now?"

"Shortly after I finished my examination, the body and all my samples underwent a reaction and dissolved into a kind of black oil, which then evaporated. At first I thought this was the disposal method that we had been looking for, but I suspect something even more sinister now." He paused and looked at his colleague, who just nodded for him to continue. "I suspect that the bodies are infected with a kind of reproductive spore. This spore is placed in the skull and initially functions as a primitive brain, animating the body but only in the most basic of manners. The spore initiates physiological changes in the body. It grows in size rapidly, taking on gigantic proportions while at the same time being covered with the alien equivalent of fungal hyphae, which would appear as hair or fur. As time passes the spore matures and eventually consumes the body of its host, transforming into a fully-fledged adult Mi-Go that then either travels into space creating a light show as it leaves the world behind or is recovered by others of its species. The semi-invisible nature of the Mi-Go might explain why no decent photographs of the sasquatch have ever been taken. Similarly, the nature of these creatures might explain why no remains or hair samples have been found. It is possible that once deceased the forces that bound the weird matter—Dr. Bishop refers to it as dark matter—might no longer be stable in our space. Here I reference not only the Akeley Case, but also the Dunwich Horror."

The labored breath was back. "And Dr. Bishop can confirm this?"

Peaslee sighed. "No, sir. In the course of the hunt Dr. Bishop and I became separated. He did not rejoin me until several hours later. By that time the body and all samples I had collected had—evaporated—for lack of a better term."

"Dr. Bishop, do you concur with your colleague's conclusions?"

There was a long pause, and when it went on too long Peaslee turned to look at his colleague. The man was staring at the floor. Finally he spoke in halting tones. "I find Dr. Peaslee's conclusions highly alarming."

Peaslee opened his mouth to speak but only a breath of exasperation escaped his lips.

Before he could formulate a response one of the seven cut him off. "Perhaps, Dr. Peaslee, you would like to wait outside while Dr. Bishop speaks his mind?"

The suddenly-wounded agent's eyes darted from Bishop to the wall of polio victims and then back. "Yes, of course," he said with resignation. Then he picked up his briefcase and headed for the exit.

As he walked through the frame he heard his colleague's voice. "You must understand, Wingate is essentially correct ..." Then the door closed and Peaslee heard nothing more.

In the weeks that followed Dr. Wingate Peaslee would try to convince himself that his actions that afternoon were the result of his frustration. That he had left the Lernaeum and the hospital to wander the grounds. His partner of three years had just betrayed his confidence. He needed to get some fresh air, to clear his head.

This is what he told the Board of Inquiry when they first questioned him. It's what he told them the second time they questioned him, and the third. He even wrote it down in his official deposition.

But the truth was something different.

Somehow, he knew. He knew something was going to happen. He didn't know what, but he knew he had to get out of there. He felt a blind lizard-brain panic to get as far away from the Lernaeum as possible, as fast as possible. So he left, without pause, and headed out of the building toward the car. He'd thought to leave his traitorous partner stranded there at

Witch Hill, it was petty revenge but in the moment that had seemed enough. He didn't know that Arthur Bishop had left a suicide note back in Washington State, or that his partner had brought a bomb into the hospital. He didn't know these things, and all parties conceded that there was no way he could have known these things, at least not consciously. The men who had interrogated him noted that he was a psychologist, specifically trained to look for the impossible, to expect the unexpected, and behave accordingly. He should have noticed that his partner was behaving oddly.

Peaslee agreed, but countered that Arthur Bishop was also a trained psychologist and likely adept at hiding his intentions. This frustrating fact seemed to satisfy everybody involved and the case was closed soon after. By June Peaslee was cleared for active duty, but the administration suggested he take another month or two of leave while they finished reorganizing the agency and figured out exactly where in the table of organization he was going to fit. Peaslee didn't argue, he was still trying to forget the screams of the patients and doctors and staff as the fifth floor of Witch Hill Hospital exploded and the rest of the structure burned to the ground. He packed his bags and went to Florida for the offseason.

PART I: A BREAK IN THE ROUTINE, AUGUST 1960

South Florida in August is a special kind of hell. In winter, the warmth that seeps up from the tropics keeps the icy cold at bay and makes the region a welcome escape for those willing and able to make the trek from the bitter winters of Canada, New York and the Midwest. In the summer however, the temperatures drift up into the nineties and beyond. From the moment the sun crests above the horizon, the days become oppressively hot, and, as mornings transition into afternoons, the near unbearable heat is magnified by rising humidity. West of the coast, over the vast marshlands men call the Everglades, the moisture churns and condenses to form foreboding storm clouds that blow east, releasing their contents as they go, drenching the coastline in violent bursts of rain, lightning and thunder. Afterward, the clouds clear and the sun sets in a magnificent skyscape of oranges, pinks and purples. This is when the great flocks of wading birds cross the sky en masse, heading back to their roosts for the night.

This is the way of Florida's dog days, and it is to this that the residents and visitors must adjust. It took Wingate Peaslee a week or so to find his rhythm. He rose just prior to the dawn and had a small glass of orange juice before he walked the beach with the rising sun. He walked north along the water's edge for a mile and then walked back. Then he had breakfast—generally consisting of two eggs, fried, with a half a grapefruit—and a cup of coffee on the patio of the Delapore House and watched the fishing boats make their way out of the inlet.

The coffee at the Delapore was served in three ways. There was café Americano, which dominated the dining room, served to vacationing guests hot, or over ice. There was also coffee in the Haitian style, a thicker, sweeter brew that was prepared for the kitchen staff as well as the management. Finally there was the thick, bitter Cubano, a relatively new addition to the kitchen of the Delapore. The new brew was introduced to the area by the sudden influx of Cuban refugees following Castro's revolution, and had since become something of a South Florida delicacy. The coffee was just the tip of the iceberg though; the revolution had had a strange impact on Florida.

The number of Cubans in South Florida prior to the revolution had been about fifty thousand, but refugees had swelled that number fourfold. They came with almost nothing on their backs, and less in their back accounts. Peaslee had gotten to know some of them, the old men played dominoes in the park and on occasion he would join them. They were all so proud, and all so lost. They were doctors, and professors, and engineers—educated men who couldn't prove they were who they said they were, let alone prove they were well-educated and trained. But to hear them talk, they all had big houses with nannies and servants and vast estates. That was a running joke amongst them and the Americans they worked and played with. If you added up all the land that people said they had owned back in Cuba, the island would have been as big as the state of Texas.

There was a particular concentration of Cuban engineers at the Delapore House. Summer being the offseason, the hotel had rented them an entire floor and a conference room. They were apparently working on forming a commercial firm, pooling their money to get licenses and certifications for a few, and then slowly working to make the rest trained, licensed and employable. Reading and writing English was apparently a sticking point. The math and science was all the same, but the examinations were all in English. So they worked together to solve their problems. Peaslee found it strange that people who were so opposed to social reform and communism in their own country were now forced to pool their resources to help each other in the United States. Peaslee found it strange, but he didn't dare mention it. His quiet observations informed him they were a proud group, and in that pride, he sensed an undercurrent of rage waiting to be kindled. He would rather not provide the spark.

He also knew that their time at Delapore House was limited. Once the season started the Cubans would have to find somewhere else to call home, as they likely wouldn't be able to—much less desire to—pay the rents at the hotel or anywhere else on Singer Island. Of course, the same could be said for Peaslee. Technically, he couldn't even afford the fees in the offseason. If it wasn't for the fact that the owners were friends of his brother and his wife, he would have had to find someplace far less fashionable. Then again, Toussaint Delapore and Lady Jane Jermyn were rather liberal in their thinking, and their financial dealings, so he wondered if perhaps he might be able to negotiate a longer stay.

After his breakfast Peaslee would go for a swim on the beach. It was unlike the rocky beaches that he was used to in New England. Here the beach was sandy, a kind of pale yellow-brown dotted with shells including small clams, scallops, conchs and drills. At the water's edge there was a plethora of such shells, a ribbon a foot or so thick just where the small waves churned the sand. Beyond this the water was clear, and the sand almost bare save for the occasional bait fish or crab. The empty landscape extended for hundreds of yards out from the beach, the bottom sloping slowly out such that even two hundred yards from the shoreline the water was barely six feet deep. But it was cool and clear and refreshing and Peaslee found some comfort swimming and basking in it. There was, he thought, something calming about the dichotomy of the hot air and the cool water that let a man's mind go clear. He could stop thinking about the world, and really relax. It was a small comfort, a small pleasure, but one he relished. As he floated there in the sea he would watch the fishing boats heading to port, presumably loaded with their fresh catch.

The vessels indicated lunch was at hand and that was his cue to swim to shore and then run back to the hotel, his sandals throwing up twin wakes of hot sand as he went. Back in his room he set about washing off the sea and the lingering sand, after which he would don a fresh cotton shirt and then head back to the patio for a lunch of grilled grouper and Yucatan shrimp. He was not fond of spicy food, and usually eschewed the greasy and peppery calamari done Rhode Island style, but there was something wonderful about the Yucatan shrimp. It was a messy but delightful concoction of large gulf shrimp, garlic, lime, cilantro and sambal, an Indonesian chili paste. Peaslee didn't know why it was called Yucatan shrimp, but frankly he enjoyed it too much to be bothered to ask. The side dish was served with noodles or rice, but he preferred Cuban bread, which made sopping up the leftover sauce easier.

After lunch he would read in the shade until the clouds began to threaten. As the storms rolled through, he often moved indoors to the bar, drank a whisky sour and then fell asleep in a lounge chair until evening.

Dinner was usually on the mainland, down at one of the restaurants on West Palm Beach's Clematis Street. There was decent food in town, particularly steaks. Beef from cattle raised just north of Lake Okeechobee seemed particularly tender and well-marbled. Afterward, he would often lounge about drinking scotch before catching the last launch back to the hotel around eleven.

This was his vacation, his retreat, it wasn't much, it wasn't very exciting, but it was his and it made him relatively happy.

Well, it should have.

Truth be told, he had become rather bored. He was a man of action, a man of secrets and secrecy. He knew the truth of the world and sometimes he just wanted to scream those truths from the top of a building and let the whole world know how insane everything was. He also knew that was the way of madness. No one would listen to him, or believe him. The local authorities would lock him up as a madman, and later, when it was convenient, JACK would find time to have him disappeared. He laughed at this thought. Since the Witch Hill fiasco the agency was undergoing reorganization and no one knew exactly what to do with him, or where to assign him. Having him disappear down some black hole, figuratively or literally was a real option. He'd seen it done to other agents. Hell, he'd done it to other agents—and civilians. Wiped them off the face of the Earth, as if they never existed. The agency was so thorough they could make a mother question whether she had given birth to her own child.

Still, nothing was set in stone. The agency was going to find a place for him. They just needed time. He just had to wait, and find some way to occupy his time—something exciting, some sort of adventure. The hotel had brochures for offshore boating, hunting in the Everglades, or bass fishing on Lake Okeechobee. He could even take a trip down to the Keys, or over to the Bahamas. But it all seemed so canned, sterile, safe … an artificial experience designed to simulate adventure and adrenaline, as opposed to letting things unfold naturally. Which is a very complicated way of saying that Dr. Wingate Peaslee was looking for something—anything—to do.

Given his mental state, the bar fight was a gift.

He hadn't even noticed what started it. One minute he was sitting at the bar minding his own business, trying and slowly failing to not feel lonely in a place full of happy people, and the next he was listening to several very loud and angry voices yelling incoherently. He couldn't see exactly what was going on, the crowd was too thick, and as the voices grew in volume the crowd just seemed to thicken. He stood up to get a better view. There were three men in uniform, they bore the insignia of the United States Air Force, and below that a badge showing a stylized anemometer indicating they were part of the Air Weather Service, the unit that amongst other things launched planes into hurricanes. They weren't exactly Marines, but they weren't administrative staff either.

"Just what exactly are you implying?" snapped one of the soldiers, he had a grey streak in his hair.

"He said that we were Nazis, fucking Nazis," said his companion, this one with a scar running down his cheek. He emphasized the word Nazi, so each time it sounded shrill and high pitched and unpleasant.

"I said no such thing, young man." came a response in a heavily accented voice. Peaslee couldn't place it but it was definitely Eastern European. "I asked if you had noticed anyone in your unit who might be sympathetic to fascist ideology."

Another voice, another soldier, this one wearing glasses. "Which sounds a lot like asking us if we're Nazis."

"That's not what I said at all."

"Listen to that accent," commented Scarface. "Does that sound Russian to you?"

"I am not Russian, I am Armenian. I mean I was Armenian."

"Right," said Greystreak, "Armenia is a part of the USSR. There aren't any Armenians anymore, just Soviets."

Peaslee stood up and made his way through the crowd, forcing his way around shoulders and elbows that really didn't want to let him pass. He pushed forward anyway, determined to intervene in what he saw as a rapidly-escalating situation. He wasn't sure what he was going to do, but he had served with some Armenians during the Second World War and he respected those men still. So while it was true that their country had fallen behind the Iron Curtain, that didn't mean they were all communists, especially one as old as the man who stood being berated by the soldiers.

From where he stood, Peaslee guessed him to be about the same age as himself—around sixty. The man's hair was cut short and round and held a considerable amount of grey. He had a full beard and mustache, trimmed neatly and both still mostly black but with some traces of grey around the edges. His head was egg shaped and rested on top of a long neck and narrow shoulders. He was very thin, and shorter than one would have expected for his arms and legs both seemed longer than they should have been. Gangly was the term that came to mind, like Ichabod Crane in that Disney film he had seen a few years back.

"We should take him outside and teach him not to talk like that," said Scarface. Glasses grunted in agreement, while Scarface reached out and took a handful of the man's shirt. That's when Peaslee, newly-arrived, put a hand on Scarface's shoulder.

"I knew a man from Armenia once, looked a lot like you. Went by the name," Peaslee paused to remember, "Ophel, Ophel Kulshedra. Helped me out of a spot of trouble down in Australia."

Scarface let go of the man's shirt and turned to look at Peaslee. "You'd be wise to stay out of this, old man." There was a growl in his voice.

"That is my name, and you are Peaslee, the Old Man," whispered the Armenian. "That's what Doc Tydon used to call you, the Terrible Old Man."

A look of confusion came over Greystreak face. "What's going on here?"

Glasses echoed his friend, "Yeah, what's going on here?"

Peaslee smiled. "What's going on here is that you're about to get your ass well and truly kicked." Scarface never saw the first punch coming, or the second, or the third. He did manage to glimpse the fourth one, the one that put him on the floor.

Glasses stepped in and landed a punch to Peaslee's gut but it wasn't much to speak of. Peaslee shrugged it off and fired back, landing a punch right on the bridge of his nose, snapping his glasses in half. The broken frames slid up his forehead and sliced a long, bloody gash. Blood blossomed into arcs before dripping down into his eyes. He was effectively blind but that didn't stop him from flailing about and swinging wildly. He almost connected with Peaslee's chin, but the old man threw a block with his right forearm and then rapid-fired three quick left-handed jabs to the man's gut. He fell back on his ass, gagging. A little vomit came up out of his mouth, it stank of bile, fish and rotgut whiskey.

That left Greystreak standing there by himself, alone and panicked. He balled his fists up, mostly in frustration, but frustration makes men do stupid things. He roared and then charged forward, meaning to tackle Peaslee, but his target sidestepped him. As he passed, Peaslee grabbed him by the back of his shirt and spun him off in another direction. He came to a stumbling stop almost right in front of the Armenian. The gangly man reached down and brought the drunken soldier to a fully-upright position.

Greystreak looked the foreigner in the eyes and sneered. "Fucking commie." Then he spit in his face.

With one hand the gangly man pushed Greystreak away while he pulled back the other one and threw a very accurate and very powerful haymaker. Greystreak's shoes left the ground and he flew through the air, an arc of spittle and blood forming a crimson-hued rainbow behind him.

"My name is Ophel Kulshedra," said the Armenian with a touch of pride in his voice. "And I am not a communist."

Somewhere in the distance, a siren wailed.

Colonel Dr. Wingate Peaslee grabbed his old friend by the arm and pulled him along. "Time to go, my friend."

"This reminds me of Bundanyabba." Kulshedra smiled. "Now that was a good time."

Peaslee shook his head and smiled. "You and I have very different memories of Bundanyabba."

They ran north, avoiding the main roads, cutting through alleyways and yards. A few times they hugged against the walls of homes and businesses while cars drove past. Peaslee didn't know whether they were police cars or not. He didn't care. The two of them skulked through the night as if they were on the run from the Gestapo. When they finally made it to the dock, their hearts were pounding and their lungs were burning but they fell into the launch with smiles on their faces and laughter pouring from their mouths.

It was the most fun Peaslee had had in weeks.

PART 2: MISSION TO MONTEVIDEO

They were sitting on the patio overlooking the inlet, watching the moon playing over the waves, and listening to the night birds calling as they scoured the shoreline for crabs and baby turtles. Peaslee had bribed the night clerk for a bottle of scotch, a bucket of ice, and two tumblers. It wasn't particularly old, or particularly good, but it was still scotch, it was still wet, and it was better than nothing. Peaslee was just happy that the wind was keeping the patio cool and the mosquitos at bay.

"Last I heard you were working for the Brits," Peaslee was almost laughing. "What was the name of that outfit? The Laundrette?

"God's Beard, that was more than a decade ago. What a bunch of bureaucrats and accountants. They actually had a manual on how to deal with secret societies, and a whole list of charge codes you had to use for your report. If you didn't do things just right you didn't get paid. A bureaucracy that was destined to collapse under its own weight."

"Careful Ophel, I still work for one of those bureaucracies."

"Yes, though I'm not sure JACK is still functional. What about that other group you use to work for, back in the forties, Beta Blue?"

Peaslee smiled. "Disavowed, defunded and disbanded. Or so I'm told. They never did play well with others. Though I'm told that some factions might have gone rogue, infiltrating other agencies and creating black budgets to keep their mission going. Not my style." He took a sip of liquor. "I prefer things above board." He took another drink, finishing the glass. "So who are you working for now?"

Ophel set his own glass back on the table and smiled slyly. "Would you believe the Institute for Intelligence and Special Operations?"

A look of surprise came over Peaslee's face. "Mossad, really? I didn't think of you as a Zionist."

"The nation of Israel has certain goals, many of those tend to align with my own."

Peaslee frowned. "So you're here on assignment?"

Ophel nodded. "I assume you know about Eichmann?"

"That was you?"

Ophel shook his head. "No, I'm not that noisy. Eitan took Eichmann out of Buenos Aires, while at the same time I acquired a different target in Montevideo."

"Care to tell me about it?"

"There isn't much to tell. As I said, Eitan went after Eichmann, there was another team in pursuit of Mengele. Can you imagine that? Can you imagine being the man to bring in the Angel of Death?"

"Last I heard Mengele was still free?"

Ophel nodded as he poured himself another scotch. "He is. Control made a mistake. They waited too long to move on Eichmann and by the time they did, Mengele had already left Buenos Aires. Paralysis by analysis."

"But …"

"When he was taken, Eichmann was carrying a valise full of papers. Most of it was junk, the detritus of a mediocre life, but there was one receipt. Eichmann had bought a selection of Egyptian statuary. Small idols of Bast, Ptah, Set, the Apes of Truth."

"What is it with Nazis and antiquities? For Nationalists, they seem strangely obsessed with the gods and artifacts of so-called lesser races."

"It's true, Hitler had hundreds of archeologists deployed around the world. Everybody talks about Reinerth and Belloq, but they were just the most visible of the Reich's servants, but the real workhorse was Simon Orne."

Peaslee tapped a finger on the table. "You know I met him once, Orne I mean. He came to Miskatonic University. He wanted access to the restricted collection, and he wanted to talk to my father. He didn't get either."

"That was very fortunate. Orne is something of an enigma."

"What do you mean by that?"

"Over the last few years we've built up dossiers on vast numbers of former members of the Reich. We've looked at all of their personal details, birth records, close relatives, primary schools, universities, fraternal organizations, business associates, all that sort of thing. Anything we could potentially use to track them down. When I found out that Eichmann was buying antiquities from somebody in Montevideo, it was easy to find the shipping address and then identify Orne. I sent for a copy of his file. It was thin, surprisingly thin." He took another drink. "The earliest reliable documentation we have of him is as a visitor to Wendy-Smith in 1929. Later that year he joined Oppenheim as an assistant in the excavations at Tell Halaf. Prior to this there is nothing."

"What do you mean, nothing?" Peaslee asked. He swirled his scotch, enjoying the sound of the ice striking the glass. He took a sip as Ophel continued.

"I mean prior to 1929 we can't find any proof that Simon Orne ever existed, at least nothing reliable. We have issued degrees, college transcripts and even rosters from various fraternities and social clubs. Documents that support the idea that Orne was real, that he went to Marcian College, that he was a member of The Pudding Club, and that he graduated with honors in 1914. However, examinations of yearbooks, of photographs, of college newsletters, reveal not one mention of anyone with the name Simon Orne. It's as if ..." he paused and then started up again. "No, that is wrong. It's not 'as if', it simply is, Simon Orne is a manufactured identity."

"So who is he then?"

"No idea, his dossier didn't have a damned clue. Whoever he was before 1929 was a complete mystery. Which is why I decided to ask him myself."

"I assume you mean under interrogation?"

"Of course."

"How did that go?"

"Not as planned." Ophel said and drained the little whiskey that remained in his glass. He eyed his empty glass with a look of satisfaction and then poured himself another drink. "Orne was running a significant import-export business. Uruguay is an incredibly fertile region. They have a saying, 'Uruguay is the cow and the port'."

"What the hell does that mean?"

"It means that the country makes most of its money from exporting wool, beef and leather. Which gives it a lot of money to spend on imports, particularly from the poorer nations in the region. Orne was ostensibly importing Mexican corn and rice, and cotton and fish from the Cayman Islands, perfect covers for smuggling cash and small artifacts through customs, or at least so I thought. Don't get me wrong, when I snuck into his warehouse and opened up a few containers I found plenty of artifacts: statuettes, idols, ceremonial weapons, and some jewelry. All the things I was expecting were there. The whole human body stuffed inside an oil drum was totally unexpected."

"Christ!"

"That isn't even the weird part. The body was old, desiccated, mummified. It still had remnants of some kind of ceremonial shroud wrapped around it. It had to be hundreds, if not thousands of years old."

"What did you do?"

"The mummy, the tomb-raiding, illegal trade in antiquities, these were not my concerns. I set up a watch and waited for my target to show up. Which he did not. Slightly after midnight a storm rolled in and the whole port was suddenly lashed with howling winds and driving rain. I was just about to pack things in when a moving van showed up. Two men in ponchos then proceeded to load five barrels, including the one containing the mummy into the back of the van. It was a ridiculous thing to see and no normal employee would undertake such a task under such conditions. Whatever they were doing was time sensitive and perhaps even best carried out under the cover of the storm. As they locked up the garage, one of them brought out a large leather valise and threw it in with the barrels. When they drove away, I followed them.

It had been easy to find Orne at his place of business. I thought about attempting to take him there, but at the warehouse Orne was surrounded by workmen. It would have been foolish to attempt anything there. But every time I tried to follow him home, I lost him in the maze that is Montevideo. The city is thoroughly European, founded by the Portuguese who were later ousted by the Spanish, who built onto and on top of the existing structures. At the beginning of the twentieth century, Europeans from all over began to immigrate into the city and it grew quickly, following European sensibilities. Thoroughfares run out from the central port, through the old city, and into the surrounding countryside estancias—ranches. The thoroughfares quarter up the city which is then gridded out with smaller connecting roads into neighborhoods. These are then subdivided by dozens of small avenues and alleyways. The city doesn't even bother to try and map any of this stuff, let alone all the byways and walkways that cut through private property, sometimes right through family courtyards. Anyway, Orne used this labyrinth of roads and pathways to elude me. I don't think he knew I was there, that I was following him. I just think that he was routinely that paranoid, always taking a different way home, always doubling back, never visiting the same store more than once, least not that I could tell. Somehow or another, he always managed to lose me. Which is why I ended up following the moving van. I hoped it would lead me to Orne's home."

"Makes sense."

"These guys weren't as slick as Orne, they took one of the main thoroughfares straight out of the city and to an isolated ranch outside the city. It was an old and dilapidated place, overgrown grass and crowded with fallen trees. Not far from the road was a kind of miniature castle, Spanish architecture but with about a dozen turrets linked together by grey stone arches. It was covered with vines and dead weeds. Off to one side a tumbledown barn attested to this once being a farm, but all signs pointed to it being long-abandoned. I parked my jeep well away from the main house in a grove of trees overgrown with brush. The wind and rain of the storm worked to my advantage, hiding both the sound of my engine and the light of the moon.

"I worked my way closer to the house while the two workmen from the truck were joined by three more from inside the house, unloaded the five barrels and moved them through a pair of double doors into the house. As the double doors closed I caught a brief glimpse of a figure in a white laboratory coat. I recognized him immediately as Simon Orne.

"Gaining entry to the house was relatively easy. It may have looked like a castle but it was designed as a ranch house, lots of doors and windows, and inevitably I found one that was unlocked and unguarded. The inside of the house was dimly lit, but this could not hide the amazing collection that Orne had amassed. The walls of the ranch held dozens upon dozens of paintings by the great masters. I saw a Rembrandt, a Matisse, and what I suspect were several Da Vincis. There were cabinets as well, rows upon rows of them and all filled with treasures looted from hundreds of cultures. The curators of the British Museum would have drooled in envy. If I had helped myself, I could have lived comfortably on my takings for the rest of my life.

"But as I have said, these were not my concerns. Instead I focused on the terrible and suggestive cacophony that was coming from deep within the very bowels of the house. A voice was reciting what I could only assume was some sort of ritual chant. The language was one I did not recognize, but the words seemed to reach into some primordial part of my brain and stirred some kind of ancestral memory. My emotional response was one of fear and loathing, for somehow I knew the invocation to be something ancient and wicked.

"I followed the chanting down a set of stone steps that seemed older than the house that surrounded them. The basalt pavers were worn from what seemed centuries of use, and the walls held traces of ancient petroglyphs, strange and antediluvian carvings in the rock. I did not pause to examine them in detail, but the impression they made on me was that these predated the colonial period by perhaps a millennia. The overwhelming motif was that of the snake, but it was in a style that I was not familiar with. It was not Incan, Aztec or Mayan. No, it was something wholly different, and I swear to you that in the swirling spirals, the snake design bore not one or two heads, but five. It was an image reminiscent of the Hindu Sheshanaga, the lord of the serpent people. But I did not tarry to study it.

"As I descended those steps, I wondered how they had gotten so far ahead of me, and I also wondered about the fetid stench that seemed to waft up out of the darkness. It was a dank and corrupting smell, like meat that had turned rotten and been corrupted by maggots. With each step, I descended deeper beneath the surface and the stink grew stronger. It was so bad that I felt compelled to pull a handkerchief and hold it to my nose. The steps were lit by widely-spaced bulbs that ran on a single wire that had been pinned to the wall with metal spikes. The bulbs flickered and did little to dispel the shadows that clung to the tunnel like moss on a tombstone.

"After a few minutes, I found myself at the terminus of the steps. They opened up into a large, cylindrical room that seemed hewn from the rock of the earth itself. A set of chains dangled from above and from these I understood how my quarry had outdistanced me so quickly. The chains were part of a crude elevator, counterweighted by a large, dangling boulder. The barrels were off to one side and their contents, five ancient mummies, had been laid out onto several tables. They lay there curled up and still, monstrous sleeping infants. Orne, in his white lab coat, was ordering his servants about in Spanish, and while they seemed a loutish bunch it quickly became apparent that they were entirely subservient to Orne. They left apparently at his order, ascending quickly by way of the elevator, leaving Orne alone.

"I decided to wait a few minutes, just to make sure that his assistants were well and truly gone. I did not want to be disturbed or outnumbered during my attempt to apprehend him. While I waited, I watched as Orne took one of those ancient husks and put it back inside one of the barrels. He then added a modicum of powder from a queerly shaped bottle, sprinkling it evenly over the body. After this he retrieved a large decanter of fluid and dressed the body with some kind of green oil; it flowed viscously out of the decanter and Orne seemed to take great delight in pouring it onto the husk of a corpse. Then he struck a match. He stared at the flame for a moment, gazed longingly at it, like a lover. Then he tossed it into the barrel. There was a great rush of air, a burst of flame and then a light grey smoke began to issue forth and climb up into the upper portions of the chamber.

"It was then that I decided to make my move. Gun in hand, I stepped out from my place of concealment and ordered Orne to slowly turn around and raise his hands. I don't know where the knife came from. One second it was there in his hand, and then the next it was in my shoulder, not deep, just enough to stay stuck-in. I felt the pain shoot into my brain, and I responded accordingly. Two shots rang out from my pistol. I saw them strike Orne, one in the chest and the second one in the throat. He fell back and down, crumbling to the floor without a sound. He lay there motionless, still as the grave. I pulled the blade from my shoulder and felt the warmth spread from the open wound. With one hand applying pressure, I kept my gun in the other and led with it as—with utmost caution—I approached the fallen villain. As far as I could see his chest wasn't moving. I nudged him with the tip of my shoe, but he didn't respond. With the full force of my boot I rolled him over. What I saw as his face came into view was impossible. There was no doubt that this was Simon Orne, but in some impossible manner he had aged decades in a matter of moments. His skin sagged with wrinkles, his hair thin and white, and his eyes rheumy and sallow. What happened next sent me into a panic. I turned to run and plowed straight into the burning barrel. It tumbled over, discharging the oil-covered body into the room. The fire spread quickly, setting flame to the examination tables and the other mummies. I looked about for something to extinguish the blaze, but there was nothing. Each second I wasted contemplating my next action the fire grew. I ran for the stairs, and as I did my eyes caught a glimpse of something that might have been useful. I grabbed it and dashed back up, back up to the surface, while behind me I could hear the flames grow into a roaring inferno.

"I reached the ground floor in a frenzy, so mad with fright that I ignored all manner of caution. I careened through the house and out the nearest door. My car, thankfully my car was exactly where I had left it. I threw my prize inside and drove like a madman through the countryside. I must have driven through the night in a kind of blind panic. I don't remember how I made it back to the safe house, but I did, and the caretaker had a nurse stitch up my shoulder.

"That was three months back. It took me a month to heal, and another month to explain myself to control. They weren't happy with me, but the valise I brought them—the object I stole from Orne's laboratory—more than made up for it. It was full of mail, letters and invoices and checks from all over the world. Even as we speak Mossad agents are setting up operations to investigate dozens of new leads. Which is why I am here in this little slice of heaven you people call Florida."

"Hang on a minute, you skipped a part." Insisted Peaslee.

"Did I?"

"You did. What was it that you saw? What was it that panicked you so? Why did you flee from Orne's body?"

Ophel lowered his eyes and nodded while tipping the rapidly-depleting bottle toward his glass. The amber liquid trickled slowly into the glass for a moment and then stopped. Ophel continued speaking. "For a long time, I did not like to think about it, but I suppose sooner or later I must, and I can think of no one better to confide in than you." He lifted the glass in solidarity and downed the shot he'd just poured. "I told you how I had shot Orne, and how he had aged almost instantly. That could have been a trick of the light, I could have just seen him from afar and not realized that he had grown old in comparison to his file photo. But what happened next was no illusion. As I watched his skin transformed from a mass of sagged and wrinkled flesh to a grey, paper-thin tissue. His eyes collapsed into something like milky prunes. In seconds, the flesh had drawn thin around the bone and drawn back from the teeth, creating a rictus smile. In mere moments the papery skin began to crack and crumble into dust. A wind came up then, and this is what drove the fire but do not ask me where it came from. I could not tell you, but what I can attest to is that the wind drove the ash away, leaving only the skeleton in its wake. It was an unnerving thing to see. I have seen dead bodies before, both fresh and ancient. I have seen strange things, and bore witness to things I cannot explain. But nothing I had seen had ever prepared for what lay there on the ground before me. The skeleton, the skeleton of Simon Orne that had mere moments before been covered with flesh, now lay bare and exposed, but it was like no skeleton I had ever seen before. The bones were black and shiny, like obsidian. What's more is that they were not like the smooth and sculpted bones of men, but rather reminiscent of the twisted and woven roots of a banyan tree. And that was not the worst of it. In the jaw, that queer, black glass, imitation of a human jaw, there were teeth, long fang-like teeth that rested in grooves in the bones of the cheeks. I don't know what Simon Orne was, but I know he wasn't a man!"

PART 3: A SERPENT IN EDEN

Ophel's tale—and the bottle of scotch—ended in the wee hours of the morning. Ophel asked the night clerk to arrange transport back to the mainland, but was disappointed to learn that the boat was unavailable till dawn. Peaslee offered his couch, but the clerk suggested a small efficiency—really a glorified closet—for the night. They agreed to brunch at half past ten, and bid each other goodnight.

Brunch was fresh fruit from the local farms and groves. The coffee was Cuban and strong. Ophel had two runny eggs on top of a seared steak while Peaslee had a cheese and spinach omelet with a ham steak. They bantered while they ate, but when the coffee was changed to mimosas Peaslee asked the hard question.

"Why are you here, Ophel?"

"As I said, Orne's papers opened up a whole new direction of research and my fellow agents have set up operations all over the world, I'm here to look at a man named Frederick Bauer."

"A former Nazi?"

"By all accounts an American, born near Philadelphia in 1935 to German immigrants Babette and Herman. He went to the Abington Friends School and then Penn State's Ogontz campus where he studied engineering. After graduating in 1956 he spent some time visiting family in Argentina, only to lose both his parents that summer. In 1957 he joined the Air Force and was assigned to the Air Weather Service. He was assigned to Palm Beach Air Force Base in 1958 where he continues to serve to this day."

"Kind of young for a Nazi, don't you think?"

"His name appears on eight receipts in Orne's bag, all for live plants. Each dated about a month apart. Then there's this." He reached into his jacket and slid a photostatic copy of a document across the table.

Peaslee looked at the paper and a strange look came across his face. "A death certificate for an Argentinian John Doe from May 1956. Why does this matter?"

Ophel sighed. "Anything that could be used to identify the man was removed: face burned off, teeth pulled, fingers cut off, though what remained met the general description of Bauer."

"You could probably find a dozen John Does to match Bauer if you tried hard enough."

Ophel nodded. "His parents were killed two days later."

"So you suspect he was killed and replaced, by whom?"

"I have no clue, but it is suspicious, and I would like to see this man and make sure he is who he says he is."

"And if he isn't?"

"Normally I would handle things myself, but as he is Air Force there are naturally complications."

"Naturally."

"Perhaps you would be interested in aiding my investigation. You are still an officer, are you not?"

"I am." Peaslee finished off his mimosa and let the offer turn over in his mind. After a moment of thought, Peaslee agreed to Ophel's request.

"There would have to be rules, I would be in charge of course."

"Of course."

"And if we do find him to be suspicious, he would have to be turned over to the proper authorities."

Ophel paused for an uncomfortable amount of time but then finally spoke. "That would be acceptable."

"So where do we find him?"

Ophel shook his head. "He hasn't been seen in weeks. The presence at the base is too small for him to be inside. He must be deployed somewhere, but I can't tell you where."

"Well, let's go ask."

They caught the noon launch for the mainland. Pelicans paddled out of the way while the small boat made its way across the calm, clear waters of the Intracoastal Waterway. The blue skies were cloud-free and it seemed to Peaslee a perfect Florida day. The boat pilot was not as agreeable, noting that a powerful storm was moving across Hispaniola, threatening to bring strong winds and torrential rains to the Florida coast. It would be a few days and nobody knew what exact direction it was going to go, but people all up and down the coast were making preparations. As they docked on the western shore, they saw the stevedores clearing the wharf of crates and barrels, coils of line, ash cans, oil cans, duffels, and anything else that could be dislodged by wind or wave or storm surge. To Peaslee it seemed like a swarm of ants crawling over a mound, to the outsider it might look like chaos but Peaslee knew it wasn't. It was organized, just along lines that only made sense to the harbormaster, and outsiders would never—could never—understand it.

They caught a cab and headed west out of the city, working their way down US 1 through the working class cracker boxes of Conch Town and then down through the more genteel neighborhoods of Northwood, with their Spanish style houses of white stucco topped with burnt red tiles. South of this was the industrial district, with the road lined with warehouses, cheap hotels, a lumberyard and several supply stores. The end of this district was capped with St. Mary's Hospital with its black-habited nuns. South of this was City of West Palm proper. The west side of the road was lined with shops and small restaurants, while the east side held another neighborhood of barrel tile roof and stucco homes, though—to be honest—only a small percentage of these could be called homes, the rest were more like mansions or miniature castles, all of them washed white, like ivory, in the bleaching sun. The roads were lined with tropical palm trees interspersed with stately oaks and gumbo limbos with their curious red peeling bark.

At Belvedere Road they turned west, crossing both the

railway track and the north spur of the barge canal that brought fruit, vegetables, and catfish from the farms out west to be shipped all up the East Coast. From there it was just another mile to the gates of what had once been known as Morrison Airfield and more recently as the Palm Beach Air Force Base, but even this was fading. The Air Force was phasing out operations and had just last year turned over operations to the county. The only real military presence remaining was the Air Weather Service, which performed weather research and hurricane reconnaissance for the armed forces.

At the gate they exited the cab and approached the guardhouse, where a soldier came out to greet them. Peaslee flashed his identification, hoping that it was still valid.

"Colonel Peaslee, AFSA, I would like to see the base commander."

The soldier took Peaslee's identification and excused himself, retreating to the guardhouse to make a phone call. The soldier's departure gave Peaslee and Ophel ample time to watch the coming and going of various aircraft. It wasn't long before Ophel turned to Peaslee with a rather curious question.

"I thought you said this place was shut down? I've counted four Sea Stallions landing since we've been standing here. Each of those is capable of discharging about thirty troops each, and equipment. Rather active and heavily-staffed for weather research." There was a touch of sarcasm in his voice.

Just then a jeep pulled up and a smart-looking lieutenant got out, conferred with the guard and then approached the two men. He handed Peaslee back his identification as he greeted the newly-arrived guests to the base.

"Colonel Dr. Peaslee, Major Kulshedra, I am Jefferies. If you come with me I'll take you to see Commander Warrington."

"It seems we are expected," said Peaslee. He smiled as Jefferies turned around and walked through the gate. He directed Opel to go first with a slight gesture of the hand. As the man passed he whispered, "You didn't tell me you were a Major."

Ophel frowned and scoffed. "A purely ceremonial title, useful on some occasions."

"Like this?"

"Exactly like this."

The ride up to the base was pleasant; Peaslee found the breeze off the ocean cooling and enjoyable. The ride through the base was less so. The breeze was far behind them, the only wind was that from the aircraft rotors and it came hot with the chemical stink of fuel. The heat of the day was so brutal it made the tarmac sweat. Peaslee could see fumes wafting up from the ground. The base itself was nothing to look at, like every other base he had ever been at. The place was dotted with drab buildings and semi-circular Quonset huts; all poorly built, all poorly maintained, and all clinging to the weed-choked earth like a myriad of hungry ticks on the back of a mangy dog.

Jeffries brought them in short order to Warrington's office, which was as non-descript as every other building, save perhaps for the presence of several parking spaces that had been properly striped in white paint and a concrete sidewalk framed by fern-like coonties leading up to the entrance. The aluminum door slammed against its wooden frame as the three men went inside. It was hotter inside, and the slowly turning ceiling fans did nothing to make things better. Warrington wasn't so much a man as a caricature, everything Peaslee had expected. Tall, with close-cut black hair, he stood as imposingly as possible; constantly puffing up his chest and displaying his broad shoulders and hips in an apparent effort to physically intimidate those around him. He chewed a fat, greasy cigar. He had once been fit, muscular even, but Peaslee could see that he had started to go soft around the middle. When Warrington greeted them, reaching out to shake hands, Peaslee noted the sweat stains under his arms and the line across his forehead. Everything about Warrington said career soldier.

"Colonel Peaslee, Major Kulshedra. Commander Robert Warrington, Air Weather Service. How can I help the two of you?"

Peaslee touched a chair, and the commander nodded. As they sat, Peaslee asked his first question. "You know who we are. How?"

Warrington smiled. "Three of my men were taken to task by

two old men last night. I would hope you wouldn't begrudge me finding out who was responsible." He took a puff off the cigar. "CIC had informed me that you were at the Delapore, and that you," he nodded at Kulshedra, "were staying at the Evernia. I wasn't told that you were working together."

"We weren't," Peaslee admitted, "at least not until your soldiers drew my attention."

"'Drew your attention.' That's a fine turn of phrase. To hear my men tell it they were insulted, provoked you might say." He took another long drag off the cigar. He pointed at Kulshedra again. "They said you called them Nazis."

Ophel Kulshedra shrugged apologetically. "That is not what I said, and it was not my intent. Obviously there was some misunderstanding."

Warrington chewed his cigar for a moment. "Of course, what I thought exactly." He smiled slyly. "So why don't you tell me exactly what you said, and what exactly your intent was?"

Peaslee shifted Warrington's attention to himself. "We would like to talk with one of your soldiers, a man named Frederick Bauer."

"The Kraut?" exclaimed Warrington. "You suspect him of something?"

"We have questions." Peaslee dodged the question. "We would like you to make him available for us to interview. Today, preferably."

Warrington looked out at the tarmac as another Sea Stallion landed and discharged another contingent of troops. "I'm afraid that will be quite out of the question."

Peaslee looked out the window at the four helicopters idling on the runway. "What exactly is it you do here, Commander Warrington?"

Warrington took the cigar out of his mouth and laid it down in an ashtray. "Do you know what the Texas Towers are?"

Peaslee nodded. "Offshore radar facilities modeled after jack-up oil rigs. There are five running from off the coast of New Jersey all the way up to Nova Scotia." Peaslee paused. "You're too far south to be servicing those."

"Yes, yes we are."

Kulshedra leaned forward. "Cuba, you're watching Cuba."

Warrington smiled slyly. "We have a variety of interests in the region, but yes, Cuba is high on our priorities."

Peaslee was suddenly coming to understand things. "Where exactly is Bauer?"

That sly smile grew wide on Warrington's face. "There's a platform about sixty miles due east of Fort Lauderdale, we call it *Babel*. Bauer is a lead engineer onboard. He makes sure the damn thing keeps running ship shape, everything from the radios, engines, the jacks, and the desalination plant. Hell, the man even makes sure that the damned greenhouse stays operational."

Kulshedra perked up. "Greenhouse?"

"Yeah, I know it sounds strange, but the men love it. The plants help clean the water and seem to have some kind of calming effect on the staff. Damned if I understand it but we have fewer complaints on *Babel* than on any of the other towers. I'm trying to get authorization to put greenhouses on the other towers, see if it works there, or if it's just a fluke."

"Can you bring him in?" Peaslee was almost insistent.

"I'm in the middle of preparing for a major storm, evacuating hundreds of troops, and you want me to bring in my best engineer." Warrington let loose a little laugh. "That is, unless you want to go on a little trip yourselves?"

A worried look passed over Kulshedra's face. "You said something about evacuating for a storm?"

Warrington waved the concern away. "Completely precautionary, standard procedure really. We can have you out there tonight and back tomorrow morning."

Peaslee shook his head. "We don't have our bags."

"No need," proclaimed Warrington, "I'll throw you and the major a kit bag," he looked the two men up and down, "and a pair of flight suits." The sly smile turned a little wicked. "What do you say, wheels up in thirty? Or have the years taken their toll on the Terrible Old Man?"

PART 4: THE NAMING OF NAMES

The Sea Stallion lurched into the sky. For the first few minutes the two men clung to straps, as if holding on for dear life would have made a difference if something catastrophic were to happen. It was stifling in the cabin and made worse by fumes leaking in from the engine compartment. They had left the doors partly open on both sides of the helicopter in order to provide some modicum of circulation. It didn't do much good. The fumes and the heat made something swell up in Peaslee's throat and he held his head near the open door in case he needed to vomit.

Far below, a city of trees and stucco and barrel tile flew by at breakneck speed. It gave way to the Intracoastal Waterway, a strip of blue water dotted with pleasure craft and sailboats. Then came the verdant strip of Orchid Island, a garden of shrubbery and manicured trees forming faux walls around the mansions and minarets that were the homes of the wealthy and well-to-do. After that, a thin run of beach the color of wheat bread. Peaslee saw a tiny woman walking on the beach, the waves crashing around her legs, her blonde hair dancing in the wind, but only for a moment. Seconds more, and the only thing Peaslee could see was the rolling blue-green swells of the open sea.

There is something about the rolling sea that can calm a man, let him lose himself in his thoughts, even lose the very thoughts themselves. There is something comforting about letting one's mind go empty. It was a luxury that Peaslee could rarely afford to indulge in, and he took what solace he could from this unexpected turn of events. At least until a hiss of static came over his headphones and Kulshedra's voice crackled in his ears. "Will you tell me how you earned the title, my friend?"

Peaslee fumbled for the switch and pulled the microphone closer to his mouth. "What are you talking about?"

"The commander, he called you Terrible Old Man, it isn't the first time I heard you called that. I heard it before, at the end of the war, back in Bundanyabba. How did you earn that nickname?"

Peaslee sighed, but made sure that the microphone wasn't

on. Kulshedra pressed on. "We have to do something to kill the time, I told you my story, now you tell me yours."

Peaslee nodded, and let Kulshedra get settled in. Then he pressed down on the microphone and began to tell his tale.

"In the summer of 1941 I took a sabbatical from my teaching duties at Miskatonic University to do a bit of research. I was interested in the psychology of group isolation and applied to the government to study aboard a ship doing an extended tour in remote areas. My goal had been to be assigned to a naval vessel touring one of the oceans. Instead, I found myself aboard the United States Coast and Geodetic Survey Ship *Maracot*, which was charting various waterways amongst the Philippines, as well as collecting examples of marine mollusks. It wasn't the most ideal of assignments; the Maracot wasn't exactly isolated. It wasn't a large ship, only two-hundred feet long with a crew of forty, five principle researchers and fifteen research assistants. The ship went to port—Zamboango—every few months for supplies, where they restocked on coal, fresh water, food and the like, and claimed any mail waiting for us there. Like I said, not ideal for my research, but then again our time at Zamboango was limited, and we were isolated in other ways. All of the crew were American, and only a handful spoke Spanish. The problem was the people of Zamboango were so far removed from Luzon—the main island—that they had never learned Spanish firsthand, they spoke a kind of Creole called Chabacano. Further south and west, around the islands we were surveying, the spoken language wasn't even related to Spanish. Still, we made ourselves understood when we had to. Money is a huge incentive, and the cache of rifles and handguns onboard didn't hurt either.

"I joined the ship in September and integrated in rather well I thought. The daily routine was mind-numbingly boring. Up at dawn, the captain would position the boat and then drop anchor. The position would then be determined and a sounding would be made. Once the location and the depth were known, the information would be recorded and a large dredge would be dropped and a square yard of the bottom would be pulled up. The stuff they pulled up with that dredge was a regular treasure trove and the only thing of interest in the early going. Most of it was sand and rock of course, bits of wood and the like. All this went right overboard. What was kept were the shells, both inhabited and uninhabited. Each day a menagerie of things like clams, scallops, snails, and crabs. There were other things as well: snails without shells, and things that looked like snails but weren't, and buckets full of starfish and things of the like. These things came up in all shapes, sizes and colors. On occasion an octopus was brought up and would scramble out of the dredge and onto the deck. This would cause some excitement. Octopuses are rather intelligent and crafty individuals, capable of eluding capture and even escaping from buckets, jars and the like. More often than not an octopus would put up a good chase and then plunge overboard, leaving the researchers disappointed but happily amused.

My research meant that I spent most of my time observing the behavior of the other researchers, their assistants, and the crew. The captain, a man named Kraus—Dan Kraus— was most accommodating and genial to my research, though he fully admitted that he didn't understand the work I was undertaking. He was an oceanographer by training and a numbers man by nature. He understood mathematics, physics, the flow of currents and tides, the particles that they carried and the sediments that they produced. He had no real taste for command, and it had only fallen to him because, at thirty-two, he was the most senior member of the crew. He was even older than any of the researchers, who were all in their late twenties, working hard to make a name for themselves in foreign climes. The same could be said of all the assistants, save that they were considerably younger, working in the shadows of their seniors.

"As I said, I was observing behavior, making notes about interactions, relationships, arguments, stresses, and what worked to diffuse them, and what didn't. I had a theory, a hypothesis really, about people and the need for human interaction. I had been corresponding with Abraham Maslow at Brooklyn College. We had met at a conference and found some of our ideas congruent. So many of our colleagues were focused on the psychology of the abnormal, but we had so little understanding about what was actually normal, or even how to define normal. It was clear from our work that normal was a relative thing, and dependent on a variety of circumstances. Maslow thought of things in terms of needs. There were undeniable physiological requirements needed to sustain life: water, food, sleep, and the like. Then there was the need for certain securities: property, resources, employment—actions that supplied access to resources. Beyond these physical things there were more abstract needs: friendship, family, intimacy, achievement, creativity, and the like. Maslow and I agreed on all these things, and a generalized hierarchical structure, but wondered how they expressed themselves in different cultures and subcultures. I was particularly interested in how things worked amongst groups that were temporarily isolated from the main for extended periods of time.

"Making my notes required me to be on deck watching the men work. The tasks they had set for themselves were not easy, and the tropical heat bordered on brutal. The men went shirtless, the sweat glistening off their youthful skin as taut muscles worked to haul in the sounding lines and the dredges. This was hard work and the crew stood side-by-side with the researchers to make sure that the schedule for the day was maintained. Only a handful of men did not participate. This included the pilot, Paiva; the cook, Denning; and two deckhands, Browning and Chapman, who were rather adept with rod and rifle and thus kept our little ship supplied with fresh meat and the occasional forage of wild fruits: mangos, rambutans, chicos, and star fruit. These two would take out the launch just after breakfast and return loaded down with fodder well before dusk.

"This was our routine, for what it was, and it deviated rather little from day to day. There were the occasional encounters with locals in their small bangka canoes, or the larger paraw with sails and outriggers, stocked with friendly, hard-working men out for a day of fishing or heading to market. Sightings of larger fishing boats—paraos—or even larger balanguays used for trading were less common. Rare were sightings of traditional war craft known as lanongs. In mid-November, one of the crew spied something on the horizon and the captain brought out his field glasses. He handed them to me and I saw a large, dark object steaming out of sight, light glinting off of its metallic hull. It was too far out for me to note any identifying marks, but Kraus frowned when he took the glasses back from me.

'Japanese,' he said, 'a gunboat.'

'Aren't they a little out of their territory?'

'The Japanese have an interesting concept of territorial rights of late.'

He left it at that, but posted a man to watch whenever we had a view of the open sea.

"It was in late November that I began to feel particularly foul. I was running a fever and my joints began to ache. On the deck, I became light-headed and took a tumble. In a matter of minutes I was confined to quarters and dosed with quinine for a rather nasty bout of malaria. When I finally came to my senses the ship had moved further south, and begun work around some island in the Sulu Sea, I don't know its name, I don't even know if it had one. There was a small village on one side, it couldn't have held more than a dozen families. We stopped in with gifts and to make our peaceful intentions clear. All was going as expected until Kraus brought out his charts and indicated exactly where we were going to be working. The village elder seemed rather concerned with a small embayment on the far side of the island. None of us spoke the local dialect, but thankfully there was a young woman who spoke a smattering of Spanish. It was she who explained things to our cook, Paiva, who then translated for us into English.

"The bay, it seemed, was merely the open water portion of a large mangrove forest that dominated most of the island. It was considered sacred to the villagers who said that a siyokoy, a kind of merman, dwelt there. When Paiva said the word 'siyokoy' the young woman shook her head and corrected the cook. I heard her use the words 'El Viejo Terrible', which Paiva translated as 'The Great Old One'. Kraus nodded his head and promised to steer clear of the region, but even through my lingering fever I knew that Kraus had no such intention.

"We started work at the point that marked the northern boundary of the sacred bay, and then worked our way clockwise around the island. As we suspected, the locals kept an eye on us with a fishing boat stationed a discreet distance from our own. This made Kraus nervous and he warned the crew and scientific staff to be on guard and remain reserved. He didn't want to give our observers any reason to get excited.

"This was somewhat prescient on his part, for on the fourth day of exploration, as we approached the other side of the sacred bay, the dredge came up and discharged its contents onto the sorting tray. It was mostly the usual bits of detritus, sand, rock and shells with a few live things with claws and fins with too few or too many legs, crawling or flopping about. The young men scrambled to grab what they could and scoop them into buckets for examination. This was not as easy as it sounded. The crabs had claws and could aggressively defend themselves, and some of the fish had razor fins and spines, some of which were rumored to be poisonous. So, gloved and armed with tongs, the dredged material was picked through by trained eyes and prizes were collected for future examination and classification. It was just after the cull was finished and the tray was to be dumped that an order to hold was shouted out by one of the primaries. The professor, a rather boring ichthyologist named Agar, came down from his perch, casually put on a pair of gloves and reached into the remaining debris. He grabbed onto something and then pulled a rather large and long object from within. At first I thought it was a stick with a large root mass at the base, and indeed it did look like two entwined branches of the mangroves that lined the shore. But it wasn't. It was a fossil of some sort, two limb bones encased in a matrix of coral, and the root mass was nothing of the sort. It was an articulated claw, with five digits in various states of integrity, one of which resembled nothing so much as a human thumb.

"There was the beginning of a low uproar amongst the staff, but Agar nixed it immediately with a harsh shush. He wrapped the specimen in a rag and whisked it away below deck where it could be examined more thoroughly, he was followed by the other doctors and the assistants. I was interested of course, fascinated really, as was the rest of the crew, but I, like them, knew that the laboratory was little more than a glorified galley.

We couldn't all fit, and there was no sense trying. Besides, I had seen something like that before, back home, not in Arkham, but in Innsmouth. And it had been a hell of a lot fresher.

"A few hours later Chapman and Browning came back with enough grouper to feed us all. Paiva seemed thrilled and set about making rice as a complement to the catch while the men cleaned the fish, preparing them for going on the grills that occupied a portion of the starboard side of the ship. Browning dipped into stores for some salt and pepper to season the meat, as well as some onions and peppers that some men liked to add to the rice which Paiva usually only did with a bit of butter and garlic.

"When the dinner bell rang the researchers came up from their studies and joined us. There is little in this world that can keep a man from a fine meal and a drink, particularly after a hard day's work. We sat there on the stern of the ship feasting on the meaty fish, most of us laughing and joking. It was, as I said, my task to make observations of the crew, and it was in this capacity that I noted that there were a minority amongst us who were not celebrating the end of the day. The researchers, those who had come up from below deck, were rather quiet, almost reserved. It was then I noticed that Agar had stopped eating. He had instead retrieved from one of the fish a pectoral fin. He had just pulled the limb away from the body and begun flexing the fleshy bit back and forth. He seemed intrigued by it, the flexibility of the structure, and the number of rays that comprised it, the flesh that bound it all together. Then I saw him do a most curious thing. He took the fin in one hand and then held it up in the air, letting the dying sunlight filter through. Then he held up his own hand behind that fin and stretched the fingers out in the strangest of manners. Then a look came over his face, a look that I thought could only be an expression of understanding, laced with awe. I lowered my head, for I knew. I like to think that there was a chance it did not have to end as it did, that if only Agar had reacted with fear rather than awe, then maybe I could have persuaded them, and we could have avoided what was to come.

"After we finished the meal and cleaned up, the senior

researchers called a meeting with Captain Kraus. The gist of the meeting was that they all agreed that they had made a significant discovery of a heretofore unknown species of marine amphibian, likely extinct for eons, but critical to the understanding of the prehistoric history of the world. The dominant currents would suggest that the fossil had come from the freshwaters that fed the sacred bay, and that if any more such specimens—the rest of the skeleton, or something similar—were to be found, then it was going to be in the bay and its tributaries. It would be a shame to let superstition stand in the way of science. I remember the words, 'This is a bad idea,' leaving my lips but I'm sure they fell on deaf ears. Within the hour the plan was formulated and our fate was sealed. I recall voicing my objections one more time, but I was reminded that despite my age and credentials, I wasn't actually part of the science team or the crew. I was an outsider without an actual say in the direction the *Maracot* went or what lines of research it pursued. I nodded and resigned myself to the inevitable.

"The captain waited until after the local boat withdrew and the sun went down before he ordered the crew on deck. They took up oars and push poles and with a unity of effort they slowly and quietly moved the *Maracot* into the bay. They kept her moving, while the scientists and their assistants used every dredge they had onboard to begin scouring the bottom for their precious samples.

"With everybody occupied, nobody saw as I slipped away into the hold, nobody heard as I smashed the lock on the gun cabinet and took a pistol and a box of ammunition. I loaded the gun and placed it inside a waterproof bag. While I was there, I grabbed some cans of water and provisions and threw them in the bag as well. Carefully, I went back up on deck and stowed my bag in an out-of-the-way spot. I bided my time and waited for the researchers to find something of interest; it didn't take long. I watched with unfeigned interest as another mass of bone and coral was pulled up and everybody rushed in to take a look. That's when I grabbed my bag, threw it in the launch and then untied it from the *Maracot*. I let it drift away before I began poling away from the ship that had been my home for the last several months. In a minute or so I was far enough away to be out of the glow of the ship's lights and outside of the point that marked the limit of the sacred bay.

"It was then that I heard the first shout of alarm. At first I thought they had finally noticed the launch was gone, but then a lone voice of alarm turned into a chorus of panic. I heard several large splashes, and some thuds that indicated something of weight hitting the deck or the side of the ship. I heard a man scream, first in fear but then in agony. It lingered in the air for a moment and then there was a spate of silence.

"It was then that I realized what I had feared had come to fruition and I started up the launch's engine to flee. The engine started and the launch lurched forward but then suddenly stopped and tilted to the starboard, throwing me off balance and slamming me into the steering column. It took me a moment to recover my senses. The darkness made things more difficult and I scuttled my way backwards into the bulkhead. At the stern of the boat something large and inhuman crawled aboard. It was easily twice my size, and it bristled with spines and fins. Its gills flashed in the starlight and its black, dead eyes stared at me without a hint of emotion. The very weight of the thing kept the bow elevated and things slid past me in the darkness. I scrambled my hand about blindly and locked my fingers down around the first thing I found. It was the bag of provisions that I had put together. I pulled it to my chest and worked my hand inside, desperately searching for the firearm I had put inside. I looked back toward the stern and the creature took a step forward. I screamed as the whole thing came into view and the true monstrosity of it weighed on my mind. I screamed again in terror as my hand wrapped around the grip of the pistol. It roared back at me, its mouth a cage of semi-translucent teeth, like icicles curved into its mouth. Its fetid breath wafted over me and, without even taking the gun out of the bag, I aimed as best I could and pulled the trigger.

"The bag tore and smoked and I saw something explode on the creature's face. It screamed and reeled backwards in agony. As it did, it grabbed the steering column and tore the wheel away. Then it was gone, with only a trail of blood and slime to prove that it had ever been there. I watched, helpless, as the launch motored away from the Maracot. Even over the engine I could hear the screams as the crew was slaughtered, but I could do nothing to help them. I just huddled in the corner as the engine drove me out of the bay and toward the deep blue sea.

"It was four days before I was found by a passing American warship. I was delirious from the sun, dehydration and malaria. I had run out of food and water the first day, and in my rush had forgotten to even get any quinine. I had no idea at the time but the warship was just one of the many evacuating the Philippines as the Japanese Navy overran the islands and the American forces fled. As I said I was delirious, and when they questioned me about what had happened I could say nothing but the name that woman had said on the island to name the gods she feared, 'El Viejo Terrible', which the soldiers on board translated as 'The Terrible Old Man'.

"It was a week before I was able to sit up and speak coherently, and by then it no longer mattered what I told them my name was. I was listed in all the accounts and all the logs as the Terrible Old Man, and the name stuck."

Ophel, who had remained quiet this whole time, put his hand on his microphone. "What did the rescuers say when you told them your story?"

Peaslee shook his head. "I never did, I never was asked. There were no questions about what had happened to the launch or to the Maracot, it was just assumed that we had encountered the Japanese, fought back and been taught a very awful lesson. I didn't see the need to tell them differently. I had seen my share of people who had seen the terrible truths of this world and chosen to speak of them, my father among them, and I had no desire to be ridiculed or branded a madman. It was better just to remain silent and let the truth die with the Maracot."

Ophel closed his eyes and seemed to reflect on what Peaslee had said. For his part Peaslee just stared at the ocean, watching the seemingly endless sea roll beneath him, its secrets forever hidden below its surface.

PART 5: BABEL

The tower stood alone and lonely, a monument to man's defiance of the very forces of nature. It was a massive steel triangle, two hundred feet on a side, supported by three huge caisson legs. On the northwest side, there were three dish antennae pointed back toward land. Above these, on the deck itself, were three spherical neoprene domes that housed various forms of tracking radar. As the helicopter banked over and around the platform, Peaslee could see that the deck was about twenty feet thick and the sides were loaded with small, motorized launches hanging from winches. On the deck, in the shadow of the spheres, were a few large equipment boxes and several control panels, but otherwise the space was clear and marked off as a landing zone for the large helicopters that ferried staff and supplies back and forth. The chopper landed with a heavy thump and then in an instant the door slid open and both Kulshedra and Peaslee were ushered out onto the deck. They passed a handful of crewmen and several crates that were quickly loaded onto the aircraft. The two investigators barely cleared the outer circle when the rotor on the helicopter revved up again and took to the sky once more. Hands went onto both of their heads and gently forced them toward an opening beneath the central sphere. A voice yelled in their ears. "Gentlemen, welcome aboard the *Babel*. I'm Curtis, the deck officer. Captain Best is waiting for you in his office. Once you're done with him I'll get you settled into your quarters for the next few days."

Peaslee shot the man a look, "We were told this would be a quick turnaround, that we would be on the next helicopter back to the base."

Curtis pointed up at the helicopter that had just dropped them off. "Change of weather," he shouted. "That was the last helicopter until the storm clears us. But don't worry, there isn't a storm that the *Babel* and Bauer can't handle."

Peaslee and Kulshedra looked at each other with a sense of foreboding as they ducked under the bulkhead and entered into the bowels of the *Babel*.

The first thing they noticed about the interior of the structure was the sound, a deep bone-penetrating thrum that made their fillings hurt. Then there was the smell. It was primarily of diesel fuel, but there was also a chemical odor that reminded Peaslee of disinfectant. Beneath that was the stench of human beings, of sweat and blood and the myriad of commensal organisms that dwell on their skins and in their hair. But there was also something else, something dry and musky, an animal smell. It reminded Peaslee of being at the zoo, or in a house infested by rats. The corridors were drab grey steel, ten feet on each side, with rails on both walls and rubber mats on the floor. Down the center of the ceiling, a double line of long fluorescent bulbs ran. They flickered on and off slightly out of time with the thrum of the engine, like a sick man breathing out of rhythm.

Peaslee and Kulshedra followed Curtis, their boots echoing against the metal walls. It was terribly hot in those halls, stifling almost, and the air was barely moving. Peaslee hated it, but noticed that Kulshedra seemed unaffected; if anything he seemed invigorated.

Kulshedra noticed Peaslee's look and shrugged. "Reminds me of Jerusalem. But there, of course, it is a dry heat."

In mere moments they were at the captain's office. It was little more than another drab metal hallway, except that it had a back wall, and a window, and a ceiling fan in place of one of the light banks. There was a desk, standard issue grey-green metallic slab, and behind it was, supposedly, Captain Best. He was a slab of an officer, and Peaslee supposed he was like many other military men who found themselves in command— proficient in what he had once done, but then promoted beyond his capabilities. Peaslee knew just by looking at him; Best may have been the officer in charge but he wasn't the one making decisions.

There was the expected exchange of pleasantries, which revealed Best's southern accent. Peaslee thought he detected a hint of condescension in Best's voice. It may have been because one of his men was being investigated, or because Peaslee was a Yankee, or because Kulshedra was working for Mossad, but it didn't matter. Not really.

"I'm told by Commander Warrington that you suspect my man Bauer of being a Nazi." Now his voice was colored with incredulity. "I've got to tell you, I have heard some hair-brained ideas in my time, but this—this is utterly ridiculous. I've known the man for years. He's as American as the next man." Best's eyes darted to Kulshedra. "You know what I mean."

Peaslee made a supplicating gesture with his hands. "You are probably right, but Bauer's name has been tied to some active investigations both by Mossad and here at home." Peaslee lied, he was good at it. "We just need to ask him some questions, clear up a few things, that's all."

Bauer looked down and tapped his fingers on his desk. Then he looked up at Peaslee and pointed in a rather friendly manner. "You can interview Bauer, ask him anything you want. Figure out the truth of things. But your friend," he glanced over at Kulshedra, "he has no jurisdiction here. He can listen in, but he doesn't go anywhere near Bauer, he doesn't get to ask any questions." He smiled in a rather unpleasant way. "This is my command, those are my rules."

Peaslee nodded ever so slightly. "Understood. Now if you don't mind we would like to get a drink, maybe a sandwich, and then I would appreciate seeing Bauer."

Best seemed pleased with Peaslee's acknowledgement that he was in charge. "Mister Curtis, show our guests some of our famous *Babel* courtesy, and then ask Mister Bauer to meet us in Room Six at 1600."

"Yes sir," answered Curtis, who led the two men away, back into the hot metal halls that all looked the same.

The sandwiches were bad. Salty meat, cheese that was mostly something else, and wilted lettuce, wedged between pieces of tasteless, spongy bread. The iced tea wasn't good either. It was tepid water into which some sugar and brown powder had been poured. The powder may have once been something green and leafy and related in some distant fashion to Camellia, but boiling, filtration, evaporation and vacuum sealing, along with various other esoteric chemical processes and contaminants had transformed it into something else entirely, something that was little more than a bitter culinary additive. It made Peaslee long for his mother's Darjeeling or his sister's coffee. Why was it that the military always seemed to view food preparation as a kind of punishment? There were cooks—not chefs, cooks—who could work wonders with the worst cuts of meat, a handful of spices, and a bag of beans. But for one reason or another the military chose to ignore such people in favor of others that they could force into producing mass quantities of nutritive pablum. To the military mind, cooking wasn't art, it was just another process to be fed raw material, standardized, where possible mechanized, and if it could also be used as a kind of corrective action, so much the better. No wonder so many soldiers packed on the pounds after retiring, they were just rediscovering the fact that food could be delicious.

Kulshedra broke the silence first. "We need to prove that Bauer isn't who he says he is, that he's been replaced by someone else."

"By whom?" asked Peaslee.

"What?"

Peaslee closed his eyes in frustration. "I've bought into your idea that Bauer could have been replaced down in South America, it's a possibility that I'm willing to entertain. But I'm also trying to figure out who and why? He's too young to be a member of Hitler's Reich. He could be a child of the first generation, born into it, raised to believe in the master race. It's a stretch but possible, but why Bauer? Why infiltrate the American military? To what point? And then why maintain contact with Simon Orne? It doesn't make sense."

Kulshedra sighed. "When it first started, did the Reich make sense? That was its greatest strength. It didn't make sense. No one took it seriously, in fact they wholly underestimated it, and laughed at it even. Let the petty little monsters spout their disgusting rhetoric all they wanted. It didn't harm anyone, no one but fanatics believed anyway. It took years for people to wake up and see what had happened to their country, but by then it was too late. The monsters had taken charge and the rest of the population had no choice but to do what they said. What if Bauer is just the beginning? What if what we've stumbled on here is just a tiny seed in a very big plan, one cog in a vast secret machine?"

Peaslee frowned. "I don't doubt there is something happening, but you work for Mossad, it's your job to find Nazis. You might subconsciously see them everywhere."

"And you, Colonel Dr. Wingate Peaslee, who do you work for now? What is it they have trained you to look for? And how does that cloud your vision?"

Peaslee bussed his table and came back with a cup of coffee that was worse than the tea. "What do you want me to ask?"

PART 6: QUESTIONS IN THE LIGHT

Room Six wasn't so much a room as an accidental box, an implied space, made out of the walls of the multiple corridors that surrounded it. It had no windows and only one door. They hadn't even bothered to paint it. They had just screwed a fluorescent light fixture onto the ceiling and thrown a table and some chairs inside. On the inside, on the wall next to the door, there was a speaker box that also housed a microphone. Peaslee noted that most of the rooms they'd seen so far had such boxes, and he'd been informed that they were connected to the bridge, and also to the radio room.

Kulshedra sat in the radio room, alone save for the on-duty communications officer. Peaslee sat in Room Six on one side of the table, facing the door as Curtis brought in Frederick Bauer. Something about Bauer made Peaslee uneasy; he was the antithesis of everything Peaslee had expected. Peaslee had thought the man would have been some paragon of Aryan ideals: tall, blue-eyed, blonde, fair, thin, and muscular. Bauer was none of these things. He was only a little over five feet tall, and more than a little overweight. Peaslee would have used the word portly. His hair was dark, almost jet black, and rather unkempt for a military man. His skin was far from pale, and reminded Peaslee of some olive-toned Sicilians he had met during the war. His eyes were tiny shards of obsidian that seemed like they could cut you just as easily as they could look at you. He smiled as he entered the room and Peaslee noticed that his teeth were small, and far too white. He moved slowly, carefully, like he was wary of something. And then there was that damned animal smell.

"Mister Bauer, please come in, have a seat." Peaslee busied himself with Kulshedra's files, shuffling the pages around as if with purpose, but really just making himself look aloof.

"Chief Engineer," said Bauer.

Peaslee looked up and snapped back, "What?"

"Chief Engineer, not Mister, everybody calls me Chief."

"I see, of course. Have a seat."

Bauer slid a chair out. It screeched across the floor, and then squeaked a little more as he sat down.

Peaslee shuffled through some more papers, mumbling to himself. "Two-two-two San Juan Boulevard."

"That's my cousin's place," Bauer said spontaneously.

"Eh?"

Bauer stuttered, "In Argentina, Cordoba."

Peaslee put a finger on a page, "Yes, yes. That's right. Nice place?"

Bauer nodded slightly. "A little European in style for my tastes, but clean and warm. It's a good neighborhood, in the heart of the city."

"So you've been there?"

"Yes."

"Just before your parents died, the year before you joined the military?"

"Yes."

"Why?"

Bauer made an empty gesture. "Why did I go to Argentina? Why did my parents die? Why did I join the military? What exactly do you want to know Mister … I'm sorry I don't know your name."

"Colonel Dr. Peaslee, and yes to all of that."

Bauer leaned back and ran a hand through his unkempt hair. "Well Colonel Dr. Peaslee, since you've asked so nicely I'll tell you the truth." There was contempt in his voice. "I went to Argentina to visit relatives where I drank excessively. While I was on vacation my parents were killed by a drunk driver. Ironic, isn't it? I joined the military to lose myself in routine and try to find some purpose in my life." Bauer chuckled. "Seriously, why am I here?"

Peaslee tapped the file. "Suspicions have been raised. There was a man involved in international trade. Turns out he was once a high level Nazi. Invoices were found in his possession. Your name was on several of them. You were shipping plants to him."

"I ship *Aspidistras* all over the world. It's an amazing plant, very tolerant of low sunlight, dry soil, poor air quality and a wide range of temperatures. I've developed a variety that is very tolerant of saline waters. We grow it here. It gives the men a place to go, to clear their heads, to feel clean, to be one with the natural world. Here, on and in this engineered monstrosity that we call *Babel*, that can be very important, necessary."

"You sound like a beatnik."

"No, I'm just a realist. I may be an engineer, but I know that people can't live disconnected from the natural world." He fumbled his words a little. "I mean they can, it's been done before, but the results were catastrophic."

"Why were you shipping *Aspidistras* to a Nazi?"

"Simon Orne is not a Nazi."

Peaslee held his breath. "I never said Simon Orne was a Nazi, I never even mentioned his name."

"Yes, yes you did."

"No, I didn't."

Bauer sighed. "It doesn't matter. Simon Orne isn't a Nazi."

"What was he then?"

"The truth?"

"I'm going to find out sooner or later."

Bauer mulled the statement over. "I'm not so sure. Did you come here alone?"

"Yes."

"You're a poor liar. Everybody knows that the helicopter brought two men."

"My assistant."

"Another lie."

Somehow, the tables had turned. If he had ever been in control, Peaslee had somehow lost it. "You were going to tell me the truth."

"I am, it doesn't matter now. Chances are we won't be getting out of here alive."

"Is that a threat?"

"There is a threat, but it isn't from me."

Peaslee was growing frustrated. "You said Orne wasn't a Nazi, what did you mean by that?"

"Exactly what I said. Simon Orne isn't a Nazi, he is actually a wizard, a member of the Brotherhood of the Dragon. He is hundreds of years old. He has been reported to have been killed at least three times that I know of. The last time was in 1928."

"We must be talking about two different men. This Simon Orne was an archeologist for the Reich, I have a report here that he was just killed a few months ago."

"Who told you that? Was it your so-called assistant? I doubt it very much."

"You make him sound like some kind of bogeyman, like Rasputin."

"Orne is much worse than Rasputin ever was. He may have worked for Hitler, scoured the planet for artifacts, sent men and women to the concentration camps, but he never bought into all that master race nonsense. "

Peaslee shook his head slightly. "There's a special term for people who worked for the Reich, who benefited from it, even though they didn't believe in it."

"Oh, what is that?"

"Nazi," Peaslee spat the word out of his mouth. He slammed the files shut and stood up. "Chief Engineer Frederick Bauer, I'm arresting you on suspicion of espionage and treason. This facility does not have a stockade, so you will be confined to this room while your quarters are searched. Then I will make arrangements for you to be transferred to the mainland where you will be held by military police while we try to figure out who and what you are."

"You won't be happy."

Peaslee stood up and walked out the door. "I haven't been happy in a very long time." He didn't look back as he ordered Curtis to secure the room.

PART 7: BEFORE THE MAELSTROM

Peaslee, Kulshedra and Captain Best stood on the deck of *Babel* as the wind whipped in off the Atlantic Ocean, driving the waves into a frothing frenzy. To the south the once blue skies had been swallowed by a roiling darkness. Even miles away they could hear the roaring winds and see the storm bands racing across the sky like the tendrils of some titanic beast.

Best pointed south and yelled above the dull roar. "That, gentlemen, is Dana, sustained winds of one hundred and sixty-five miles per hour, generating waves more than forty feet high. That makes her a Force Twelve Hurricane, one of the most dangerous storms ever seen. And she's heading right toward us."

"And how do we get out of the way?" begged Peaslee.

Best laughed. "We don't, we stay here and we keep *Babel* operational. That's the job, Colonel. It's what we signed up to do." He turned back to look at Peaslee and Kulshedra. "There's the two of you, me, Bauer, Curtis, Schulman and Strauss. I know that you think that Bauer is a criminal, but he's the best engineer I've ever known, and he's our best chance of keeping *Babel* afloat, and the rest of us alive." Best let that sink in. "Let's get through this and then, when it's all over, you can have Bauer, but right now I need him to do his job."

"Fine," conceded Peaslee, "but we are going to search Bauer's rooms and this so-called greenhouse of his. He is to stay clear of these areas."

"Agreed," said Best. "At the same time you two are going to help us in the best way you can."

"How is that?" queried Kulshedra.

"When you're done searching, make sure the shutters are secure. After that—" Best paused and looked out at the raging seas. "After that stay out of our way and do as you're told, and we just might get through this."

As they retreated back inside of *Babel*, the seas boiled with a terrible froth while the black wind howled in the distance.

Bauer's room was merely the terminus of a hallway with a door fitted into the front and a small, slotted window in the rear. A framed sheet of metal was hinged to the wall and supported by two outer legs. A thin mattress with some folded bedding turned it into a bed. The whole thing could be folded up against the wall if need be. Along both walls there were similar such constructs; one side had a desk with a small bench, while the other held several sets of shelves filled with books beneath which was stowed a large, well-worn footlocker.

While Peaslee looked at the books, Kulshedra pulled the footlocker out and lifted it onto the bed. It took a little effort, but the stuck latch finally came loose and the lid lifted up with a creak. Kulshedra rummaged around inside. There were some clothes, a cap, a tin of shoeshine, a spare pair of boots, and an address book. Kulshedra flipped through it and spied something interesting.

"Orne's name is in here, along with dozens of other names all over the world. Control is going to be absolutely thrilled." He waved it in the air as if it were a trophy. "Have you found anything?"

Peaslee made a noncommittal noise. "These are all engineering manuals and design documents. There's nothing here that you wouldn't expect ..." His voice trailed off as he reached out and pulled a black volume from the stacks. "Well this is a surprise."

Kulshedra stepped over, "What is it?"

"Something I've never actually seen before—*Die Offenbarungen des Yig*, roughly The Revelations of Yig. I actually thought it to be apocryphal. There's a passing reference to it in *Cultes des Goules*, the central text of some European faith involving serpents. The believers professed it to have originated in the pre-human civilization of serpent men."

"Written in German?"

Peaslee winced as he flipped through the pages. "This one is in German and English. Not all faiths are as strict about translations as the Hebrews and the Muslims. Look at the Bible, how many languages is that in now? And services are held in Latin, but Biblical scholars believe the book was assembled in

Greek from texts from a number of dialects including Hebrew and Aramaic." He turned the book over in his hand. "Don't even get me started on the rather sordid history of the *Necronomicon*."

"So what is our young Mister Bauer doing with it?"

"An excellent question, but I think something is becoming clear."

"What is that?"

"Bauer may fall more in my purview than yours."

"You mean he isn't a Nazi?"

"Perhaps, perhaps not. Let us not get ahead of ourselves." He tucked the book in his pocket. "I still want to look at the greenhouse." He looked about the room. "Where's his kit?"

Kulshedra looked around confused. "His what?"

Peaslee flipped through the trunk frantically. "His toiletry kit, a razor, shaving cream, soap, shampoo. Where is it?"

Kulshedra scanned once more. "It's not here, he probably keeps it in the shower room."

Peaslee gave Kulshedra an incredulous look. "I find that highly unlikely." He flipped through the footlocker one more time. "What kind of soldier doesn't have a toiletry kit?"

"One who doesn't need one," joked Kulshedra.

Peaslee didn't say a word, he just went over to the window, found the crank and rolled the storm shutters closed. Outside, the waves began to crash against the legs in a thunderous beat that almost drowned out the droning hum of the engines.

The greenhouse occupied a corner of the lower level with long, slotted windows of tempered glass along the outer walls. The contents of the room were not what Peaslee had expected. The greenhouses he was familiar with were complex collections of various species, layered to take full advantage of the various intensities of sun and shade. Bauer's creation was something else completely; it was a room of nothing but *Aspidistras*, row upon row of them. Bauer had filled the floor with pots, and above these had laid out tables full of the same, and on the wall the shelves were laden as well. There were hundreds of pots and in them, hundreds of plants. It took a moment but Peaslee realized that the plants were not simply stacked willy-nilly, but rather were subtly arranged in a sublime spiral that radiated out from a single central point. There—in the vertex of the entire room—sat a piece of brown rock about seven inches across. It had been squared off at one point, but now the edges were ragged and chipped in several places. The roots of several plants had grown over it, entwining it in their tendrils as if they were somehow enamored with it, or perhaps with some power that resided within. As he studied it he could make out some rough markings, as if it had once been inscribed with some décor that had been worn away with the passing of years that had stretched into centuries, if not eons. Even so, he thought that he could make out some details: a serpent perhaps, the head of a crocodile, and a cluster of markings that he thought for sure were meant to be stars.

Kulshedra found the stone vile, and sneered in disgust at it. "More evidence of your depraved cult, my friend." He clambered through the pots and dislodged the stone from where it resided. "We should destroy this immediately."

Peaslee took it from his hands, "Why the rush? I'll admit that I'm more suspicious than ever of Bauer, but that doesn't give us the right to confiscate or destroy private property." He worked his way back into the pots and tried his best to put the piece of rock back where it belonged.

When he finished, he brushed some debris from his pants and headed for the window. "Would you mind giving me a hand?"

Together, they shuttered the room from the elements. With each crank of the handle the window shrank in size, and the light grew dimmer and dimmer. With one last turn the room went dark. Peaslee sighed, realizing that the very process of trying to save the greenhouse was at the same time cutting it off from the very source of its life. How many days could the plants in this room survive without light?

The howling winds seemed to grow more terrible with each passing minute.

Dinner wasn't much to speak of. The radioman, Strauss, had done what he could, but it was little more than dumping bags into pots and dishing out a slab of grey meat covered in a salty brown gravy with a lump of lukewarm mashed potatoes and some lima beans on the side. It was just the two of them and Best, eating at a long Formica table in a large steel box with bad lights and ceiling fans that barely moved and did little to cool the place down. The only thing that made the meal passable was the bottle of scotch that Best had brought.

"Strictly against policy. No booze on the boat so to speak. I took this off a helicopter pilot who spent the night and thought it would be fun to throw a party with some of the deck crew. Normally I would just dump it down the drain, but it turned out to be a rather decent vintage." He took a sip from his tin cup. "It might also help us get through the next twelve hours."

"Where's Bauer?" asked Peaslee.

"Doing what he needs to do to keep us functional. All of the windows have been shuttered, the antennae have been secured, and the boats have been loaded with emergency supplies. You'll both be issued emergency bags—food, water, first aid kit, life jacket, flare gun, et cetera." He took another drink. "We're going to try and ride this out. We're sitting on top of three legs. One houses the generator, one the fuel tank, and the third is empty. Under normal conditions this isn't a problem, but these aren't normal conditions. Bauer's going to have to keep us anchored and balanced as well. He's going to do that by flooding the third leg and partially flooding the other two. The fuel tank is double-hulled, but the generator room isn't. It can only be flooded so deep, any more and the power will go. But that might not be enough to keep us balanced. We lose one leg and the others might not be enough to keep us in place. If that happens, we might have to blow the clamps and set ourselves adrift. In forty-foot seas, that is going to be anything but pleasant." He took another sip. "Finish your meal, it'll be the last hot food you'll have for a while. Get a shower and then get some rest. Once the storm hits, you'll be too wound up to sleep. After twelve hours or so you'll start to get tired. Coffee and food will help, but only for so long. You'll start becoming inattentive, make mistakes, and doze off. You will crash. When that happens, and it will, make sure you're in a safe and secure place."

Kulshedra took a shot. "Where would that be?"

"There's a room off command, reinforced structure,

bulkheads, airtight. We only go there if the structure fails."

"How will we know?"

"You'll know, but just in case you're a little dense there's a claxon that would wake the dead."

PART 8: THE FALL OF BABEL

There was no claxon. Despite this, Peaslee awoke with a jolt. The room was off-kilter and he could feel the whole construct shifting slightly counter-clockwise. It threw him out of bed and against the wall. He bounced off and fell toward the floor. He caught himself against the bed, but still slammed his shoulder into a piece of the frame. He staggered to his feet and almost fell against the door. He held onto the frame as he swung out into the hall, the whole of everything seesawing up and down, left and right. It was like being in a funhouse, except the metal was screeching and the wind was howling like a wounded dog.

Peaslee called for Kulshedra, but there was no answer. He pounded on the door, and when the floor shifted once more he grabbed onto the handle and swung inside. The room was the mirror image of his own, with one small but important difference—there was nobody inside. Kulshedra was not there, and based on the well-made bed, he hadn't slept there at all.

"Damn it," Peaslee cursed as he fell back into his own room. He grabbed the bag that Best had given him, and was thankful that he had slept with his boots on. He chuckled at that. He hadn't done that for years, hadn't had to do that for years. He couldn't remember the last time he had roughed it, but he knew the rules for filling out expense reports and claiming his per diem. He'd been too comfortable for too long, and he was going to pay for it now. None of that mattered now though, where the hell was Kulshedra?

Where the hell was everybody?

He ran down the hall, careening off the walls as the floor violently swayed beneath his feet. It didn't feel like they were floating free, it felt like they were spinning, slowly but definitely rotating about, and dragging something large in the process. Down the hall he went, battling for every yard, every step. It was hard enough but then the lights flickered and Peaslee realized that the generator wasn't running, he hadn't noticed over the sound of the wind. The lights flickered again and Peaslee saw the dim light seeping in through the seams in the walls. There was water too, he ran his hand along the wall and tasted it. Freshwater, rain, well at least we aren't sinking, he thought to himself, at least not yet.

He came to a turn. There was something on the floor ahead, something large, but in the flickering light he couldn't make it out until he staggered his way down, nearly falling on top of it. It was a body, a bloody body in a uniform. An officer's uniform. The man inside was battered and bloodied but still recognizable as Captain Best, and amazingly enough he was still breathing.

Peaslee rolled him over and lifted his head. Blood sprayed from his mouth as Best coughed and tried to speak. "Ba-Ba-Bauer." He managed to spit out.

"Bauer did this?"

Best shook his head weakly. "Protect Bauer, protect *Babel*."

Peaslee nodded, "From whom? Best, who did this?"

Best pulled something from his waist and shoved it into Peaslee's hand, his sidearm. Best looked at Peaslee and pleaded with his eyes. "Kulshedra, he's not what he seems, he wants to destroy *Babel*, he's uncoupling the legs." Then he coughed again, violently this time. A spasm travelled down the man's body. He convulsed, flopping about on the floor while Peaslee tried in vain to hold him still. It took a moment but he did finally settle down and grow still. Peaslee cursed and let the body gently down to the floor.

Something above shuddered and screeched. Peaslee could hear metal tearing against metal, cables whipping through the air, ventilation shafts collapsing, blowing out air with deep bellows like titanic pipe organs. A huge support beam pierced the hall just yards from where he stood. It was like a sword through the heart of a dragon and it came with a torrent of rain like hot, foaming blood. Peaslee checked the gun—Smith & Wesson Model 15, with a four-inch barrel, six shots, fully loaded. It was cold and heavy, but it felt good in his hand. It made him feel capable, like he had a chance. He stood up and moved forward down the hall, bouncing against the walls as he ran. He didn't know where he was running to, he just knew he had to run.

A few minutes in and things began to look familiar. A turn here, another there, and then suddenly he was in front of Best's office. It had to be somewhere near, just around the corner. He careened down the hall and finally found what he was looking for. He forced his way through a bent and crumpled door and into the command center. The lights were off but a yellow emergency light was on in the corner. It cast a soft glow over the room, but it was enough to see that the room had been destroyed. Someone had taken a fire axe to the panels, chopped them up until they weren't functional anymore, and then buried the weapon in the chest of Strauss, the radioman. Strauss' hands were wrapped around the handle. Peaslee supposed he had tried to pull it out before he had succumbed to his wounds. That wouldn't have helped; he would just have bled to death faster.

Peaslee checked the panels; they might not have been functional anymore, but some of the lights still flickered on. There was a section labeled Support Towers, with lights next to each number; two of these lights were red, the third was still green. "Thank goodness for small favors." Peaslee muttered.

Something fell behind a door to his right. Peaslee swung the gun in that direction as the door swung open. There was a short shadow, with a flashlight in one hand and a length of pipe in the other. It was Bauer. Peaslee took a stance and steadied the gun.

Bauer lowered the flashlight. "Don't mess around Peaslee, we don't have time for heroics. Kulshedra killed everybody else and if we don't act quickly we'll be next." Then he waved the flashlight and went back into the side room. For some reason, following some instinct he couldn't explain, Peaslee lowered the gun and followed.

The lights in the side room were on, they were weak but they were on. Bauer was packing up files into plastic bags and loading them into waterproof boxes. Even from a distance Peaslee could see that they were transcriptions of communications, but they weren't in English—they weren't in any language Peaslee could recognize, in some ways they were more like pictograms than letters.

"What did he tell you?" Bauer said to no one in particular as he shoved more pages into a bag. "That Orne was a Nazi? That I was?" He shook his head and cursed. "He used you to get here, to get to me."

Peaslee stood there in the low orange glow. "What are you? I know you aren't a Nazi, but what are you?"

Bauer slammed a ream of papers down onto the table. "I'm an American, Dr. Peaslee. First and foremost I'm an American. After what Kulshedra and his kind did to my parents I needed to make sure that someone stood up to them."

"His kind?"

Bauer was obviously annoyed. He grabbed a letter opener from the table and made sure that Peaslee saw it. Then he held up his other arm, flexing his hand open and shut. Before he could do anything to stop him, Bauer took the blade and jabbed it into his forearm. Peaslee gasped as he rotated the blade around the limb, the meat parting like fat as it cut through. To Peaslee's surprise there was very little blood, almost none at all really.

When he completed the circuit he withdrew the blade, it glistened moist in the light. "There are hundreds of us, thousands maybe." He laid the blade back down on the table. "We aren't infiltrators, we're just people, citizens, we believe in the American dream." He grabbed the fingers of the cut hand with his other hand and pulled. "We're as loyal as any other immigrant population. Maybe even more so." The flesh peeled away with a sickening, sucking sound. What was underneath was dark, glistening, and scaled. Bauer flexed it. The fingertips were clawed and there was a digit missing. "We just happen to be older than you, millions of years older."

"You're clearly kin to the inhabitants of Innsmouth, what did they call them there? Deep Ones?" Peaslee's hand made sure he knew where his gun was.

"Deep Ones? The fifth slaves? No, we aren't that old, we were the sixth slaves, bred from reptiles. We served our masters the Q'Hrell for millions of years until they retreated and went dormant. Like all the other slave races, most of us perished in the great cataclysm. Some of us survived, no more than a handful really. It took us generations just to come out of the underground shelters. Your kind were better adapted to the new ecology, you bred faster than we ever could. Still we eventually raised up a new nation for ourselves, one that rivaled yours, but when the ice came we were once again ill-prepared, and your species became the dominant one on the planet."

With the one arm bared he continued to pack the bags and waterproof containers. "We are determined to survive, several decades back we decided to reveal ourselves to President Roosevelt. He recognized that we might be valuable both against the Nazis and the Soviets. So we struck up a deal."

"Operation Paperclip."

"Something similar, they called it Project Pegasus. Do you know the myth?"

Peaslee nodded. "When Perseus cut off the head of Medusa the winged horse sprang forth from the stump. Pegasus later goes on to help the hero Bellerophon in his battle against the Chimera."

"You're classically educated, Dr. Peaslee. Do you know what happened to the other two Gorgons, Medusa's sisters?"

Peaslee shook his head.

"Everybody forgets the other two." Bauer sighed. "Pegasus is spawned by the death of Medusa, but the other Gorgons still abide. The symbolism works in multiple ways. Not all of my kind agreed with the decision to align ourselves with you Americans. Some preferred to stay hidden, others used the war to establish a new nation of our own."

"Cuba?"

"No, no. Cuba is much too prominent." He walked over to a wall with a map of the Caribbean. He pointed to a small group of islands south of Cuba. "The Cayman Islands, officially a dependency of Jamaica, but for the last decade they've slowly cut ties, isolated themselves. The British have been covering it up as best they could. Jamaica is in the process of becoming an independent nation. When that happens the Caymans will be cut free. We need to be prepared for what happens next."

"*Babel* was spying on the Caymans, these reptile men—Cuba was just a cover."

"Yes."

"And Ophel Kulshedra isn't a Mossad agent."

"No, that's probably true, but he could be working for both Israel and the Caymans."

"But I knew him during the war."

"We are a very long-lived species. Kulshedra has fought in many of your wars, not always on the winning or the right side."

"And Simon Orne, how does he fit into all of this? Was he one of you?"

"Orne, or Orme as he was first named, was part of a group called the Brotherhood of the Dragon. Men that we recruited centuries back to help us make headway in the world. We taught them science and magicks, and showed them how to defy death. They were supposed to be our agents, our allies, but they made mistakes. They lived too long in one place. People got suspicious when they noticed that they hadn't aged." He closed the top of one box and cranked the seal tight. "It was a disaster for all involved."

"So he really wasn't a Nazi."

"I told you."

"What about this?" He pulled the book out of his jacket. *"The Revelations of Yig?"*

Bauer shrugged. "Wisdom of our God, the paragon of us all. Guidance on how to live."

"And the *Aspidistras*?"

"Just a very old species of plant that has been with us for a very long time. It gives us a kind of mental comfort."

"And the rock in the garden? Why did Kulshedra want to destroy it?"

"It's old, very old. Pre-cataclysmic. There are five of them, or so legend says. Supposedly if you put them together, they will reveal some great truth."

"And what is that?"

"I'm not sure, it's just a legend. Our recorded history says that we were the sixth sentient slave species made on this planet to serve the Q'Hrell, the star-headed things that came from beyond space to inhabit the Earth. The first had been the protoplasmic shoggothim, then came the worms of the Earth.

The spiderlings were next, and after them the great cones that were stolen and used to wage war. You said you know the Deep Ones, you must also know how they were corrupted by those of R'lyeh. We came sixth, and while we seem to have endured we were also likely the greatest disappointment."

Bauer took the book from Peaslee's hands. "It's all here you know, our need to repent, to find a way to atone. Our technology wasn't like yours. We bred our workforce, made living machines, tweaked the genetics when we had to. When we knew the end was near, we were determined that our masters wouldn't be alone. That they would have someone to rely on when they finally woke up."

The door burst open, Kulshedra was suddenly there with a gun in his hand. He screamed once, "LISALL!" and then wildly opened fire.

Peaslee fell to the floor, dodging the shots, but Bauer wasn't as lucky. He took two slugs to the left shoulder, and as he spun a third struck him in his temple. He flew back and smashed into the wall. Peaslee had cover and aimed carefully. One shot and Kulshedra was hit in the chest. The double agent flew back through the door. Peaslee scrambled forward and took up a position to the side of the entrance. He could hear Kulshedra moaning as he stumbled down the shifting halls.

He meant to go after the man, but Bauer called him back. He was holding the book in his hand. "Take this, I've marked the page. Read it. Understand why we have done what we have done. All this," he waved at the documents. "Get this into the safe room and make sure they get back to Command."

Peaslee nodded. "I'll make sure Kulshedra pays."

Bauer coughed and shook his head. "Kulshedra isn't important. He's a small cog in a great machine. The United States needs these documents; it needs to know what the Caymans are planning. Nothing else matters."

Peaslee shook the man's hand and agreed. "Thank you. I'll tell them you died a hero."

Bauer smiled weakly. "What else could I do, I'm an American."

Then his eyes closed and Peaslee was left alone. He grabbed

the book and the last crate and lugged it over to the safe room. It wasn't easy, and given the motion of the station it was more like pushing the box three steps forward only to have it slide back two. It was a task for Sisyphus, made all the more difficult by Peaslee having to be on guard against another attack. What should have been two minutes took ten, and after all of it he was battered and bruised and gasping for air.

His chest heaving, he wondered briefly about what Kulshedra could be up to but just then he heard a buzzing sound that came from the active light panel. The last remaining green light went out, and a red one came on instead. The long-awaited claxon finally sounded and a terrible wrenching sound shook the whole station. He grabbed the door and slammed it shut. He spun the interior valve wheel and sealed himself inside. The whole room shifted as he looked around. There were a dozen padded chairs covered with straps, but only one that seemed to be larger than the others and next to a large lever. There were also five or six crates like the one he just loaded in. These were strapped to the floor. He saw an empty space and shoved the last crate into it just as the floor shifted again and he was thrown sideways. The lights flashed as he crawled up and over to the crate. He lashed it into place, running a strap through both handles and then clipping it off.

He went to stand up but the floor shifted and spun. Suddenly he was back at the carnival, crawling along the floor of the tiltawhirl. Only this time there was no girl to impress. He clambered into the command chair and pulled the harness over his head and put his arms through holes cut for a man twice his build. He reached down between his legs and grabbed the lock. He struggled for a moment but finally got everything aligned. There was a satisfying click and he finally took a deep breath and relaxed. He stared at the lever. There were letters in bright red stenciled onto the side. FOR EMERGENCY USE ONLY. Under this someone had written in pen, *Command is not responsible for what happens next.*

He laughed, reached out his hand, and took the lever. He squeezed the release and pulled back. He felt something go thunk beneath his feet, and suddenly he felt himself falling, his stomach trying to climb up into his throat, but only for a second. The room hit the surface of the water hard. The gun fell from his hand. He reached for it but a wave upended the now floating capsule. Peaslee's head snapped back and hit the headrest with a thud. He gasped and then, mercifully, fell unconscious.

PART 9: REVELATIONS

Three days after the *Babel* broke up, a helicopter saw Peaslee's flare and four hours later the Coast Guard Cutter *Sentinel* brought him aboard, tired and hungry but mostly unhurt. They wrapped him in blankets while they hooked a line to the pod. As the crew scrambled to bring the pod aboard, he heard the captain cry out. "Radio it in, two survivors recovered."

Peaslee didn't miss a beat. "Belay that order." He threw off the blanket and pulled out his identification, almost shoving it in the captain's face. "Take me to him."

The captain motioned a crewman and they led Peaslee down into the ship and into the sickbay. Kulshedra was there, sitting on the side of a bed, a cup of soup in his hand. He saw Peaslee and frowned.

Peaslee dismissed the orderly with a gesture, then sat down next to his old friend. "Well, this is awkward," Kulshedra said as he took a gulp.

Peaslee was quiet for a moment, opened his mouth to speak, but then decided not to. Another moment passed and he finally sighed. "I'm not here to kill you, I need you alive to prove everything that has happened here. Bauer told me about Project Pegasus, and about the Caymans."

"Did you believe him?"

"I had three days alone with the radio surveillance transcripts. If it's disinformation it's a hell of a setup."

"Is that all you read?"

Peaslee reached into his coat and pulled a book from within. *Die Offenbarungen des Yig* dropped to the deck between them. "Interesting read, I particularly like the part where the serpent men realize that they've been abandoned by their makers in favor of another species and that they might go extinct. I memorized the passage, 'And so the People, they took from the trees the small and noisome beast that the Masters had raised up, and made it so that in generations to come the beast would become not as it was, but as the people were themselves. And one day it would populate the Earth, and when the Masters woke once more, would be recognized as descendants of the People—an almost People, that would be more than suitable to serve the Masters in their stead.' Is that a fair translation?"

A grimace crossed Kulshedra's face. "It is a fair translation of a heretical text."

"Is that what you called Bauer before you shot him, a heretic?"

"I don't owe you an explanation."

"Because?"

"Because you are a lesser thing. The creation of a race that abandoned us, that chose small furry things to be their servants instead of us. That thought we would perish when the meteor storms came, but they were wrong. We did survive, and they cursed us with vermin that have now overrun the world."

Peaslee nodded and was going to respond, but the captain walked in with a scrap of paper in his hand. Peaslee went over and took the page from him. The two whispered back and forth and then the captain shook his hand and left.

Peaslee came back with the paper in his hand. "The agency I work for has finally finished reorganizing. I've been worried they were going to terminate me—fire me, or maybe worse. Turns out, I was on the wrong track." He handed the paper to Kulshedra.

Kulshedra read it and started to laugh. "They put you in charge of JACK."

Peaslee laughed back. "They put me in charge." He took the paper back and reached into his coat. "I lied to you, Ophel. That story I told you about how I became known as The Terrible Old Man. I lied."

"How so?"

"I never got off the *Maracot*. I stayed on board and armed

myself. When the Deep Ones came aboard, I waited until they dealt with the crew and then I came up and I slaughtered them all. There were nine of them and I killed them one by one, a gun in each hand, a bandolier full of explosives, a pair of knives at my waist. The locals saw it all happen, watched me kill their gods and then blow up the ship, and swim to shore. I killed their old gods and became their new one. At least until the Japanese arrived."

Kulshedra stared at him, there was a bit of awe in his black eyes. "You did no such thing."

"I did," Peaslee nodded slightly. "I killed them, made sure they were dead. Just like I'll make sure you are dead as well."

"You said you weren't going to kill me."

"That was when I needed proof, but now I'm I charge, I don't need to prove anything. You wanted to know why they call me the Terrible Old Man."

Peaslee slid the gun into Kulshedra's belly and pulled the trigger twice. As he stood up, he watched the light leave Kulshedra's eyes but then put the gun up to the man's head and pulled the trigger one more time. Then he set the gun down on the bed.

"Now you know." He bent down and picked up the copy of the *Revelations of Yig*. "Load of good that did you."

At the door, the captain held the orderly back while Peaslee walked out.

While crewmen cleaned up his mess, the new head of JACK made his way back up topside and found a lonely spot on the rail. He watched the sea as it rolled and thought about what he had seen, what he had learned, what Bauer had told him. He looked at the *Die Offenbarungen des Yig*, the so-called *Revelations of Yig* and tried to put it all in context, tried to make sense of it. It clawed at him, ate at his mind, at his psyche, at the very things that made him human. What was he going to do? Reptilian monsters had infiltrated the nation, and even enlisted in the military. Who knows what other institutions they had penetrated. How far had they insinuated themselves? Was it benign as Bauer had said, or was there something more sinister to their motives?

What was he to do?

He let the book fall from his hand. It hit the ocean, but whatever noise it made was swallowed up by the crash of the boat driving through the sea. It floated there, just for a moment or two. And then the *Revelations of Yig* sank beneath the waves, lost to the abyss forever.

CODA: THE RETURN

BY DAVID HAMBLING

New Delhi, 2020

Two soft taps sounded. Martinez looked around blearily, dazed by jet lag and bourbon, unable to locate the source of the sound, until the door entered his field of view and the tapping sound suddenly made sense.

Martinez padded over the thick carpet on shoeless feet and put his eye to the spyhole.

On the other side was a woman in her thirties in what he guessed was a fashionable suit, achieving a look that was both businesslike and stylish. Considerably better than his own rumpled appearance, the mirror by the door informed him. Her face was half concealed by an oyster silk mask, but she was still recognizable as the woman in the picture he had been sent.

He swung the door open and stood back.

"Come in," he said. "There's plenty of room and we can't talk with you standing out there. I'm Martinez, obviously."

"Pleased to meet you," she said, in the clear tones of a British television announcer, not attempting an elbow-bump or any of the other new Covid-era greetings. "Victoria Murray."

He backed out of the way and she made her way to the far side of the room. They had not given Martinez a suite, but his hotel room was spacious enough to have a sleeping area with two queen-sized beds at one end and a living area with two armchairs and a sofa grouped around a glass-topped table. An imposing nineteenth-century writing desk took up one corner, equipped with a full range of hotel stationary and an array of electrical outlets. Apart from a few touches like fire exit instructions in different languages, it could have been anywhere. Although the tiny lizard which had flitted across the bathroom floor was a reminder he was not in America.

Murray settled in an armchair and, after a moment's hesitation and seeing his bare face, removed her mask.

Martinez was very aware that his shoes were lying by the bed, that he had not shaved, and that there was an open bottle of Jack Daniels on the coffee table next to a plastic glass.

"The flight from London is only eight hours," she said conversationally. "The plane was empty and I never have any trouble sleeping on flights."

"Four hours from Oklahoma to Washington, a six-hour layover and fourteen hours to Delhi," he said, sitting on the other armchair at a safe distance. "Plus a few extra hours getting The Thing into the country when I arrived. What day is this again?"

"'The Thing,'" she said. "Is that what you call it?"

"Operational security," he said. "Can't let people know it's a piece of rock. It's in that case on the desk."

The Thing had its own, custom-made travel case, an aviation-grade aluminum block that might carry professional photographic gear or scientific equipment. It was rigged with numerous sensors and alarms. Getting through airport security, even with all the documentation, had not been easy. Indian customs had been even more of a nightmare.

"You should put it in the wall safe," she said. "But I suppose you've only just arrived. Should I come back later?"

"No, this is fine," he said. "This is all new to me—I just read the field reports on the flight. Do you work with…this stuff?"

"New to me as well," she said, shaking her head. "I'm usually involved in diplomatic issues connected with the colonial era. This is all very, very strange."

"My usual beat is more to do with Native Americans," he said. "The reports make the X-Files look like a documentary series. Shape-changing alien lizards walking among us—really?"

"Exactly," she said. "But alien lizards with magic. It takes some suspension of disbelief."

"There are only about few data points spread out over a hundred years," he went on. "Half of them are contradictory. How did this stone get from New England to Florida? After that it's radio silence since 1970. Unless you count for the Weekly World News reports about Queen Elizabeth being one of them."

"Most of it was on your side of the pond," she said. "This JACK organization was real, but the rest of it—well, I can see why you needed a drink."

"That wasn't it," he said. "It's crazy, but then so is any religion when you get down to it. The Children of Yig believe some weird things, but then so do Scientologists. They just seem to be arguing about whether we are supposed to be serving an actual god, a figurative one… or a god who happens to be an alien astronaut."

"But their actual god is a snake, and their alien astronauts are in a frozen city under Antarctica," she said. "Oh, and they think they're reptiles."

"We're all descended from reptiles," said Martinez, enjoying the experience of meeting someone who was even more outraged than he was. He had spent several hours on the flight reading through the material on his ultra-secure laptop, with its layers of software protection and a filter on the screen so it could only be read from a frustratingly narrow angle.

"So they're just another crazy religion at war with themselves."

"America was founded on religious struggles," he said. "This splinter group, who stole the stone—they're like the Mormons."

"Oh well, it all makes perfect sense when you put it like that," she said sarcastically.

"You were talking about why I needed a drink," he said. "Take a look in the wardrobe."

She shot him a quizzical look. There were three wardrobes in the room, two built-in and one freestanding. The door of one of the built-in wardrobes was half open and she went over to peer inside.

It could have been a shop window mannequin wearing a dark suit. It was lying face-down, in an attitude more suited to a dummy than a live human. All she could see was the dark blonde hair; definitely not an Indian.

"They cut his throat," said Martinez. "But he's lying on some plastic dry-cleaning bags, so he won't make too much mess."

Murray's jaw hung open as she looked from the body to Martinez and he realized he had been acting far too casual.

"You didn't...?"

"No! I just opened the wardrobe to hang up my stuff and he was there," said Martinez.

"Who is he?" she asked.

"I didn't check him for ID," Martinez admitted. "I think he's Russian."

His handlers had warned Martinez that the Russians were grumbling about the handover, even though they did not actually oppose it. The Russians did not want to give them back the original, they wanted to hand over a copy instead—and they wanted their technicians to get a good look at the original. They were turned down on all counts.

The hotel was likely to be swarming with Russians. It would be swarming with CIA too, but his handler had assured him that Martinez would not see them. Presumably, there would be MI5 or whoever the British used for security too. The dead man looked too pale though, his watch was Eastern European, and his suit was not from any Western tailor.

"You shouldn't disturb evidence," said Martinez, seeing Murray donning thin plastic gloves.

"I know." She went briskly through the dead man's pockets. The ID she turned up was almost certainly fake, but the name on it was Russian. "That's the first thing that's made sense."

"If you say so."

She tossed the plastic ID card back in the wardrobe and pulled the door fully closed, then pocketed her gloves.

"You haven't told anyone?"

He had been about to call his handlers. Now that Murray had arrived though he was calming down and it seemed less like an emergency and more like something that could wait.

"The Indians won't like it," she said.

"Telling them would be game over," he said. "As soon as the Indians get involved, the deal is off."

Martinez did not know much about Indian politics. But he knew that Narendra Modi's nationalist government was not sympathetic. They would probably view the operation as interference in internal affairs. America dealing with an Indian Muslim group would be bad enough; dealing with an even more contentious religious faction, and with the collusion of the British, would be intolerable.

"You're right, of course," she said, then stepped away from the wardrobe and crossed back to her seat, with just one backward glance. "That does make the whole thing look less like a bad joke and more... serious."

"Throat-cutting seems to be something they do," said Martinez. "Our reptilian friends, lizard-men, Children of Yig or whatever. I assume they're sending us a message."

"Or sending the Russians a message," she said. "Or quite possibly, it's one group of them sending a message to a different group. If the reports are right there's a lot of in-fighting."

Something pinged and she reached for her handbag; a moment later Martinez's own phone signaled a text alert.

"It's happening," she said. "I'd better let you get ready."
"See you in the lobby in ten minutes," he said, trying to remember where he had put his tie.

The lobby had a more regional Indian flavor than the rooms, being lavishly decorated with slightly kitsch reminders to visitors that they were in the subcontinent. A pair of huge wooden elephants were stationed on either side of the reception desk, and the walls were hung with a modern artist's panoramic rendering of tigers stalking through long grass. In one corner an Indian jazz quartet were working through standards at a level which would not disrupt conversation, and waiters crisscrossed with trays of cocktails, afternoon tea, lassi and diet cokes. As in the rooms, smoked glass and blinds kept the real Delhi at bay.

Martinez, cleaned and tidied up and looking businesslike with the aluminum case by his side, surveyed the room. Murray was a pace behind him.

"Spot the spook," said Martinez.

Two men at the bar wearing Stetsons were too obviously American stereotypes to be CIA, unless the Company now thought double bluff was a smart idea. The black couple—if they were a couple—sitting side-by-side and looking outwards were a better bet. Martinez picked out a couple of Eastern European types as possible FSB—or would it be GRU?—types.

His gaze ran along the mezzanine level where other hotel guests could be looking down on them from behind a row of ugly, dark green potted plants.

"Oh, I think we're being watched," said Murray. "And I bet some of the Chinese are here on government business."

The text said their contact would be at the north-east end of the room. A glance at his phone's compass gave him the right direction. Clearly their contact was not the group of five Sikh businessmen loudly arguing over a deal, or the Scandinavian tourists—mother, father and two small children—but the Indian woman sitting alone two tables away.

Folding wickerwork panels displayed works by local artists. Behind her was what appeared to be a distorted blown-up photograph of a painting of an apple. Crawling from it was a worm, except that the distortion made the worm look more like a snake.

It could not be a coincidence.

A man was sitting on his own on the other side of the panel, facing the other direction. All Martinez could see were his tasseled shoes and a shopping bag from some department store. Maybe he was engrossed in his phone, or a magazine. Or maybe he was listening in .

"You are here for the handover?" the seated woman asked as they approached, with a glance at the metal case. "You are the American, and this is the British representative?"

"That's us," said Martinez, sinking into a seat.

Murray introduced them.

"I'm Anita Devi," said their contact. She could have been an executive with any multinational; like the hotel rooms, she would not look out of place anywhere in the world. A slimline designer laptop case and a suede handbag were arranged negligently up by her feet. "Representing—shall we say, the Children of Yig."

Martinez let out a breath. Speaking the name out loud made the whole thing seem even more ridiculous than it was already.

Playing spies was not his usual field. Playing spies with alien lizards was too ridiculous.

"I don't think you're from the usual agency that deals with us," said Devi.

"I didn't even know there was a usual agency," said Martinez. "In fact, I hadn't even heard of the Children of Yig until yesterday. Or was it the day before—what day is it now?"

"I see," said Devi.

"Same here," said Murray. "I was drafted in at the last minute."

"But they acquainted you with enough of the history," said Devi. "In some senses the return of the stone is an historic event. But I understand it might be contentious for both your governments... please express our thanks to your superiors."

Martinez was watching her closely. She certainly seemed human enough, with nothing to suggest there was a reptile lurking behind those entirely ordinary features. If the reports were accurate though, they could go out in society and pass as human for years. The Russians apparently had a scanner which could tell the difference, but the CIA report had dismissed it as false security. If the lizard people allowed some of their people to be detected, it was only so others could slip past as genuine. Their ability to infiltrate drove the Russians crazy.

"They haven't told us much about it," said Murray. "We don't really know who you are or what you represent."

"The Children of Yig have always been rather enigmatic," said Devi, with the smile perfected by unhelpful customer services representatives. "Not exactly a political party, nor a religious movement. In fact, it's a description some of us only use when dealing with outsiders, a mask we wear for your benefit. A rather meaningless term, in fact."

"We weren't expecting a briefing," said Murray, returning a similar smile. "We're just here to confirm the handover has taken place."

"I assume you'll be taking it back to the temple of Rthan," said Martinez.

"You'll be tracking it with satellites, drones or whatever electronic gadgets you use these days," said Devi. "But of course it will be returning to where it belongs."

"I gather it's important to you," said Murray. "I've seen it compared to the Koh-i-Noor."

They were interrupted by a man in a camouflage jacket and jeans who dumped his backpack on the table in front of them and sat down next to Devi. He was a Westerner with ragged facial hair and the pale complexion of a life spent indoors.

"This is a bomb," he said calmly. "Six pounds of C4 plastic explosive wrapped round with two-inch nails. It'll take out everyone in the room. Human or non-human."

Sweet Jesus, thought Martinez hearing the man's voice, *he's an American. One of ours.*

And that was before he noticed the patch sewn over the left arm of the cammo jacket: a big red Q.

Murray, who must have picked up the accent too, threw Martinez a questioning look as if to ask 'Do you know anything about this?'

"This is the controller," said the man, partly opening his right hand to show a small black plastic device like an electronic key fob. "Dead man's switch—if I let go of it, then everything goes up. End Of. So no fast moves."

Martinez had the sudden conviction that he was going to be in the newspaper headlines, as one of the foreigners killed in a terrorist bomb attack on an Indian hotel. The government would probably blame Muslim extremists, and the State Department would not argue with them. He fought a temptation to reach out and put his hand on the backpack, as though that would stop it from exploding.

The stone though, sheathed in Kevlar and titanium, would survive. Martinez was oddly sure of that. More care had been taken to protect it than in keeping him or Murray safe.

"We understand," said Devi, unperturbed.

"Somebody's security has messed up big time," muttered Murray, still looking at Martinez.

The man with the bomb looked around the table. Seemingly satisfied with their reaction, he sat back and seemed to relax a little.

"This really isn't a good idea," said Martinez, looking at the bomb. If it was a bomb. How the hell could he have gotten it in here?

"I'll tell you what isn't a good idea," said the man. "Giving that rock back to Them. That's it there, isn't it?"

"What's your objection, exactly?" asked Murray. "The stone is theirs, after all."

"My objection? My objection?" The man leaned forward, fixing on her intently. "You're going to give a major technological artefact back to a group of reptiles that want to wipe out the human race? It's people like you—" he stabbed at her with one finger "—traitors like you who are the real problem. People in the government working for Them."

"That's not our understanding of the arrangement," said Murray evenly.

"Maybe the problem is with your 'understanding'," he shot back, making air quotes. "Maybe you don't really 'understand' any of this."

"Perhaps if you explain your views, we can talk this through," said Martinez. He was aware of movement in his peripheral vision but did not want to move his head. Some of the people in the lobby had stood up almost as soon as the backpack hit the table. He assumed they had been listening in, with shotgun mic or bugging devices, probably there was a microphone built into the aluminum case. He just hoped they knew what to do.

"No, I want her to talk," said the man, pointing at Devi. "I want this all out in the open."

"You're recording this," Martinez deduced, seeing a glass button on the man's breast pocket. It did not match the other buttons on his jacket.

"Tell us who you are," the man ordered Devi. "Tell us what you want with that rock."

Or what? Thought Martinez. *You're really going to blow us all up if she doesn't give the right answer?*

"My name is Anita Devi," she said. "As you must know, I'm here to meet representatives from America and Britain to discuss the return of an item of cultural heritage. It is a stone which was looted from India in the twentieth century by a well-meaning but misguided Christian missionary, at a time when the country was under British control. The item was only recently recovered by divers off the Florida coast."

"Exactly," said Murray.

"That's pretty much my brief," said Martinez. "Though I admit, this whole area is all new to me."

The bomber scanned them with quick, anxious glances, figuring out how much he believed, how much he wanted to believe.

"Bullshit," he said. "This conspiracy goes right to the heart of everything. The reptiles have always been here, behind everything. They want world domination."

"You just said they wanted to wipe us out," said Murray. "That's not very consistent."

"Tell me about the rock," the bomber said to Devi. "How does the technology work?"

"Cultural objects are not 'technology,'" said Devi. "They start by having symbolic value, like a crown which simply reminds people who is king. Then it takes on a life of its own, becomes revered, a religious relic able to work miracles because of its association. At the lowest level, religion degenerates into superstition and people think it's just a magic tool."

"I'm not drinking that Kool-Aid," said the bomber. "How about we talk about how something that worked as a crude psychic focus can be refined into a single active element—"

Martinez recognized something in the phrasing from the Revelations of Yig, the heretical bible of the American splinter faction.

"What you want is proof," said Devi, seeming keen to interrupt him. "You want this."

In her hand was a tiny pearl-handled tool, like a miniature Swiss Army knife with a nail file and scissors. She unfolded a blade.

The bomber shrank back as though she might stab him, but Devi just held out one hand, palm uppermost and slowly and deliberately sliced across the flesh. The bomber watched in amazed fascination. Red blood welled up and overflowed almost at once. Putting down the tool, Devi staunched the bleeding at once with a wad of tissues.

Movement caught Martinez's eye. Something copper-colored had poked its head out of a hole in the shopping bag of the man on the other side of the wicker screen. It glided towards the bomber, disappearing from Martinez's view as it approached his chair from behind.

"There," said Devi. "Does that convince you I am not, as you say, one of 'them'?"

"It doesn't prove anything," the bomber said quickly, and leaned forward to take possession of the little knife, keeping his eyes on her the whole time.

"What do you want?" asked Martinez.

The bomber looked around the table again, as if they would make a move if he didn't keep looking directly at them.

"I want the code," he said. "The key to the pictographic code you people use."

"The world's archaeologists are still working on that alphabet—" Devi started, but he had already moved on.

"And I want the rock. You, CIA, open the case—slowly."

"Sure," said Martinez. There was a combination dial and a lock; the key was on a chain around his wrist. He opened the case with slow, careful movements. Inside, resting on dark velvet, was an unremarkable triangle of brown stone.

Martinez slowly rotated the case around to give the bomber a good look inside. As he looked up, he saw a group of men in shades moving on the mezzanine. Shielded from the people beside them by the aspidistra plants, they were hastily setting up a device on a tripod.

The bomber gave a sudden yelp. Something metallic reared up by his ankle and he flailed ineffectually at it.

At that moment Devi grabbed the bomber's right hand in both of hers and held on, as the bomber tried to bat away the snake with his free hand. Martinez saw it strike twice more.

"Shit!" said the bomber, but not so loud or alarmed as Martinez would have expected. He sounded like he had just spilled his drink. The bomber tried to pull his hand back from Devi, then struggled with both hands to free the remote control, but Devi's grip must have been more powerful than it looked.

Martinez and Murray sat frozen, not knowing what to do, as the bomber struck Devi across the face. The blow was badly aimed, as though the bomber was half drunk. Martinez sensed the people around them falling silent and turning to look at the struggle. A moment later two large men in dark suits converged on their table and hauled the bomber to his feet.

"Wha—wha—" the bomber was slurring, and almost fell back into his seat. The venom was working fast. Confusion and panic raced across his features, and the two suited men expertly folded his arms back and half-carried him away.

"I've got it," said Devi, blood leaking from her fist, still firmly closed around the remote.

"Jesus," said Murray, watching as they dragged the bomber though a side door.

Unobserved by anyone except Martinez, the snake slithered back into its shopping bag.

Around them the conversation resumed, louder now. Nobody was looking in their direction. The men on the mezzanine with the telescope had disappeared, too.

"Let's conclude this before anything else happens," said Martinez, taking the stone from the case and placing it in front of Devi. "Our people can deal with the bomb—if it is a bomb."

"It is a bomb," said Devi. "One of you had better take this."

She passed the remote to Murray, showing her how to keep the button depressed. Murray took it as though handling a live snake.

"Thank you," said Devi, unfastening the drawstring on her suede handbag and slipping the stone inside. It fit exactly. The bag, which had looked full, must have been stuffed with soft padding material. Unless it was some kind of inter-dimensional portal. Neither would have surprised Martinez.

"What a mess," said Murray as Devi walked away, unruffled and unhurried, suede handbag over her shoulder, laptop case in one hand and a fistful of tissue in the other. Nobody was following her, as far as Martinez could tell.

"Yeah," said Martinez, closing the case and lifting it away from the table. "Let's just sit tight here and see how long it takes the cavalry to come and get us."

He had a phone number for emergencies, but calling them now would be a distraction. His handlers would have seen everything, must be scrambling to talk to a bomb tech if they did not have one on the scene.

"Any idea who the man was?" she asked.

"Some random. A conspiracy theorist, not a pro."

"There was a leak," she said. "Somebody clued him in. Do you know who those men were who took him? They didn't look Indian."

Martinez shook his head. He had not noticed anything about them except that they had the build of nightclub bouncers and their matching suits which made them look like hotel staff. Which must have been the idea.

"You didn't see the snake, did you?" he asked.

"Snake?"

The man on the other side of the wicker panel had gone, and the shopping bag with him. But surely Martinez's handlers would have seen everything. They would be taking whatever steps needed to be taken… if they were not too busy dealing with the threat of an apparently American-made bomb in a crowded Indian hotel lobby.

"Doesn't matter," said Martinez.

"They never told me what the deal was," said Murray. Martinez could not tell whether she was just making conversation or fishing for information. "What we get in exchange for the rock. Are your people asking for something?"

"They sent me to hand the rock over and be diplomatic about it," he said, spreading his hands. "That's all she wrote."

He was looking at the backpack: big, black, ominous, pregnant with threat. If it was a professional job it would have anti-tamper devices, and maybe a timer circuit too so it would go off after a set period if it was not deactivated. Much more dangerous than any inert piece of rock. A serpent's egg ready to hatch in a burst of flame and bring evil into the world.

"My theory is that the rock is in exchange for doing nothing and not interfering," she said. "They must be wondering whether they should step in and take charge of the world before we wreck it. I think this is a bribe to keep them away."

"Nice theory," he said.

He had expected his handlers to move in quicker than this. Had something gone wrong? Something else besides having the handover interrupted by a mad bomber?

"What's your theory?" she asked.

There was something not quite right about the way she asked the question. Something also about the way she was holding the remote control. Something about her calm attitude that might not just be English reserve.

Martinez suddenly felt that his answer was going to be very important.

"My theory?"

"About the Children of Yig. About this whole affair. What do you think, Martinez? What will you tell your people?"

He closed his eyes. Even if he dived like a Hollywood stuntman behind the nearest sofa, he would not survive the blast. Surely she would not survive either. Or did she simply not care?

"Martinez?" she repeated.

"I think sometimes it's better not to take the fruit of the tree of knowledge," he said. "I'm ignorant and sometimes that's better."

Seconds passed. He expected her to speak again, but she said nothing.

When Martinez eventually opened his eyes again, he was alone.

ABOUT THE AUTHORS

David Hambling lives in darkest Norwood, South London with his wife and cat. He is a journalist and his fiction, starting with the collection, 'The Dulwich Horror & Others', explores the Cthulhu mythos in his own locale. He continues the theme in a number of novels including the popular Harry Stubbs adventures, set in the 1920s, and the epic fantasy 'War of the God Queen', and has contributed to the anthologies 'Black Wings' V and VI (PS publishing) and 'Time Loopers: Four Tales From a Time War'.

Keep track of his fiction at the Shadows From Norwood page on Facebook: https://www.facebook.com/ShadowsFromNorwood

Matthew Davenport hails from Des Moines, Iowa where he lives with his wife, Ren, and daughter, Willow. When his scattered author brain isn't earning weird looks from the ladies of his life, he enjoys reading sci-fi and horror, tinkering with electronics, and doing escape rooms.

Matt is the author of the Andrew Doran series, the Broken Nights series (along with his brother, Michael), The Trials of Obed Marsh, and Satan's Salesman among other titles.

He's also a self-styled student of the Cthulhu Mythos and exercises that influence in his stories and as an editor at the blog Shoggoth.net

You can keep track of Matthew through his twitter account @spazenport.

Mark Howard Jones was born in South Wales on the 26th anniversary of H P Lovecraft's death. He is the editor of the anthology 'Cthulhu Cymraeg: Lovecraftian Tales From Wales' (SD Publishing) and 'Cthulhu Cymraeg II' (Fugitive Fiction). His Lovecraftian fiction appears in the anthologies 'Black Wings' III , V and VI (PS publishing),'The Madness Of Cthulhu' II (Titan Books) 'Gothic Lovecraft' (Cycatrix Press) and 'His Own Most Fantastic Creation' (PS Publishing) . He lives in Cardiff, the capital of Wales."

Pete Rawlik is the author of more than fifty short stories, the novels 'Reanimators', 'The Weird Company', and 'Reanimatrix', as well as 'The Peaslee Papers', a chronicle of the distant past, the present, and the far future, and the short-story collection 'Strange Company and Others.' As editor he has produced 'The Legacy of the Reanimator' and 'The Chromatic Court'. His short story 'Revenge of the Reanimator' was nominated for a New Pulp Award. He is a regular member of the Lovecraft Ezine Podcast and a frequent contributor to the New York Review of Science Fiction.

Curious about other Crossroad Press books?
Stop by our site:
http://store.crossroadpress.com
We offer quality writing
in digital, audio, and print formats.